THE KILLER

STEWART EDWARD WHITE

1st WORLD
LIBRARY
Literary Society

The Killer

Stewart Edward White

© 1st World Library, 2006
PO Box 2211
Fairfield, IA 52556
www.1stworldlibrary.com
First Edition

LCCN: 2006910003

Softcover ISBN: 978-1-4218-3408-5
Hardcover ISBN: 978-1-4218-3308-8
eBook ISBN: 978-1-4218-3508-2

Purchase *"The Killer"*
as a traditional bound book at:
www.1stWorldLibrary.com/purchase.asp?ISBN=978-1-4218-3408-5

1st World Library is a literary, educational organization
dedicated to:

- Creating a free internet library of downloadable ebooks

- Hosting writing competitions and offering book
publishing scholarships.

Interested in more 1st World Library books?
contact: literacy@1stworldlibrary.com
Check us out at: www.1stworldlibrary.com

1st World Library Literary Society

Giving Back to the World

"If you want to work on the core problem, it's early school literacy."

- James Barksdale, former CEO of Netscape

"No skill is more crucial to the future of a child, or to a democratic and prosperous society, than literacy."

- Los Angeles Times

Literacy... means far more than learning how to read and write... The aim is to transmit... knowledge and promote social participation."

- UNESCO

"Literacy is not a luxury, it is a right and a responsibility. If our world is to meet the challenges of the twenty-first century we must harness the energy and creativity of all our citizens."

- President Bill Clinton

"Parents should be encouraged to read to their children, and teachers should be equipped with all available techniques for teaching literacy, so the varying needs and capacities of individual kids can be taken into account."

- Hugh Mackay

CONTENTS

THE KILLER

CHAPTER I

I want to state right at the start that I am writing this story twenty years after it happened solely because my wife and Senor Buck Johnson insist on it. Myself, I don't think it a good yarn. It hasn't any love story in it; and there isn't any plot. Things just happened, one thing after the other. There ought to be a yarn in it somehow, and I suppose if a fellow wanted to lie a little he could make a tail-twister out of it. Anyway, here goes; and if you don't like it, you know you can quit at any stage of the game.

It happened when I was a kid and didn't know any better than to do such things. They dared me to go up to Hooper's ranch and stay all night; and as I had no information on either the ranch or its owner, I saddled up and went. It was only twelve miles from our Box Springs ranch—a nice easy ride. I should explain that heretofore I had ridden the Gila end of our range, which is so far away that only vague rumours of Hooper had ever reached me at all. He was reputed a tough old devil with horrid habits; but that meant little to me. The tougher and horrider they came, the better they suited me—so I thought. Just to make everything entirely clear I will add that this was in the year of 1897 and the Soda Springs valley in Arizona.

By these two facts you old timers will gather the setting of my tale. Indian days over; "nester" days with frame houses and vegetable patches not yet here. Still a few guns packed for business purposes; Mexican border handy; no railroad in to Tombstone yet; cattle rustlers lingering in the Galiuros; train hold-ups and homicide yet prevalent but frowned upon; favourite tipple whiskey toddy with sugar; but the old fortified ranches all gone; longhorns crowded out by shorthorn blaze-head Herefords or near-Herefords; some indignation against Alfred Henry Lewis's *Wolfville* as a base libel; and, also but, no gasoline wagons or pumps, no white collars, no tourists pervading the desert, and the Injins still wearing blankets and overalls at their reservations instead of bead work on the railway platforms when the Overland goes through. In other words, we were wild and wooly, but sincerely didn't know it.

While I was saddling up to go take my dare, old Jed Parker came and leaned himself up against the snubbing post of the corral. He watched me for a while, and I kept quiet, knowing well enough that he had something to say.

"Know Hooper?" he asked.

"I've seen him driving by," said I.

I had: a little humped, insignificant figure with close-cropped white hair beneath a huge hat. He drove all hunched up. His buckboard was a rattletrap, old, insulting challenge to every little stone in the road; but there was nothing the matter with the horses or their harness. We never held much with grooming in Arizona, but these beasts shone like bronze. Good sizeable horses, clean built—well, I better not get started talking horse! They're the reason I had never really sized up the old man the few times I'd passed him.

"Well, he's a tough bird," said Jed.

"Looks like a harmless old cuss—but mean," says I.

"About this trip," said Jed, after I'd saddled and coiled my rope—"don't, and say you did."

Stewart Edward White

I didn't answer this, but led my horse to the gate.

"Well, don't say as how I didn't tell you all about it," said Jed, going back to the bunk house.

Miserable old coot! I suppose he thought he *had* told me all about it! Jed was always too loquacious!

But I hadn't racked along more than two miles before a man cantered up who was perfectly able to express himself. He was one of our outfit and was known as Windy Bill. Nuff said!

"Hear you're goin' up to stay the night at Hooper's," said he. "Know Hooper?"

"No, I don't," said I, "are you another of these Sunbirds with glad news?"

"Know about Hooper's boomerang?"

"Boomerang!" I replied, "what's that?"

"That's what they call it. You know how of course we all let each other's strays water at our troughs in this country, and send 'em back to their own range at round up."

"Brother, you interest me," said I, "and would you mind informing me further how you tell the dear little cows apart?"

"Well, old Hooper don't, that's all," went on Windy, without paying me any attention. "He built him a chute leading to the water corrals, and half way down the chute he built a gate that would swing across it and open a hole into a dry corral. And he had a high platform with a handle that ran the gate. When any cattle but those of his own brands came along, he had a man swing the gate and they landed up into the dry corral. By and by he let them out on the range again."

"Without water?"

"Sure! And of course back they came into the chute. And so on. Till they died, or we came along and drove them back home."

"Windy," said I, "you're stuffing me full of tacks."

"I've seen little calves lyin' in heaps against the fence like drifts of tumbleweed," said Windy, soberly; and then added, without apparent passion, "The old—!"

Looking at Windy's face, I knew these words for truth.

"He's a bad *hombre*," resumed Windy Bill after a moment. "He never does no actual killing himself, but he's got a bad lot of oilers[A] there, especially an old one named Andreas and another one called Ramon, and all he has to do is to lift one eye at a man he don't like and that man is as good as dead— one time or another."

This was going it pretty strong, and I grinned at Windy Bill.

"All right," said Windy, "I'm just telling you."

"Well, what's the matter with you fellows down here?" I challenged. "How is it he's lasted so long? Why hasn't someone shot him? Are you all afraid of him or his Mexicans?"

"No, it ain't that, exactly. I don't know. He drives by all alone, and he don't pack no gun ever, and he's sort of runty—and—I do'no *why* he ain't been shot, but he ain't. And if I was you, I'd stick home."

Windy amused but did not greatly persuade me. By this time I was fairly conversant with the cowboy's sense of humour. Nothing would have tickled them more than to bluff me out of a harmless excursion by means of scareful tales. Shortly Windy Bill turned off to examine a distant bunch of cattle; and so I rode on alone.

Stewart Edward White

It was coming on toward evening. Against the eastern mountains were floating tinted mists; and the canons were a deep purple. The cattle were moving slowly so that here and there a nimbus of dust caught and reflected the late sunlight into gamboge yellows and mauves. The magic time was near when the fierce, implacable day-genius of the desert would fall asleep and the soft, gentle, beautiful star-eyed night-genius of the desert would arise and move softly. My pony racked along in the desert. The mass that represented Hooper's ranch drew imperceptibly nearer. I made out the green of trees and the white of walls and building.

CHAPTER II

Hooper's ranch proved to be entirely enclosed by a wall of adobe ten feet high and whitewashed. To the outside it presented a blank face. Only corrals and an alfalfa patch were not included. A wide, high gateway, that could be closed by massive doors, let into a stable yard, and seemed to be the only entrance. The buildings within were all immaculate also: evidently Old Man Hooper loved whitewash. Cottonwood trees showed their green heads; and to the right I saw the sloped shingled roof of a larger building. Not a living creature was in sight. I shook myself, saying that the undoubted sinister feeling of utter silence and lifelessness was compounded of my expectations and the time of day. But that did not satisfy me. My aroused mind, casting about, soon struck it: I was missing the swarms of blackbirds, linnets, purple finches, and doves that made our own ranch trees vocal. Here were no birds. Laughing at this simple explanation of my eerie feeling, I passed under the gate and entered the courtyard.

It, too, seemed empty. A stable occupied all one side; the other three were formed by bunk houses and necessary out-buildings. Here, too, dwelt absolute solitude and absolute silence. It was uncanny, as though one walked in a vacuum. Everything was neat and shut up and whitewashed and apparently dead. There were no sounds or signs of occupancy. I was as much alone as though I had been in the middle of an ocean. My mind, by now abnormally sensitive and alert, leaped on this idea. For the same reason, it insisted—lack of life: there were no birds here, not even *flies*! Of course, said I, gone to

Stewart Edward White

bed in the cool of evening: why should there be? I laughed aloud and hushed suddenly; and then nearly jumped out of my skin. The thin blue curl of smoke had caught my eye; and I became aware of the figure of a man seated on the ground, in the shadow, leaning against the building. The curl of smoke was from his cigarette. He was wrapped in a *serape* which blended well with the cool colour of shadow. My eyes were dazzled with the whitewash—natural enough—yet the impression of solitude had been so complete. It was uncanny, as though he had materialized out of the shadow itself. Silly idea! I ranged my eye along the row of houses, and I saw three other figures I had missed before, all broodingly immobile, all merged in shadow, all watching me, all with the insubstantial air of having as I looked taken body from thin air.

This was too foolish! I dismounted, dropped my horse's reins over his head, and sauntered to the nearest figure. He was lost in the dusk of the building and of his Mexican hat. I saw only the gleam of eyes.

"Where will I find Mr. Hooper?" I asked.

The figure waved a long, slim hand toward a wicket gate in one side of the enclosure. He said no word, nor made another motion; and the other figures sat as though graved from stone.

After a moment's hesitation I pushed open the wicket gate, and so found myself in a smaller intimate courtyard of most surprising character. Its centre was green grass, and about its border grew tall, bright flowers. A wide verandah ran about three sides. I could see that in the numerous windows hung white lace curtains. Mind you, this was in Arizona of the 'nineties!

I knocked at the nearest door, and after an interval it opened and I stood face to face with Old Man Hooper himself.

He proved to be as small as I had thought, not taller than my own shoulder, with a bent little figure dressed in wrinkled and baggy store clothes of a snuff brown. His bullet head had been cropped so that his hair stood up like a short-bristled white brush. His rather round face was brown and lined. His hands, which grasped the doorposts uncompromisingly to bar the way, were lean and veined and old. But all that I found in my recollections afterward to be utterly unimportant. His eyes were his predominant, his formidable, his compelling characteristic. They were round, the pupils very small, the irises large and of a light flecked blue. From the pupils radiated fine lines. The blank, cold, inscrutable stare of them bored me through to the back of the neck. I suppose the man winked occasionally, but I never got that impression. I've noticed that owls have this same intent, unwinking stare—and wildcats.

"Mr. Hooper," said I, "can you keep me over night?"

It was a usual request in the old cattle country. He continued to stare at me for some moments.

"Where are you from?" he asked at length. His voice was soft and low; rather purring.

I mentioned our headquarters on the Gila: it did not seem worth while to say anything about Box Springs only a dozen miles away. He stared at me for some time more.

"Come in," he said, abruptly; and stood aside.

This was a disconcerting surprise. All I had expected was permission to stop, and a direction as to how to find the bunk house. Then a more or less dull evening, and a return the following day to collect on my "dare." I stepped into the dimness of the hallway; and immediately after into a room beyond.

Again I must remind you that this was the Arizona of the 'nineties. All the ranch houses with which I was acquainted, and I knew about all of them, were very crudely done. They comprised generally a half dozen rooms with adobe walls and

Stewart Edward White

rough board floors, with only such furnishings as deal tables, benches, homemade chairs, perhaps a battered old washstand or so, and bunks filled with straw. We had no such things as tablecloths and sheets, of course. Everything was on a like scale of simple utility.

All right, get that in your mind. The interior into which I now stepped, with my clanking spurs, my rattling *chaps*, the dust of my sweat-stained garments, was a low-ceilinged, dim abode with faint, musty aromas. Carpets covered the floors; an old-fashioned hat rack flanked the door on one side, a tall clock on the other. I saw in passing framed steel engravings. The room beyond contained easy chairs, a sofa upholstered with hair cloth, an upright piano, a marble fireplace with a mantel, in a corner a triangular what-not filled with objects. It, too, was dim and curtained and faintly aromatic as had been the house of an old maiden aunt of my childhood, who used to give me cookies on the Sabbath. I felt now too large, and too noisy, and altogether mis-dressed and blundering and dirty. The little old man moved without a sound, and the grandfather's clock outside ticked deliberately in a hollow silence.

I sat down, rather gingerly, in the chair he indicated for me.

"I shall be very glad to offer you hospitality for the night," he said, as though there had been no interim. "I feel honoured at the opportunity."

I murmured my thanks, and a suggestion that I should look after my horse.

"Your horse, sir, has been attended to, and your *cantinas*[B] are undoubtedly by now in your room, where, I am sure, you are anxious to repair."

He gave no signal, nor uttered any command, but at his last words a grave, elderly Mexican appeared noiselessly at my elbow. As a matter of fact, he came through an unnoticed door at the back, but he might as well have materialized from the thin air for the start that he gave me. Hooper instantly arose.

"I trust, sir, you will find all to your liking. If anything is lacking, I trust you will at once indicate the fact. We shall dine in a half hour—"

He seized a small implement consisting of a bit of wire screen attached to the end of a short stick, darted across the room with the most extraordinary agility, thwacked a lone house fly, and returned.

"—and you will undoubtedly be ready for it," he finished his speech, calmly, as though he had not moved from his tracks.

I murmured my acknowledgments. My last impression as I left the room was of the baleful, dead, challenging stare of the man's wildcat eyes.

The Mexican glided before me. We emerged into the court, walked along the verandah, and entered a bedroom. My guide slipped by me and disappeared before I had the chance of a word with him. He may have been dumb for all I know. I sat down and tried to take stock.

Stewart Edward White

CHAPTER III

The room was small, but it was papered, it was rugged, its floor was painted and waxed, its window—opening into the court, by the way—was hung with chintz and net curtains, its bed was garnished with sheets and counterpane, its chairs were upholstered and in perfect repair and polish. It was not Arizona, emphatically not, but rather the sweet and garnished and lavendered respectability of a Connecticut village. My dirty old *cantinas* lay stacked against the washstand. At sight of them I had to grin. Of course I travelled cowboy fashion. They contained a toothbrush, a comb, and a change of underwear. The latter item was sheer, rank pride of caste.

It was all most incongruous and strange. But the strangest part, of course, was the fact that I found myself where I was at that moment. Why was I thus received? Why was I, an ordinary and rather dirty cowpuncher, not sent as usual to the men's bunk house? It could not be possible that Old Man Hooper extended this sort of hospitality to every chance wayfarer. Arizona is a democratic country, Lord knows: none more so! But owners are not likely to invite in strange cowboys unless they themselves mess with their own men. I gave it up, and tried unsuccessfully to shrug it off my mind, and sought distraction in looking about me. There was not much to see. The one door and one window opened into the court. The other side was blank except that near the ceiling ran a curious, long, narrow opening closed by a transom-like sash. I had never seen anything quite like it, but concluded that it must be a sort of loop hole for musketry in the old days. Probably they had some kind of scaffold to stand on.

I pulled off my shirt and took a good wash: shook the dust out of my clothes as well as I could; removed my spurs and *chaps*; knotted my silk handkerchief necktie fashion; slicked down my wet hair, and tried to imagine myself decently turned out for company. I took off my gun belt also; but after some hesitation thrust the revolver inside the waistband of my drawers. Had no reason; simply the border instinct to stick to one's weapon.

Then I sat down to wait. The friendly little noises of my own movements left me. I give you my word, never before nor since have I experienced such stillness. In vain I told myself that with adobe walls two feet thick, a windless evening, and an hour after sunset, stillness was to be expected. That did not satisfy. Silence is made up of a thousand little noises so accustomed that they pass over the consciousness. Somehow these little noises seemed to lack. I sat in an aural vacuum. This analysis has come to me since. At that time I only knew that most uneasily I missed something, and that my ears ached from vain listening.

At the end of the half hour I returned to the parlour. Old Man Hooper was there waiting. A hanging lamp had been lighted. Out of the shadows cast from it a slender figure rose and came forward.

"My daughter, Mr.—" he paused.

"Sanborn," I supplied.

"My dear, Mr. Sanborn has most kindly dropped in to relieve the tedium of our evening with his company—his distinguished company." He pronounced the words suavely, without a trace of sarcastic emphasis, yet somehow I felt my face flush. And all the time he was staring at me blankly with his wide, unblinking, wildcat eyes.

The girl was very pale, with black hair and wide eyes under a fair, wide brow. She was simply dressed in some sort of white stuff. I thought she drooped a little. She did not look at me, nor speak to me; only bowed slightly.

We went at once into a dining room at the end of the little dark hall. It was lighted by a suspended lamp that threw the illumination straight down on a table perfect in its appointments of napery, silver, and glass. I felt very awkward and dusty in my cowboy rig; and rather too large. The same Mexican served us, deftly. We had delightful food, well cooked. I do not remember what it was. My attention was divided between the old man and his daughter. He talked, urbanely, of a wide range of topics, displaying a cosmopolitan taste, employing a choice of words and phrases that was astonishing. The girl, who turned out to be very pretty in a dark, pale, sad way, never raised her eyes from her plate.

It was the cool of the evening, and a light breeze from the open window swung the curtains. From the blackness outside a single frog began to chirp. My host's flow of words eddied, ceased. He raised his head uneasily; then, without apology, slipped from his chair and glided from the room. The Mexican remained, standing bolt upright in the dimness.

For the first time the girl spoke. Her voice was low and sweet, but either I or my aroused imagination detected a strained under quality.

"Ramon," she said in Spanish, "I am chilly. Close the window."

The servant turned his back to obey. With a movement rapid as a snake's dart the girl's hand came from beneath the table, reached across, and thrust into mine a small, folded paper. The next instant she was back in her place, staring down as before in apparent apathy. So amazed was I that I recovered barely soon enough to conceal the paper before Ramon turned back from his errand.

The next five minutes were to me hours of strained and bewildered waiting. I addressed one or two remarks to my companion, but received always monosyllabic answers. Twice I caught the flash of lanterns beyond the darkened window; and a subdued, confused murmur as though several people were walking about stealthily. Except for this the night had again fallen deathly still. Even the cheerful frog had hushed.

At the end of a period my host returned, and without apology or explanation resumed his seat and took up his remarks where he had left them.

The girl disappeared somewhere between the table and the sitting room. Old Man Hooper offered me a cigar, and sat down deliberately to entertain me. I had an uncomfortable feeling that he was also amusing himself, as though I were being played with and covertly sneered at. Hooper's politeness and suavity concealed, and well concealed, a bitter irony. His manner was detached and a little precise. Every few moments he burst into a flurry of activity with the fly whacker, darting here and there as his eyes fell upon one of the insects; but returning always calmly to his discourse with an air of never having moved from his chair. He talked to me of Praxiteles, among other things. What should an Arizona cowboy know of Praxiteles? and why should any one talk to him of that worthy Greek save as a subtle and hidden expression of contempt? That was my feeling. My senses and mental apperceptions were by now a little on the raw.

That, possibly, is why I noticed the very first chirp of another frog outside. It continued, and I found myself watching my host covertly. Sure enough, after a few repetitions I saw subtle signs of uneasiness, of divided attention; and soon, again without apology or explanation, he glided from the room. And at the same instant the old Mexican servitor came and pretended to fuss with the lamps.

My curiosity was now thoroughly aroused, but I could guess no means of satisfying it. Like the bedroom, this parlour gave

Stewart Edward White

out only on the interior court. The flash of lanterns against the ceiling above reached me. All I could do was to wander about looking at the objects in the cabinet and the pictures on the walls. There was, I remember, a set of carved ivory chessmen and an engraving of the legal trial of some English worthy of the seventeenth century. But my hearing was alert, and I thought to hear footsteps outside. At any rate, the chirp of the frog came to an abrupt end.

Shortly my host returned and took up his monologue. It amounted to that. He seemed to delight in choosing unusual subjects and then backing me into a corner with an array of well-considered phrases that allowed me no opening for reply nor even comment. In one of my desperate attempts to gain even a momentary initiative I asked him, apropos of the piano, whether his daughter played.

"Do you like music?" he added, and without waiting for a reply seated himself at the instrument.

He played to me for half an hour. I do not know much about music; but I know he played well and that he played good things. Also that, for the first time, he came out of himself, abandoned himself to feeling. His close-cropped head swayed from side to side; his staring, wildcat eyes half closed—

He slammed shut the piano and arose, more drily precise than ever.

"I imagine all that is rather beyond your apperceptions," he remarked, "and that you are ready for your bed. Here is a short document I would have you take to your room for perusal. Good-night."

He tendered me a small, folded paper which I thrust into the breast pocket of my shirt along with the note handed me earlier in the evening by the girl. Thus dismissed I was only too delighted to repair to my bedroom.

There I first carefully drew together the curtains; then examined the first of the papers I drew from my pocket. It proved to be the one from the girl, and read as follows:

I am here against my will. I am not this man's daughter. For God's sake if you can help me, do so. But be careful for he is a dangerous man. My room is the last one on the left wing of the court. I am constantly guarded. I do not know what you can do. The case is hopeless. I cannot write more. I am watched.

I unfolded the paper Hooper himself had given me. It was similar in appearance to the other, and read:

I am held a prisoner. This man Hooper is not my father but he is vindictive and cruel and dangerous. Beware for yourself. I live in the last room in the left wing. I am watched, so cannot write more.

The handwriting of the two documents was the same. I stared at one paper and then at the other, and for a half hour I thought all the thoughts appropriate to the occasion. They led me nowhere, and would not interest you.

Stewart Edward White

CHAPTER IV

After a time I went to bed, but not to sleep. I placed my gun under my pillow, locked and bolted the door, and arranged a string cunningly across the open window so that an intruder—unless he had extraordinary luck—could not have failed to kick up a devil of a clatter. I was young, bold, without nerves; so that I think I can truthfully say I was not in the least frightened. But I cannot deny I was nervous—or rather the whole situation was on my nerves. I lay on my back staring straight at the ceiling. I caught myself gripping the sheets and listening. Only there was nothing to listen to. The night was absolutely still. There were no frogs, no owls, no crickets even. The firm old adobe walls gave off no creak nor snap of timbers. The world was muffled—I almost said smothered. The psychological effect was that of blank darkness, the black darkness of far underground, although the moon was sailing the heavens.

How long that lasted I could not tell you. But at last the silence was broken by the cheerful chirp of a frog. Never was sound more grateful to the ear! I lay drinking it in as thirstily as water after a day on the desert. It seemed that the world breathed again, was coming alive after syncope. And then beneath that loud and cheerful singing I became aware of duller half-heard movements; and a moment or so later yellow lights began to flicker through the transom high at the blank wall of the room, and to reflect in wavering patches on the ceiling. Evidently somebody was afoot outside with a lantern.

I crept from the bed, moved the table beneath the transom, and climbed atop. The opening was still a foot or so above my head. Being young, strong, and active, I drew myself up by the strength of my arms so I could look—until my muscles gave out!

I saw four men with lanterns moving here and there among some willows that bordered what seemed to be an irrigating ditch with water. They were armed with long clubs. Old Man Hooper, in an overcoat, stood in a commanding position. They seemed to be searching. Suddenly from a clump of bushes one of the men uttered an exclamation of triumph. I saw his long club rise and fall. At that instant my tired fingers slipped from the ledge and I had to let myself drop to the table. When a moment later I regained my vantage point, I found that the whole crew had disappeared.

Nothing more happened that night. At times I dozed in a broken sort of fashion, but never actually fell into sound sleep. The nearest I came to slumber was just at dawn. I really lost all consciousness of my surroundings and circumstances, and was only slowly brought to myself by the sweet singing of innumerable birds in the willows outside the blank wall. I lay in a half stupor enjoying them. Abruptly their music ceased. I heard the soft, flat *spat* of a miniature rifle. The sound was repeated. I climbed back on my table and drew myself again to a position of observation.

Old Man Hooper, armed with a .22 calibre rifle, was prowling along the willows in which fluttered a small band of migratory birds. He was just drawing bead on a robin. At the report the bird fell. The old man darted forward with the impetuosity of a boy, although the bird was dead. An impulse of contempt curled my lips. The old man was childish! Why should he find pleasure in hunting such harmless creatures? and why should he take on triumph over retrieving such petty game? But when he reached the fallen bird he did not pick it up for a possible pot-pie as I thought he would do. He ground it into the soft earth with the heel of his boot, stamping on the poor thing

Stewart Edward White

again and again. And never have I seen on human countenance such an expression of satisfied malignity!

I went to my door and looked out. You may be sure that the message I had received from the unfortunate young lady had not been forgotten; but Old Man Hooper's cynical delivery of the second paper had rendered me too cautious to undertake anything without proper reconnaissance. The left wing about the courtyard seemed to contain two apartments—at least there were two doors, each with its accompanying window. The window farthest out was heavily barred. My thrill at this discovery was, however, slightly dashed by the further observation that also all the other windows into the courtyard were barred. Still, that was peculiar in itself, and not attributable—as were the walls and remarkable transoms—to former necessities of defence. My first thought was to stroll idly around the courtyard, thus obtaining a closer inspection. But the moment I stepped into the open a Mexican sauntered into view and began to water the flowers. I can say no more than that in his hands that watering pot looked fairly silly. So I turned to the right and passed through the wicket gate and into the stable yard. It was natural enough that I should go to look after my own horse.

The stable yard was for the moment empty; but as I walked across it one of its doors opened and a very little, wizened old man emerged leading a horse. He tied the animal to a ring in the wall and proceeded at once to currying.

I had been in Arizona for ten years. During that time I had seen a great many very fine native horses, for the stock of that country is directly descended from the barbs of the *conquistadores*. But, though often well formed and as tough and useful as horseflesh is made, they were small. And no man thought of refinements in caring for any one of his numerous mounts. They went shaggy or smooth according to the season; and not one of them could have called a curry comb or brush out of its name.

The beast from which the wizened old man stripped a *bona fide* horse blanket was none of these. He stood a good sixteen hands; his head was small and clean cut with large, intelligent eyes and little, well-set ears; his long, muscular shoulders sloped forward as shoulders should; his barrel was long and deep and well ribbed up; his back was flat and straight; his legs were clean and—what was rarely seen in the cow country— well proportioned—the cannon bone shorter than the leg bone, the ankle sloping and long and elastic—in short, a magnificent creature whose points of excellence appeared one by one under close scrutiny. And the high lights of his glossy coat flashed in the sun like water.

I walked from one side to the other of him marvelling. Not a defect, not even a blemish could I discover. The animal was fairly a perfect specimen of horseflesh. And I could not help speculating as to its use. Old Man Hooper had certainly never appeared with it in public; the fame of such a beast would have spread the breadth of the country.

During my inspection the wizened little man continued his work without even a glance in my direction. He had on riding breeches and leather gaiters, a plaid waistcoat and a peaked cap; which, when you think of it, was to Arizona about as incongruous as the horse. I made several conventional remarks of admiration, to which he paid not the slightest attention. But I know a bait.

"I suppose you claim him as a Morgan," said I.

"Claim, is it!" grunted the little man, contemptuously.

"Well, the Morgan is not a real breed, anyway," I persisted. "A sixty-fourth blood will get one registered. What does that amount to?"

The little man grunted again.

"Besides, though your animal is a good one, he is too short and

Stewart Edward White

straight in the pasterns," said I, uttering sheer, rank, wild heresy.

After that we talked; at first heatedly, then argumentatively, then with entire, enthusiastic agreement. I saw to that. Allowing yourself to be converted from an absurd opinion is always a sure way to favour. We ended with antiphonies of praise for this descendant of Justin Morgan.

"You're the only man in all this God-forsaken country that has the sense of a Shanghai rooster!" cried the little man in a glow. "They ride horses and they know naught of them; and they laugh at a horseman! Your and, sir!" He shook it. "And is that your horse in number four? I wondered! He's the first animal I've seen here properly shod. They use the rasp, sir, on the outside the hoof, and on the clinches, sir; and they burn a seat for the shoe; and they pare out the sole and trim the frog— bah! You shoe your own horse, I take it. That's right and proper! Your hand again, sir. Your horse has been fed this hour agone."

"I'll water him, then," said I.

But when I led him forth I could find no trough or other facilities until the little man led me to a corner of the corral and showed me a contraption with a close-fitting lid to be lifted.

"It's along of the flies," he explained to me. "They must drink, and we starve them for water here, and they go greedy for their poison yonder." He indicated flat dishes full of liquid set on shelves here and about. "We keep them pretty clear."

I walked over, curiously, to examine. About and in the dishes were literally quarts of dead insects, not only flies, but bees, hornets, and other sorts as well. I now understood the deadly silence that had so impressed me the evening before. This was certainly most ingenious; and I said so.

But at my first remark the old man became obstinately silent, and fell again to grooming the Morgan horse. Then I became aware that he was addressing me in low tones out of the corner of his mouth.

"Go on; look at the horse; say something," he muttered, busily polishing down the animal's hind legs. "You're a man who *saveys* a horse—the only man I've seen here who does. *Get out!* Don't ask why. You're safe now. You're not safe here another day. Water your horse; eat your breakfast; then *get out!*"

And not another word did I extract. I watered my horse at the covered trough, and rather thoughtfully returned to the courtyard.

I found there Old Man Hooper waiting. He looked as bland and innocent and harmless as the sunlight on his own flagstones—until he gazed up at me, and then I was as usual disconcerted by the blank, veiled, unwinking stare of his eyes.

"Remarkably fine Morgan stallion you have, sir," I greeted him. "I didn't know such a creature existed in this part of the world."

But the little man displayed no gratification.

"He's well enough. I have him more to keep Tim happy than anything else. We'll go in to breakfast."

I cast a cautious eye at the barred window in the left wing. The curtains were still down. At the table I ventured to ask after Miss Hooper. The old man stared at me up to the point of embarrassment, then replied drily that she always breakfasted in her room. The rest of our conversation was on general topics. I am bound to say it was unexpectedly easy. The old man was a good talker, and possessed social ease and a certain charm, which he seemed to be trying to exert. Among other things, I remember, he told me of the Indian councils he used to hold in the old days.

"They were held on the willow flat, outside the east wall," he said. "I never allowed any of them inside the walls." The suavity of his manner broke fiercely and suddenly. "Everything inside the walls is mine!" he declared with heat. "Mine! mine! mine! Understand? I will not tolerate in here anything that is not mine; that does not obey my will; that does not come when I say come; go when I say go; and fall silent when I say be still!"

A wild and fantastic idea suddenly illuminated my understanding.

"Even the crickets, the flies, the frogs, the birds," I said, audaciously.

He fixed his wildcat eyes upon me without answering.

"And," I went on, deliberately, "who could deny your perfect right to do what you will with your own? And if they did deny that right what more natural than that they should be made to perish—or take their breakfasts in their rooms?"

I was never more aware of the absolute stillness of the house than when I uttered these foolish words. My hand was on the gun in my trouser-band; but even as I spoke a sickening realization came over me that if the old man opposite so willed, I would have no slightest chance to use it. The air behind me seemed full of menace, and the hair crawled on the back of my neck. Hooper stared at me without sign for ten seconds; his right hand hovered above the polished table. Then he let it fall without giving what I am convinced would have been a signal.

"Will you have more coffee—my guest?" he inquired. And he stressed subtly the last word in a manner that somehow made me just a trifle ashamed.

At the close of the meal the Mexican familiar glided into the room. Hooper seemed to understand the man's presence, for he arose at once.

"Your horse is saddled and ready," he told me, briskly. "You will be wishing to start before the heat of the day. Your *cantinas* are ready on the saddle."

He clapped on his hat and we walked together to the corral. There awaited us not only my own horse, but another. The equipment of the latter was magnificently reminiscent of the old California days—gaily-coloured braided hair bridle and reins; silver *conchas*; stock saddle of carved leather with silver horn and cantle; silvered bit bars; gay Navajo blanket as corona; silver corners to skirts, silver *conchas* on the long *tapaderos*. Old Man Hooper, strangely incongruous in his wrinkled "store clothes," swung aboard.

"I will ride with you for a distance," he said.

We jogged forth side by side at the slow Spanish trot. Hooper called my attention to the buildings of Fort Shafter glimmering part way up the slopes of the distant mountains, and talked entertainingly of the Indian days, and how the young officers used to ride down to his ranch for music.

After a half hour thus we came to the long string of wire and the huge, awkward gate that marked the limit of Hooper's "pasture." Of course the open range was his real pasture; but every ranch enclosed a thousand acres or so somewhere near the home station to be used for horses in active service. Before I could anticipate him, he had sidled his horse skillfully alongside the gate and was holding it open for me to pass. I rode through the opening murmuring thanks and an apology. The old man followed me through, and halted me by placing his horse square across the path of mine.

"You are now, sir, outside my land and therefore no longer my guest," he said, and the snap in his voice was like the crackling of electricity. "Don't let me ever see you here again. You are keen and intelligent. You spoke the truth a short time since.

You were right. I tolerate nothing in my place that is not my own—no man, no animal, no bird, no insect nor reptile even—that will not obey my lightest order. And these creatures, great or small, who will not—*or even cannot*—obey my orders must go—or die. Understand me clearly?

"You have come here, actuated, I believe, by idle curiosity, but without knowledge. You made yourself—ignorantly—my guest; and a guest is sacred. But now you know my customs and ideas. I am telling you. Never again can you come here in ignorance; therefore never again can you come here as a guest; and never again will you pass freely."

He delivered this drily, precisely, with frost in his tones, staring balefully into my eyes. So taken aback was I by this unleashed hostility that for a moment I had nothing to say.

"Now, if you please, I will take both notes from that poor idiot: the one I handed you and the one she handed you."

I realized suddenly that the two lay together in the breast pocket of my shirt; that though alike in tenor, they differed in phrasing; and that I had no means of telling one from the other.

"The paper you gave me I read and threw away," I stated, boldly. "It meant nothing to me. As to any other, I do not know what you are talking about."

"You are lying," he said, calmly, as merely stating a fact. "It does not matter. It is my fancy to collect them. I should have liked to add yours. Now get out of this, and don't let me see your face again!"

"Mr. Hooper," said I, "I thank you for your hospitality, which has been complete and generous. You have pointed out the fact that I am no longer your guest. I can, therefore, with propriety, tell you that your ideas and prejudices are noted with interest; your wishes are placed on file for future reference; I don't give a damn for your orders; and you can go to hell!"

"Fine flow of language. Educated cowpuncher," said the old man, drily. "You are warned. Keep off. Don't meddle with what does not concern you. And if the rumour gets back to me that you've been speculating or talking or criticizing—"

"Well?" I challenged.

"I'll have you killed," he said, simply; so simply that I knew he meant it.

"You are foolish to make threats," I rejoined. "Two can play at that game. You drive much alone."

"I do not work alone," he hinted, darkly. "The day my body is found dead of violence, that day marks the doom of a long list of men whom I consider inimical to me—like, perhaps, yourself." He stared me down with his unwinking gaze.

CHAPTER V

I returned to Box Springs at a slow jog trot, thinking things over. Old Man Hooper's warning sobered, but did not act as a deterrent of my intention to continue with the adventure. But how? I could hardly storm the fort single handed and carry off the damsel in distress. On the evidence I possessed I could not even get together a storming party. The cowboy is chivalrous enough, but human. He would not uprise spontaneously to the point of war on the mere statement of incarcerated beauty —especially as ill-treatment was not apparent. I would hardly last long enough to carry out the necessary proselyting campaign. It never occurred to me to doubt that Hooper would fulfill his threat of having me killed, or his ability to do so.

So when the men drifted in two by two at dusk, I said nothing of my real adventures, and answered their chaff in kind.

"He played the piano for me," I told them the literal truth, "and had me in to the parlour and dining room. He gave me a room to myself with a bed and sheets; and he rode out to his pasture gate with me to say good-bye," and thereby I was branded a delicious liar.

"They took me into the bunk house and fed me, all right," said Windy Bill, "and fed my horse. And next morning that old Mexican Joe of his just nat'rally up and kicked me off the premises."

"Wonder you didn't shoot him," I exclaimed.

"Oh, he didn't use his foot. But he sort of let me know that the place was unhealthy to visit more'n once. And somehow I seen he meant it; and I ain't never had no call to go back."

I mulled over the situation all day, and then could stand it no longer. On the dark of the evening I rode to within a couple of miles of Hooper's ranch, tied my horse, and scouted carefully forward afoot. For one thing I wanted to find out whether the system of high transoms extended to all the rooms, including that in the left wing: for another I wanted to determine the "lay of the land" on that blank side of the house. I found my surmise correct as to the transoms. As to the blank side of the house, that looked down on a wide, green, moist patch and the irrigating ditch with its stunted willows. Then painstakingly I went over every inch of the terrain about the ranch; and might just as well have investigated the external economy of a mud turtle. Realizing that nothing was to be gained in this manner, I withdrew to my strategic base where I rolled down and slept until daylight. Then I saddled and returned toward the ranch.

I had not ridden two miles, however, before in the boulder-strewn wash of Arroyo Seco I met Jim Starr, one of our men.

"Look here," he said to me. "Jed sent me up to look at the Elder Springs, but my hoss has done cast a shoe. Cain't you ride up there?"

"I cannot," said I, promptly. "I've been out all night and had no breakfast. But you can have my horse."

So we traded horses and separated, each our own way. They sent me out by Coyote Wells with two other men, and we did not get back until the following evening.

The ranch was buzzing with excitement. Jim Starr had not returned, although the ride to Elder Springs was only a two-hour affair. After a night had elapsed, and still he did not return, two men had been sent. They found him half way to Elder Springs with a bullet hole in his back. The bullet was that of a rifle. Being plainsmen they had done good detective work of its kind, and had determined—by the direction of the bullet's flight as evidenced by the wound—that it had been fired from a point above. The only point above was the low "rim" that ran for miles down the Soda Springs Valley. It was of black lava and showed no tracks. The men, with a true sense of values, had contented themselves with covering Jim Starr with a blanket, and then had ridden the rim for some miles in both directions looking for a trail. None could be discovered. By this they deduced that the murder was not the result of chance encounter, but had been so carefully planned that no trace would be left of the murderer or murderers.

No theory could be imagined save the rather vague one of personal enmity. Jim Starr was comparatively a newcomer with us. Nobody knew anything much about him or his relations. Nobody questioned the only man who could have told anything; and that man did not volunteer to tell what he knew.

I refer to myself. The thing was sickeningly clear to me. Jim Starr had nothing to do with it. I was the man for whom that bullet from the rim had been intended. I was the unthinking, shortsighted fool who had done Jim Starr to his death. It had never occurred to me that my midnight reconnoitring would leave tracks, that Old Man Hooper's suspicious vigilance would even look for tracks. But given that vigilance, the rest followed plainly enough. A skillful trailer would have found his way to where I had mounted; he would have followed my horse to Arroyo Seco where I had met with Jim Starr. There he would have visualized a rider on a horse without one shoe coming as far as the Arroyo, meeting me, and returning whence he had come; and me at once turning off at right angles. His natural conclusion would be that a messenger had brought me orders and had returned. The fact that we had shifted mounts he could not have read, for the reason—as I only too distinctly remembered—that we had made the change in the boulder and rock stream bed which would show no clear traces.

The thought that poor Jim Starr, whom I had well liked, had been sacrificed for me, rendered my ride home with the convoy more deeply thoughtful than even the tragic circumstances warranted. We laid his body in the small office, pending Buck Johnson's return from town, and ate our belated meal in silence. Then we gathered around the corner fireplace in the bunk house, lit our smokes, and talked it over. Jed Parker joined us. Usually he sat with our owner in the office.

Hardly had we settled ourselves to discussion when the door opened and Buck Johnson came in. We had been so absorbed that no one had heard him ride up. He leaned his forearm against the doorway at the height of his head and surveyed the silenced group rather ironically.

"Lucky I'm not nervous and jumpy by nature," he observed. "I've seen dead men before. Still, next time you want to leave one in my office after dark, I wish you'd put a light with him, or tack up a sign, or even leave somebody to tell me about it. I'm sorry it's Starr and not that thoughtful old horned toad in the corner."

Jed looked foolish, but said nothing. Buck came in, closed the door, and took a chair square in front of the fireplace. The glow of the leaping flames was full upon him. His strong face and bulky figure were revealed, while the other men sat in half shadow. He at once took charge of the discussion.

"How was he killed?" he inquired, "bucked off?"

"Shot," replied Jed Parker.

Buck's eyebrows came together.

"Who?" he asked.

He was told the circumstances as far as they were known, but declined to listen to any of the various deductions and surmises.

"Deliberate murder and not a chance quarrel," he concluded. "He wasn't even within hollering distance of that rim-rock. Anybody know anything about Starr?"

"He's been with us about five weeks," proffered Jed, as foreman. "Said he came from Texas."

"He was a Texican," corroborated one of the other men. "I rode with him considerable."

"What enemies did he have?" asked Buck.

But it developed that, as far as these men knew, Jim Starr had had no enemies. He was a quiet sort of a fellow. He had been to town once or twice. Of course he might have made an enemy, but it was not likely; he had always behaved himself. Somebody would have known of any trouble—

"Maybe somebody followed him from Texas."

"More likely the usual local work," Buck interrupted. "This man Starr ever met up with Old Man Hooper or Hooper's men?"

But here was another impasse. Starr had been over on the Slick Rock ever since his arrival. I could have thrown some light on the matter, perhaps, but new thoughts were coming to me and I kept silence.

Shortly Buck Johnson went out. His departure loosened tongues, among them mine.

"I don't see why you stand for this old *hombre* if he's as bad as you say," I broke in. "Why don't some of you brave young warriors just naturally pot him?"

And that started a new line of discussion that left me even more thoughtful than before. I knew these men intimately. There was not a coward among them. They had been tried and hardened and tempered in the fierceness of the desert. Any one of them would have twisted the tail of the devil himself; but they were off Old Man Hooper. They did not make that admission in so many words; far from it. And I valued my hide enough to refrain from pointing the fact. But that fact remained: they were off Old Man Hooper. Furthermore, by the time they had finished recounting in intimate detail some scores of anecdotes dealing with what happened when Old Man Hooper winked his wildcat eye, I began in spite of myself to share some of their sentiments. For no matter how flagrant the killing, nor how certain morally the origin, never had the most brilliant nor the most painstaking effort been able to connect with the slayers nor their instigator. He worked in the dark by hidden hands; but the death from the hands was as certain as the rattlesnake's. Certain of his victims, by luck or cleverness, seemed to have escaped sometimes as many as three or four attempts but in the end the old man's Killers got them.

A Jew drummer who had grossly insulted Hooper in the Lone Star Emporium had, on learning the enormity of his crime, fled to San Francisco. Three months later Soda Springs awoke to find pasted by an unknown hand on the window of the Emporium a newspaper account of that Jew drummer's taking off. The newspaper could offer no theory and merely recited the fact that the man suffered from a heavy-calibred bullet. But always the talk turned back at last to that crowning atrocity, the Boomerang, with its windrows of little calves, starved for water, lying against the fence.

"Yes," someone unexpectedly answered my first question at last, "someone could just naturally pot him easy enough. But I got a hunch that he couldn't get fur enough away to feel safe afterward. The fellow with a hankering for a good *useful* kind of suicide could get it right there.

Any candidates? You-all been looking kinda mournful lately,

Stewart Edward White

Windy; s'pose you be the human benefactor and rid the world of this yere reptile."

"Me?" said Windy with vast surprise, "me mournful? Why, I sing at my work like a little dicky bird. I'm so plumb cheerful bull frogs ain't in it. You ain't talking to me!"

But I wanted one more point of information before the conversation veered.

"Does his daughter ever ride out?" I asked.

"Daughter?" they echoed in surprise.

"Or niece, or whoever she is," I supplemented impatiently.

"There's no woman there; not even a Mex," said one, and "Did you see any sign of any woman?" keenly from Windy Bill.

But I was not minded to be drawn.

"Somebody told me about a daughter, or niece, or something," I said, vaguely.

CHAPTER VI

I lay in my bunk and cast things up in my mind. The patch of moonlight from the window moved slowly across the floor. One of the men was snoring, but with regularity, so he did not annoy me. The outside silence was softly musical with all the little voices that at Hooper's had so disconcertingly lacked. There were crickets—I had forgotten about them—and frogs, and a hoot owl, and various such matters, beneath whose influence customarily my consciousness merged into sleep so sweetly that I never knew when I had lost them. But I was never wider awake than now, and never had I done more concentrated thinking.

For the moment, and for the moment, only, I was safe. Old Man Hooper thought he had put me out of the way. How long would he continue to think so? How long before his men would bring true word of the mistake that had been made? Perhaps the following day would inform him that Jim Starr and not myself had been reached by his killer's bullet. Then, I had no doubt, a second attempt would be made on my life. Therefore, whatever I was going to do must be done quickly.

I had the choice of war or retreat. Would it do me any good to retreat? There was the Jew drummer who was killed in San Francisco; and others whose fates I have not detailed. But why should he particularly desire my extinction? What had I done or what knowledge did I possess that had not been equally done and known by any chance visitor to the ranch? I remembered the notes in my shirt pocket; and, at the risk of awakening some of my comrades, I lit a candle and studied them. They were undoubtedly written by the same hand. To whom had the other been smuggled? and by what means had it come into Old Man Hooper's possession? The answer hit me so suddenly, and seemed intrinsically so absurd, that I blew out the candle and lay again on my back to study it.

And the more I studied it, the less absurd it seemed, not by the light of reason, but by the feeling of pure intuition. I knew it as sanely as I knew that the moon made that patch of light through the window. The man to whom that other note had been surreptitiously conveyed by the sad-eyed, beautiful girl of the iron-barred chamber was dead; and he was dead because Old Man Hooper had so willed. And the former owners of the other notes of the "Collection" concerning which the old man had spoken were dead, too—dead for the same reason and by the same hidden hands.

Why? Because they knew about the girl? Unlikely. Without doubt Hooper had, as in my case, himself made possible that knowledge. But I remembered many things; and I knew that my flash of intuition, absurd as it might seem at first sight, was true. I recalled the swift, darting onslaughts with the fly whackers, the fierce, vindictive slaughter of the frogs, his early-morning pursuit of the flock of migrating birds. Especially came clear to my recollection the words spoken at breakfast:

"Everything inside the walls is mine! Mine! Mine! Understand? I will not tolerate anything that is not mine; that does not obey my will; that does not come when I say come; go when I say go; and fall silent when I say be still!"

My crime, the crime of these men from whose dead hands the girl's appeals had been taken for the "Collection," was that of curiosity! The old man would within his own domain reign supreme, in the mental as in the physical world. The chance cowboy, genuinely desirous only of a resting place for the night, rode away unscathed; but he whom the old man convicted of a prying spirit committed a lese-majesty that could not be forgiven. And I had made many tracks during my night reconnaissance.

And the same flash of insight showed me that I would be followed wherever I went; and the thing that convinced my intuitions—not my reason—of this was the recollection of the old man stamping the remains of the poor little bird into the mud by the willows. I saw again the insane rage of his face; and I felt cold fingers touching my spine.

On this I went abruptly and unexpectedly to sleep, after the fashion of youth, and did not stir until Sing, the cook, routed us out before dawn. We were not to ride the range that day because of Jim Starr, but Sing was a person of fixed habits. I plunged my head into the face of the dawn with a new and light-hearted confidence. It was one of those clear, nile-green sunrises whose lucent depths go back a million miles or so; and my spirit followed on wings. Gone were at once my fine-spun theories and my forebodings of the night. Life was clean and clear and simple. Jim Starr had probably some personal enemy. Old Man Hooper was undoubtedly a mean old lunatic, and dangerous; very likely he would attempt to do me harm, as he said, if I bothered him again, but as for following me to the ends of the earth—

The girl was a different matter. She required thought. So, as I was hungry and the day sparkling, I postponed her and went in to breakfast.

CHAPTER VII

By the time the coroner's inquest and the funeral in town were over it was three o'clock of the afternoon. As I only occasionally managed Soda Springs I felt no inclination to hurry on the return journey. My intention was to watch the Overland through, to make some small purchases at the Lone Star Emporium, to hoist one or two at McGrue's, and to dine sumptuously at the best—and only—hotel. A programme simple in theme but susceptible to variations.

The latter began early. After posing kiddishly as a rough, woolly, romantic cowboy before the passengers of the Overland, I found myself chaperoning a visitor to our midst. By sheer accident the visitor had singled me out for an inquiry.

"Can you tell me how to get to Hooper's ranch?" he asked.

So I annexed him promptly in hope of developments.

He was certainly no prize package, for he was small, pale, nervous, shifty, and rat-like; and neither his hands nor his eyes were still for an instant. Further to set him apart he wore a hard-boiled hat, a flaming tie, a checked vest, a coat cut too tight for even his emaciated little figure, and long toothpick shoes of patent leather. A fairer mark for cowboy humour would be difficult to find; but I had a personal interest and a determined character so the gang took a look at me and bided their time.

But immediately I discovered I was going to have my hands full. It seemed that the little, shifty, rat-faced man had been possessed of a small handbag which the negro porter had failed to put off the train; and which was of tremendous importance. At the discovery it was lacking my new friend went into hysterics. He ran a few feet after the disappearing train; he called upon high heaven to destroy utterly the race of negro porters; he threatened terrible reprisals against a delinquent railroad company; he seized upon a bewildered station agent over whom he poured his troubles in one gush; and he lifted up his voice and wept—literally wept! This to the vast enjoyment of my friends.

"What ails the small party?" asked Windy Bill coming up.

"He's lost the family jewels!" "The papers are missing." "Sandy here (meaning me) won't give him his bottle and it's past feeding time." "Sandy's took away his stick of candy and won't give it back." "The little son-of-a-gun's just remembered that he give the nigger porter two bits," were some of the replies he got.

On the general principle of "never start anything you can't finish," I managed to quell the disturbance; I got a description of the bag, and arranged to have it wired for at the next station. On receiving the news that it could not possibly be returned before the following morning, my protege showed signs of another outburst. To prevent it I took him firmly by the arm and led him across to McGrue's. He was shivering as though from a violent chill.

The multitude trailed interestedly after; but I took my man into one of McGrue's private rooms and firmly closed the door.

"Put that under your belt," I invited, pouring him a half tumbler of McGrue's best, "and pull yourself together."

He smelled it.

"It's only whiskey," he observed, mournfully. "That won't help much."

"You don't know this stuff," I encouraged.

He took off the half tumbler without a blink, shook his head, and poured himself another. In spite of his scepticism I thought his nervousness became less marked.

"Now," said I, "if you don't mind, why do you descend on a peaceful community and stir it all up because of the derelictions of an absent coon? And why do you set such store by your travelling bag? And why do you weep in the face of high heaven and outraged manhood? And why do you want to find Hooper's ranch? And why are you and your vaudeville make up?"

But he proved singularly embarrassed and nervous and uncommunicative, darting his glance here and there about him, twisting his hands, never by any chance meeting my eye. I leaned back and surveyed him in considerable disgust.

"Look here, brother," I pointed out to him. "You don't seem to realize. A man like you can't get away with himself in this country except behind footlights—and there ain't any footlights. All I got to do is to throw open yonder door and withdraw my beneficent protection and you will be set upon by a pack of ravening wolves with their own ideas of humour, among whom I especially mention one Windy Bill. I'm about the only thing that looks like a friend you've got."

He caught at the last sentence only.

"You my friend?" he said, breathlessly, "then tell me: is there a doctor around here?"

"No," said I, looking at him closely, "not this side of Tucson. Are you sick?"

"Is there a drug store in town, then?"

"Nary drug store."

He jumped to his feet, knocking over his chair as he did so.

"My God!" he cried in uncontrollable excitement, "I've got to get my bag! How far is it to the next station where they're going to put it off? Ain't there some way of getting there? I got to get to my bag."

"It's near to forty miles," I replied, leaning back.

"And there's no drug store here? What kind of a bum tank town is this, anyhow?"

"They keep a few patent medicines and such over at the Lone Star Emporium—" I started to tell him. I never had a chance to finish my sentence. He darted around the table, grabbed me by the arm, and urged me to my feet.

"Show me!" he panted.

We sailed through the bar room under full head of steam, leaving the gang staring after us open-mouthed. I could feel we were exciting considerable public interest. At the Lone Star Emporium the little freak looked wildly about him until his eyes fell on the bottle shelves. Then he rushed right in behind the counter and began to paw them over. I headed off Sol Levi, who was coming front making war medicine.

"*Loco*," says I to him. "If there's any damage, I'll settle."

It looked like there was going to be damage all right, the way he snatched up one bottle after the other, read the labels, and thrust them one side. At last he uttered a crow of delight, just like a kid.

"How many you got of these?" he demanded, holding up a

bottle of soothing syrup.

"You only take a tablespoon of that stuff—" began Sol.

"How many you got—how much are they?" interrupted the stranger.

"Six—three dollars a bottle," says Sol, boosting the price.

The little man peeled a twenty off a roll of bills and threw it down.

"Keep the other five bottles for me!" he cried in a shaky voice, and ran out, with me after him, forgetting his change and to shut the door behind us.

Back through McGrue's bar we trailed like one of these moving-picture chases and into the back room.

"Well, here we are home again," said I.

The stranger grabbed a glass and filled it half full of soothing syrup.

"Here, you aren't going to drink that!" I yelled at him. "Didn't you hear Sol tell you the dose is a spoonful?"

But he didn't pay me any attention. His hand was shaking so he could hardly connect with his own mouth, and he was panting as though he'd run a race.

"Well, no accounting for tastes," I said. "Where do you want me to ship your remains?"

He drank her down, shut his eyes a few minutes, and held still. He had quit his shaking, and he looked me square in the face.

"What's it *to* you?" he demanded. "Huh? Ain't you never seen a guy hit the hop before?"

He stared at me so truculently that I was moved to righteous wrath; and I answered him back. I told him what I thought of him and his clothes and his conduct at quite some length. When I had finished he seemed to have gained a new attitude of aggravating wise superiority.

"That's all right, kid; that's all right," he assured me; "keep your hair on. I ain't such a bad scout; but you gotta get used to me. Give me my hop and I'm all right. Now about this Hooper; you say you know him?"

"None better," I rejoined. "But what's that to you? That's a fair question."

He bored me with his beady rat eyes for several seconds.

"Friend of yours?" he asked, briefly.

Something in the intonations of his voice induced me to frankness.

"I have good cause to think he's trying to kill me," I replied.

He produced a pocketbook, fumbled in it for a moment, and laid before me a clipping. It was from the Want column of a newspaper, and read as follows:

A.A.B.—Will deal with you on your terms. H.H.

"A.A.B. that's me—Artie Brower. And H.H.—that's him—Henry Hooper," he explained. "And that lil' piece of paper means that's he's caved, come off, war's over. Means I'm rich, that I can have my own ponies if I want to, 'stead of touting somebody else's old dogs. It means that I got old H.H. —Henry Hooper—where the hair is short, and he's got to come my way!"

His eyes were glittering restlessly, and the pupils seemed to be unduly dilated. The whiskey and opium together—probably an unaccustomed combination—were too much for his ill-balanced control. Every indication of his face and his narrow eyes was for secrecy and craft; yet for the moment he was opening up to me, a stranger, like an oyster. Even my inexperience could see that much, and I eagerly took advantage of my chance.

"You are a horseman, then?" I suggested.

"Me a horseman? Say, kid, you didn't get my name. Brower—Artie Brower. Why, I've ridden more winning races than any other man on the Pacific Coast. That's how I got onto old H.H. I rode for him. He knows a good horse all right—the old skunk. Used to have a pretty string."

"He's got at least one good Morgan stallion now," said I. "I've seen him at Hooper's ranch."

"I know the old crock—trotter," scorned the true riding jockey. "Probably old Tim Westmore is hanging around, too. He's in love with that horse."

"Is he in love with Hooper, too?" I asked.

"Just like I am," said the jockey with a leer.

"So you're going to be rich," said I. "How's that?"

He leered at me again, going foxy.

"Don't you wish you knew! But I'll tell you this: old H.H. is going to give me all I want—just because I ask him to."

I took another tack, affecting incredulity.

"The hell he is! He'll hand you over to Ramon and that will be the last of a certain jockey."

"No, he won't do no such trick. I've fixed that; and he knows it. If he kills me, he'll lose *all* he's got 'stead of only part."

"You're drunk or dreaming," said I. "If you bother him, he'll just plain have you killed. That's a little way of his."

"And if he does a friend of mine will just go to a certain place and get certain papers and give 'em to a certain lawyer—and then where's old H.H.? And he knows it, damn well. And he's going to be good to Artie and give him what he wants. We'll get along fine. Took him a long time to come to it; but I didn't take no chances while he was making up his mind; you can bet on that."

"Blackmail, eh?" I said, with just enough of a sneer to fire him.

"Blackmail nothing!" he shouted. "It ain't blackmail to take away what don't belong to a man at all!"

"What don't belong to him?"

"Nothing. Not a damn thing except his money. This ranch. The oil wells in California. The cattle. Not a damn thing. That was the agreement with his pardner when they split. And I've got the agreement! Now what you got to say?"

"Say? Why its *loco*! Why doesn't the pardner raise a row?"

"He's dead."

"His heirs then?"

"He hasn't got but one heir—his daughter." My heart skipped a beat in the amazement of a half idea. "And she knew nothing about the agreement. Nobody knows but old H.H.—and me." He sat back, visibly gloating over me. But his mood was passing. His earlier exhilaration had died, and with it was dying the expansiveness of his confidence. The triumph of his last speech savoured he slipped again into his normal self. He looked at me suspiciously, and raised his whiskey to cover

Stewart Edward White

his confusion.

"What's it to yuh, anyway?" he muttered into his glass darkly. His eyes were again shifting here and there; and his lips were snarled back malevolently to show his teeth.

At this precise moment the lords of chance willed Windy Bill and others to intrude on our privacy by opening the door and hurling several whiskey-flavoured sarcasms at the pair of us. The jockey seemed to explode after the fashion of an over-inflated ball. He squeaked like a rat, leaped to his feet, hurled the chair on which he had been sitting crash against the door from which Windy Bill *et al* had withdrawn hastily, and ended by producing a small wicked-looking automatic—then a new and strange weapon—and rushing out into the main saloon. There he announced that he was known to the cognoscenti as Art the Blood and was a city gunman in comparison with which these plain, so-called bad men were as sucking doves to the untamed eagle. Thence he glanced briefly at their ancestry as far as known; and ended by rushing forth in the general direction of McCloud's hotel.

"Suffering giraffes!" gasped Windy Bill after the whirlwind had passed. "Was that the scared little rabbit that wept all them salt tears over at the depot? What brand of licker did you feed him, Sandy?"

I silently handed him the bottle.

"Soothing syrup—my God!" said Windy in hushed tones.

CHAPTER VIII

At that epoch I prided myself on being a man of resource; and I proceeded to prove it in a fashion that even now fills me with satisfaction. I annexed the remainder of that bottle of soothing syrup; I went to Sol Levi and easily procured delivery of the other five. Then I strolled peacefully to supper over at McCloud's hotel. Pathological knowledge of dope fiends was outside my ken—I could not guess how soon my man would need another dose of his "hop," but I was positively sure that another would be needed. Inquiry of McCloud elicited the fact that the ex-jockey had swallowed a hasty meal and had immediately retired to Room 4. I found Room 4 unlocked, and Brower lying fully clothed sound asleep across the bed. I did not disturb him, except that I robbed him of his pistol. All looked safe for awhile; but just to be certain I took Room 6, across the narrow hall, and left both doors open. McCloud's hotel never did much of a room business. By midnight the cowboys would be on their way for the ranches. Brower and myself were the only occupants of the second floor.

For two hours I smoked and read. The ex-jockey did not move a muscle. Then I went to bed and to a sound sleep; but I set my mind like an alarm clock, so that the slightest move from the other room would have fetched me broad awake. City-bred people may not know that this can be done by most outdoor men. I have listened subconsciously to horsebells for so many nights, for example, that even on stormy nights the cessation of that faint twinkle will awaken me, while the crash of the elements or even the fall of a tree would not in the slightest

Stewart Edward White

disturb my tired slumbers. So now, although the songs and stamping and racket of the revellers below stairs in McCloud's bar did not for one second prevent my falling into deep and dreamless sleep, Brower's softest tread would have reached my consciousness.

However, he slept right through the night, and was still dead to the world when I slipped out at six o'clock to meet the eastbound train. The bag—a small black Gladstone—was aboard in charge of the baggageman. I had no great difficulty in getting it from my friend, the station agent. Had he not seen me herding the locoed stranger? I secreted the black bag with the five full bottles of soothing syrup, slipped the half-emptied bottle in my pocket, and returned to the hotel. There I ate breakfast, and sat down for a comfortable chat with McCloud while awaiting results.

Got them very promptly. About eight o'clock Brower came downstairs. He passed through the office, nodding curtly to McCloud and me, and into the dining room where he drank several cups of coffee. Thence he passed down the street toward Sol Levi's. He emerged rather hurriedly and slanted across to the station.

"In about two minutes," I observed to McCloud, "you're going to observe yon butterfly turn into a stinging lizard. He's going to head in this direction; and he'll probably aim to climb my hump. Such being the case, and the affair being private, you'll do me a favour by supervising something in some remote corner of the premises."

"Sure," said McCloud, "I'll go twist that Chink washee-man. Been intending to for a week." And he stumped out on his wooden foot.

The comet hit at precisely 7:42 by McCloud's big clock. Its head was Brower at high speed and tension; and its tail was the light alkali dust of Arizona mingled with the station agent. No irresistible force and immovable body proposition in mine; I gave to the impact.

"Why, sure, I got 'em for you," I answered. "You left your dope lying around loose so I took care of it for you. As for your bag; you seemed to set such store by it that I got that for you, too."

Which deflated that particular enterprise for the moment, anyway. The station agent, too mad to spit, departed before he should be tempted beyond his strength to resist homicide.

"I suppose you're taking care of my gun for me, too," said Brower; but his irony was weak. He was evidently off the boil.

"Your gun?" I echoed. "Have you lost your gun?"

He passed his hand across his eyes. His super-excitement had passed, leaving him weak and nervous. Now was the time for my counter-attack.

"Here's your gun," said I, "didn't want to collect any lead while you were excited, and I've got your dope," I repeated, "in a safe place." I added, "and you'll not see any of it again until you answer me a few questions, and answer them straight."

"If you think you can roll me for blackmail," he came back with some decision, "you're left a mile."

"I don't want a cent; but I do want a talk."

"Shoot," said he.

"How often do you have to have this dope—for the best results; and how much of it at a shot?"

He stared at me for a moment, then laughed.

"What's it to yuh?" he repeated his formula.

"I want to know."

"I get to needing it about once a day. Three grains will carry me by."

"All right; that's what I want to know. Now listen to me. I'm custodian of this dope, and you'll get your regular ration as long as you stick with me."

"I can always hop a train. This ain't the only hamlet on the map," he reminded me.

"That's always what you can do if you find we can't work together. That's where you've got me if my proposition doesn't sound good."

"What is your proposition?" he asked after a moment.

"Before I tell you, I'm going to give you a few pointers on what you're up against. I don't know how much you know about Old Man Hooper, but I'll bet there's plenty you *don't* know about."

I proceeded to tell him something of the old man's methods, from the "boomerang" to vicarious murder.

"And he gets away with it?" asked Brower when I had finished.

"He certainly does," said I. "Now," I continued, "you may be solid as a brick church, and your plans may be water-tight, and old Hooper may kill the fatted four-year-old, for all I know. But if I were you, I wouldn't go sasshaying all alone out to Hooper's ranch. It's altogether *too* blame confiding and innocent."

"If anything happens to me, I've left directions for those contracts to be recorded," he pointed out. "Old Hooper knows that."

"Oh, sure!" I replied, "just like that! But one day your trustworthy friend back yonder will get a letter in your well-known hand-write that will say that all is well and the goose hangs high, that the old man is a prince and has come through, and that in accordance with the nice, friendly agreement you have reached he—your friend—will hand over the contract to a very respectable lawyer herein named, and so forth and so on, ending with your equally well-known John Hancock."

"Well, that's all right."

"I hadn't finished the picture. In the meantime, you will be getting out of it just one good swift kick, and that is all."

"I shouldn't write any such letter. Not 'till I felt the feel of the dough."

"Not at first you wouldn't," I said, softly. "Certainly not at first. But after a while you would. These renegade Mexicans—like Hooper's Ramon, for example—know a lot of rotten little tricks. They drive pitch-pine splinters into your legs and set fire to them, for one thing. Or make small cuts in you with a knife, and load them up with powder squibs in oiled paper—so the blood won't wet them—and touch them off. And so on. When you've been shown about ten per cent, of what old Ramon knows about such things, you'll write most any kind of a letter."

"My God!" he muttered, thrusting the ridiculous derby to the back of his head.

"So you see you'd look sweet walking trustfully into Hooper's claws. That's what that newspaper ad was meant for. And when the respectable lawyer wrote that the contract had been delivered, do you know what would happen to you?"

The ex-jockey shuddered.

"But you've only told me part of what I want to know," I pursued. "You got me side tracked. This daughter of the dead pardner—this girl, what about her? Where is she now?"

"Europe, I believe."

"When did she go?"

"About three months ago."

"Any other relatives?"

"Not that I know of."

"H'm," I pondered. "What does she look like?"

"She's about medium height, dark, good figure, good-looking all right. She's got eyes wide apart and a wide forehead. That's the best I can do. Why?"

"Anybody heard from her since she went to Europe?"

"How should I know?" rejoined Brower, impatiently. "What you driving at?"

"I think I've seen her. I believe she's not in Europe at all. I believe she's a prisoner at the ranch."

"My aunt!" ejaculated Brower. His nervousness was increasing—the symptoms I was to recognize so well. "Why the hell don't you just shoot him from behind a bush? I'll do it, if you won't."

"He's too smooth for that." And I told him what Hooper had told me. "His hold on these Mexicans is remarkable. I don't doubt that fifty of the best killers in the southwest have lists of the men Old Man Hooper thinks might lay him out. And every man on that list would get his within a year—without any doubt. I don't doubt that partner's daughter would go first of all. You, too, of course."

"My aunt!" groaned the jockey again.

"He's a killer," I went on, "by nature, and by interest—a bad combination. He ought to be tramped out like a rattlesnake. But this is a new country, and it's near the border. I expect he's got me marked. If I have to I'll kill him just like I would a rattlesnake; but that wouldn't do me a whole lot of good and would probably get a bunch assassinated. I'd like to figure something different. So you see you'd better come on in while the coming is good."

"I see," said the ex-jockey, very much subdued. "What's your idea? What do you want me to do?"

That stumped me. To tell the truth I had no idea at all what to do.

"I don't want you to go out to Hooper's ranch alone," said I.

"Trust me!" he rejoined, fervently.

"I reckon the first best thing is to get along out of town," I suggested. "That black bag all the plunder you got?"

"That's it."

"Then we'll go out a-horseback."

We had lunch and a smoke and settled up with McCloud. About mid-afternoon we went on down to the livery corral. I knew the keeper pretty well, of course, so I borrowed a horse and saddle for Brower. The latter looked with extreme disfavour on both.

"This is no race meet," I reminded him. "This is a means of transportation."

"Sorry I ain't got nothing better," apologized Meigs, to whom I had confided my companion's profession—I had to account for such a figure somehow. "All my saddle hosses went off with a mine outfit yesterday."

"What's the matter with that chestnut in the shed?"

"He's all right; fine beast. Only it ain't mine. It belongs to amon."

"Ramon from Hooper's?"

"Yeah."

"I'd let you ride my horse and take Meigs's old skate myself," I said to Brower, "but when you first get on him this bronc of mine is a rip-humming tail twister. Ain't he, Meigs?"

"He's a bad *caballo*," corroborated Meigs.

"Does he buck?" queried Brower, indifferently.

"Every known fashion. Bites, scratches, gouges, and paws. Want to try him?"

"I got a headache," replied Brower, grouchily. "Bring out your old dog."

When I came back from roping and blindfolding the twisted dynamite I was engaged in "gentling," I found that Brower was saddling the mournful creature with my saddle. My expostulation found him very snappy and very arbitrary. His opium-irritated nerves were beginning to react. I realized that he was not far short of explosive obstinacy. So I conceded the point; although, as every rider knows, a cowboy's saddle and a cowboy's gun are like unto a toothbrush when it comes to lending. Also it involved changing the stirrup length on the livery saddle. I needed things just right to ride Tiger through the first five minutes.

When I had completed this latter operation, Brower had just finished drawing tight the cinch. His horse stood dejectedly. When Brower had made fast the latigo, the horse—as such dispirited animals often do—heaved a deep sigh. Something snapped beneath the slight strain of the indrawn breath.

"Dogged if your cinch ain't busted!" cried Meigs with a loud laugh. "Lucky for you your friend did borrow your saddle! If you'd clumb Tiger with that outfit you could just naturally have begun pickin' out the likely-looking she-angels."

I dropped the stirrup and went over to examine the damage. Both of the quarter straps on the off side had given way. I found that they had been cut nearly through with a sharp knife. My eye strayed to Ramon's chestnut horse standing under the shed.

CHAPTER IX

We jogged out to Box Springs by way of the lower alkali flats. It is about three miles farther that way; but one can see for miles in every direction. I did not one bit fancy the canons, the mesquite patches, and the open ground of the usual route.

I beguiled the distance watching Brower. The animal he rode was a hammer-headed, ewe-necked beast with a disconsolate eye and a half-shed winter coat. The ex-jockey was not accustomed to a stock saddle. He had shortened his stirrups beyond all reason so that his knees and his pointed shoes and his elbows stuck out at all angles. He had thrust his derby hat far down over his ears, and buttoned his inadequate coat tightly. In addition, he was nourishing a very considerable grouch, attributable, I suppose, to the fact that his customary dose was just about due. Tiger could not be blamed for dancing wide. Evening was falling, the evening of the desert when mysterious things seem to swell and draw imminent out of unguessed distances. I could not help wondering what these gods of the desert could be thinking of us.

However, as we drew imperceptibly nearer the tiny patch of cottonwoods that marked Box Springs, I began to realize that it would be more to the point to wonder what that gang of hoodlums in the bunk house was going to think of us. The matter had been fairly well carried off up to that moment, but I could not hope for a successful repetition. No man could continue to lug around with him so delicious a vaudeville sketch without some concession to curiosity. Nor could any mortal for long wear such clothes in the face of Arizona without being required to show cause. He had got away with it last night, by surprise; but that would be about all.

At my fiftieth attempt to enter into conversation with him, I unexpectedly succeeded. I believe I was indicating the points of interest. You can see farther in Arizona than any place I know, so there was no difficulty about that. I'd pointed out the range of the Chiracahuas, and Cochise's Stronghold, and the peaks of the Galiuros and other natural sceneries; I had showed him mesquite and yucca, and mescal and soapweed, and sage, and sacatone and niggerheads and all the other known vegetables of the region. Also I'd indicated prairie dogs and squinch owls and Gambel's quail and road runners and a couple of coyotes and lizards and other miscellaneous fauna. Not to speak of naming painstakingly the ranches indicated by the clumps of trees that you could just make out as little spots in the distance—Box Springs, the O.T., the Double H, Fort Shafter, and Hooper's. He waked up and paid a little attention at this; and I thought I might get a little friendly talk out of him. A cowboy rides around alone so much he sort of likes to josh when he has anybody with him. This "strong silent" stuff doesn't go until you've used around with a man quite some time.

I got the talk, all right, but it didn't have a thing to do with topography or natural history. Unless you call the skate he was riding natural history. That was the burden of his song. He didn't like that horse, and he didn't care who knew it. It was an uncomfortable horse to ride on, it required exertion to keep in motion, and it hurt his feelings. Especially the last. He was a horseman, a jockey, he'd ridden the best blood in the equine world; and here he was condemned through no fault of his own to straddle a cross between a llama and a woolly toy sheep. It hurt his pride. He felt bitterly about it. Indeed, he fairly harped on the subject.

"Is that horse of yours through bucking for the day?" he asked at last.

"Certain thing. Tiger never pitches but the once."

"Let me ride him a ways. I'd like to feel a real horse to get the taste of this kangaroo out of my system."

I could see he was jumpy, so I thought I'd humour him.

"Swing on all at once and you're all right," I advised him. "Tiger don't like fumbling in getting aboard."

He grunted scornfully.

"Those stirrups are longer than the ones you've been using. Want to shorten them?"

He did not bother to answer, but mounted in a decisive manner that proved he was indeed a horseman, and a good one. I climbed old crow bait and let my legs hang.

The jockey gathered the reins and touched Tiger with his heels. I kicked my animal with my stock spurs and managed to extract a lumbering sort of gallop.

"Hey, slow up!" I called after a few moments. "I can't keep up with you."

Brower did not turn his head, nor did Tiger slow up. After twenty seconds I realized that he intended to do neither. I ceased urging on my animal, there was no use tiring us both; evidently the jockey was enjoying to the full the exhilaration of a good horse, and we would catch up at Box Springs. I only hoped the boys wouldn't do anything drastic to him before my arrival.

So I jogged along at the little running walk possessed by even the most humble cattle horse, and enjoyed the evening. It was going on toward dusk and pools of twilight were in the bottomlands. For the moment the world had grown smaller, more intimate, as the skies expanded. The dust from Brower's going did not so much recede as grow littler, more toy-like. I watched idly his progress.

At a point perhaps a mile this side the Box Springs ranch the road divides: the right-hand fork leading to the ranch house, the left on up the valley. After a moment I noticed that the dust was on the left-hand fork. I swore aloud.

"The damn fool has taken the wrong road!" and then after a moment, with dismay: "He's headed straight for Hooper's ranch!"

I envisaged the full joy and rapture of this thought for perhaps half a minute. It sure complicated matters, what with old Hooper gunning on my trail, and this partner's daughter shut up behind bars. Me, I expected to last about two days unless I did something mighty sudden. Brower I expected might last approximately half that time, depending on how soon Ramon *et al* got busy. The girl I didn't know anything about, nor did I want to at that moment. I was plenty worried about my own precious hide just then. And if you think you are going to get a love story out of this, I warn you again to quit right now; you are not.

Brower was going to walk into that gray old spider's web like a nice fat fly. And he was going to land without even the aid and comfort of his own particular brand of Dutch courage. For safety's sake, and because of Tiger's playful tendencies when first mounted, we had tied the famous black bag—which now for convenience contained also the soothing syrup—behind the cantle of Meigs's old nag. Which said nag I now possessed together with all appurtenances and attachments thereunto appertaining I tried to speculate on the reactions of Old Man Hooper, Ramon, Brower and no dope, but it was too much for me. My head was getting tired thinking about all these complicated things, anyhow. I was accustomed to nice, simple jobs with my head, like figuring on the shrinkage of beef cattle, or the inner running of a two-card draw. All this annoyed me. I began to get mad. When I got mad enough I cussed and came to a decision: which was to go after Old Man Hooper and all his works that very night. Next day wouldn't do; I wanted action right off quick. Naturally I had no plans, nor even a glimmering of what I was going to do about it; but you bet you I was going to do something! As soon as it was dark I was going right on up there. Frontal attack, you understand. As to details, those would take care of themselves as the affair developed. Having come to which sapient decision I shoved the whole irritating mess over the edge of my mind and rode on quite happy. I told you at the start of this yarn that I was a kid.

My mind being now quite easy as to my future actions, I gave thought to the first step. That was supper. There seemed to me no adequate reason, with a fine, long night before me, why I shouldn't use a little of the shank end of it to stoke up for the rest. So I turned at the right-hand fork and jogged slowly toward our own ranch.

Of course I had the rotten luck to find most of the boys still at the water corral. When they saw who was the lone horseman approaching through the dusk of the spring twilight, and got a good fair look at the ensemble, they dropped everything and came over to see about it, headed naturally by those mournful blights, Windy Bill and Wooden. In solemn silence they examined my outfit, paying not the slightest attention to me. At the end of a full minute they looked at each other.

"What do you think, Sam?" asked Windy.

"My opinion is not quite formed, suh," replied Wooden, who was a Texican. "But my first examination inclines me to the belief that it is a hoss."

"Yo're wrong, Sam," denied Windy, sadly; "yo're judgment is confused by the fact that the critter carries a saddle. Look at the animile itself."

"I have done it," continued Sam Wooden; "at first glance I

should agree with you. Look carefully, Windy. Examine the details; never mind the *toot enscramble*. It's got hoofs."

"So's a cow, a goat, a burro, a camel, a hippypottamus, and the devil," pointed out Windy.

"Of course I may be wrong," acknowledged Wooden. "On second examination I probably am wrong. But if it ain't a hoss, then what is it? Do you know?"

"It's a genuine royal gyasticutus," esserted Windy Bill, positively. "I seen one once. It has one peculiarity that you can't never fail to identify it by."

"What's that?"

"It invariably travels around with a congenital idiot."

Wooden promptly conceded that, but claimed the identification not complete as he doubted whether, strictly speaking, I could be classified as a congenital idiot. Windy pointed out that evidently I had traded Tiger for the gyasticutus. Wooden admitted that this proved me an idiot, but not necessarily a congenital idiot.

This colloquy—and more like it—went on with entire gravity. The other men were hanging about relishing the situation, but without a symptom of mirth. I was unsaddling methodically, paying no attention to anybody, and apparently deaf to all that was being said. If the two old fools had succeeded in eliciting a word from me they would have been entirely happy; but I knew that fact, and shut my lips.

I hung my saddle on the rack and was just about to lead the old skate to water when we all heard the sound of a horse galloping on the road.

"It's a light boss," said somebody after a moment, meaning a horse without a burden.

We nodded and resumed our occupation. A stray horse coming in to water was nothing strange or unusual. But an instant later, stirrups swinging, reins flapping, up dashed my own horse, Tiger.

CHAPTER X

All this being beyond me, and then some, I proceeded methodically to carry out my complicated plan; which was, it will be remembered, to eat supper and then to go and see about it in person. I performed the first part of this to my entire satisfaction but not to that of the rest. They accused me of unbecoming secrecy; only they expressed it differently. That did not worry me, and in due time I made my escape. At the corral I picked out a good horse, one that I had brought from the Gila, that would stay tied indefinitely without impatience. Then I lighted me a cigarette and jogged up the road. I carried with me a little grub, my six-gun, the famous black bag, and an entirely empty head.

The night was only moderately dark, for while there was no moon there were plenty of those candle-like desert stars. The little twinkling lights of the Box Springs dropped astern like lamps on a shore. By and by I turned off the road and made a wide detour down the sacatone bottoms, for I had still some sense; and roads were a little too obvious. The reception committee that had taken charge of my little friend might be expecting another visitor—me. This brought my approach to the blank side of the ranch where were the willow trees and the irrigating ditch. I rode up as close as I thought I ought to. Then I tied my horse to a prominent lone Joshua-tree that would be easy to find, unstrapped the black bag, and started off. The black bag, however, bothered me; so after some thought I broke the lock with a stone and investigated the contents, mainly by feel. There were a lot of clothes and toilet articles and such junk, and a number of undetermined hard things like round wooden boxes. Finally I withdrew to the shelter of a *barranca* where I could light matches. Then I had no difficulty in identifying a nice compact little hypodermic outfit, which I slipped into a pocket. I then deposited the bag in a safe place where I could find it easily.

Leaving my horse I approached the ranch under cover of the willows. Yes, I remembered this time that I left tracks, but I did not care. My idea was to get some sort of decisive action before morning. Once through the willows I crept up close to the walls. They were twelve or fifteen feet high, absolutely smooth; and with one exception broken only by the long, narrow loopholes or transoms I have mentioned before. The one exception was a small wicket gate or door. I remembered the various sorties with torches after the chirping frogs, and knew that by this opening the hunting party had emerged. This and the big main gate were the only entrances to the enclosure.

I retired to the vicinity of the willows and uttered the cry of the barred owl. After ten seconds I repeated it, and so continued. My only regret was that I could not chirp convincingly like a frog. I saw a shadow shift suddenly through one of the transoms, and at once glided to the wall near the little door. After a moment or so it opened to emit Old Man Hooper and another bulkier figure which I imagined to be that of Ramon. Both were armed with shotguns. Suddenly it came to me that I was lucky not to have been able to chirp convincingly like a frog. They hunted frogs with torches and in a crowd. Those two carried no light and they were so intent on making a sneak on the willows and the supposititious owl that I, flattened in the shadow of the wall, easily escaped their notice. I slipped inside the doorway.

This brought me into a narrow passage between two buildings. The other end looked into the interior court. A careful reconnaissance showed no one in sight, so I walked boldly along the verandah in the direction of the girl's room. Her note had said she was constantly guarded; but I could see no one in sight, and I had to take a chance somewhere. Two seconds' talk would do me: I wanted to know in which of the numerous rooms the old man slept. I had a hunch it would be a good idea to share that room with him. What to do then I left to the hunch.

But when I was half way down the verandah I heard the wicket door slammed shut. The owl hunters had returned more quickly than I had anticipated. Running as lightly as possible I darted down the verandah and around the corner of the left wing. This brought me into a narrow little garden strip between the main house and the wall dividing the court from the corrals and stable yards. Footsteps followed me but stopped. A hand tried the door knob to the corner room.

"Nothing," I heard Hooper's voice replying to a question. "Nothing at all. Go to sleep."

The fragrant smell of Mexican tobacco reached my nostrils. After a moment Ramon—it was he—resumed a conversation in Spanish:

"I do not know, senor, who the man was. I could but listen; it was not well to inquire nor to show too much interest. His name, yes; Jim Starr, but who he is—" I could imagine the shrug. "It is of no importance."

"It is of importance that the other man still lives," broke in Hooper's harsher voice. "I will not have it, I say! Are you sure of it?"

"I saw him. And I saw his horse at the Senor Meigs. It was the brown that bucks badly, so I cut the quarter straps of his saddle. It might be that we have luck; I do not count on it. But rest your mind easy, senor, it shall be arranged."

"It better be."

Stewart Edward White

"But there is more, senor. The senor will remember a man who rode in races for him many years ago, one named Artie—"

"Brower!" broke in Hooper. "What about him?"

"He is in town. He arrived yesterday afternoon."

Hooper ejaculated something.

"And more, he is all day and all night with this Sanborn."

Hooper swore fluently in English.

"Look, Ramon!" he ordered, vehemently. "It is necessary to finish this Sanborn at once, without delay."

"*Bueno*, senor."

"It must not go over a single day."

"Haste makes risk, senor."

"The risk must be run."

"*Bueno*, senor. And also this Artie?"

"No! no! no!" hastened Hooper. "Guard him as your life! But send a trusty man for him to-morrow with the buckboard. He comes to see me, in answer to my invitation."

"And if he will not come, senor?" inquired Ramon's quiet voice.

"Why should he not come?"

"He has been much with Sanborn."

"It's necessary that he come," replied Hooper, emphasizing

each word.

"*Bueno*, senor."

"Who is to be on guard?"

"Cortinez, senor."

"I will send him at once. Do me the kindness to watch for a moment until I send him. Here is the key; give it to him. It shall be but a moment."

"*Bueno*, senor," replied Ramon.

He leaned against the corner of the house. I could see the half of his figure against the sky and the dim white of the walls.

The night was very still, as always at this ranch. There was not even a breeze to create a rustle in the leaves. I was obliged to hold rigidly motionless, almost to hush my breathing, while the figure bulked large against the whitewashed wall. But my eyes, wide to the dimness, took in every detail of my surroundings. Near me stood a water barrel. If I could get a spring from that water barrel I could catch one of the heavy projecting beams of the roof.

After an apparently interminable interval the sound of footsteps became audible, and a moment later Ramon moved to meet his relief. I seized the opportunity of their conversation and ascended to the roof. It proved to be easy, although the dried-out old beam to which for a moment I swung creaked outrageously. Probably it sounded louder to me than the actual fact. I took off my boots and moved cautiously to where I could look down into the court. Ramon and his companion were still talking under the verandah, so I could not see them; but I waited until I heard one of them move away. Then I went to seat myself on the low parapet and think things over.

The man below me had the key to the girl's room. If I could

get the key I could accomplish the first step of my plan—indeed the only step I had determined upon. The exact method of getting the key would have to develop. In the meantime, I gave passing wonder to the fact, as developed by the conversation between Hooper and Ramon, that Brower was not at the ranch and had not been heard of at the ranch. Where had Tiger dumped him, and where now was he lying? I keenly regretted the loss of a possible ally; and, much to my astonishment, I found within myself a little regret for the man himself.

The thought of the transom occurred to me. I tiptoed over to that side and looked down. The opening was about five feet below the parapet. After a moment's thought I tied a bit of stone from the coping in the end of my silk bandana and lowered it at arm's length. By swinging it gently back and forth I determined that the transom was open. With the stub of the pencil every cowboy carried to tally with I scribbled a few words on an envelope which I wrapped about the bit of coping. Something to the effect that I was there, and expected to gain entrance to her room later, and to be prepared. Then I lowered my contraption, caused it to tap gently a dozen times on the edge of the transom, and finally swung it with a rather nice accuracy to fly, bandana and all, through the opening. After a short interval of suspense I saw the reflection of a light and so knew my message had been received.

There was nothing to do now but return to a point of observation. On my way I stubbed my stockinged foot against a stone *metate* or mortar in which Indians and Mexicans make their flour. The heavy pestle was there. I annexed it. Dropped accurately from the height of the roof it would make a very pretty weapon. The trouble, of course, lay in that word "accurately."

But I soon found the fates playing into my hands. At the end of a quarter hour the sentry emerged from under the verandah, looked up at the sky, yawned, stretched, and finally sat down with his back against the wall of the building opposite. Inside of ten minutes he was sound asleep and snoring gently.

I wanted nothing better than that. The descent was a little difficult to accomplish noiselessly, as I had to drop some feet, but I managed it. After crouching for a moment to see if the slight sounds had aroused him, I crept along the wall to where he sat. The stone pestle of the *metate* I had been forced to leave behind me, but I had the heavy barrel of my gun, and I was going to take no chances. I had no compunctions as to what I did to any one of this pack of mad dogs. Cautiously I drew it from its holster and poised it to strike. At that instant I was seized and pinioned from behind.

CHAPTER XI

I did not struggle. I would have done so if I had been able, but I was caught in a grip so skillful that the smallest move gave me the most exquisite pain. At that time I had not even heard the words *jiu jitsu*, but I have looked them up since. Cortinez, the sleepy sentry, without changing his position, had opened his eyes and was grinning at me.

I was forced to my feet and marched to the open door of the corner room. There I was released, and turned around to face Hooper himself. The old man's face was twisted in a sardonic half-snarl that might pass for a grin; but there was no smile in his unblinking wildcat eyes. There seemed to be trace neither of the girl nor the girl's occupation.

"Thank you for your warning of your intended visit," said Hooper in silky tones, indicating my bandana which lay on the table. "And now may I inquire to what I owe the honour of this call? Or it may be that the visit was not intended for me at all. Mistake in the rooms, perhaps. I often shift and change my quarters, and those of my household; especially if I suspect I have some reason for doing so. It adds interest to an otherwise uneventful life."

He was eying me sardonically, evidently gloating over the situation as he found it.

"How did you get on that roof? Who let you inside the walls?" he demanded, abruptly.

I merely smiled at him.

"That we can determine later," he observed, resuming command of himself.

I measured my chances, and found them at present a minus quantity. The old man was separated from me by a table, and he held my own revolver ready for instant use. So I stood tight and waited.

The room was an almost exact replica of the one in which I had spent the night so short a time before; the same long narrow transom near the ceiling, the same barred windows opening on the court, the same closet against the blank wall. Hooper had evidently inhabited it for some days, for it was filled with his personal belongings. Indeed he must have moved in *en bloc* when his ward had been moved out, for none of the furnishings showed the feminine touch, and several articles could have belonged only to the old man personally. Of such was a small iron safe in one corner and a tall old-fashioned desk crammed with papers.

But if I decided overt action unwise at this moment, I decidedly went into action the next. Hooper whistled and four Mexicans appeared with ropes. Somehow I knew if they once hog-tied me I would never get another chance. Better dead now than helpless in the morning, for what that old buzzard might want of me.

One of them tossed a loop at me. I struck it aside and sailed in.

It had always been my profound and contemptuous belief that I could lick any four Mexicans. Now I had to take that back. I could not. But I gave the man argument, and by the time they had my elbows lashed behind me and my legs tied to the legs of one of those big solid chairs they like to name as "Mission style," I had marked them up and torn their pretty clothes and smashed a lot of junk around the place and generally got them so mad they would have knifed me in a holy second if it had not been for Old Man Hooper. The latter held up the lamp where it wouldn't get smashed and admonished them in no uncertain terms that he wanted me alive and comparatively undamaged. Oh, sure! they mussed me up, too. I wasn't very pretty, either.

The bravos withdrew muttering curses, as the story books say; and after Hooper had righted the table and stuck the lamp on it, and taken a good look at my bonds, he withdrew also.

Most of my time until the next thing occurred was occupied in figuring on all the things that might happen to me. One thing I acknowledged to myself right off the reel: the Mexicans had sure trussed me up for further orders! I could move my hands, but I knew enough of ropes and ties to realize that my chances of getting free were exactly nothing. My plans had gone perfectly up to this moment. I had schemed to get inside the ranch and into Old Man Hooper's room; and here I was! What more could a man ask?

The next thing occurred so soon, however, that I hadn't had time to think of more than ten per cent. of the things that might happen to me. The outside door opened to admit Hooper, followed by the girl. He stood aside in the most courtly fashion.

"My dear," he said, "here is Mr. Sanborn, who has come to call on you. You remember Mr. Sanborn, I am sure. You met him at dinner; and besides, I believe you had some correspondence with him, did you not? He has taken so much trouble, so very much trouble to see you that I think it a great pity his wish should not be fulfilled. Won't you sit down here, my dear?"

She was staring at me, her eyes gone wide with wonder and horror. Half thinking she took her seat as indicated. Instantly the old man had bound her elbows at the back and had lashed her to the chair. After the first start of surprise she made no resistance.

"There," said Hooper, straightening up after the accomplishment of this task; "now I'm going to leave you to your visit. You can talk it all over. Tell him all you please, my dear. And you, sir, tell her all you know. I think I can arrange so your confidences will go no further."

For the first time I heard him laugh, a high, uncertain cackle. The girl said nothing, but she stared at him with level, blazing eyes. Also for the first time I began to take an interest in her.

"Do you object to smoking?" I asked her, suddenly.

She blinked and recovered.

"Not at all," she answered.

"Well then, old man, be a sport. Give me the makings. I can get my hands to my mouth."

The old man transferred his baleful eyes on me. Then without saying a word he placed in my hands a box of tailor-made cigarettes and a dozen matches.

"Until morning," he observed, his hand on the door knob. He inclined in a most courteous fashion, first to the one of us, then to the other, and went out. He did not lock the door after him, and I could hear him addressing Cortinez outside. The girl started to speak, but I waved my shackled hand at her for silence. By straining my ears I could just make out what was said.

"I am going to bed," Hooper said. "It is not necessary to stand guard. You may get your blankets and sleep on the verandah."

After the old man's footsteps had died, I turned back to the girl opposite me and looked her over carefully. My first impression of meekness I revised. She did not look to be one bit meek. Her lips were compressed, her nostrils wide, her level eyes unsubdued. A person of sense, I said to myself, well balanced, who has learned when it is useless to kick against the pricks, but who has not necessarily on that account forever renounced all kicking. It occurred to me that she must have had to be pretty thoroughly convinced before she had come to this frame of mind. When she saw that I had heard all I wanted of the movements outside, she spoke hurriedly in her low, sweet voice:

"Oh, I am so distressed! This is all my doing! I should have known better—"

"Now," I interrupted her, decisively, "let's get down to cases. You had nothing to do with this; nothing whatever. I visited this ranch the first time out of curiosity, and to-night because I knew that I'd have to hit first to save my own life. You had no influence on me in either case."

"You thought this was my room—I wrote you it was," she countered, swiftly.

"I wanted to see you solely and simply that I might find out how to get at Hooper. This is all my fault; and we're going to cut out the self-accusations and get down to cases."

I afterward realized that all this was somewhat inconsiderate and ungallant and slightly humiliating; I should have taken the part of the knight-errant rescuing the damsel in distress, but at that moment only the direct essentials entered my mind.

"Very well," she assented in her repressed tones.

"Do you think he is listening to what we say; or has somebody listening?"

"I am positive not."

"Why?"

"I lived in this room for two months, and I know every inch

of it."

"He might have some sort of a concealed listening hole somewhere, just the same."

"I am certain he has not. The walls are two feet thick."

"All right; let it go at that. Now let's see where we stand. In the first place, how do you dope this out?"

"What do you mean?"

"What does he intend to do with us?"

She looked at me straight, eye to eye.

"In the morning he will kill you—unless you can contrive something."

"Cheering thought."

"There is no sense in not facing situations squarely. If there is a way out, that is the only method by which it may be found."

"True," I agreed, my admiration growing. "And yourself; will he kill you, too?"

"He will not. He does not dare!" she cried, proudly, with a flash of the eyes.

I was not so sure of that, but there was no object in saying so.

"Why has he tied you in that chair, then, along with the condemned?" I asked.

"You will understand better if I tell you who I am."

"You are his deceased partner's daughter; and everybody thinks you are in Europe," I stated.

"How in the world did you know that? But no matter; it is true. I embarked three months ago on the Limited for New York intending, as you say, to go on a long trip to Europe. My father and I had been alone in the world. We were very fond of each other. I took no companion, nor did I intend to. I felt quite independent and able to take care of myself. At the last moment Mr. Hooper boarded the train. That was quite unexpected. He was on his way to the ranch. He persuaded me to stop over for a few days to decide some matters. You know, since my father's death I am half owner."

"Whole owner," I murmured.

"What did you say?"

"Nothing. Go ahead. Sure you don't mind my smoking?" I lit one of the tailor-mades and settled back. Even my inexperienced youth recognized the necessity of relief this long-continued stubborn repression must feel. My companion had as yet told me nothing I did not already know or guess; but I knew it would do her good to talk, and I might learn something valuable.

"We came out to the ranch, and talked matters over quite normally; but when it came time for my departure, I was not permitted to leave. For some unexplained reason I was a prisoner, confined absolutely to the four walls of this enclosure. I was guarded night and day; and I soon found I was to be permitted conversation with two men only, Mexicans named Ramon and Andreas."

"They are his right and left hand," I commented.

"So I found. You may imagine I did not submit to this until I found I had to. Then I made up my mind that the only possible thing to do was to acquiesce, to observe, and to wait my chance."

"You were right enough there. Why do you figure he did this?"

"I don't know!" she cried with a flash of thwarted despair. "I have racked my brains, but I can find no motive. He has not asked me for a thing; he has not even asked me a question. Unless he's stark crazy, I cannot make it out!"

"He may be that," I suggested.

"He may be; and yet I doubt it somehow. I don't know why; but I *feel* that he is sane enough. He is inconceivably cruel and domineering. He will not tolerate a living thing about the place that will not or cannot take orders from him. He kills the flies, the bees, the birds, the frogs, because they are not his. I believe he would kill a man as quickly who stood out even for a second against him here. To that extent I believe he is crazy: a sort of monomania. But not otherwise. That is why I say he will kill you; I really believe he would do it."

"So do I," I agreed, grimly. "However, let's drop that for right now. Do you know a man named Brower, Artie Brower?"

"I don't think I ever heard of him. Why?"

"Never mind for a minute. I've just had a great thought strike me. Just let me alone a few moments while I work it out."

I lighted a second cigarette from the butt of the first and fell into a study. Cortinez breathed heavily outside. Otherwise the silence was as dead as the blackness of the night. The smoke from my cigarettes floated lazily until it reached the influence of the hot air from the lamp; then it shot upward toward the ceiling. The girl watched me from under her level brows, always with that air of controlled restraint I found so admirable.

"I've got it," I said at last, "—or at least I think I have. Now listen to me, and believe what I've got to say. Here are the facts: first, your father and Hooper split partnership a while back. Hooper took his share entirely in cash; your father took his probably part in cash, but certainly all of the ranch and cattle. Get that clear? Hooper owns no part of the ranch and cattle. All right. Your father dies before the papers relating to this agreement are recorded. Nobody knew of those papers except your father and Hooper. So if Hooper were to destroy those papers, he'd still have the cash that had been paid him, and an equal share in the property. That plain?"

"Perfectly," she replied, composedly. "Why didn't he destroy them?"

"Because they had been stolen by this man Brower I asked you about—an ex-jockey of Hooper's. Brower held them for blackmail. Unless Hooper came through Brower would record the papers."

"Where do I come in?"

"Easy. I'm coming to that. But answer me this: who would be your heir in case you died?"

"Why—I don't know!"

"Have you any kin?"

"Not a soul!"

"Did you ever make a will?"

"I never thought of such a thing!"

"Well, I'll tell you. If you were to die your interest in this property would go to Hooper."

"What makes you think so? I thought it would go to the state."

"I'm guessing," I acknowledged, "but I believe I'm guessing straight. A lot of these old Arizona partnerships were made just that way. Life was uncertain out here. I'll bet the old original partnership between your father and Hooper provides that in case of the extinction of one line, the other will inherit. It's a very common form of partnership in a new country like this. You can see for yourself it's a sensible thing to provide."

"You may be right," she commented. "Go on."

"You told me a while ago it was best to face any situation squarely. Now brace up and face this. You said a while ago that Hooper would not dare kill you. That is true for the moment. But there is no doubt in my mind that he has intended from the first to kill you, because by that he would get possession of the whole property."

"I cannot believe it!" she cried.

"Isn't the incentive enough? Think carefully, and answer honestly: don't you think him capable of it?"

"Yes—I suppose so," she admitted, reluctantly, after a moment. She gathered herself as after a shock. "Why hasn't he done so? Why has he waited?"

I told her of the situation as it concerned Brower. While the dissolution of partnership papers still existed and might still be recorded, such a murder would be useless. For naturally the dissolution abrogated the old partnership agreement. The girl's share of the property would, at her demise intestate, go to the state. That is, provided the new papers were ever recorded.

"Then I am safe until—?" she began.

"Until he negotiates or otherwise settles with Brower. Until he has destroyed all evidence."

"Then everything seems to depend on this Brower," she said, knitting her brows anxiously. "Where is he?"

I did not answer this last question. My eyes were riveted on the door knob which was slowly, almost imperceptibly, turning.

Cortinez continued to breathe heavily in sleep outside. The intruder was evidently at great pains not to awaken the guard. A fraction of an inch at a time the door opened. A wild-haired, wild-eyed head inserted itself cautiously through the crack. The girl's eyes widened in surprise and, I imagine, a little in fear. I began to laugh, silently, so as not to disturb Cortinez. Mirth overcame me; the tears ran down my cheeks.

"It's so darn complete!" I gasped, answering the girl's horrified look of inquiry. "Miss Emory, allow me to present Mr. Artie Brower!"

CHAPTER XII

Brower entered the room quickly but very quietly, and at once came to me. His eyes were staring, his eyelids twitched, his hands shook. I recognized the symptoms.

"Have you got it? Have you got it with you?" he whispered, feverishly.

"It's all right. I can fix you up. Untie me first," I replied.

He began to fumble with the knots of my bonds too hastily and impatiently for effectiveness. I was trying to stoop over far enough to see what he was doing when my eye caught the shadow of a moving figure outside. An instant later Tim Westmore, the English groom attached to the Morgan stallion, came cautiously through the door, which he closed behind him. I attempted unobtrusively to warn Brower, but he only looked up, nodded vaguely, and continued his fumbling efforts to free me. Westmore glanced at us all curiously, but went at once to the big windows, which he proceeded to swing shut. Then he came over to us, pushed Brower one side, and most expeditiously untied the knots. I stood up stretching in the luxury of freedom, then turned to perform a like office for Miss Emory. But Brower was by now frantic. He seized my arm and fairly shook me, big as I was, in the urgence of his desire. He was rapidly losing all control and caution.

"Let him have it, sir," urged Westmore in a whisper. "I'll free the young lady."

Stewart Edward White

I gave Brower the hypodermic case. He ran to the wash bowl for water. During the process of preparation he uttered little animal sounds under his breath. When the needle had sunk home he lay back in a chair and closed his eyes.

In the meantime, I had been holding a whispered colloquy with Westmore.

"He sneaked in on me at dark, sir," he told me, "on foot. I don't know how he got in without being seen. They'd have found his tracks anyway in the morning. I don't think he knew quite what he wanted to do. Him and me were old pals, and he wanted to ask me about things. He didn't expect to stay, I fancy. He told me he had left his horse tied a mile or so down the road. Then a while back orders came to close down, air tight. We're used to such orders. Nobody can go out or come in, you understand. And there are guards placed. That made him uneasy. He told me then he was a hop fiend. I've seen them before, and I got uneasy, too. If he came to the worst I might have to tie and gag him. I know how they are."

"Go ahead," I urged. He had stopped to listen.

"I don't like that Cortinez being so handy like out there," he confessed.

"Hooper told him he could sleep. He's not likely to pay attention to us. Miss Emory and I have been talking aloud."

"I hope not. Well, then, Ramon came by and stopped to talk to me for a minute. I had to hide Artie in a box-stall and hope to God he kept quiet. He wasn't as bad as he is now. Ramon told me about you being caught, and went on. After that nothing must do but find you. He thought you might have his dope. He'd have gone into the jaws of hell after it. So I came along to keep him out of mischief."

"What are you going to do now?" asked the girl, who had kicked off her slippers and had been walking a few paces to and fro.

"I don't know, ma'am. We've got to get away."

"We?"

"You mean me, too? Yes, ma'am! I have stood with the doings of this place as long as I can stand them. Artie has told me some other things. Are you here of your free will, ma'am?" he asked, abruptly.

"No," she replied.

"I suspected as much. I'm through with the whole lot of them."

Brower opened his eyes. He was now quite calm.

"Hooper sold the Morgan stallion," he whispered, smiled sardonically, and closed his eyes again.

"Without telling me a word of it!" added Tim with heat. "He ain't delivered him yet."

"Well, I don't blame you. Now you'd better quietly sneak back to your quarters. There is likely to be trouble before we get through. You, too, Brower. Nobody knows you are here."

Brower opened his eyes again.

"I can get out of this place now I've had me hop," said he, decidedly. "Come on, let's go."

"We'll all go," I agreed; "but let's see what we can find here first. There may be some paper—or something—"

"What do you mean? What sort of papers? Hadn't we better go at once?"

"It is supposed to be well known that the reason Hooper isn't assassinated from behind a bush is because in that case his killers are in turn to assassinate a long list of his enemies. Only nobody is sure: just as nobody is really sure that he has killers at all. You can't get action on an uncertainty."

She nodded. "I can understand that."

"If we could get proof positive it would be no trick at all to raise the country."

"What sort of proof?"

"Well, I mentioned a list. I don't doubt his head man— Ramon, I suppose, the one he'd trust with carrying out such a job—must have a list of some sort. He wouldn't trust to memory."

"And he wouldn't trust it to Ramon until after he was dead!" said the girl with sudden intuition. "If it exists we'll find it here."

She started toward the paper-stuffed desk, but I stopped her.

"More likely the safe," said I.

Tim, who was standing near it, tried the handle.

"It's locked," he whispered.

I fell on my knees and began to fiddle with the dial, of course in vain. Miss Emory, with more practical decision of character, began to run through the innumerable bundles and loose papers in the desk, tossing them aside as they proved unimportant or not germane to the issue. I had not the slightest knowledge of the constructions of safes but whirled the knob hopelessly in one direction or another trying to listen for clicks, as somewhere I had read was the thing to do. As may be imagined, I arrived nowhere. Nor did the girl. We looked at each other in chagrin at last.

"There is nothing here but ranch bills and accounts and business letters," she confessed.

I merely shook my head.

At this moment Brower, whom I had supposed to be sound asleep, opened his eyes.

"Want that safe open?" he asked, drowsily.

He arose, stretched, and took his place beside me on the floor. His head cocked one side, he slowly turned the dials with the tips of fingers I for the first time noticed were long and slim and sensitive. Twice after extended, delicate manipulations he whirled the knob impatiently and took a fresh start. On the proverbial third trial he turned the handle and the door swung open. He arose rather stiffly from his knees, resumed his place in the armchair, and again closed his eyes.

It was a small safe, with few pigeon holes. A number of blue-covered contracts took small time for examination. There were the usual number of mine certificates not valuable enough for a safe deposit, some confidential memoranda and accounts having to do with the ranch.

"Ah, here is something!" I breathed to the eager audience over my shoulder. I held in my hands a heavy manila envelope, sealed, inscribed "Ramon. (To be destroyed unopened.)"

"Evidently we were right: Ramon has the combination and is to be executor," I commented.

I tore open the envelope and extracted from it another of the blue-covered documents.

"It's a copy, unsigned, of that last agreement with your father," I said, after a disappointed glance. "It's worth keeping," and I thrust it inside my shirt.

But this particular pigeon hole proved to be a mine. In it were several more of the same sort of envelope, all sealed, all addressed to Ramon. One was labelled as the Last Will, one as Inventory, and one simply as Directions. This last had a further warning that it was to be opened only by the one addressed. I determined by hasty examination that the first two were only what they purported to be, and turned hopefully to a perusal of the last. It was in Spanish, and dealt at great length with the disposition and management of Hooper's extensive interests. I append a translation of the portion of this remarkable document, having to do with our case.

"These are my directions," it began, "as to the matter of which we have many times spoken together. I have many enemies, and many who think they have cause to wish my death. They are cowards and soft and I do not think they will ever be sure enough to do me harm. I do not fear them. But it may be that one or some of them will find it in their souls to do a deed against me. In that case I shall be content, for neither do I fear the devil. But I shall be content only if you follow my orders. I add here a list of my enemies and of those who have cause to wish me ill. If I am killed, it is probable that some one of these will have done the deed. Therefore they must all die. You must see to it, following them if necessary to the ends of the earth. You will know how; and what means to employ. When all these are gone, then go you to the highest rock on the southerly pinnacle of Cochise's Stronghold. Ten paces northwest is a gray, flat slab. If you lift this slab there will be found a copper box. In the box is the name of a man. You will go to this man and give him the copper box and in return he will give to you one hundred thousand dollars. I know well, my Ramon, that your honesty would not permit you to seek the copper box before the last of my enemies is dead. Nevertheless, that you may admire my recourse, I have made an arrangement. If the gray slab on Cochise's Stronghold is ever disturbed before the whole toll is paid, you will die very suddenly and unpleasantly. I know well that you, my Ramon, would not disturb it; and I hope for your sake that nobody else will do so. It is not likely. No one is fool enough to climb Cochise's Stronghold for pleasure; and this gray slab is one among many."

At this time I did not read carefully the above cheerful document. My Spanish was good enough, but took time in the translating. I dipped into it enough to determine that it was what we wanted, and flipped the pages to come to the list of prospective victims. It covered two sheets, and a glance down the columns showed me that about every permanent inhabitant of the Soda Springs Valley was included. I found my own name in quite fresh ink toward the last.

"This is what we want," I said in satisfaction, rising to my feet. I sketched in a few words the purport of the document.

"Let me see it," said the girl.

I handed it to her. She began to examine carefully the list of names, her face turning paler as she read. Tim Westmore looked anxiously over her shoulder. Suddenly I saw his face congest and his eyes bulge.

"Why! why!" he gasped, "I'm there! What've I ever done, I ask you that? The old—" he choked, at a loss and groping. Then his anger flared up. "I've always served him faithful and done what I was told," he muttered, fiercely. "I'll do him in for this!"

"I am here," observed Miss Emory.

"Yes, and that sot in the chair!" whispered Tim, fiercely.

Again Brower proved he was not asleep by opening one eye.

"Thanks for them kind words," said he.

"We've got to get out of here," stated Tim with conviction.

"That idea just got through your thick British skull?" queried Artie, rousing again.

"I wish we had some way to carry the young lady—she can't walk," said Westmore, paying no attention.

"I have my horse tied out by the lone Joshua-tree," I answered him.

"I'm going to take a look at that Cortinez," said the little Englishman, nodding his satisfaction at my news as to the horse. "I'm not easy about him."

"He'll sleep like a log until morning," Miss Emory reassured me. "I've often stepped right over him where he has been on guard and walked all around the garden."

"Just the same I'm going to take a look," persisted Westmore.

He tiptoed to the door, softly turned the knob and opened it. He found himself face to face with Cortinez.

CHAPTER XIII

I had not thought of the English groom as a man of resource, but his action in this emergency proved him. He cast a fleeting glance over his shoulder. Artie Brower was huddled down in his armchair practically out of sight; Miss Emory and I had reseated ourselves in the only other two chairs in the room, so that we were in the same relative positions as when we had been bound and left. Only the confusion of the papers on the floor and the open safe would have struck an observant eye.

"It is well that you come," said Tim to Cortinez in Spanish. "The senor sent me to conduct these two to the East Room and I like not the job alone. Enter."

He held the door with one hand and fairly dragged Cortinez through with the other. Instantly he closed the door and cast himself on Cortinez's back. I had already launched myself at the Mexican's throat.

The struggle was violent but brief. Fortunately I had not missed my spring at our enemy's windpipe, so he had been unable to shout. The noise of our scuffle sounded loud enough within the walls of the room; but those walls were two feet thick, and the door and windows closed.

"Get something to gag him with, and the cords," panted Tim to the girl.

Brower opened his eyes again.

Stewart Edward White

"I can beat that," he announced.

He produced his hypodermic and proceeded to mix a gunful of the dope.

"This'll fix him," he observed, turning back the Mexican's sleeve. "You can lay him outside and if anybody comes along they'll think he's asleep—as usual."

This we did when the dope had worked.

It was now high time to think of our next move. For weapons we had the gun and knife taken from Cortinez and the miserable little automatic belonging to Brower. That was all. It was perfectly evident that we could not get out through the regular doorways, as, by Tim's statement, they were all closed and guarded. On my representation it was decided to try the roof.

We therefore knotted together the cord that had bound me and two sheets from the bed, and sneaked cautiously out on the verandah, around the corner to the water barrel, and so to the vantage point of the roof.

The chill of the night was come, and the stars hung cold in the sky. It seemed that the air would snap and crackle were some little resolving element to be dropped into its suspended hush. Not a sound was to be heard except a slow drip of water from somewhere in the courtyard.

It was agreed that I, as the heaviest, should descend first. I landed easily enough and steadied the rope for Miss Emory who came next. While I was waiting I distinctly heard, from the direction of the willows, the hooting of an owl. Furthermore, it was a great horned owl, and he seemed to have a lot to say. You remember what I told you about setting your mind so that only one sort of noise will arouse it, but that one instantly? I knew perfectly well that Old Man Hooper's mind was set to all these smaller harmless noises that most people never notice at all, waking or sleeping—frogs, crickets, owls. And therefore I was convinced that sooner or later that old man and his foolish ideas and his shotgun would come projecting right across our well-planned getaway. Which was just what happened, and almost at once. Probably that great horned owl had been hooting for some time, but we had been too busy to notice. I heard the wicket door turning on its hinges, and ventured a warning hiss to Brower and Tim Westmore, who had not yet descended. An instant later I could make out shadowy forms stealing toward the willows. Evidently those who served Old Man Hooper were accustomed to broken rest.

We kept very quiet, straining our eyes at the willows. After an interval a long stab of light pierced the dusk and the round detonation of old-fashioned black powder shook the silence. There came to us the babbling of voices released. At the same instant the newly risen moon plastered us against that whitewashed wall like insects pinned in a cork-lined case. The moonlight must have been visibly creeping down to us for some few minutes, but so absorbed had I been in the doings of the party in the willows, and so chuckleheaded were the two on the roof, that actually none of us had noticed!

I dropped flat and dragged the girl down with me. But there remained that ridiculous, plainly visible rope; and anyway a shout relieved me of any doubt as to whether we had been seen. Brower came tumbling down on us, and with one accord we three doubled to the right around the walls of the ranch. A revolver shot sang by us, but we were not immediately pursued. Our antagonists were too few and too uncertain of our numbers and arms.

It was up to us to utilize the few minutes before the ranch should be aroused. We doubled back through the willows and across the mesquite flat toward the lone Joshua-tree where I had left my horse. I held the girl's hand to help her when she stumbled, while Brower scuttled along with surprising endurance for a dope wreck. Nobody said anything, but saved their wind.

"Where's Tim?" I asked at a check when we had to scramble across a *barranca*.

"He went back into the ranch the way we came," replied Artie with some bitterness.

It was, nevertheless, the wisest thing he could have done. He had not been identified with this outfit except by Cortinez, and Cortinez was safe for twelve hours.

We found the Joshua-tree without difficulty.

"Now," said I, "here is the plan. You are to take these papers to Senor Buck Johnson, at the Box Springs ranch. That's the next ranch on the fork of the road. Do you remember it?"

"Yes," said Brower, who had waked up and seemed quite sober and responsible. "I can get to it."

"Wake him up. Show him these papers. Make him read them. Tell him that Miss Emory and I are in the Bat-eye Tunnel. Remember that?"

"The Bat-eye Tunnel," repeated Artie.

"Why don't *you* go?" inquired the girl, anxiously.

"I ride too heavy; and I know where the tunnel is," I replied. "If anybody else was to go, it would be you. But Artie rides light and sure, and he'll have to ride like hell. Here, put these papers inside your shirt. Be off!"

Lights were flickering at the ranch as men ran to and fro with lanterns. It would not take these skilled *vaqueros* long to catch their horses and saddle up. At any moment I expected to see the massive doors swing open to let loose the wolf pack.

Brower ran to my horse—a fool proceeding, especially for an experienced horseman—and jerked loose the tie rope. Badger is a good reliable cow horse, but he's not a million years old, and he's got some natural equine suspicions. I kind of lay a good deal of it to that fool hard-boiled hat. At any rate, he snorted and sagged back on the rope, hit a yucca point, whirled and made off. Artie was game. He hung on until he was drug into a bunch of *chollas*, and then he had to let go. Badger departed into the distance, tail up and snorting.

"Well, you've done it now!" I observed to Brower, who, crying with nervous rage and chagrin, and undoubtedly considerably stuck up with *cholla* spines, was crawling to his feet.

"Can't we catch him? Won't he stop?" asked Miss Emory. "If he gets to the ranch, won't they look for you?"

"He's one of my range ponies: he won't stop short of the Gila."

I cast over the chances in my mind, weighing my knowledge of the country against the probabilities of search. The proportion was small. Most of my riding experience had been farther north and to the west. Such obvious hole-ups as the one I had suggested—the Bat-eye Tunnel—were of course familiar to our pursuers. My indecision must have seemed long, for the girl broke in anxiously on my meditations.

"Oughtn't we to be moving?"

"As well here as anywhere," I replied. "We are under good cover; and afoot we could not much better ourselves as against mounted men. We must hide."

"But they may find the trampled ground where your horse has been tied."

"I hope they do."

"You hope they do!"

"Sure. They'll figure that we must sure have moved away. They'll never guess we'd hide near at hand. At least that's what I hope."

"How about tracks?"

"Not at night. By daylight maybe."

"But then to-morrow morning they can—"

"To-morrow morning is a long way off."

"Look!" cried Brower.

The big gates of the ranch had been thrown open. The glare of a light—probably a locomotive headlight—poured out. Mounted figures galloped forth and swerved to right or left, spreading in a circle about the enclosure. The horsemen reined to a trot and began methodically to quarter the ground, weaving back and forth. Four detached themselves and rode off at a swift gallop to the points of the compass. The mounted men were working fast for fear, I suppose, that we may have possessed horses. Another contingent, afoot and with lanterns, followed more slowly, going over the ground for indications. I could not but admire the skill and thoroughness of the plan.

"Our only chance is in the shadow from the moon," I told my companions. "If we can slip through the riders, and get in their rear, we may be able to follow the *barranca* down. Any of those big rocks will do. Lay low, and after a rider has gone over a spot, try to get to that spot without being seen."

We were not to be kept long in suspense. Out of all the three hundred and sixty degrees of the circle one of the swift outriders selected precisely our direction! Straight as an arrow he came for us, at full gallop. I could see the toss of his horse's mane against the light from the opened door. There was no time to move. All we could do was to cower beneath our rock, muscles tense, and hope to be able to glide around the shadow as he passed.

But he did not pass. Down into the shallow *barranca* he slid with a tinkle of shale, and drew rein within ten feet of our lurking place.

We could hear the soft snorting of his mount above the thumping of our hearts. I managed to get into a position to steal a glimpse. It was difficult, but at length I made out the statuesque lines of the horse, and the rider himself, standing in his stirrups and leaning slightly forward, peering intently about him. The figures were in silhouette against the sky, but nobody ever fooled me as to a horse. It was the Morgan stallion, and the rider was Tim Westmore. Just as the realization came to me, Tim uttered a low, impatient whistle.

It's always a good idea to take a chance. I arose into view—but I kept my gun handy.

"Thank God!" cried Tim, fervently, under his breath. "I remembered you'd left your horse by this Joshua: it's the only landmark in the dark. Saints!" he ejaculated in dismay as he saw us all. "Where's your horse?"

"Gone."

"We can't all ride this stallion—"

"Listen," I cut in, and I gave him the same directions I had previously given Brower. He heard me attentively.

"I can beat that," he cut me off. He dismounted. "Get on here, Artie. Ride down the *barranca* two hundred yards and you'll come to an alkali flat. Get out on that flat and ride like hell for Box Springs."

"Why don't you do it?"

"I'm going back and tell 'em how I was slugged and robbed of my horse."

"They'll kill you if they suspect; dare you go back?"

"I've been back once," he pointed out. He was helping Brower aboard.

"Where did you get that bag?" he asked.

"Found it by the rock where we were hiding: it's mine," replied Brower.

Westmore tried to get him to leave it, but the little jockey was obstinate. He kicked his horse and, bending low, rode away.

"You're right: I beg your pardon," I answered Westmore's remark to me. "You don't look slugged."

"That's easy fixed," said Tim, calmly. He removed his hat and hit his forehead a very solid blow against a projection of the conglomerate boulder. The girl screamed slightly.

"Hush!" warned Tim in a fierce whisper. He raised his hand toward the approaching horsemen, who were now very near. Without attention to the blood streaming from his brow he bent his head to listen to the faint clinking of steel against rock that marked the stallion's progress toward the alkali flat. The searchers were by now dangerously close, and Tim uttered a smothered oath of impatience. But at last we distinctly heard the faint, soft thud of galloping hoofs.

The searchers heard it, too, and reined up to listen. Tim thrust into my hand the 30-30 Winchester he was carrying together with a box of cartridges. Then with a leap like a tiger he gained the rim of the *barranca*. Once there, however, his forces seemed to desert him. He staggered forward calling in a weak voice. I could hear the volley of rapid questions shot at him by the men who immediately surrounded him; and his replies.

Then somebody fired a revolver thrice in rapid succession and the whole cavalcade swept away with a mighty crackling of brush. Immediately after Tim rejoined us. I had not expected this.

Relieved for the moment we hurried Miss Emory rapidly up the bed of the shallow wash. The tunnel mentioned was part of an old mine operation, undertaken at some remote period before the cattle days. It entered the base of one of those isolated conical hills, lying like islands in the plain, so common in Arizona. From where we had hidden it lay about three miles to the northeast. It was a natural and obvious hide out, and I had no expectation of remaining unmolested. My hope lay in rescue.

We picked our way under cover of the ravine as long as we could, then struck boldly across the plain. Nobody seemed to be following us. A wild hope entered my heart that perhaps they might believe we had all made our escape to Box Springs.

As we proceeded the conviction was borne in on me that the stratagem had at least saved us from immediate capture. Like most men who ride I had very sketchy ideas of what three miles afoot is like—at night—in high heels. The latter affliction was common to both Miss Emory and myself. She had on a sort of bedroom slipper, and I wore the usual cowboy boots. We began to go footsore about the same time, and the little rolling volcanic rocks among the bunches of *sacatone* did not help us a bit. Tim made good time, curse him. Or rather, bless him; for as I just said, if he had not tolled away our mounted pursuit we would have been caught as sure as God made little green apples. He seemed as lively as a cricket, in spite of the dried blood across his face.

The moon was now sailing well above the horizon, throwing the world into silver and black velvet. When we moved in the open we showed up like a train of cars; but, on the other hand, the shadow was a cloak. It was by now nearly one o'clock in the morning.

Miss Emory's nerve did not belie the clear, steadfast look of her eye; but she was about all in when we reached the foot of Bat-eye Butte. Tim and I had discussed the procedure as we walked. I was for lying in wait outside; but Tim pointed out that the tunnel entrance was well down in the boulders, that even the sharpest outlook could not be sure of detecting an approach through the shadows, and that from the shelter of the roof props and against the light we should be able to hold off a large force almost indefinitely. In any case, we would have to gamble on Brewer's winning through, and having sense enough in his opium-saturated mind to make a convincing yarn of it. So after a drink at the *tenaja* below the mine we entered the black square of the tunnel.

The work was old, but it had been well done. They must have dragged the timbers down from the White Mountains. Indeed a number of unused beams, both trunks of trees and squared, still lay around outside. From time to time, since the original operations, some locoed prospector comes projecting along and does a little work in hopes he may find something the other fellow had missed. So the passage was crazy with props and supports, new and old, placed to brace the ageing overhead timbers. Going in they were a confounded nuisance against the bumped head; but looking back toward the square of light they made fine protections behind which to crouch. In this part of the country any tunnel would be dry. It ran straight for about a hundred and fifty feet.

We groped our way about seventy-five feet, which was as far as we could make out the opening distinctly, and sat down to wait. I still had the rest of the tailor-made cigarettes, which I shared with Tim. We did not talk, for we wished to listen for sounds outside. To judge by her breathing, I think Miss Emory dozed, or even went to sleep.

About an hour later I thought to hear a single tinkle of shale. Tim heard it, too, for he nudged me. Our straining ears caught nothing further, however; and I, for one, had relaxed from my tension when the square of light was darkened by a figure. I was nearest, so I raised Cortinez's gun and fired. The girl uttered a scream, and the figure disappeared. I don't know yet whether I hit him or not; we never found any blood.

We made Miss Emory lie down behind a little slide of rock, and disposed ourselves under shelter.

"We can take them as fast as they come," exulted Tim.

"I don't believe there are more than two0 or three of them," I observed. "It would be only a scouting party. They will go for help."

As there was no longer reason for concealment, we talked aloud and freely.

Now ensued a long waiting interim. We could hear various sounds outside as of moving to and fro. The enemy had likewise no reason for further concealment.

"Look!" suddenly cried Tim. "Something crawling."

He raised the 30-30 and fired. Before the flash and the fumes had blinded me I, too, had seen indistinctly something low and prone gliding around the corner of the entrance. That was all we could make out of it, for as you can imagine the light was almost non-existent. The thing glided steadily, untouched or unmindful of the shots we threw at it. When it came to the first of the crazy uprights supporting the roof timbers it seemed to hesitate gropingly. Then it drew slowly back a foot or so, and darted forward. The ensuing thud enlightened us. The thing was one of the long, squared timbers we had noted outside; and it was being used as a battering ram.

"They'll bring the whole mountain down on us!" cried Tim, springing forward.

But even as he spoke, and before he had moved two feet, that catastrophe seemed at least to have begun. The prop gave way:

the light at the entrance was at once blotted out; the air was filled with terrifying roaring echoes. There followed a succession of crashes, the rolling of rocks over each other, the grinding slide of avalanches great and small. We could scarcely breathe for the dust. Our danger was that now the thing was started it would not stop: that the antique and inadequate supports would all give way, one bringing down the other in succession until we were buried. Would the forces of equilibrium establish themselves through the successive slight resistances of these rotted, worm-eaten old timbers before the constricted space in which we crouched should be entirely eaten away?

After the first great crash there ensued a moment's hesitation. Then a second span succumbed. There followed a series of minor chutes with short intervening silences. At last so long an interval of calm ensued that we plucked up courage to believe it all over. A single stone rolled a few feet and hit the rock floor with a bang. Then, immediately after, the first-deafening thunder was repeated as evidently another span gave way. It sounded as though the whole mountain had moved. I was almost afraid to stretch out my hand for fear it would encounter the wall of debris. The roar ceased as abruptly as it had begun. Followed then a long silence. Then a little cascading tinkle of shale. And another dead silence.

"I believe it's over," ventured Miss Emory, after a long time.

"I'm going to find out how bad it is," I asserted.

I moved forward cautiously, my arms extended before me, feeling my way with my feet. Foot after foot I went, encountering nothing but the props. Expecting as I did to meet an obstruction within a few paces at most, I soon lost my sense of distance; after a few moments it seemed to me that I must have gone much farther than the original length of the tunnel. At last I stumbled over a fragment, and so found my fingers against a rough mass of debris.

"Why, this is fine!" I cried to the others, "I don't believe more than a span or so has gone!"

I struck one of my few remaining matches to make sure. While of course I had no very accurate mental image of the original state of things, still it seemed to me there was an awful lot of tunnel left. As the whole significance of our situation came to me, I laughed aloud.

"Well," said I, cheerfully, "they couldn't have done us a better favour! It's a half hour's job to dig us out, and in the meantime we are safe as a covered bridge. We don't even have to keep watch."

"Provided Brower gets through," the girl reminded us.

"He'll get through," assented Tim, positively. "There's nothing on four legs can catch that Morgan stallion."

I opened my watch crystal and felt of the hands. Half-past two.

"Four or five hours before they can get here," I announced.

"We'd better go to sleep, I think," said Miss Emory.

"Good idea," I approved. "Just pick your rocks and go to it."

I sat down and leaned against one of the uprights, expecting fully to wait with what patience I might the march of events. Sleep was the farthest thing from my thoughts. When I came to I found myself doubled on my side with a short piece of ore sticking in my ribs and eighteen or twenty assorted cramp-pains in various parts of me. This was all my consciousness had room to attend to for a few moments. Then I became dully aware of faint tinkling sounds and muffled shoutings from the outer end of the tunnel. I shouted in return and made my way as rapidly as possible toward the late entrance.

Stewart Edward White

A half hour later we crawled cautiously through a precarious opening and stood blinking at the sunlight.

CHAPTER XIV

A group of about twenty men greeted our appearance with a wild cowboy yell. Some of the men of our outfit were there, but not all; and I recognized others from as far south as the Chiracahuas. Windy Bill was there with Jed Parker; but Senor Johnson's bulky figure was nowhere to be seen. The other men were all riders—nobody of any particular standing or authority. The sun made it about three o'clock of the afternoon. Our adventures had certainly brought us a good sleep!

After we had satisfied our thirst from a canteen we began to ask and answer questions. Artie Brower had made the ranch without mishap, had told his story, and had promptly fallen asleep. Buck Johnson, in his usual deliberate manner, read all the papers through twice; pondered for some time while the more excited Jed and Windy fidgeted impatiently; and then, his mind made up, acted with his customary decision. Three men he sent to reconnoitre in the direction of the Bat-eye Tunnel with instructions to keep out of trouble and to report promptly. His other riders he dispatched with an insistent summons to all the leading cattlemen as far south as the Chiracahua Range, as far east as Grant's Pass, as far west as Madrona. Such was Buck Johnson's reputation for level-headedness that without hesitation these men saddled and rode at their best speed. By noon the weightiest of the Soda Spring Valley had gathered in conclave.

"That's where we faded out," said Jed Parker. "They sent us up to see about you-all. The scouts from up here come back with their little Wild West story about knocking down this yere mountain on top of you. We had to believe them because they brought back a little proof with them. Mex guns and spurs and such plunder looted off'n the deceased on the field of battle. Bill here can tell you."

"They was only two of them," said Windy Bill, diffident for the first time in his life, "and we managed to catch one of 'em foul. We been digging here for too long. We ain't no prairie dogs to go delving into the bosom of the earth. We thought you must be plumb deceased anyhow: we couldn't get a peep out of you. I was in favour of leavin' you lay myself. This yere butte seemed like a first-rate imposing tomb; and I was willing myself to carve a few choice sentiments on some selectedrock. Sure I can carve! But Jed here allowed that you owed him ten dollars and maybe had some money in your pocket—"

"Shut up, Windy," I broke in. "Can't you see the young lady—"

Windy whirled all contrition and apologies.

"Don't you mind me, ma'am," he begged. "They call me Windy Bill, and I reckon that's about right. I don't mean nothing. And we'd have dug all through this butte before—"

"I know that. It isn't your talk," interrupted Miss Emory, "but the sun is hot—and—haven't you anything at all to eat?"

"Suffering giraffes!" cried Windy above the chorus of dismay. "Lunkheads! chumps! Of all the idiot plays ever made in this territory!" He turned to the dismayed group. "Ain't any one of you boys had sense enough to bring any grub?"

But nobody had. The old-fashioned Arizona cowboy ate only twice a day. It would never occur to him to carry a lunch for noon. Still, they might have considered a rescue party's probable needs.

We mounted and started for the Box Springs ranch. They had at least known enough to bring extra horses.

"Old Hooper knows the cat is out of the bag now," I suggested as we rode along.

"He sure does."

"Do you think he'll stick: or will he get out?"

"He'll stick."

"I don't know—" I argued, doubtfully.

"I do," with great positiveness.

"Why are you so sure?"

"There are men in the brush all around his ranch to see that he does."

"For heaven's sake how many have you got together?" I cried, astonished.

"About three hundred," said Jed.

"What's the plan?"

"I don't know. They were chewing over it when I left. But I'll bet something's going to pop. There's a bunch of 'em on that sweet little list you-all dug up."

We rode slowly. It was near five o'clock when we pulled down the lane toward the big corrals. The latter were full of riding horses, and the fences were topped with neatly arranged saddles. Men were everywhere, seated in rows on top rails, gathered in groups, leaning idly against the ranch buildings. There was a feeling of waiting.

Stewart Edward White

We were discovered and acclaimed with a wild yell that brought everybody running. Immediately we were surrounded. Escorted by a clamouring multitude we moved slowly down the lane and into the enclosure.

There awaited us a dozen men headed by Buck Johnson. They emerged from the office as we drew up. At sight of them the cowboys stopped, and we moved forward alone. For here were the substantial men of this part of the territory, the old timers, who had come in the early days and who had persisted through the Indian wars, the border forays, the cattle rustlings, through drought and enmity and bad years. A grim, elderly, four-square, unsmiling little band of granite-faced pioneers, their very appearance carried a conviction of direct and, if necessary, ruthless action. At sight of them my heart leaped. Twenty-four hours previous my case had seemed none too joyful. Now, mainly by my own efforts, after all, I was no longer alone.

They did not waste time in vain congratulations or query. The occasion was too grave for such side issues. Buck Johnson said something very brief to the effect that he was glad to see us safe.

"If this young lady will come in first," he suggested.

But I was emboldened to speak up.

"This young lady has not had a bite to eat since last night," I interposed.

The senor bent on me his grave look.

"Thank you," said he. "Sing!" he roared, and then to the Chinaman who showed up in a nervous hover: "Give this lady grub, savvy? If you'll go with him, ma'am, he'll get you up something. Then we'd like to see you."

"I can perfectly well wait—" she began.

"I'd rather not, ma'am," said Buck with such grave finality that she merely bowed and followed the cook.

CHAPTER XV

They had no tender feelings about me, however. Nobody cared whether I ever ate or not. I was led into the little ranch office and catechized to a fare-ye-well. They sat and roosted and squatted about, emitting solemn puffs of smoke and speaking never a word; and the sun went down in shafts of light through the murk, and the old shadows of former days crept from the corners. When I had finished my story it was dusk.

And on the heels of my recital came the sound of hoofs in a hurry; and presently loomed in the doorway the gigantic figure of Tom Thorne, the sheriff. He peered, seeing nothing through the smoke and the twilight; and the old timers sat tight and smoked.

"Buck Johnson here?" asked Thorne in his big voice.

"Here," replied the senor.

"I am told," said Thorne, directly, "that there is here an assembly for unlawful purposes. If so, I call on you in the name of the law to keep the peace."

"Tom," rejoined Buck Johnson, "I want you to make me your deputy."

"For what purpose?"

"There is a dispossession notice to be served hereabouts; a

trespasser who must be put off from property that is not his."

"You men are after Hooper, and I know it. Now you can't run your neighbours' quarrels with a gun, not anymore. This is a country of law now."

"Tom," repeated Buck in a reasoning tone, "come in. Strike a light if you want to: and take a look around. There's a lot of your friends here. There's Jim Carson over in the corner, and Donald Macomber, and Marcus Malley, and Dan Watkins."

At this slow telling of the most prominent names in the southwest cattle industry Tom Thorne took a step into the room and lighted a match. The little flame, held high above his head, burned down to his fingers while he stared at the impassive faces surrounding him. Probably he had thought to interfere dutifully in a local affair of considerable seriousness; and there is no doubt that Tom Thorne was never afraid of his duty. But here was Arizona itself gathered for purposes of its own. He hardly noticed when the flame scorched his fingers.

"Tom," said Buck Johnson after a moment, "I heerd tell of a desperate criminal headed for Grant's Pass, and I figure you can just about catch up with him if you start right now and keep on riding. Only you'd better make me your deputy first. It'll sort of leave things in good legal responsible hands, as you can always easy point out if asked."

Tom gulped.

"Raise your right hand," he commanded, curtly, and administered the oath. "Now I leave it in your hands to preserve the peace," he concluded. "I call you all to witness."

"That's all right, Tom," said Buck, still in his crooning tones, taking the big sheriff by the elbow and gently propelling him toward the door, "now as to this yere criminal over toward Grant's Pass, he was a little bit of a runt about six foot three tall; heavy set, weight about a hundred and ten; light complected with black hair and eyes. You can't help but find him. Tom's a good sort," he observed, coming back, "but he's young. He don't realize yet that when things get real serious this sheriff foolishness just nat'rally bogs down. Now I reckon we'd better talk to the girl."

I made a beeline for the cook house while they did that and filled up for three. By the time I had finished, the conference was raised, and men were catching and saddling their mounts. I did not intend to get left out, you may be sure, so I rustled around and borrowed me a saddle and a horse, and was ready to start with the rest.

We jogged up the road in a rough sort of column, the old timers riding ahead in a group of their own. No injunction had been laid as to keeping quiet; nevertheless, conversation was sparse and low voiced. The men mostly rode in silence smoking their cigarettes. About half way the leaders summoned me, and I trotted up to join them.

They wanted to know about the situation of the ranch as I had observed it. I could not encourage them much. My recollection made of the place a thoroughly protected walled fortress, capable of resisting a considerable assault.

"Of course with this gang we could sail right over them," observed Buck, thoughtfully, "but we'd lose a considerable of men doing it."

"Ain't no chance of sneaking somebody inside?" suggested Watkins.

"Got to give Old Man Hooper credit for some sense," replied the senor, shortly.

"We can starve 'em out," suggested somebody.

"Unless I miss the old man a mile he's already got a messenger headed for the troops at Fort Huachuca," interposed

Macomber. "He ain't fool enough to take chances on a local sheriff."

"You're tooting he ain't," approved Buck Johnson. "It's got to be quick work."

"Burn him out," said Watkins.

"It's the young lady's property," hesitated my boss. "I kind of hate to
destroy it unless we have to."

At this moment the Morgan stallion, which I had not noticed before, was reined back to join our little group. Atop him rode the diminutive form of Artie Brower whom I had thought down and out. He had evidently had his evening's dose of hop and under the excitation of the first effect had joined the party. His derby hat was flattened down to his ears. Somehow it exasperated me.

"For heaven's sake why don't you get you a decent hat!" I muttered, but to myself. He was carrying that precious black bag.

"Blow a hole in his old walls!" he suggested, cheerfully. "That old fort was built against Injins. A man could sneak up in the shadow and set her off. It wouldn't take but a dash of soup to stick a hole you could ride through a-horseback."

"Soup?" echoed Buck.

"Nitroglycerine," explained Watkins, who had once been a miner.

"Oh, sure!" agreed Buck, sarcastically. "And where'd we get it?"

"I always carry a little with me just for emergencies," asserted Brower, calmly, and patted his black bag.

There was a sudden and unanimous edging away.

"For the love of Pete!" I cried. "Was there some of that stuff in there all the time I've been carrying it around?"

"It's packed good: it can't go off," Artie reassured us. "I know my biz."

"What in God's name do you want such stuff for!" cried Judson.

"Oh, just emergencies," answered Brower, vaguely, but I remembered his uncanny skill in opening the combination of the safe. Possibly that contract between Emory and Hooper had come into his hands through professional activities. However, that did not matter.

"I can make a drop of soup go farther than other men a pint," boasted Artie. "I'll show you: and I'll show that old—"

"You'll probably get shot," observed Buck, watching him closely.

"W'at t'hell," observed Artie with an airy gesture.

"It's the dope he takes," I told Johnson aside. "It only lasts about so long. Get him going before it dies on him."

"I see. Trot right along," Buck commanded.

Taking this as permission Brower clapped heels to the stallion and shot away like an arrow.

"Hold on! Stop! Oh, damn!" ejaculated the senor. "He'll gum the whole game!" He spurred forward in pursuit, realized the hopelessness of trying to catch the Morgan, and reined down again to a brisk travelling canter. We surmounted the long, slow rise this side of Hooper's in time to see a man stand out in the brush, evidently for the purpose of challenging the horseman. Artie paid him not the slightest attention, but swept by magnificently, the great stallion leaping high in his restrained vitality. The outpost promptly levelled his rifle. We saw the vivid flash in the half light. Brower reeled in his saddle, half fell, caught himself by the stallion's mane and clung, swinging to and fro. The horse, freed of control, tossed his head, laid back his ears, and ran straight as an arrow for the great doors of the ranch.

We uttered a simultaneous groan of dismay. Then with one accord we struck spurs and charged at full speed, grimly and silently. Against the gathering hush of evening rose only the drum-roll of our horses' hoofs and the dust cloud of their going. Except that Buck Johnson, rising in his stirrups, let off three shots in the air; and at the signal from all points around the beleagured ranch men arose from the brush and mounted concealed horses, and rode out into the open with rifles poised.

The stallion thundered on; and the little jockey managed to cling to the saddle, though how he did it none of us could tell. In the bottomland near the ranch he ran out of the deeper dusk into a band of the strange, luminous after-glow that follows erratically sunset in wide spaces. Then we could see that he was not only holding his seat, but was trying to do something, just what we could not make out. The reins were flying free, so there was no question of regaining control.

A shot flashed at him from the ranch; then a second; after which, as though at command, the firing ceased. Probably the condition of affairs had been recognized.

All this we saw from a distance. The immensity of the Arizona country, especially at dusk when the mountains withdraw behind their veils and mystery flows into the bottomlands, has always a panoramic quality that throws small any human-sized activities. The ranch houses and their attendant trees look like toys; the bands of cattle and the men working them are as though viewed through the reverse lenses of a glass; and the very details of mesquite or *sacatone* flats, of alkali shallow or of oak grove are blended into broad washes of tone. But now the distant, galloping horse with its swaying mannikin charging on the ranch seemed to fill our world. The great forces of portent that hover aloof in the dusk of the desert stooped as with a rush of wings. The peaceful, wide spaces and the veiled hills and the brooding skies were swept clear. Crisis filled our souls: crisis laid her hand on every living moving thing in the world, stopping it in its tracks so that the very infinities for a brief, weird period seemed poised over the running horse and the swaying, fumbling man.

At least that is the way it affected me; and subsequent talk leads me to believe that that it is how it affected every man jack of us. We all had different ways of expressing it. Windy Bill subsequently remarked: "I felt like some old Injun He-God had just told me to crawl in my hole and give them that knew how a chanct."

But I know we all stopped short, frozen in our tracks, and stared, and I don't believe man, *or* horse, drew a deep breath.

Nearer and nearer the stallion drew to the ranch. Now he was within a few yards. In another moment he would crash head on, at tremendous speed, into the closed massive doors. The rider seemed to have regained somewhat of his strength. He was sitting straight in the saddle, was no longer clinging. But apparently he was making no effort to regain control. His head was bent and he was still fumbling at something. The distance was too great for us to make out what, but that much we could see.

On flew the stallion at undiminished speed. He was running blind; and seemingly nothing could save him from a crash. But at almost the last moment the great doors swung back. Those within had indeed realized the situation and were meeting it. At the same instant Brower rose in his stirrups and brought his arm forward in a wide, free swing. A blinding glare flashed across the world. We felt the thud and heave of a tremendous explosion. Dust obliterated everything.

"Charge, you coyotes! Charge!" shrieked Buck Johnson.

And at full speed, shrieking like fiends, we swept across flats.

Stewart Edward White

CHAPTER XVI

There was no general resistance. We tumbled pell mell through the breach into the courtyard, encountering only terror-stricken wretches who cowered still dazed by the unexpectedness and force of the explosion. In the excitement order and command were temporarily lost. The men swarmed through the ranch buildings like locusts. Senor Buck Johnson and the other old timers let them go; but I noticed they themselves scattered here and there keeping a restraining eye on activities. There was to be no looting: and that was early made plain.

But before matters had a chance to go very far we were brought up all standing by the sound of shots outside. A rush started in that direction: but immediately Buck Johnson asserted his authority and took command. He did not intend to have his men shot unnecessarily.

By now it was pitch dark. A reconnaissance disclosed a little battle going on down toward the water corrals. Two of our men, straying in that direction, had been fired upon. They had promptly gone down on their bellies and were shooting back.

"I think they've got down behind the water troughs," one of these men told me as I crawled up alongside. "Cain't say how many there is. They shore do spit fire considerable. I'm just cuttin' loose where I see the flash. When I shoot, you prepare to move and move lively. One of those horned toads can sure shoot some; and it ain't healthy to linger none behind your own flash."

The boys, when I crawled back with my report, were eager to pile in and rush the enemy.

"Just put us a hoss-back, senor," pleaded Windy Bill, "and we'll run right over them like a Shanghai rooster over a little green snake. They can't hit nothing moving fast in the dark."

"You'll do just what I say," rejoined Buck Johnson, fiercely. "Cow hands are scarce, and I don't aim to lose one except in the line of business. If any man gets shot to-night, he's out of luck. He'd better get shot good and dead; or he'll wish he had been. That goes! There can't be but a few of those renegades out there, and we'll tend to them in due order. Watkins," he addressed that old timer, "you tend to this. Feel around cautious. Fill up the place full of lead. Work your men around through the brush until you get them surrounded, and then just squat and shoot and wait for morning."

Watkins sent out a dozen of the nearest men to circle the water troughs in order to cut off further retreat, if that were projected. Then he went about methodically selecting others to whom he assigned various stations.

"Now you get a-plenty of catteridges," he told them, "and you lay low and shoot 'em off. And if any of you gets shot I'll sure skin him alive!"

In the meantime, the locomotive lantern had been lit so that the interior of the courtyard was thrown into brilliant light. Needless to say the opening blown in the walls did *not* face toward the water corrals. Of Artie Brower and the Morgan stallion we found hardly a trace. They had been literally blown to pieces. Not one of us who had known him but felt in his heart a kindly sorrow for the strange little man. The sentry who had fired at him and who had thus, indirectly, precipitated the catastrophe, was especially downcast.

"I told him to stop, and he kep' right on a-going, so I shot at him," he explained. "What else was I to do? How was I to know he didn't belong to that gang? He acted like it."

But when you think of it how could it have come out better? Poor, weak, vice-ridden, likeable little beggar, what could the future have held for him? And it is probable that his death saved many lives.

The prisoners were brought in—some forty of them, for Old Man Hooper maintained only the home ranch and all his cow hands as well as his personal bravos were gathered here. Buck Johnson separated apart seven of them, and ordered the others into the stables under guard.

"Bad *hombres*, all of them," he observed to Jed Parker. "We'll just nat'rally ship them across the line very *pronto*. But these seven are worse than bad *hombres*. We'll have to see about them."

But neither Andreas, Ramon, nor Old Man Hooper himself were among those present.

"Maybe they slipped out through our guards; but I doubt it," said Buck. "I believe we've identified that peevish lot by the water troughs."

The firing went on quite briskly for a while; then slackened, and finally died to an occasioned burst, mainly from our own side. Under our leader's direction the men fed their horses and made themselves comfortable. I was summoned to the living quarters to explain on the spot the events that had gone before. Here we examined more carefully and in detail the various documents—the extraordinary directions to Ramon; the list of prospective victims to be offered at the tomb, so to speak, of Old Man Hooper; and the copy of the agreement between Emory and Hooper. The latter, as I had surmised, stated in so many words that it superceded and nullified an old partnership agreement. This started us on a further search which was at last rewarded by the discovery of that original partnership. It contained, again as I had surmised, the not-uncommon clause that in case of the death of one or the other of the partners without direct heirs the common property should revert to the other. I felt very stuck on myself for a good guesser. The only trouble was that the original of the second agreement was lacking: we had only a copy, and of course without signatures. It will be remembered that Brower said he had deposited it with a third party, and that third party was to us unknown. We could not even guess in what city he lived. Of course we could advertise. But Windy Bill who—leaning his long figure against the wall—had been listening in silence—a pretty fair young miracle in itself—had a good idea, which was the real miracle, in my estimation.

"Look here," he broke in, "if I've been following the plot of this yere dime novel correctly, it's plumb easy. Just catch Jud—Jud—you know, the editor of the *Cochise Branding Iron*, and get him to telegraph a piece to the other papers that Artie Brower, celebrated jockey et ceterer, has met a violent death at Hooper's ranch, details as yet unknown. That's the catchword, as I *savey* it. When this yere third party sees that, he goes and records the paper, and there you are!"

Windy leaned back dramatically and looked exceedingly pleased with himself.

"Yes, that's it," approved Buck, briefly, which disappointed Windy, who was looking for high encomium.

At this moment a messenger came in from the firing party to report that apparently all opposition had ceased. At least there had been for some time no shooting from the direction of the water troughs; a fact concealed from us by the thickness of the ranch walls. Buck Johnson immediately went out to confer with Watkins.

"I kind of think we've got 'em all," was the latter's opinion. "We haven't had a sound out of 'em for a half hour. It may be a trick, of course."

"Sure they haven't slipped by you?" suggested the senor,

"Pretty certain. We've got a close circle."

"Well, I wouldn't take chances in the dark. Just lay low 'till morning."

We returned to the ranch house where, after a little further discussion, I bedded down and immediately fell into a deep sleep. This was more and longer continued excitement than I was used to.

I was afoot with the first stirrings of dawn, you may be sure, and out to join the party that moved with infinite precaution on the water troughs as soon as it was light enough to see clearly. We found them riddled with bullets and the water all run out. Gleaming brass cartridges scattered, catching the first rays of the sun, attested the vigour of the defence. Four bodies lay huddled on the ground under the partial shelter of the troughs. I saw Ramon, his face frowning and sinister even in death, his right hand still grasping tenaciously the stock of his Winchester; and Andreas flat on his face; and two others whom I did not recognize. Ramon had been hit at least four times. But of Hooper himself was no hide nor hair! So certain had we been that he had escaped to this spot with his familiars that we were completely taken aback at his absence.

"We got just about as much sense as a bunch of sheepmen!" cried Buck Johnson, exasperated. "He's probably been hiding out somewhere about the place. God knows where he is by now!"

But just as we were about to return to the ranch house we were arrested by a shout from one of the cowboys who had been projecting around the neighbourhood. He came running to us. In his hand he held a blade of *sacatone* on which he pointed out a single dark spot about the size of the head of a pin. Buck seized it and examined it closely.

"Blood, all right," he said at last. "Where did you get this, son?"

The man, a Chiracahua hand named Curley something-or-other, indicated a *sacatone* bottom a hundred yards to the west.

"You got good eyes, son," Buck complimented him. "Think you can make out the trail?"

"Do'no," said Curley. "Used to do a considerable of tracking."

"Horses!" commanded Buck.

We followed Curley afoot while several men went to saddle up. On the edge of the two-foot jump-off we grouped ourselves waiting while Curley, his brows knit tensely, quartered here and there like a setter dog. He was a good trailer, you could see that in a minute. He went at it right. After quite a spell he picked up a rock and came back to show it. I should never have noticed anything—merely another tiny black spot among other spots—but Buck nodded instantly he saw it.

"It's about ten rods west of whar I found the grass," said Curley. "Looks like he's headed for that water in Cockeye Basin. From thar he could easy make Cochise when he got rested."

"Looks likely," agreed Buck. "Can't you find no footprints?"

"Too much tramped up by cowboys and other jackasses," said Curley. "It'll come easier when we get outside this yere battlefield."

He stood erect, sizing up the situation through half-squinted eyes.

"You-all wait here," he decided. "Chances are he kept right on up the broad wash."

He mounted one of the horses that had now arrived and rode at a lope to a point nearly half a mile west. There he dismounted and tied his horse to the ground. After rather a prolonged search he raised his hand over his head and described several small horizontal circles in the air.

"Been in the army, have you?" muttered Buck; "well, I will say you're a handy sort of leather-leg to have around. He gave the soldier signal for 'assemble'," he answered Jed Parker's question.

We rode over to join Curley.

"It's all right; he came this way," said the latter; but he did not trouble to show us indications. I am a pretty fair game trailer myself, but I could make out nothing.

We proceeded slowly, Curley afoot leading his horse. The direction continued to be toward Cockeye. Sometimes we could all see plain footprints; again the trail was, at least as far as I was concerned, a total loss. Three times we found blood, once in quite a splash. Occasionally even Curley was at fault for a few moments; but in general he moved forward at a rapid walk.

"This Curley person is all right," observed Windy Bill after a while, "I was brung up to find my way about, and I can puzzle out most anywhere a critter has gone and left a sign; but this yere Curley can track a humming bird acrost a granite boulder!"

After a little while Curley stopped for us to catch up.

"Seems to me no manner of doubt but what he's headed for Cockeye," he said. "There ain't no other place for him to go out this way. I reckon I can pick up enough of this trail just riding along. If we don't find no sign at Cockeye, we can just naturally back track and pick up where he turned off. We'll save time that-away, and he's had plenty of time to get thar and back again."

So Curley mounted and we rode on at a walk on the horse trail that led up the broad, shallow wash that came out of Cockeye.

Curley led, of course. Then rode Buck Johnson and Watkins and myself. I had horned in on general principles, and nobody kicked. I suppose they thought my general entanglement with this extraordinary series of events entitled me to more than was coming to me as ordinary cow hand. For a long time we proceeded in silence. Then, as we neared the hills, Buck began to lay out his plan.

"When we come up on Cockeye," he was explaining, "I want you to take a half dozen men or so and throw around the other side on the Cochise trail—"

His speech was cut short by the sound of a rifle shot. The country was still flat, unsuited for concealment or defence. We were riding carelessly. A shivering shock ran through my frame and my horse plunged wildly. For an instant I thought I must be hit, then I saw that the bullet had cut off cleanly the horn of my saddle—within two inches of my stomach!

Surprise paralyzed us for the fraction of a second. Then we charged the rock pile from which the shot had come.

We found there Old Man Hooper seated in a pool of his own blood. He had been shot through the body and was dead. His rifle lay across a rock, trained carefully on the trail. How long he had sat there nursing the vindictive spark of his vitality nobody will ever know—certainly for some hours. And the shot delivered had taken from him the last flicker of life.

"By God, he was sure game!" Buck Johnson pronounced his epitaph.

CHAPTER XVII

We cleaned up at the ranch and herded our prisoners together and rode back to Box Springs. The seven men who had been segregated from the rest by Buck Johnson were not among them. I never found out what had become of them nor who had executed whatever decrees had been pronounced against them. There at the home ranch we found Miss Emory very anxious, excited, and interested. Buck and the others in authority left me to inform her of what had taken place.

I told you some time back that this is no love story; but I may as well let you in on the whole sequel to it, and get it off my chest. Windy's scheme brought immediate results. The partnership agreement was recorded, and after the usual legal red-tape Miss Emory came into the property. She had to have a foreman for the ranch, and hanged if she didn't pick on me! Think of that; me an ordinary, forty-dollar cow puncher! I tried to tell her that it was all plumb foolishness, that running a big cattle ranch was a man-sized job and took experience, but she wouldn't listen. Women are like that. She'd seen me blunder in and out of a series of adventures and she thought that settled it, that I was a great man. After arguing with her quite some time about it, I had to give in; so I spit on my hands and sailed in to do my little darndest. I expected the men who realized fully how little I knew about it all would call me a brash damn fool or anyway give me the horse laugh; but I fooled myself. They were mightily decent. Jed Parker or Sam Wooden or Windy Bill were always just happening by and roosting on the corral rails. Then if I listened to them—and I always did—I learned a heap about what I ought to do. Why, even Buck Johnson himself came and stayed at the ranch with me for more than a week at the time of the fall round-up: and he never went near the riding, but just projected around here and there looking over my works and ways. And in the evenings he would smoke and utter grave words of executive wisdom which I treasured and profited by.

If a man gives his whole mind to it, he learns practical things fast. Even a dumb-head Wop gets his English rapidly when he's where he has to talk that or nothing. Inside of three years I had that ranch paying, and paying big. It was due to my friends whom I had been afraid of, and I'm not ashamed to say so. There's Herefords on our range now instead of that lot of heady long-horns Old Man Hooper used to run; and we're growing alfalfa and hay in quantity for fattening when they come in off the ranges. Got considerable hogs, too, and hogs are high—nothing but pure blood Poland. I figure I've added fully fifty per cent., if not more, to the value of the ranch as it came to me. No, I'm not bragging; I'm explaining how came it I married my wife and figured to keep my self-respect. I'd have married her anyhow. We've been together now fifteen years, and I'm here to say that she's a humdinger of a girl, game as a badger, better looking every day, knows cattle and alfalfa and sunsets and sonatas and Poland hogs—but I said this was no love story, and it isn't!

The day following the taking of the ranch and the death of Old Man Hooper we put our prisoners on horses and started along with them toward the Mexican border. Just outside of Soda Springs whom should we meet up with but big Tom Thorne, the sheriff.

"Evenin', Buck," said he.

"Evenin'," replied the senor.

"What you got here?"

"This is a little band of religious devotees fleein' persecution," said Buck.

"And what are you up to with them?" asked Thorne.

"We're protecting them out of Christian charity from the dangers of the road until they reach the Promised Land."

"I see," said Thorne, reflectively. "Whereabouts lays this Promised Land?"

"About sixty mile due south."

"You sure to get them all there safe and sound—I suppose you'd be willing to guarantee that nothing's going to happen to them, Buck?"

"I give my word on that, Tom."

"All right," said Thorne, evidently relieved. He threw his leg over the horn of his saddle. "How about that little dispossession matter, deputy? You ain't reported on that."

"It's all done and finished."

"Have any trouble?"

"Nary trouble," said Senor Buck Johnson, blandly, "all went off quiet and serene."

THE ROAD AGENT

CHAPTER I

The Sierra Nevadas of California are very wide and very high. Kingdoms could be lost among the defiles of their ranges. Kingdoms have been found there. One of them was Bright's Cove.

It happened back in the seventies. Old Man Bright was prospecting. He had come up from the foothills accompanied by a new but stolid Indian wife. After he had grubbed around a while on old Italian bar and had succeeded in washing out a little colour, she woke up and took a slight interest in the proceedings.

"You like catch dat?" she grunted, contemptuously. "Heap much over dere!"

She waved an arm. Old Man Bright girded his loins and packed his jackass. After incredible scramblings the two succeeded in surmounting the ranges and in dropping sheer to the mile-wide round valley through which flowed the river— the broad, swift mountain river, with the snow-white rapids and the swirling translucent green of very thick grass. They were very glad to reach the grass at the bottom, but a little doubtful on how to get out. The big mountains took root at the very edge of the tiny round valley; the river flowed out of a gorge at one end and into a gorge at the other.

Stewart Edward White

"Guess the sun don't rise here 'til next morning," commented Old Man Bright. The squaw was too busy even to grunt.

In six years Old Man Bright was worth six million dollars, all taken from the ledges of Bright's Cove. Of this amount he had been forced to let go of a small proportion for mill machinery and labour. He had also invested twenty-five thousand dollars in a road. It was a steep road, and a picturesque. It wound in and out and around, by loops, lacets, and hairpins, dropping down the face of the mountain in unheard-of grades and turns. Nothing was ever hauled up it, save yellow bars of bullion—so that did not matter. Down it, with a shriek of brakes, a cloud of dust, a clank of harness and a rumble of oaths, came divers matters, such as machinery, glassware, whiskey, mirrors, ammunition, and pianos. From any one of a dozen bold points on this road one could see far down and far up its entire white, thread-like length. The tiny crawling teams each with its puff of dust crawling with it; the great tumbled peaks of the Sierras; the river so far below as to resemble a little stream, the round Cove with its toy houses and its distant ant-like industry—all these were plainly to be seized by a glance of whatever eye cared to look.

As time went on a great many teams and pack trains and saddle animals climbed up and down that road. Bright's Cove became quite a town. Old Man Bright made six millions; other men aggregated nearly four millions more; still others acquired deep holes and a deficit. It might be remarked in passing that the squaw acquired experience, a calico dress or so, and a final honourable discharge. Being an Indian she quite cheerfully went back to pounding acorns in a *metate*.

In the fifth year of prosperity there drifted into camp two men, possessed of innocence, three mules, and a thousand dollars. They retained the mules; and, it is to be presumed, at least a portion of the innocence.

The thousand dollars went to the purchase of the Lost Dog from Barney Fallan. The Lost Dog consisted quite simply of a hole in the ground guarded by an excellent five stamp-mill. The latter's existence could only be explained by the incurable optimism of Barney Fallan—certainly not by the contents of the hole in the ground. To the older men of the camp it seemed a shame, for the newcomers were nice, fresh-cheeked, clear-eyed lads to whom everything was new and strange and wonderful, their enthusiasm was contagious, and their cheerful command of vernacular exceedingly heart-warming. California John, then a man in his forties, tried to head off the deal.

"Look here, son," said he to Gaynes. "Don't do it. There's nothin' in it. Take my word."

"But Fallan's got a good stamp-mill all ready for business, and the ledge—"

"Son," said California John, "every once in a while the Lord gets to experimentin' makin' brains for a new species of jackass, and when he runs out of donkeys to put 'em in—"

"Meaning me?" demanded Gaynes, his fair skin turning a deep red.

"Not at all. Meanin' Barney Fallan."

Nevertheless the Babes, as the Gaynes brothers were speedily nicknamed, paid over their good thousand for Barney's worthless prospect with the imposing but ridiculous stamp-mill. There they set cheerfully to work. After a week's desperate and clanking experiment they got the machinery under way and began to run rock through the crushers.

"It ain't even ore!" expostulated California John. "Why, son, it's only country rock. Go down on your shaft until you strike a pan test, anyway! You're wasting time and fuel and—Oh, hell!" he broke off hopelessly at the sight of the two cherubic faces upturned respectful but unconvinced.

"But you never can tell where you will find gold," broke in

Stewart Edward White

Jimmy, eagerly. "That's been proved over and over again. I heard one fellow say once that they thought they'd never find gold in hornblende. But they did."

California John stumped home in indignant disgust.

"Damn little ijits!" he exploded. "Pigheaded! Stubborn as a pair of mules!" The recollection of the scrubbed red cheeks, the clear, puppy-dog, frank brown eyes, the close-curling brown hair, forced his lips to a wry grin. "Just like I was at that age," he admitted. He sighed. "Well, they'll drop their little pile, of course. The only ray of hope's the experience that old Bible fellow had with them turkey buzzards—or was it ravens?"

The Babes pecked away for about a month, full of tribulation and questions. They seemed to depend almost equally on optimism and chance, in both of which they had supreme faith. A huge horseshoe was tacked over the door of the stamp-mill. Jimmy Gaynes always spat over his right shoulder before doing a day's work. They never walked under the short ladders leading to the hoppers. Neither would they permit visitors to their shafts. To California John and his friend Tibbetts they interposed scandalized objections.

"It's bad luck to let another man in your shaft!" cried George. "I'm no high-brow on this mining proposition, but I know enough for that."

"Bad as playing opposite a cross-eyed man," said Jimmy.

"Or holding Jacks full on Eights," supplemented George, conclusively.

"You're about as wise as a treeful of owls," said California John, sarcastically. "But, Lord love you, I ain't cherishin' any very burnin' ambition to crawl down your snake hole."

The Babes used up their provisions; they went about as far as they could on credit; they harrowed the feelings of the community—and then, in a very mild way, they struck it. Together they drifted down the single street of the camp, arm in arm, an elaborate nonchalance steadying their steps. Near the horse trough they paused.

"Gold," said Jimmy, oracularly, to George, "is where you find it."

"Likewise horse sense," quoth George.

Whereupon they whooped wildly and descended on the astonished group. To it they exhibited yellow dust to the value of an hundred dollars. "And more where that came from," said they.

"What kind of rock did you find it in?" demanded Tibbetts, after he had recovered his breath from the youngsters' enthusiastic man-handling.

"Oh, a kind of red, pasty-looking rock," said they.

"Show us," demanded the miners.

"What?" cried Jimmy, astounded, "and give Old Man Luck the backhand slap just when he's decided to buy a corner lot in the Gaynes Addition? Not on your saccharine existence!"

"But we'll show you some more of this to-morrow Q.M.," said George.

They bought drinks all round, and paid their various bills, and departed again feverishly to the Lost Dog whence rose smoke and clankings. And next day, sure enough, they left their work just long enough to exhibit another respectable little clean-up of fifty dollars or so.

"And we're just getting into it!" said George, triumphantly.

California John and all the rest of his good friends rejoiced exceedingly and genuinely. They liked the Babes. The little strike of the Lost Dog quite overshadowed in importance the fact that old man Bright's "Clarice" had run into a fabulously rich pocket.

The end of the month drew near. The Lost Dog had produced nearly eight hundred dollars. The Babes waxed important and talked largely of their moneyed interests.

"I think," said Jimmy, importantly, "that we will decide to keep three hundred dollars to boost the game; and nail down the rest where moths won't corrupt. Where do you fellows salt your surplus, anyway?"

"There's an express goes out pretty soon," someone explained, "with the clean-up of the Clarice. We send our dust out with that; and I reckon you can fix it with Bright."

They saw Bright, but ran up against an unexpected difficulty. Old Man Bright received them with considerable surliness. He considered himself as the originator, discoverer, inventor, and almost the proprietor of Bright's Cove and all it contained. Therefore, when he first heard of the new strike, he walked up to the Lost Dog to see what it looked like. The Babes, panic stricken at the intended affront to "Old Man Luck," headed him off. Bright had not the least belief in the reason given. He surveyed them with disfavour.

"I can't take your package," he told them. "Send it out yourself."

"And that old skunk has cleaned up a hundred thousand this month!" complained Jimmy, pathetically, to the group around the horse trough. "And he won't even take a pore little five hundred package of dust out to some suffering bank! I suppose I'll have to cache it in a tomato can for Johnson's old billy goat to chew up."

"Bring it over and I'll shove it in with mine," suggested

California John.

So it was done. The express, carrying nearly four hundred pounds of gold dust, set forth over the steep road. In two hours the driver and messenger sailed in, bung-eyed with excitement. They had been held up by a single road agent.

"He come out right on that point of rocks where you can see the whole valley," said the driver in answer to many questions, "right where the heavy grade is and the thick chaparral. We was busy climbing; and he had us before we could wink. Made us drop off the dust and 'bout face. He was a big, tall feller; and had a sawed-off Winchester. Once, when we stopped, he dropped a bullet right behind us. He must have watched us all the way to camp."

The camp turned out. As the men passed the Lost Dog someone yelled to the Babes. George, covered with mud, came to the door of the mill.

"Gee!" said he. "Lucky we saved out that three hundred. I'm powerful sorry for that suffering bank. I'll join you as soon as I can get Jimmy up out of the shaft." Before the party had gone a mile they were joined by the brothers boyishly eager over this new excitement.

The men toiled up the road to where the robbery had taken place. Plainly to be seen were the marks of the man's boots. The tracks of a single horse, walking, followed the man.

"He packed off the dust, and he had an almighty big horse to carry it," pronounced someone.

They followed the trail. It led a half mile to a broad sheet of rock. There it disappeared. On one side the bank rose twenty or thirty feet. On the other it fell away nearly a hundred. On the other side of the sheet of rock stretched the dusty road unbroken by anything more recent than the wheel-tracks of the day before. It was as though man and horse had taken unto themselves wings.

Immediately Bright took active charge of the posse.

"Stand here, on this rock," he commanded. "This road's been tracked up too much already. You, John, and Tibbetts and Simmins, there, come 'long with me to see what you can make out."

The old mountaineers retraced their steps, examining carefully every inch of the ground. They returned vastly puzzled.

"No sabe," California John summed up their investigations. "There's the man's track leadin' his hoss. The hoss had on new shoes, and the robber did his own shoeing. So we ain't got any blacksmiths to help us."

"How do you know he shod the horse himself?" asked Jimmy Gaynes.

"Shoes just alike on front and back feet. Shows he must just have tacked on ready-made shoes. A blacksmith shapes 'em different. Those tracks leads right up to this rock: and here they quit. If you can figger how a horse, a man, and nigh four hundredweight of gold dust got off this rock, I'll be obleeged."

The men looked up at the perpendicular cliff to their right; over the sheer precipice at their left; and upon the untracked deep, white dust ahead.

"Furthermore," California John went on, impressively, after a moment, "where did that man and that hoss come from in the beginning? Not from up this way. They's no fresh tracks comin' down the road no more than they's fresh tracks goin' up. Not from camp. They's no tracks whatsomever on the road below, except our'n and the stage outfit's."

"Are you sure of that?" asked Jimmy, his eyes shining with interest.

"Sartin sure," replied California John, positively. "We didn't take no chances on that."

"Then he must have come into the road from up the mountain or down the mountain."

"Where?" demanded California John. "A man afoot might scramble down in one or two places; but not a hoss. They ain't no tracks either side the muss-up where the express was stopped. And at that p'int the mountain is straight up and down, like it is here."

They talked it over, and argued it, and reexamined the evidence, but without avail. The stubborn facts remained: Between the hold-up and the sheet of rock was one set of tracks going one way; elsewhere, nothing.

CHAPTER II

Nearly a year passed. If it had not been for the very tangible loss of a hundred and fifty thousand dollars, the little community at Bright's Cove might almost have come to doubt the evidence of their senses and the accuracy of their memories, so fantastic on sober reflection did all the circumstances become. Even the indisputable four hundred pounds of gold could not quite avert an unconfessed suspicion of the uncanny. Miners are superstitious folk. Old Man Bright remembered the parting and involved curses of his squaw before she went back to her acorns and pine nuts. To Tibbetts alone he imparted a vague hint of the imaginings into which he had fallen. But he brooded much, seeking a plausible theory that would not force him back on the powers of darkness. This he did not find.

Nor did any other man. It remained a mystery, a single bizarre anomaly in the life of the camp. For some time thereafter the express went heavily guarded. The road was patrolled. Jimmy or George Gaynes in person accompanied each shipment of dust. Their pay streak held out, increased steadily in value. They would hire no assistance for the actual mining in the shaft, although they had several hands to work at the mill. One month they cleaned up twelve thousand dollars.

"You bet I'm going," said Jimmy, "I don't care if it is only a little compared to what Bright and you fellows are sending. It's a heap sight to us, and I'm going to see it safe to the city. No more spooks in mine. I got my fingers crossed. Allah skazallalum! I don't know what a ghost would want with cash assets, but they seemed to use George's and my little old five hundred, all right."

Twelve months went by. Two expresses a month toiled up the road. Nothing happened. Finally Jimmy decided that four good working days a month were a good deal to pay for apparently useless supervision. Three men comprised the shot-gun guard. They, with the driver, were considered ample.

"You'll have to get on without me," said Jimmy to them in farewell. "Be good boys. We've got the biggest clean-up yet aboard you."

They started on the twenty-fifth trip since the hold-up. After a time, far up the mountain was heard a single shot. Inside of two hours the express drew sorrowfully into camp. The driver appeared to be alone. In the bottom of the wagon were the three guards weak and sick. The gold sacks were very much absent.

"Done it again," said the driver. "Ain't more than got started afore the whole outfit's down with the belly-ache. Too much of that cursed salmon. Told 'em so. I didn't eat none. That road agent hit her lucky this trip sure. He was all organized for business. Never showed himself at all. Just opened fire. Sent a bullet through the top of my hat. He's either a damn good shot or a damn poor one. I hung up both hands and yelled we was down and out. What could I do? This outfit couldn't a fit a bumble bee. And I couldn't git away, or git hold of no gun, or see anything to shoot, if I did. He was behind that big rock."

The men nodded. They were many of them hard hit, but they had lived too long in the West not to recognize the justice of the driver's implied contention that he had done his best.

"He told me to throw out them sacks, and to be damn quick about it," went on the driver. "Then I drove home."

"What sort of a lookin' fellow was he?" asked someone. "Same one as last year?"

"I never seen him," said the driver. "He hung behind his rock. He was organized for shoot, and if the messengers hadn't happened to' a' been out of it, I believe he could have killed us all."

"What did his hoss look like?" inquired California John.

"He didn't have no horse," stated the driver. "Leastways, not near him. There was no cover. He might have been around a p'int. And I can sw'ar to this: there weren't no tracks of no kind from there to camp."

They caught up horses and started out. When they came to the Lost Dog, they stopped and looked at each other.

"Poor old Babes," said Simmins. "Biggest clean-up yet; and first time one of 'em didn't go 'long."

"I'm glad they didn't," said Tibbetts. "That agent would have killed 'em shore!"

They called out the Gaynes brothers and broke the news. For once the jovial youngsters had no joke to make.

"This is getting serious," said Jimmy, seriously. "We can't afford to lose that much."

George whistled dolefully, and went into the corral for the mules.

The party toiled up the mountain. Plainly in the dust could be made out the trail of the express ascending and descending. Plain also were the signs where the driver had dumped out the gold bags and turned around. From that point the tracks of a man and a horse led to the sheet of rock. Beyond that, nothing.

The men stared at each other a little frightened. Somebody swore softly.

"Boys," said Bright in a strained voice, "do you know how much was in that express? A half million! There's nary earthly hoss can carry over half a ton! And this one treads as light as a saddler."

They looked at each other blankly. Several even glanced in apprehension at the sky.

In a perfunctory manner, for the sake of doing something, those skilled in trail-reading went back over the ground. Nothing was added to the first experience. At the point of robbery magically had appeared a man and—if the stage driver's solemn assertion that at the time of the hold-up no animal was in sight could be believed—subsequently, when needed, a large horse. Whence had they come? Not along the road in either direction: the unbroken, deep dust assured that. Not down the mountain from above, for the cliff rose sheer for at least three hundred feet. Jimmy Gaynes, following unconsciously the general train of conjecture, craned his neck over the edge of the road. The broken jagged rock and shale dropped off an hundred feet to a tangle of manzanita and snowbrush.

California John looked over, too.

"Couldn't even get sheep up that," said he, "let alone a sixteen-hand horse."

Old Man Bright was sunk in a superstitious torpor. He had lost hundreds of thousands where he would have hated to spend pennies; yet the financial part of the loss hardly touched him. He mumbled fearfully to himself, and took not the slightest interest in the half-hearted attempts to read the mystery. When the others moved, he moved with them, because he was afraid to be left alone.

After the men had assured themselves again and again that the horse and the man had apparently materialized from thin air exactly at the point of robbery, they again followed the tracks to the broad sheet of rock. Whither had the robber gone? Back into the thin air whence he had come. There was no other solution. No tracks ahead; an absolute and physical impossibility of anything without wings getting up or down the flanking precipices—these were the incontestable facts.

After this second robbery a gloom descended on Bright's Cove which lasted through many months. Old Man Bright hunted out the squaw with whom he had first discovered the diggings, and set her up in an establishment with gay curtains, glass danglers and red doileys. Each month he paid for her provisions and sent to her a sum of money. In this manner, at least, the phantom road agent had furthered the ends of justice. The sop to the powers of darkness appeared to be effective in this respect: no more hold-ups occurred; no more mysterious tracks appeared in the dust; gradually men's minds swung back to the balanced and normal, and the life of the camp went forward on its appointed way.

Nevertheless, certain effects remained. Each express went out heavily guarded, and preceded and followed by men on horseback. Strangely enough the gamblers left camp. In a little more than a year Old Man Bright fell into a settled melancholia from which his millions never helped him to the very day of his death a little more than a year later.

In the meantime, however varied the fortunes of the other mines and prospects, the Lost Dog continued to work toward a steadily increasing paying basis. It never reached the proportions of the Clarice, but turned out an increasing value of dust at each clean-up. The Gaynes boys two years before had been in debt for their groceries. Now they were said to have shipped out something like three or four hundred thousand dollars' worth of gold. Their friends used to wander down for the regular clean-up, just to rejoice over the youngsters' deserved good luck. The little five stamp-mill crunched away steadily; the water flowed; and in the riffles the heavy gold dust accumulated.

"Why don't you-all put up a big mill, throw in a crew of men, and get busy?" they were asked.

"I'll tell you," replied George, "it's because we know a heap sight more about mining than we did when we came here. We have just one claim, and from all indications it's only a pocket. The Clarice is on a genuine lode; but we're likely to run into a 'horse' or pinch out most any minute. When we do, it's all over but a few faint cries of fraud. And we can empty that pocket just as well with a little jerkwater outfit like this as we could with a big crew and a real mill. It'll take a little longer; but we're pulling it and quick enough."

"Those Babes have more sense than we gave 'em credit for," commented California John. "Their heads are level. They're dead right about it's bein' a pocket. The stuff they run through there is the darndest mixture *I* ever see gold in."

Two months after this conversation the Babes drifted into camp to announce that the expected pinch had come.

"We're going," said Jimmy. "We have a heap plenty dust salted away; and there's not a colour left in the Lost Dog. The mill machinery is for sale cheap. Any one can have the Lost Dog who wants it. We're going out to see what makes the wheels go 'round. You boys have a first claim on us wherever you find us. You've sure been good to us. If you catch that spook, send us one of his tail feathers. It would be worth just twelve thousand five hundred to us."

They sold the stamp-mill for almost nothing; packed eight animals with heavy things they had accumulated; and departed up the steep white road, over the rim to the outer world whence came no word of them more. The camp went on prospering. Old Man Bright died. The heavily guarded express continued to drag out yellow gold by the hundredweight.

About six weeks after the departure of the Babes, California John saddled up his best horse, put on his best overalls, strapped about him his shiny worn Colt's .45 and departed for his semi-annual visit to the valleys and the towns. A week later he returned. It was about dusk. At the water trough he dismounted.

"Boys," said he, quietly, "I've been held up." He eyed them quizzically. "Up by the slide rock," he continued, "and by the spook."

"Who was he?" "What was it?" they cried, starting to their feet.

"It was Jimmy Gaynes," replied California John.

"The Babe?" someone broke the stunned silence at last.

"Precisely."

"Well, I'll be damned!" cried Tibbetts.

"Did he get much off you?" asked a miner after another pause.

"He never took a thing."

And on that, being much besieged, California John sat him down and told of his experience.

CHAPTER III

California John was discursive and interested and disinclined to be hurried. He crossed one leg over the other and lit his pipe.

"I was driftin' down the road busy with my own idees—which ain't many," he began, "when I was woke up all to once by someone givin' me advice. I took the advice. Wasn't nothin' else to do. All I could see was a rock and a gun barrel. That was enough. So I histed my hands as per commands and waited for the next move." He chuckled. "I wasn't worryin'. Had to squeeze my dust bag to pay my hotel bill when I left the city."

"'Drop yore gun in the road,' says the agent."

"I done so. "

"Now dismount."

"I climbed down." And then Jimmy Gaynes rose up from behind that rock and laughed at me.

"'The joke's on me!' said I, and reached down for my gun."

"'Better leave that!' said Jimmy pretty sharp. I know that tone of voice, so I straightened up again."

"'Well, Jimmy,' said I, 'she lays if you say so. But where'd you

Stewart Edward White

come from; and what for do you turn road agent and hold up your old friends?'"

"'I'm holdin' you up,' Jimmy answered, 'because I want to talk to you for ten minutes. As for where I come from, that's neither here nor there.'"

"'Of course,' said I, 'I'm one of these exclusive guys that needs a gun throwed on him before he'll talk with the plain people like you.'"

"'Now don't get mad,' says Jimmy. 'But light yore pipe, and set down on that rock, and you'll see in a minute why I *pre*ferred to corner the gatling market.'"

"Well, I set down and lit up, and Jimmy done likewise, about ten feet away."

"'I've come back a long ways to talk to one of you boys, and I've shore hung around this road some few hours waitin' for some of you terrapins to come along. Ever found out who done those two hold-ups?'"

"'Nope,' said I, 'and don't expect to.'"

"'Well, I done it,' says he."

"I looked him in the eye mighty severe."

"'You're one of the funniest little jokers ever hit this trail,' I told him. 'If that's your general line of talkee-talkee I don't wonder you don't want me to have no gun.'"

"'Never*the*less,' he insists, 'I done it. And I'll tell you just how it was done. Here's yore old express crawlin' up the road. Here I am behind this little old rock. You know what happened next I reckon—from experience.'"

"'I reckon I know that,' says I, 'but how did you get behind that rock without leavin' no tracks?'"

"I climbed up the cliff out of the canon, and I just walked up the canon from the Lost Dog through the brush."

"'Yes,' says I, 'that might be: a man could make out to shinny up. But how—'"

"'One thing to a time. Then I ordered them dust sacks throwed out, and the driver to 'bout-face and retreat.'"

"'Sure,' says I, 'simple as a wart on a kid's nose. There was you with a half ton of gold to fly off with! Come again.'"

"'I then dropped them sacks off the edge of the cliff where they rolled into the brush. After a while I climbed down after them, and was on hand when your posse started out. Then I carried them home at leisure.'"

"'What did you do with your hoss?' I asked him, mighty sarcastic. 'Seems to me you overlook a few bets.'

"'I didn't have no hoss,' says he."

"But the real hold-up—"

"You mean them tracks. Well, just to amuse you fellows, I walked in the dust up to that flat rock. Then I clamped a big pair of horseshoes on hind-side before and walked back again."

California John's audience had been listening intently. Now it could no longer contain itself, but broke forth into exclamations indicative of various emotions.

"That's why them front and back tracks was the same size!" someone cried.

"Gee, you're bright!" said California John. "That's what I told him. I also told him he was a wonder, but how did he manage to slip out near a ton of dust up that road without our knowing it?

"'You did know it,' says he. 'Did you fellows really think there was any gold-bearing ore in the Lost Dog? We just run that dust through the mill along with a lot of worthless rock, and shipped it out open and above board as our own mill run. There never was an ounce of dust come out of the Lost Dog, and there never will.' Then he give me back my gun— emptied—we shook hands, and here I be."

After the next burst of astonishment had ebbed, and had been succeeded by a rather general feeling of admiration, somebody asked California John if Jimmy had come back solely for the purpose of clearing up the mystery. California John had evidently been waiting for this question. He arose and knocked the ashes from his pipe.

"Bring a candle," he requested the storekeeper, and led the way to the abandoned Lost Dog. Into the tunnel he led them, to the very end. There he paused, holding aloft his light. At his feet was a canvas which, being removed, was found to cover neatly a number of heavy sacks.

"Here's our dust," said California John, "every ounce of it, he said. He kept about six hundred thousand or so that belonged to Bright: but he didn't take none of ours. He come back to tell me so."

The men crowded around for closer inspection.

"I wonder why he done that?" Tibbetts marvelled.

"I asked him that," replied California John, grimly, "He said his conscience never would rest easy if he robbed us babes."

Tibbetts broke the ensuing silence.

"Was 'babes' the word he used?" he asked, softly.

"'Babes' was the word," said California John.

THE TIDE

A short story, say the writers of text books and the teachers of sophomores, should deal with but a single episode. That dictum is probably true; but it admits of wider interpretation than is generally given it. The teller of tales, anxious to escape from restriction but not avid of being cast into the outer darkness of the taboo, can in self-justification become as technical as any lawyer. The phrase "a single episode" is loosely worded. The rule does not specify an episode in one man's life; it might be in the life of a family, or a state, or even of a whole people. In that case the action might cover many lives. It is a way out for those who have a story to tell, a limit to tell it within, but who do not wish to embroil themselves too seriously with the august Makers of the Rules.

CHAPTER I

The time was 1850, the place that long, soft, hot dry stretch of blasted desolation known as the Humboldt Sink. The sun stared, the heat rose in waves, the mirage shimmered, the dust devils of choking alkali whirled aloft or sank in suffocation on the hot earth. Thus it had been since in remote ages the last drop of the inland sea had risen into a brazen sky. But this year had brought something new. A track now led across the desert. It had sunk deep into the alkali, and the soft edges had closed over it like snow, so that the wheel marks and the hoof marks and the prints of men's feet looked old. Almost in a straight line it led to the west. Its perspective, dwindling to nothingness, corrected the deceit of the clear air. Without it the cool, tall mountains looked very near. But when the eye followed the trail to its vanishing, then, as though by magic, the Ranges drew back, and before them denied dreadful forces of toil, thirst, exhaustion, and despair. For the trail was marked. If the wheel ruts had been obliterated, it could still have been easily followed. Abandoned goods, furniture, stores, broken-down wagons, bloated carcasses of oxen or horses, bones bleached white, rattling mummies of dried skin, and an almost unbroken line of marked and unmarked graves—like the rout of an army, like the spent wash of a wave that had rolled westward—these in double rank defined the road.

The buzzards sailing aloft looked down on the Humboldt Sink as we would look upon a relief map. Near the centre of the map a tiny cloud of white dust crawled slowly forward. The buzzards stooped to poise above it.

Stewart Edward White

Two ox wagons plodded along. A squirrel—were such a creature possible—would have stirred disproportionately the light alkali dust; the two heavy wagons and the shuffling feet of the beasts raised a cloud. The fitful furnace draught carried this along at the slow pace of the caravan, which could be seen only dimly, as through a dense fog.

The oxen were in distress. Evidently weakened by starvation, they were proceeding only with the greatest difficulty. Their tongues were out, their legs spread, spasmodically their eyes rolled back to show the whites, from time to time one or another of them uttered a strangled, moaning bellow. They were white with the powdery dust, as were their yokes, the wagons, and the men who plodded doggedly alongside. Finally, they stopped. The dust eddied by; and the blasting sun fell upon them.

The driver of the leading team motioned to the other. They huddled in the scanty shade alongside the first wagon. Both men were so powdered and caked with alkali that their features were indistinguishable. Their red-rimmed, inflamed eyes looked out as though from masks.

The one who had been bringing up the rear looked despairingly toward the mountains.

"We'll never get there!" he cried.

"Not the way we are now," replied the other. "But I intend to get there."

"How?"

"Leave your wagon, Jim; it's the heaviest. Put your team on here."

"But my wagon is all I've got in the world!" cried the other, "and we've got near a keg of water yet! We can make it! The oxen are pulling all right!"

His companion turned away with a shrug, then thought better of it and turned back.

"We've thrown out all we owned except bare necessities," he explained, patiently. "Your wagon is too heavy. The time to change is while the beasts can still pull."

"But I refuse!" cried the other. "I won't do it. Go ahead with your wagon. I'll get mine in, John Gates, you can't bulldoze me."

Gates stared him in the eye.

"Get the pail," he requested, mildly.

He drew water from one of the kegs slung underneath the wagon's body. The oxen, smelling it, strained weakly, bellowing. Gates slowly and carefully swabbed out their mouths, permitted them each a few swallows, rubbed them pityingly between the horns. Then he proceeded to unyoke the four beasts from the other man's wagon and yoked them to his own. Jim started to say something. Gates faced him. Nothing was said.

"Get your kit," Gates commanded, briefly, after a few moments. He parted the hanging canvas and looked into the wagon. Built to transport much freight it was nearly empty. A young woman lay on a bed spread along the wagon bottom. She seemed very weak.

"All right, honey?" asked Gates, gently.

She stirred, and achieved a faint smile.

"It's terribly hot. The sun strikes through," she replied. "Can't we let some air in?"

"The dust would smother you."

"Are we nearly there?"

"Getting on farther every minute," he replied, cheerfully.

Again the smothering alkali rose and the dust cloud crawled.

Four hours later the traveller called Jim collapsed face downward. The oxen stopped. Gates lifted the man by the shoulders. So exhausted was he that he had not the strength nor energy to spit forth the alkali with which his fall had caked his open mouth. Gates had recourse to the water keg. After a little he hoisted his companion to the front seat.

At intervals thereafter the lone human figure spoke the single word that brought his team to an instantaneous dead stop. His first care was then the woman, next the man clinging to the front seat, then the oxen. Before starting he clambered to the top of the wagon and cast a long, calculating look across the desolation ahead. Twice he even further reduced the meagre contents of the wagon, appraising each article long and doubtfully before discarding it. About mid-afternoon he said abruptly:

"Jim, you've got to walk."

The man demurred weakly, with a touch of panic.

"Every ounce counts. It's going to be a close shave. You can hang on to the tail of the wagon."

Yet an hour later Jim, for the fourth time, fell face downward, but now did not rise. Gates, going to him, laid his hand on his head, pushed back one of his eyelids, then knelt for a full half minute, staring straight ahead. Once he made a tentative motion toward the nearly empty water keg, once he started to raise the man's shoulders. The movements were inhibited. A brief agony cracked the mask of alkali on his countenance. Then stolidly, wearily, he arose. The wagon lurched forward. After it had gone a hundred yards and was well under way in its painful forward crawl, Gates, his red-rimmed, bloodshot eyes fixed and glazed, drew the revolver from its holster and went back.

At sundown he began to use the gad. The oxen were trying to lie down. If one of them succeeded, it would never again arise. Gates knew this. He plied the long, heavy whip in both hands. Where the lash fell it bit out strips of hide. It was characteristic of the man that though heretofore he had not in all this day inflicted a single blow on the suffering animals, though his nostrils widened and his terrible red eyes looked for pity toward the skies, yet now he swung mercilessly with all his strength.

Dusk fell, but the hot earth still radiated, the powder dust rose and choked. The desert dragged at their feet; and in the twilight John Gates thought to hear mutterings and the soft sound of wings overhead as the dread spirits of the wastes stooped low. He had not stopped for nearly two hours. This was the last push; he must go straight through or fail.

And when the gleam of the river answered the gleam of the starlight he had again to rouse his drained energies. By the brake, by directing the wagon into an obstruction, by voice and whip he fought the frantic beasts back to a moaning standstill. Then pail by pail he fed them the water until the danger of overdrinking was past. He parted the curtains. In spite of the noise outside the woman, soothed by the breath of cooler air, had fallen asleep.

Some time later he again parted the curtains.

"We're here, honey," he said, "good water, good grass, shade. The desert is past. Wake up and take a little coffee."

She smiled at him.

"I'm so tired."

"We're going to rest here a spell,"

She drank the coffee, ate some of the food he brought her, thrust back her hair, breathed deep of the cooling night.

"Where's Jim?" she asked at last.

"Jim got very tired," he said, "Jim's asleep."

$$* \quad * \quad * \quad * \quad *$$

Three months later. The western slant of the Sierras just where the canon clefts begin to spread into foothills. On a flat near— too near—the stream-bed was a typical placer-mining camp of the day. That is, three or four large, rough buildings in a row, twenty or thirty log cabins scattered without order, and as many tents.

The whole population was gathered interestedly in the largest structure, which was primarily a dance hall. Ninety-five per cent. were men, of whom the majority were young men. A year ago the percentage would have been nearer one hundred, but now a certain small coterie of women had drifted in, most of them with a keen eye for prosperity. The red or blue shirt, the nondescript hat, and the high, mud-caked boots of the miner preponderated. Here and there in the crowd, however, stood a man dressed in the height of fashion. There seemed no middle ground. These latter were either the professional gamblers, the lawyers, or the promoters.

A trial was in progress, to which all paid deep attention. Two men disputed the ownership of a certain claim. Their causes were represented by ornate individuals whose evident zest in the legal battle was not measured by prospective fees. Nowhere in the domain and at no time in the history of the law has technicality been so valued, has the game of the courts possessed such intellectual interest, has substantial justice been so uncertain as in the California of the early 'fifties. The lawyer could spread himself unhampered; and these were so doing.

In the height of the proceedings a man entered from outside and took his position leaning against the rail of the jury box. That he was a stranger was evident from the glances of curiosity, cast in his direction. He was tall, strong, young, bearded, with a roving, humorous bold eye.

The last word was spoken. A rather bewildered-looking jury filed out. Ensued a wait. The jury came back. It could not agree; it wanted information. Both lawyers supplied it in abundance. The foreman, who happened to be next the rail against which the newcomer was leaning, cast on him a quizzical eye.

"Stranger," said he, "mout you be able to make head er tail of all that air?"

The other shook his head.

"I'm plumb distracted to know what to do; and dear knows we all want to git shet of this job. Thar's a badger fight—"

"Where is this claim, anyway?"

"Right adown the road. Location notice is on the first white oak you come to. Cain't miss her."

"If I were you," said the stranger after a pause, "I'd just declare the claim vacant. Then neither side would win."

At this moment the jury rose to retire again. The stranger unobtrusively gained the attention of the clerk and from him begged a sheet of paper. On this he wrote rapidly, then folded it, and moved to the outer door, against the jamb of which he took his position. After another and shorter wait, the jury returned.

"Have you agreed on your verdict, gentlemen?" inquired the judge.

"We have," replied the lank foreman. "We award that the claim belongs to neither and be declared vacant."

At the words the stranger in the doorway disappeared. Two minutes later the advance guard of the rush that had comprehended the true meaning of the verdict found the white oak tree in possession of a competent individual with a Colt's revolving pistol and a humorous eye.

"My location notice, gentlemen," he said, calling attention to a paper freshly attached by wooden pegs.

"Honey-bug claim'," they read, "'John Gates'," and the usual phraseology.

"But this is a swindle, an outrage!" cried one of the erstwhile owners.

"If so it was perpetrated by your own courts," said Gates, crisply. "I am within my rights, and I propose to defend them."

Thus John Gates and his wife, now strong and hearty, became members of this community. His intention had been to proceed to Sacramento. An incident stopped him here.

The Honey-bug claim might or might not be a good placer mine—time would show—but it was certainly a wonderful location. Below the sloping bench on which it stood the country fell away into the brown heat haze of the lowlands, a curtain that could lift before a north wind to reveal a landscape magnificent as a kingdom. Spreading white oaks gave shade, a spring sang from the side hill on which grew lofty pines, and back to the east rose the dark or glittering Sierras. The meadow at the back was gay with mariposa lilies, melodious with bees and birds, aromatic with the mingled essences of tarweed, lads-love, and the pines. At this happy elevation the sun lay warm and caressing, but the air tasted cool.

"I could love this," said the woman.

"You'll have a chance," said John Gates, "for when we've made our pile, we'll always keep this to come back to."

At first they lived in the wagon, which they drew up under one of the trees, while the oxen recuperated and grew fat on the abundant grasses. Then in spare moments John Gates began the construction of a house. He was a man of tremendous energy, but also of many activities. The days were not long enough for him. In him was the true ferment of constructive civilization. Instinctively he reached out to modify his surroundings. A house, then a picket fence, split from the living trees; an irrigation ditch; a garden spot; fruit trees; vines over the porch; better stables; more fences; the gradual shaping from the wilderness of a home—these absorbed his surplus. As a matter of business he worked with pick and shovel until he had proved the Honey-bug hopeless, then he started a store on credit. Therein he sold everything from hats to 42 calibre whiskey. To it he brought the same overflowing play-spirit that had fashioned his home.

"I'm making a very good living," he answered a question; "that is, if I'm not particular on how well I live," and he laughed his huge laugh.

He was very popular. Shortly they elected him sheriff. He gained this high office fundamentally, of course, by reason of his courage and decision of character; but the immediate and visible causes were the Episode of the Frazzled Mule, and the Episode of the Frying Pan. The one inspired respect; the other amusement.

The freight company used many pack and draught animals. One day one of its mules died. The *mozo* in charge of the corrals dragged the carcass to the superintendent's office. That individual cursed twice; once at the mule for dying, and once at the *mozo* for being a fool. At nightfall another mule died. This time the *mozo*, mindful of his berating, did not deliver

Stewart Edward White

the body, but conducted the superintendent to see the sad remains.

"Bury it," ordered the superintendent, disgustedly. Two mules at $350—quite a loss.

But next morning another had died; fairly an epidemic among mules. This carcass also was ordered buried. And at noon a fourth. The superintendent, on his way to view the defunct, ran across John Gates.

"Look here, John," queried he, "do you know anything about mules?"

"Considerable," admitted Gates.

"Well, come see if you can tell me what's killing ours off."

They contemplated the latest victim of the epidemic.

"Seems to be something that swells them up," ventured the superintendent after a while.

John Gates said nothing for some time. Then suddenly he snatched his pistol and levelled it at the shrinking *mozo*.

"Produce those three mules!" he roared, "*mucho pronto*, too!" To the bewildered superintendent he explained. "Don't you see? this is the same old original mule. He ain't never been buried at all. They've been stealing your animals pretending they died, and using this one over and over as proof!"

This proved to be the case; but John Gates was clever enough never to tell how he surmised the truth.

"That mule looked to me pretty frazzled," was all he would say.

The frying-pan episode was the sequence of a quarrel. Gates

was bringing home a new frying pan. At the proper point in the discussion he used his great strength to smash the implement over his opponent's head so vigorously that it came down around his neck like a jagged collar! Gates clung to the handle, however, and by it led his man all around camp, to the huge delight of the populace.

As sheriff he was effective, but at times peculiar in his administration. No man could have been more zealous in performing his duty; yet he never would mix in the affairs of foreigners. Invariably in such cases he made out the warrants in blank, swore in the complaining parties themselves as deputies, and told them blandly to do their own arresting! Nor at times did he fail to temper his duty with a little substantial justice of his own. Thus he was once called upon to execute a judgment for $30 against a poor family. Gates went down to the premises, looked over the situation, talked to the man—a poverty-stricken, discouraged, ague-shaken creature—and marched back to the offices of the plaintiffs in the case.

"Here," said he, calmly, laying a paper and a small bag of gold dust on their table, "is $30 and a receipt in full."

The complainant reached for the sack. Gates placed his hand over it.

"Sign the receipt," he commanded. "Now," he went on after the ink had been sanded, "there's your $30. It's yours legally; and you can take it if you want to. But I want to warn you that a thousand-dollar licking goes with it!"

The money—from Gates's own pocket—eventually found its way to the poor family!

They had three children, two boys and a girl of which one boy died.

In five years the placers began to play out. One by one the more energetic of the miners dropped away. The nature of the community changed. Small hill ranches or fruit farms took the place of the mines. The camp became a country village. Old time excitement calmed, the pace of life slowed, the horizon narrowed.

John Gates, clear-eyed, energetic, keen brained, saw this tendency before it became a fact.

"This camp is busted," he told himself.

It was the hour to fulfill the purpose of the long, terrible journey across the plains, to carry out the original intention to descend from the Sierras to the golden valleys, to follow the struggle.

"Reckon it's time to be moving," he told his wife.

But now his own great labours asserted their claim. He had put four years of his life into making this farm out of nothing, four years of incredible toil, energy, and young enthusiasm. He had a good dwelling and spacious corrals, an orchard started, a truck garden, a barley field, a pasture, cattle, sheep, chickens, his horses—all his creation from nothing. One evening at sundown he found his wife in the garden weeping softly.

"What is it, honey?" he asked.

"I was just thinking how we'd miss the garden," she replied.

He looked about at the bright, cheerful flowers, the vine-hung picket fence, the cool verandah, the shady fig tree already of some size. Everything was neat and trim, just as he liked it. And the tinkle of pleasant waters, the song of a meadow lark, the distant mellow lowing of cows came to his ears; the smell of tarweed and of pines mingled in his nostrils.

"It's a good place for children," he said, vaguely.

Neither knew it, but that little speech marked the ebb of the wave that had lifted him from his eastern home, had urged him across the plains, had flung him in the almost insolent triumph of his youth high toward the sun. Now the wash receded.

CHAPTER II

It was indeed a good place for children. Charley and Alice Gates grew tall and strong, big boned, magnificent, typical California products. They went to the district school, rode in the mountains, helped handle the wild cattle. At the age of twelve Charley began to accompany the summer incursions into the High Sierras in search of feed. At the age of sixteen he was entrusted with a bunch of cattle. In these summers he learned the wonder of the high, glittering peaks, the blueness of the skies in high altitudes, the multitude of the stars, the flower-gemmed secret meadows, the dark, murmuring forests. He fished in the streams, and hunted on the ridges. His camp was pitched within a corral of heavy logs. It was very simple. Utensils depending from trees, beds beneath canvas tarpaulins on pine needles, saddlery, riatas, branding irons scattered about. No shelter but the sky. A wonderful roving life.

It developed taciturnity and individualism. Charley Gates felt no necessity for expression as yet; and as his work required little cooeperation from his fellow creatures he acknowledged as little responsibility toward them. Thus far he was the typical mountaineer.

But other influences came to him; as, indeed, they come to all. But young Charley was more susceptible than most, and this—on the impulse of the next tide resurgent—saved him from his type. He liked to read; he did not scorn utterly and boisterously the unfortunate young man who taught the school; and, better than all, he possessed just the questioning mind that refuses to accept on their own asseveration only the conventions of life or the opinions of neighbours. If he were to drink, it would be because he wanted to; not because his companions considered it manly. If he were to enter the sheep war, it would be because he really considered sheep harmful to the range; not because of the overwhelming—and contagious —prejudice.

In one thing only did he follow blindly his sense of loyalty: He hated the Hydraulic Company.

Years after the placers failed someone discovered that the wholesale use of hydraulic "giants" produced gold in paying quantities. Huge streams of water under high pressure were directed against the hills, which melted like snow under the spring sun. The earth in suspension was run over artificial riffles against which the heavier gold collected. One such stream could accomplish in a few hours what would have cost hand miners the better part of a season.

But the debris must go somewhere. A rushing mud and boulder-filled torrent tore down stream beds adapted to a tenth of their volume. It wrecked much of the country below, ripping out the good soil, covering the bottomlands many feet deep with coarse rubble, clay, mud, and even big rocks and boulders. The farmers situated below such operations suffered cruelly. Even to this day the devastating results may be seen above Colfax or Sacramento.

John Gates suffered with the rest. His was not the nature to submit tamely, nor to compromise. He had made his farm with his own hands, and he did not propose to see it destroyed. Much money he expended through the courts; indeed the profits of his business were eaten by a never-ending, inconclusive suit. The Hydraulic Company, securely entrenched behind the barriers of especial privilege, could laugh at his frontal attacks. It was useless to think of force. The feud degenerated into a bitter legal battle and much petty guerrilla warfare on both sides.

Stewart Edward White

To this quarrel Charley had been bred up in a consuming hate of the Hydraulic Company, all its works, officers, bosses, and employees. Every human being in any way connected with it wore horns, hoofs, and a tail. In company with the wild youths of the neighbourhood he perpetrated many a raid on the Company's property. Beginning with boyish openings of corrals to permit stock to stray, these raids progressed with the years until they had nearly arrived at the dignity of armed deputies and bench warrants.

The next day of significance to our story was October 15, 1872. On that date fire started near Flour Gold and swept upward. October is always a bad time of year for fires in foothill California—between the rains, the heat of the year, everything crisp and brown and brittle. This threatened the whole valley and water shed. The Gateses turned out, and all their neighbours, with hoe, mattock, axe, and sacking, trying to beat, cut, or scrape a "break" wide enough to check the flames. It was cruel work. The sun blazed overhead and the earth underfoot. The air quivered as from a furnace. Men gasped at it with straining lungs. The sweat pouring from their bodies combined with the parching of the superheated air induced a raging thirst. No water was to be had save what was brought to them. Young boys and women rode along the line carrying canteens, water bottles, and food. The fire fighters snatched hastily at these, for the attack of the fire permitted no respite. Twice they cut the wide swath across country; but twice before it was completed the fire crept through and roared into triumph behind them. The third time the line held, and this was well into the second day.

Charley Gates had fought doggedly. He had summoned the splendid resources of youth and heritage, and they had responded. Next in line to his right had been a stranger. This latter was a slender, clean-cut youth, at first glance seemingly of delicate physique. Charley had looked upon him with the pitying contempt of strong youth for weak youth. He considered that the stranger's hands were soft and effeminate, he disliked his little trimmed moustache, and especially the cool, mocking, appraising glance of his eyes. But as the day, and the night, and the day following wore away, Charley raised his opinion. The slender body possessed unexpected reserve, the long, lean hands plied the tools unweariedly, the sensitive face had become drawn and tired, but the spirit behind the mocking eyes had not lost the flash of its defiance. In the heat of the struggle was opportunity for only the briefest exchanges. Once, when Charley despairingly shook his empty canteen, the stranger offered him a swallow from his own. Next time exigency crowded them together, Charley croaked:

"Reckon we'll hold her."

Toward evening of the second day the westerly breeze died, and shortly there breathed a gentle air from the mountains. The danger was past.

Charley and the stranger took long pulls from their recently replenished canteens. Then they sank down where they were, and fell instantly asleep. The projecting root of a buckthorn stuck squarely into Charley's ribs, but he did not know it; a column of marching ants, led by a non-adaptable commander, climbed up and over the recumbent form of the stranger, but he did not care.

They came to life in the shiver of gray dawn, wearied, stiffened, their eyes swelled, their mouths dry.

"You're a sweet sight, stranger," observed Charley.

"Same to you and more of 'em," rejoined the other.

Charley arose painfully.

"There's a little water in my canteen yet," he proffered. "What might you call yourself? I don't seem to know you in these parts."

"Thanks," replied the other. "My name's Cathcart; I'm from

just above."

He drank, and lowered the canteen to look into the flaming, bloodshot eyes of his companion.

"Are you the low-lived skunk that's running the Hydraulic Company?" demanded Charley Gates.

The stranger laid down the canteen and scrambled painfully to his feet.

"I am employed by the Company," he replied, curtly, "but please to understand I don't permit you to call me names."

"Permit!" sneered Charley.

"Permit," repeated Cathcart.

So, not having had enough exercise in the past two days, these young game cocks went at each other. Charley was much the stronger rough-and-tumble fighter; but Cathcart possessed some boxing skill. Result was that, in their weakened condition, they speedily fought themselves to a standstill without serious damage to either side.

"Now perhaps you'll tell me who the hell you think you are!" panted Cathcart, fiercely.

At just beyond arm's length they discussed the situation, at first belligerently with much recrimination, then more calmly, at last with a modicum of mutual understanding. Neither seceded from his basic opinion. Charley Gates maintained that the Company had no earthly business ruining his property, but admitted that with all that good gold lying there it was a pity not to get it out. Cathcart stoutly defended a man's perfect right to do as he pleased with his own belongings, but conceded that something really ought to be done about overflow waters.

"What are you doing down here fighting fire, anyway?" demanded Charley, suddenly. "It couldn't hurt your property. You could turn the 'giants' on it, if it ever came up your way."

"I don't know. I just thought I ought to help out a little," said Cathcart, simply.

For three years more Charley ran his father's cattle in the hills. Then he announced his intention of going away. John Gates was thunderstruck. By now he was stranded high and dry above the tide, fitting perfectly his surroundings. Vaguely he had felt that his son would stay with him always. But the wave was again surging upward. Charley had talked with Cathcart.

"This is no country to draw a salary in," the latter had told him, "nor to play with farming or cows. It's too big, too new, there are too many opportunities. I'll resign, and you leave; and we'll make our fortunes."

"How?" asked Charley.

"Timber," said Cathcart.

They conferred on this point. Cathcart had the experience of business ways; Charley Gates the intimate knowledge of the country; there only needed a third member to furnish some money. Charley broke the news to his family, packed his few belongings, and the two of them went to San Francisco.

Charley had never seen a big city. He was very funny about it, but not overwhelmed. While willing, even avid, to go the rounds and meet the sporting element, he declined to drink. When pressed and badgered by his new acquaintances, he grinned amiably.

"I never play the other fellows' game," he said. "When it gets to be my game, I'll join you."

The new partners had difficulty in getting even a hearing.

"It's a small business," said capitalists, "and will be. The demand for lumber here is limited, and it is well taken care of by small concerns near at hand."

"The state will grow and I am counting on the outside market," argued Cathcart.

But this was too absurd! The forests of Michigan, Wisconsin, and Minnesota were inexhaustible! As for the state growing to that extent; of course we all believe it, but when it comes to investing good money in the belief—

At length they came upon one of the new millionaires created by the bonanzas of Virginia City.

"I don't know a damn thing about your timber, byes," said he, "but I like your looks. I'll go in wid ye. Have a seegar; they cost me a dollar apiece."

The sum invested was absurdly, inadequately small.

"It'll have to spread as thin as it can," said Cathcart.

They spent the entire season camping in the mountains. By the end of the summer they knew what they wanted; and immediately took steps to acquire it. Under the homestead laws each was entitled to but a small tract of Government land. However, they hired men to exercise their privileges in this respect, to take up each his allotted portion, and then to convey his rights to Cathcart and Gates. It was slow business, for the show of compliance with Government regulations had to be made. But in this manner the sum of money at their disposal was indeed spread out very thin.

For many years the small, nibbling lumbering operations their limited capital permitted supplied only a little more than a bare living and the taxes. But every available cent went back into the business. It grew. Band saws replaced the old circulars; the new mills delivered their product into flumes that carried it forty miles to the railroad. The construction of this flume was a tremendous undertaking, but by now the firm could borrow on its timber. To get the water necessary to keep the flume in operation the partners—again by means of "dummies"—filed on the water rights of certain streams. To take up the water directly was without the law; but a show of mineral stain was held to justify a "mineral claim," so patents were obtained under that ruling. Then Charley had a bright idea.

"Look here, Cliff," he said to Cathcart. "I know something about farming; I was brought up on a farm. This country will grow anything anywhere if it has water. That lower country they call a desert, but that's only because it hasn't any rainfall. We're going to have a lot of water at the end of that flume—"

They bought the desert land at fifty cents an acre; scraped ditches and checks; planted a model orchard, and went into the real estate business. In time a community grew up. When hydro-electric power came into its own Cathcart & Gates from their various water rights furnished light for themselves, and gradually for the towns and villages round-about. Thus their affairs spread and became complicated. Before they knew it they were wealthy, very wealthy. Their wives—for in due course each had his romance—began to talk of San Francisco.

All this had not come about easily. At first they had to fight tooth and nail. The conditions of the times were crude, the code merciless. As soon as the firm showed its head above the financial horizon, it was swooped upon. Business was predatory. They had to fight for what they got; had to fight harder to hold it. Cathcart was involved continually in a maze of intricate banking transactions; Gates resisted aggression within and without, often with his own two fists. They learned to trust no man, but they learned also to hate no man. It was all part of the game. More sensitive temperaments would have failed; these succeeded. Cathcart became shrewd, incisive, direct, cold, a little hard; Charley Gates was burly, hearty, a trifle bullying. Both were in all circumstances quite unruffled; and in some circumstances ruthless.

About 1900 the entire holdings of the Company were capitalized, and a stock company was formed. The actual management of the lumbering, the conduct of the farms and ranches, the running of the hydro-electric systems of light and transportation, were placed in the hands of active young men. Charley Gates and his partner exercised over these activities only the slightest supervision; auditing accounts, making an occasional trip of inspection. Affairs would quite well have gone on without them; though they would have disbelieved and resented that statement.

The great central offices in San Francisco were very busy—all but the inner rooms where stood the partners' desks. One day Cathcart lit a fresh cigar, and slowly wheeled his chair.

"Look here, Charley," he proposed, "we've got a big surplus. There's no reason why we shouldn't make a killing on the side."

"As how?" asked Gates.

Cathcart outlined his plan. It was simply stock manipulation on a big scale; although the naked import was somewhat obscured by the complications of the scheme. After he had finished Gates smoked for some time in silence.

"All right, Cliff," said he, "let's do it."

And so by a sentence, as his father before him, he marked the farthest throw of the wave that had borne him blindly toward the shore. In the next ten years Cathcart and Gates made forty million dollars. Charley seemed to himself to be doing a tremendous business, but his real work, his contribution to the episode in the life of the commonwealth, ceased there. Again the wave receded.

CHAPTER III

The third generation of the Gates family consisted of two girls and a boy. They were brought up as to their early childhood in what may be called moderate circumstances. A small home near the little mill town, a single Chinese servant, a setter dog, and plenty of horses formed their entourage. When Charles, Jr., was eleven, and his sisters six and eight, however, the family moved to a pretentious "mansion" on Nob Hill in San Francisco. The environment of childhood became a memory: the reality of life was comprised in the super-luxurious existence on Nob Hill.

It was not a particularly wise existence. Whims were too easily realized, consequences too lightly avoided, discipline too capricious. The children were sent to private schools where they met only their own kind; they were specifically forbidden to mingle with the "hoodlums" in the next street; they became accustomed to being sent here and there in carriages with two servants, or later, in motor cars; they had always spending money for the asking.

"I know what it is like to scrimp and save, and my children are going to be spared that!" was Mrs. Gates's creed in the matter.

The little girls were always dressed alike in elaborately simple clothes, with frilly, starched underpinnies, silk stockings, high boots buttoned up slim legs; and across their shoulders, from beneath wonderful lingerie hats, hung shining curls. The latter were not natural, but had each day to be elaborately

Stewart Edward White

constructed. They made a dainty and charming picture.

"Did you ever see anything so sweet in all your life!" was the invariable feminine exclamation.

Clara and Ethel-May always heard these remarks. They conducted themselves with the poise and *savoir faire* of grown women. Before they were twelve they could "handle" servants, conduct polite conversations in a correctly artificial accent, and adapt their manners to another's station in life.

Charley Junior's development was sharply divided into two periods, with the second of which alone we have to do. The first, briefly, was repressive. He was not allowed to play with certain boys, he was not permitted to stray beyond certain bounds, he was kept clean and dressed-up, he was taught his manners. In short, Mrs. Gates tried—without knowing what she was doing—to use the same formula on him as she had on Ethel-May and Clara.

In the second period, he was a grief to his family. Roughly speaking, this period commenced about the time he began to be known as "Chuck" instead of Charley.

There was no real harm in the boy. He was high spirited, full of life, strong as a horse, and curious. Possessed of the patrician haughty good looks we breed so easily from shirtsleeves, free with his money, known as the son of his powerful father, a good boxer, knowing no fear, he speedily became a familiar popular figure around town. It delighted him to play the prince, either incognito or in person; to "blow off the crowd," to battle joyously with longshoremen; to "rough house" the semi-respectable restaurants. The Barbary Coast knew him, Taits, Zinkands, the Poodle Dog, the Cliff House, Franks, and many other resorts not to be spoken of so openly. He even got into the police courts once or twice; and nonchalantly paid a fine, with a joke at the judge and a tip to the policeman who had arrested him. There was too much drinking, too much gambling, too loose a companionship, altogether too much spending; but in this case the life was redeemed from its usual significance by a fantastic spirit of play, a generosity of soul, a regard for the unfortunate, a courtliness toward all the world, a refusal to believe in meanness or sordidness or cruelty. Chuck Gates was inbred with the spirit of *noblesse oblige*.

As soon as motor cars came in Chuck had the raciest possible. With it he managed to frighten a good many people half out of their wits. He had no accidents, partly because he was a very good heady driver, and partly because those whom he encountered were quick witted. One day while touring in the south he came down grade around a bend squarely upon a car ascending. Chuck's car was going too fast to be stopped. He tried desperately to wrench it from the road, but perceived at once that this was impossible without a fatal skid. Fortunately the only turnout for a half mile happened to be just at that spot. The other man managed to jump his car out on this little side ledge and to jam on his brakes at the very brink, just as Chuck flashed by. His mud guards slipped under those at the rear of the other car.

"Close," observed Chuck to Joe Merrill his companion, "I was going a little too fast," and thought no more of it.

But the other man, being angry, turned around and followed him into town. At the garage he sought Chuck out.

"Didn't you pass me on the grade five miles back?" he inquired.

"I may have done so," replied Chuck, courteously.

"Don't you realize that you were going altogether too fast for a mountain grade? that you were completely out of control?"

"I'm afraid I'll have to admit that that is so."

"Well," said the other man, with difficulty suppressing his anger. "What do you suppose would have happened if I hadn't

Stewart Edward White

just been able to pull out?"

"Why," replied Chuck, blandly, "I suppose I'd have had to pay heavily; that's all."

"Pay!" cried the man, then checked himself with an effort, "so you imagine you are privileged to the road, do whatever damage you please—and *pay!* I'll just take your number."

"That is unnecessary. My name is Charles Gates," replied Chuck, "of San Francisco."

The man appeared never to have heard of this potent cognomen. A month later the trial came off. It was most inconvenient. Chuck was in Oregon, hunting. He had to travel many hundreds of miles, to pay an expensive lawyer. In the end he was fined. The whole affair disgusted him, but he went through with it well, testified without attempt at evasion. It was a pity; but evidently the other man was no gentleman.

"I acknowledged I was wrong," he told Joe Merrill. He honestly felt that this would have been sufficient had the cases been reversed. In answer to a question as to whether he considered it fair to place the burden of safety on the other man, he replied:

"Among motorists it is customary to exchange the courtesies of the road—and sometimes the discourtesies," he added with a faint scorn.

The earthquake and fire of 1906 caught him in town. During three days and nights he ran his car for the benefit of the sufferers; going practically without food or sleep, exercising the utmost audacity and ingenuity in getting supplies, running fearlessly many dangers.

For the rest he played polo well, shot excellently at the traps, was good at tennis, golf, bridge. Naturally he belonged to the best clubs both city and country. He sailed a yacht expertly, was a keen fisherman, hunted. Also he played poker a good deal and was noted for his accurate taste in dress.

His mother firmly believed that he caused her much sorrow; his sisters looked up to him with a little awe; his father down on him with a fiercely tolerant contempt.

For Chuck had had his turn in the offices. His mind was a good one; his education both formal and informal, had trained it fairly well; yet he could not quite make good. Energetic, ambitious, keen young men, clambering upward from the ruck, gave him points at the game and then beat him. It was humiliating to the old man. He could not see the perfectly normal reason. These young men were striving keenly for what they had never had. Chuck was asked merely to add to what he already had more than enough of by means of a game that itself did not interest him.

Late one evening Chuck and some friends were dining at the Cliff House. They had been cruising up toward Tomales Bay, and had had themselves put ashore here. No one knew of their whereabouts. Thus it was that Chuck first learned of his father's death from apoplexy in the scareheads of an evening paper handed him by the majordomo. He read the article through carefully, then went alone to the beach below. It had been the usual sensational article; and but two sentences clung to Chuck's memory: "This fortunate young man's income will actually amount to about ten dollars a minute. What a significance have now his days—and nights!"

He looked out to sea whence the waves, in ordered rank, cast themselves on the shore, seethed upward along the sands, poised, and receded. His thoughts were many, but they always returned to the same point. Ten dollars a minute—roughly speaking, seven thousand a day! What would he do with it? "What a significance have now his days—and nights!"

His best friend, Joe Merrill, came down the path to him, and stood silently by his side.

"I'm sorry about your governor, old man," he ventured; and then, after a long time:

"You're the richest man in the West."

Chuck Gates arose. A wave larger than the rest thundered and ran hissing up to their feet.

"I wonder if the tide is coming in or going out," said Chuck, vaguely.

CLIMBING FOR GOATS

CHAPTER I

Near the point at which the great Continental Divide of the Rocky Mountains crosses the Canadian border another range edges in toward it from the south. Between these ranges lies a space of from twenty to forty miles; and midway between them flows a clear, wonderful river through dense forests. Into the river empty other, tributary, rivers rising in the bleak and lofty fastnesses of the mountains to right and left. Between them, in turn, run spur systems of mountains only a little less lofty than the parent ranges. Thus the ground plan of the whole country is a good deal like that of a leaf: the main stem representing the big river, the lateral veins its affluents; the tiny veins its torrents pouring from the sides of its mountains and glaciers; and the edges of the leaf and all spaces standing for mountains rising very sheer and abrupt from the floor of the densely forested stream valleys. In this country of forty miles by five hundred, then, are hundreds of distinct ranges, thousands of peaks, and innumerable valleys, pockets, and "parks." A wilder, lonelier, grander country would be hard to find. Save for the Forest Service and a handful of fur trappers, it is uninhabited. Its streams abound in trout; its dense forests with elk and white-tailed deer; its balder hills with blacktail deer; its upper basins with grizzly bears; its higher country with sheep and that dizzy climber the Rocky Mountain goat.

He who would enter this region descends at a little station on

Stewart Edward White

the Great Northern, and thence proceeds by pack train at least four days, preferably more, out into the wilderness. The going is through forests, the tree trunks straight and very close together, so that he will see very little of the open sky and less of the landscape. By way of compensation the forest itself is remarkably beautiful. Its undergrowth, though dense, is very low and even, not more than a foot or so off the ground; and in the Hunting Moon the leaves of this undergrowth have turned to purest yellow, without touch or trace of red, so that the sombre forest is carpeted with gold. Here and there shows a birch or aspen, also bright, pure light yellow, as though a brilliant sun were striking down through painted windows. Groups of yellow-leafed larches add to the splendour. And close to the ground grow little flat plants decked out with red or blue or white wax berries, Christmas fashion.

In this green-and-gold room one journeys for days. Occasionally a chance opening affords a momentary glimpse of hills or of the river sweeping below; but not for long. It is a chilly room. The frost has hardened the mud in the trail. One's feet and hands ache cruelly. At night camp is made near the banks of the river, whence always one may in a few moments catch as many trout as are needed, fine, big, fighting trout.

By the end of three or four days the prospect opens out. Tremendous cliffs rise sheer from the bottom of the valley; up tributary canons one can see a dozen miles to distant snow ranges glittering and wonderful. Nearer at hand the mountains rise above timber line to great buttes and precipices.

CHAPTER II

THE FIRST CLIMB

Fisher, Frank, and I had been hunting for elk in the dense forests along the foot of one of these mountains; and for a half day, drenched with sweat, had toiled continuously up and down steep slopes, trying to go quietly, trying to keep our wind, trying to pierce the secrets of the leafy screen always about us. We were tired of it.

"Let's go to the top and look for goats," suggested Frank. "There are some goat cliffs on the other side of her. It isn't very far."

It was not very far, as measured by the main ranges, but it was a two hours' steady climb nearly straight up. We would toil doggedly for a hundred feet, or until our wind gave out and our hearts began to pound distressingly; then we would rest a moment. After doing this a few hundred times we would venture a look upward, confidently expecting the summit to be close at hand. It seemed as far as ever. We suffered a dozen or so of these disappointments, and then learned not to look up. This was only after we had risen above timber line to the smooth, rounded rock-and-grass shoulder of the mountain. Then three times we made what we thought was a last spurt, only to find ourselves on a "false summit." After a while we grew resigned, we realized that we were never going to get anywhere, but were to go on forever, without ultimate purpose and without hope, pushing with tired legs, gasping with

Stewart Edward White

inadequate lungs. When we had fully made up our minds to that, we arrived. This is typical of all high-mountain climbing—the dogged, hard, hopeless work that can never reach an accomplishment; and then at last the sudden, unexpected culmination.

We topped a gently rounding summit; took several deep breaths into the uttermost cells of our distressed lungs; walked forward a dozen steps—and found ourselves looking over the sheer brink of a precipice. So startlingly unforeseen was the swoop into blue space that I recoiled hastily, feeling a little dizzy. Then I recovered and stepped forward cautiously for another look. As with all sheer precipices, the lip on which we stood seemed slightly to overhang, so that in order to see one had apparently to crane away over, quite off balance. Only by the strongest effort of the will is one able to rid oneself of the notion that the centre of gravity is about to plunge one off head first into blue space. For it was fairly blue space below our precipice. We could see birds wheeling below us; and then below them again, very tiny, the fall away of talus, and the tops of trees in the basin below. And opposite, and all around, even down over the horizon, were other majestic peaks, peers of our own, naked and rugged. From camp the great forests had seemed to us the most important, most dominant, most pervading feature of the wilderness. Now in the high sisterhood of the peaks we saw they were as mantles that had been dropped about the feet.

Across the face of the cliff below us ran irregular tiny ledges; buttresses ended in narrow peaks; "chimneys" ran down irregularly to the talus. Here were supposed to dwell the goats.

We proceeded along the crest, spying eagerly. We saw tracks; but no animals. By now it was four o'clock, and past time to turn campward. We struck down the mountain on a diagonal that should take us home. For some distance all went well enough. To be sure, it was very steep, and we had to pay due attention to balance and sliding. Then a rock wall barred our way. It was not a very large rock wall. We went below it. After a hundred yards we struck another. By now the first had risen until it towered far above us, a sheer, gray cliff behind which the sky was very blue. We skirted the base of the second and lower cliff. It led us to another; and to still another. Each of these we passed on the talus beneath it; but with increasing difficulty, owing to the fact that the wide ledges were pinching out. At last we found ourselves cut off from farther progress. To our right rose tier after tier of great cliffs, serenely and loftily unconscious of any little insects like ourselves that might be puttering around their feet. Straight ahead the ledge ceased to exist. To our left was a hundred-foot drop to the talus that sloped down to the canon. The canon did not look so very far away, and we desired mightily to reach it. The only alternative to getting straight down was to climb back the weary way we had come; and that meant all night without food, warm clothing, or shelter on a snow-and-ice mountain.

Therefore, we scouted that hundred-foot drop to our left very carefully. It seemed hopeless; but at last I found a place where a point of the talus ran up to a level not much below our own. The only difficulty was that between ourselves and that point of talus extended a piece of sheer wall. I slung my rifle over my back, and gave myself to a serious consideration of that wall. Then I began to work out across its face.

The principle of safe climbing is to maintain always three points of suspension: that it to say, one should keep either both footholds and one handhold, or both handholds and one foothold. Failing that, one is taking long chances. With this firmly in mind, I spidered out across the wall, testing every projection and cranny before I trusted any weight to it. One apparently solid projection as big as my head came away at the first touch, and went bouncing off into space. Finally I stood, or rather sprawled, almost within arm's length of a tiny scrub pine growing solidly in a crevice just over the talus. Once there, our troubles were over; but there seemed no way of crossing. For the moment it actually looked as though four feet only would be sufficient to turn us back.

Stewart Edward White

At last, however, I found a toehold half way across. It was a very slight crevice, and not more than two inches deep. The toe of a boot would just hold there without slipping. Unfortunately, there were no handholds above it. After thinking the matter over, however, I made up my mind to violate, for this occasion only, the rules for climbing. I inserted the toe, gathered myself, and with one smooth swoop swung myself across and grabbed that tiny pine!

Fisher now worked his way out and crossed in the same manner. But Frank was too heavy for such gymnastics. Fisher therefore took a firm grip on the pine, inserted his toe in the crevice, and hung on with all his strength while Frank crossed on his shoulders!

CHAPTER III

THE SECOND AND THIRD CLIMBS

Once more, lured by the promise of the tracks we had seen, we climbed this same mountain, but again without results. By now, you may be sure, we had found an easier way home! This was a very hard day's work, but uneventful.

Now, four days later, I crossed the river and set off above to explore in the direction of the Continental Divide. Of course I had no intention of climbing for goats, or, indeed, of hunting very hard for anything. My object was an idle go-look-see. Equally, of course, after I had rammed around most happily for a while up the wooded stream-bed of that canon, I turned sharp to the right and began to climb the slope of the spur, running out at right angles to the main ranges that constituted one wall of my canon. It was fifteen hundred nearly perpendicular feet of hard scrambling through windfalls. Then when I had gained the ridge, I thought I might as well keep along it a little distance. And then, naturally, I saw the main peaks not so *very* far away; and was in for it!

On either side of me the mountain dropped away abruptly. I walked on a knife edge, steeply rising. Great canons yawned close at either hand, and over across were leagues of snow mountains.

In the canon from which I had emerged a fine rain had been falling. Here it had turned to wet sleet. As I mounted, the

Stewart Edward White

slush underfoot grew firmer, froze, then changed to dry, powdery snow. This change was interesting and beautiful, but rather uncomfortable, for my boots, soaked through by the slush, now froze solid and scraped various patches of skin from my feet. It was interesting, too, to trace the change in bird life as the altitude increased. At snow line the species had narrowed down to a few ravens, a Canada jay, a blue grouse or so, nuthatches, and brown creepers. I saw one fresh elk track, innumerable marten, and the pad of a very large grizzly.

The ridge mounted steadily. After I had gained to 2,300 feet above the canon I found that the ridge dipped to a saddle 600 feet lower. It really grieved me to give up that hard-earned six hundred, and then to buy it back again by another hard, slow, toilsome climb. Again I found my way barred by some unsuspected cliffs about sixty feet in height. Fortunately, they were well broken; and I worked my way to the top by means of ledges.

Atop this the snow suddenly grew deeper and the ascent more precipitous. I fairly wallowed along. The timber line fell below me. All animal life disappeared. My only companions were now at spaced-out and mighty intervals the big bare peaks that had lifted themselves mysteriously from among their lesser neighbours, with which heretofore they had been confused. In spite of very heavy exertions, I began to feel the cold; so I unslung my rucksack and put on my buckskin shirt. The snow had become very light and feathery. The high, still buttes and crags of the main divide were right before me. Light fog wreaths drifted and eddied slowly, now concealing, now revealing the solemn crags and buttresses. Over everything— the rocks, the few stunted and twisted small trees, the very surface of the snow itself—lay a heavy rime of frost. This rime stood out in long, slender needles an inch to an inch and a half in length, sparkling and fragile and beautiful. It seemed that a breath of wind or even a loud sound would precipitate the glittering panoply to ruin; but in all the really awesome silence and hushed breathlessness of that strange upper world there was nothing to disturb them. The only motion was that of the idly-drifting fog wreaths; the only sound was that made by the singing of the blood in my ears! I felt as though I were in a world holding its breath.

It was piercing cold. I ate a biscuit and a few prunes, tramping energetically back and forth to keep warm. I could see in all directions now: an infinity of bare peaks, with hardly a glimpse of forests or streams or places where things might live. Goats are certainly either fools or great poets.

After a half hour of fruitless examination of the cliffs I perforce had to descend. The trip back was long. It had the added interest in that it was bringing me nearer water. No thirst is quite so torturing as that which afflicts one who climbs hard in cold, high altitudes. The throat and mouth seem to shrivel and parch. Psychologically, it is even worse than the desert thirst because in cold air it is unreasonable. Finally it became so unendurable that I turned down from the spur-ridge long before I should otherwise have done so, and did a good deal of extra work merely to reach a little sooner the stream at the bottom of the canon. When I reached it, I found that here it flowed underground.

CHAPTER IV

OTHER CLIMBS

For ten days we hunted and fished. When the opportunity offered, we made a goat-survey of a new place. Finally, as time grew short, we realized that we must concentrate our energies in one effort if we were to get specimens of this most desirable of all American big game. Therefore Fisher, Frank, Harry, and I, leaving our other two companions and the majority of the horses at the base camp, packed a few days' provisions and started in for the highest peaks of all.

We journeyed up an unknown canon eighteen miles long, heavily wooded in the bottoms, with great mountains overhanging, and with a beautiful clear trout stream singing down its bed. The first day we travelled ten hours. One man was always in front cutting out windfalls or other obstructions. I should be afraid to guess how many trees we chopped through that day. Another man scouted ahead for the best route amid difficulties. The other two performed the soul-destroying task of getting the horses to follow the appointed way. After three o'clock we began to hope for horse feed. At dark we reluctantly gave it up. The forest remained unbroken. We had to tie the poor, unfed horses to trees, while we ourselves searched diligently and with only partial success for tiny spots level enough and clear enough for our beds. It was very cold that night; and nobody was comfortable; the horses least of all.

Next morning we were out and away by daylight. If we could not find horse feed inside of four hours, we would be forced to retreat. Three hours of the four went by. Then Harry and I held the horses while our companions scouted ahead rapidly. We nearly froze, for in that deep valley the sun did not rise until nearly noon. Through an opening we could see back to a tremendous sheer butte rising more than three thousand feet[C] by a series of very narrow terraced ledges. We named it the Citadel, so like was it to an ancient proud fortress.

Fisher reported first. He had climbed a tree, but had seen no feed. Ten minutes later Frank returned. He had found the track of an ancient avalanche close under the mountain, and in that track grew coarse grasses. We pushed on, and there made camp.

It was a queer enough camp. Our beds we spread in the various little spots among the roots and hummocks we imagined to look the most even. The fire we had to build in quite another place. All around us the lodge-pole pines, firs, and larches grew close and dark and damp. Only to the west the snow ranges showed among the treetops like great, looming white clouds.

For two days we lived high among the glaciers and snow crags, taking tremendous tramps, seeing wonderful peaks, frozen lakes, sheer cliffs, the tracks of grizzlies in numbers, the tiny sources of great streams, and the infinity of upper spaces. But no goats; and no tracks of goats. Little by little we eliminated the possibilities of the country accessible to us. Leagues in all directions, as far as the eye could reach, was plenty of other country, all equally good for goats; but it was not within reach of us from this canon; and our time was up. Finally, we dropped back and made camp at the last feed; a mile or so below the Citadel. Two ranges at right angles here converged, and the Citadel rose like a tower at the corner. Here was our last chance.

Stewart Edward White

CHAPTER V

GOATS

As we were finishing breakfast my eye was attracted to a snow speck on the mountainside some two thousand feet above us and slightly westward that somehow looked to me different from other snow specks. For nearly a minute I stared at it through my glasses. At last the speck moved. The game was in sight!

We drew straws for the shot, and Fisher won. Then we began our climb. It was the same old story of pumping lungs and pounding hearts; but with the incentive before us we made excellent time. A shallow ravine and a fringe of woods afforded us the cover we needed. At the end of an hour and a half we crawled out of our ravine and to the edge of the trees. There across a steep canon and perhaps four hundred yards away were the goats, two of them, lying on the edge of small cliffs. We could see them very plainly, but they were too far for a sure shot. After examining them to our satisfaction we wormed our way back.

"The only sure way," I insisted, "is to climb clear to the top of the ridge, go along it on the other side until we are above and beyond the goats, and then to stalk them down hill."

That meant a lot more hard work; but in the end the plan was adopted. We resumed our interminable and toilsome climbing.

The ridge proved to be of the knife-edge variety, and covered with snow. From a deep, wide, walled-in basin on the other side rose the howling of two brush wolves. We descended a few feet to gain safe concealment; walked as rapidly as possible to the point above the goats; and then with the utmost caution began our descent.

In the last two hundred yards is the essence of big-game stalking. The hunter must move noiselessly, he must keep concealed; he must determine *at each step* just what the effect of that step has been in the matters of noise and of altering the point of view. It is necessary to spy sharply, not only from the normal elevation of a man's shoulders, but also stooping to the waist line, and even down to the knees. An animal is just as suspicious of legs as of heads; and much more likely to see them.

The shoulder of the mountain here consisted of a series of steep grass curves ending in short cliff jump-offs. Scattered and stunted trees and tree groups grew here and there. In thirty minutes we had made our distance and recognized the fact that our goats must be lying at the base of the next ledge. Motioning Harry to the left and Fisher to the front, I myself moved to the right to cut off the game should it run in that direction. Ten seconds later I heard Fisher shoot; then Harry opened up; and in a moment a goat ran across the ledge fifty yards below me. With a thrill of the greatest satisfaction I dropped the gold bead of my front sight on his shoulder!

The bullet knocked him off the edge of the cliff. He fell, struck the steep grass slope, and began to roll. Over and over and over he went, gathering speed like a snowball, getting smaller and smaller until he disappeared in the brush far below, a tiny spot of white.

No one can appreciate the feeling of relaxed relief that filled me. Hard and dangerous climbs, killing work, considerable hardship and discomfort had at length their reward. I could now take a rest. The day was young, and I contemplated with something like rapture a return to camp, and a good puttery day skinning out that goat. In addition I was suffering now from a splitting headache, the effects of incipient snow-blindness, and was generally pretty wobbly.

And then my eye wandered to the left, whence that goat had come. I saw a large splash of blood; at a spot *before* I had fired! It was too evident that the goat had already been wounded by Fisher; and therefore, by hunter's law, belonged to him!

I set my teeth and turned up the mountain to regain the descent we had just made. At the knife-edge top I stopped for a moment to get my breath and to survey the country. Diagonally across the basin where the wolves were howling, half way down the ridge running at right angles to my own, I made out two goats. They were two miles away from me on an air line. My course was obvious. I must proceed along my ridge to the Citadel, keeping always out of sight; surmount that fortress; descend to the second ridge; walk along the other side of it until I was above those goats, and then sneak down on them.

I accomplished the first two stages of my journey all right, though with considerably more difficulty in spots than I should have anticipated. The knife edge was so sharp and the sides so treacherous that at times it was almost impossible to travel anywhere but right on top. This would not do. By a little planning, however, I managed to reach the central "keep" of the Citadel: a high, bleak, broken pile, flat on top, with snow in all the crevices, and small cliffs on all sides. From this advantage I could cautiously spy out the lay of the land.

Below me fifty feet dipped the second ridge, running nearly at right angles. It sloped abruptly to the wolf basin, but fell sheer on the other side to depths I could not at that time guess.[D] A very few scattered, stunted, and twisted trees huddled close down to the rock and snow. This saddle was about fifty feet in width and perhaps five hundred yards in length. It ended in another craggy butte very much like the Citadel.

My first glance determined that my original plan would not do. The goats had climbed from where I had first seen them, and were now leisurely topping the saddle. To attempt to descend would be to reveal myself. I was forced to huddle just where I was. My hope was that the goats would wander along the saddle toward me, and not climb the other butte opposite. Also I wanted them to hurry, please, as the snow in which I sat was cold, and the wind piercing.

This apparently they were not inclined to do. They paused, they nibbled at some scanty moss, they gazed at the scenery, they scratched their ears. I shifted my position cautiously—and saw below me,[E] lying on the snow at the very edge of the cliff, a tremendous billy! He had been there all the time; and I had been looking over him!

At the crack of the Springfield he lurched forward and toppled slowly out of sight over the edge of the cliff. The two I had been stalking instantly disappeared. But on the very top of the butte opposite appeared another. It was a very long shot,[F] but I had to take chances, for I could not tell whether or not the one I had just shot was accessible or not. On a guess I held six inches over his back. The goat gave one leap forward into space. For twenty feet he fell spread-eagled and right side up as though flying. Then he began to turn and whirl. As far as my personal testimony could go, he is falling yet through that dizzy blue abyss.

"Good-bye, billy," said I, sadly. It looked then as though I had lost both.

I worked my way down the face of the Citadel until I was just above the steep snow fields. Here was a drop of six feet. If the snow was soft, all right. If it was frozen underneath, I would be very likely to toboggan off into space. I pried loose a small rock and dropped it, watching with great interest how it lit. It sunk with a dull plunk. Therefore I made my leap, and found myself waist deep in feathery snow.

Stewart Edward White

With what anxiety I peered over the edge of that precipice the reader can guess. Thirty feet below was a four-foot ledge. On the edge of that ledge grew two stunted pines about three feet in height—and only two. Against those pines my goat had lodged! In my exultation I straightened up and uttered a whoop. To my surprise it was answered from behind me. Frank had followed my trail. He had killed a nanny and was carrying the head. Everybody had goats!

After a great deal of man[oe]uvring we worked our way down to the ledge by means of a crevice and a ten-foot pole. Then we tied the goat to the little trees, and set to work. I held Frank while he skinned; and then he held me while I skinned. It was very awkward. The tiny landscape almost directly beneath us was blue with the atmosphere of distance. A solitary raven discovered us, and began to circle and croak and flop.

"You'll get your meal later," we told him.

Far below us, like suspended leaves swirling in a wind, a dense flock of snowbirds fluttered.

We got on well enough until it became necessary to sever the backbone. Then, try as we would, we could not in the general awkwardness reach a joint with a knife. At last we had a bright idea. I held the head back while Frank shot the vertebrae in two with his rifle!

Then we loosed the cords that held the body. It fell six hundred feet, hit a ledge, bounded out, and so disappeared toward the hazy blue map below. The raven folded his wings and dropped like a plummet, with a strange rushing sound. We watched him until the increasing speed of his swoop turned us a little dizzy, and we drew back. When we looked a moment later he had disappeared into the distance—straight down!

Now we had to win our way out. The trophy we tied with a rope. I climbed up the pole, and along the crevice as far as the rope would let me, hauled up the trophy, jammed my feet and back against both sides of the "chimney." Frank then clambered past me; and so repeat.

But once in the saddle we found we could not return the way we had come. The drop-off into the feather snow settled that. A short reconnaissance made it very evident that we would have to go completely around the outside of the Citadel, at the level of the saddle, until we had gained the other ridge. This meant about three quarters of a mile against the tremendous cliff.

We found a ledge and started. Our packs weighed about sixty pounds apiece, and we were forced to carry them rather high. The ledge proved to be from six to ten feet wide, with a gentle slope outward. We could not afford the false steps, nor the little slips, nor the overbalancings so unimportant on level ground. Progress was slow and cautious. We could not but remember the heart-stopping drop of that goat after we had cut the rope; and the swoop of the raven. Especially at the corners did we hug close to the wall, for the wind there snatched at us eagerly.

The ledge held out bravely. It had to; for there was no possible way to get up or down from it. We rounded the shoulder of the pile. Below us now was another landscape into which to fall—the valley of the stream, with its forests and its high cliffs over the way. But already we could see our ridge. Another quarter mile would land us in safety.

Without warning the ledge pinched out. A narrow tongue of shale, on so steep a slope that it barely clung to the mountain, ran twenty feet to a precipice. A touch sent its surface rattling merrily down and into space. It was only about eight feet across; and then the ledge began again.

We eyed it. Three steps would take us across. Alternative: return along the ledge to attack the problem *ab initio*.

"That shale is going to start," said Frank. "If you stop, she'll sure carry you over the ledge. But if you keep right on going, *fast*, I believe your weight will carry you through."

We readjusted our packs so they could not slip and overbalance us; we measured and re-measured with our eyes just where those steps would fall; we took a deep breath—and we *hustled*. Behind us the fine shale slid sullenly in a miniature avalanche that cascaded over the edge. Our "weight had carried us through!"

In camp, we found that Harry's shooting had landed a kid, so that we had a goat apiece.

We rejoined the main camp next day just ahead of a big snowstorm that must have made travel all but impossible. Then for five days we rode out, in snow, sleet, and hail. But we were entirely happy, and indifferent to what the weather could do to us now.

MOISTURE, A TRACE

Last fall I revisited Arizona for the first time in many years. My ultimate destination lay one hundred and twenty-eight miles south of the railroad. As I stepped off the Pullman I drew deep the crisp, thin air; I looked across immeasurable distance to tiny, brittle, gilded buttes; I glanced up and down a ramshackle row of wooden buildings with crazy wooden awnings, and I sighed contentedly. Same good old Arizona.

The Overland pulled out, flirting its tail at me contemptuously. A small, battered-looking car, grayed and caked with white alkali dust, glided alongside, and from under its swaying and disreputable top emerged someone I knew. Not individually. But by many campfires of the past I had foregathered with him and his kind. Same old Arizona, I repeated to myself.

This person bore down upon me and gently extracted my bag from my grasp. He stood about six feet three; his face was long and brown and grave; his figure was spare and strong. Atop his head he wore the sacred Arizona high-crowned hat, around his neck a bright bandana; no coat, but an unbuttoned vest; skinny trousers, and boots. Save for lack of spurs and *chaps* and revolver he might have been a moving-picture cowboy. The spurs alone were lacking from the picture of a real one.

He deposited my bag in the tonneau, urged me into a front seat, and crowded himself behind the wheel. The effect was that of a grown-up in a go-cart. This particular brand of tin car

Stewart Edward White

had not been built for this particular size of man. His knees were hunched up either side the steering column; his huge, strong brown hands grasped most competently that toy-like wheel. The peak of his sombrero missed the wrinkled top only because he sat on his spine. I reflected that he must have been drafted into this job, and I admired his courage in undertaking to double up like that even for a short journey.

"Roads good?" I asked the usual question as I slammed shut the door.

"Fair, suh," he replied, soberly.

"What time should we get in?" I inquired.

"Long 'bout six o'clock, suh," he informed me.

It was then eight in the morning—one hundred and twenty-eight miles—ten hours—roads good, eh?—hum.

He touched the starter. The motor exploded with a bang. We moved.

I looked her over. On the running board were strapped two big galvanized tanks of water. It was almost distressingly evident that the muffler had either been lost or thrown away. But she was hitting on all four. I glanced at the speedometer dial. It registered the astonishing total of 29,250 miles.

We swung out the end of the main street and sailed down a road that vanished in the endless gentle slope of a "sink." Beyond the sink the bank rose again, gently, to gain the height of the eyes at some *mesas*. Well I know that sort of country. One journeyed for the whole day, and the *mesas* stayed where they were; and in between were successively vast stretches of mesquite, or alkali, or lava outcrops, or *sacatone* bottoms, each seeming, while one was in it, to fill all the world forever, without end; and the day's changes were of mirage and the shifting colours of distant hills.

It was soon evident that my friend's ideas of driving probably coincided with his ideas of going up a mountain. When a mounted cowboy climbs a hill he does not believe in fussing with such nonsense as grades; he goes straight up. Similarly, this man evidently considered that, as roads were made for travel and distance for annihilation, one should turn on full speed and get there. Not one hair's breadth did he deign to swerve for chuck-hole or stone; not one fractional mile per hour did he check for gully or ditch. We struck them head-on, bang! did they happen in our way. Then my head hit the disreputable top. In the mysterious fashion of those who drive freight wagons my companion remained imperturbably glued to his seat. I had neither breath nor leisure for the country or conversation.

Thus one half hour. The speedometer dial showed the figures 29,260. I allowed myself to think of a possible late lunch at my friend's ranch.

We slowed down. The driver advanced the hand throttle the full sweep of the quadrant, steered with his knees, and produced the "makings." The faithful little motor continued to hit on all four, but in slow and painful succession, each explosion sounding like a pistol shot. We had passed already the lowest point of the "sink," and were climbing the slope on the other side. The country, as usual, looked perfectly level, but the motor knew different.

"I like to hear her shoot," said the driver, after his first cigarette. "That's why I chucked the muffler. Its plumb lonesome out yere all by yourself. A hoss is different."

"Who you riding for?"

"Me? I'm riding for me. This outfit is mine."

It didn't sound reasonable; but that's what I heard.

"You mean you drive this car—as a living—"

"Correct."

"I should think you'd get cramped!" I burst out.

"Me? I'm used to it. I bet I ain't missed three days since I got her—and that's about a year ago."

He answered my questions briefly, volunteering nothing. He had never had any trouble with the car; he had never broken a spring; he'd overhauled her once or twice; he averaged sixteen actual miles to the gallon. If I were to name the car I should have to write advt. after this article to keep within the law. I resolved to get one. We chugged persistently along on high gear; though I believe second would have been better. Presently we stopped and gave her a drink. She was boiling like a little tea kettle, and she was pretty thirsty.

"They all do it," said Bill. Of course his name was Bill. "Especially the big he-ones. High altitude. Going slow with your throttle wide open. You're all right if you got plenty water. If not, why then ketch a cow and use the milk. Only go slow or you'll git all clogged up with butter."

We clambered aboard and proceeded. That distant dreamful *mesa* had drawn very near. It was scandalous. The aloof desert whose terror, whose beauty, whose wonder, whose allure was the awe of infinite space that could be traversed only in toil and humbleness, had been contracted by a thing that now said 29,265.

"At this rate we'll get there before six o'clock," I remarked, hopefully.

"Oh, this is County Highway!" said Bill.

As we crawled along, still on high gear—that tin car certainly pulled strongly—a horseman emerged from a fold in the hills. He was riding a sweat-covered, mettlesome black with a rolling eye. His own eye was bitter, and likewise the other features of his face. After trying in vain to get the frantic animal within twenty feet of our *mitrailleuse,* he gave it up.

"Got anything for me?" he shrieked at Bill.

Bill leisurely turned off the switch, draped his long legs over the side of the car, and produced his makings.

"Nothing, Jim. Expaicting of anything?"

"Sent for a new grass rope. How's feed down Mogallon way?"

"Fair. That a bronco you're riding?"

"Just backed him three days ago."

"Amount to anything?"

"That," said Jim, with an extraordinary bitterness, "is already a gaited hoss. He has fo' gaits now."

"Four gaits," repeated Bill, incredulously. "I'm in the stink wagon business. I ain't aiming to buy no hosses. What four gaits you claim he's got?"

"Start, stumble, fall down *and* git up," said Jim.

Shortly after this joyous *rencontre* we topped the rise, and, looking back, could realize the grade we had been ascending.

The road led white and straight as an arrow to dwindle in perspective to a mere thread. The little car leaped forward on the invisible down grade. Again I anchored myself to one of the top supports. A long, rangy fowl happened into the road just ahead of us, but immediately flopped clumsily, half afoot, half a-wing, to one side in the brush, like a stampeded hen.

"Road runner," said Bill, with a short laugh. "Remember how they used to rack along in front of a hoss for miles, keeping just ahead, lettin' out a link when you spurred up? Aggravatin' fowl! They got over tryin' to keep ahead of gasoline."

In the white alkaline road lay one lone, pyramidal rock. It was about the size of one's two fists and all its edges and corners were sharp. Probably twenty miles of clear space lay on either flank of that rock. Nevertheless, our right front wheel hit it square in the middle. The car leaped straight up, the rock popped sidewise, and the tire went off with a mighty bang. Bill put on the brakes, deliberately uncoiled himself, and descended.

"Seems like tires don't last no time at all in this country," he remarked, sadly. He walked around the car and began to examine the four wrecks he carried as spares. After some inspection of their respective merits, he selected one. "I just somehow kain't git over the notion she ought to sidestep them little rocks and holes of her own accord," he exclaimed. "A hoss is a plumb, narrow-minded critter, but he knows enough for that."

While he changed the tire—which incidentally involved patching one of half a dozen over-worn tubes—I looked her over more in detail. The customary frame, strut rods, and torsion rods had been supplemented by the most extraordinary criss-cross of angle-iron braces it has ever been my fortune to behold. They ran from anywhere to everywhere beneath that car. I began to comprehend her cohesiveness.

"Jim Coles, blacksmith at the O T, puts them braces in all our cars," explained Bill. "He's got her down to a system."

The repair finished and the radiator refilled we resumed the journey. It was now just eleven o'clock. The odometer reading was 29,276. The temperature was well up toward 100 degrees. But beneath the disreputable top, and while in motion, the heat was not noticeable. Nevertheless, the brief stop had brought back poignantly certain old days—choking dust, thirst, the heat of a heavy sun, the long day that led one nowhere—

The noon mirages were taking shape, throwing stately and slow their vast illusions across the horizon. Lakes glimmered; distant ranges took on the forms of phantasm, rising higher, flattening, reaching across space the arches of their spans, rendering unreal a world of beauty and dread. That in the old days was the deliberate fashion the desert had of searing men's souls with her majesty. Slowly, slowly, the changes melted one into the other; massively, deliberately the face of the world was altered; so that at last the poor plodding human being, hot, dry, blinded, thirsty, felt himself a nothing in the presence of eternities. Well I knew that old spell of the desert. But now! Honestly, after a few minutes I began to feel sorry for the poor old desert! Its spells didn't work for the simple reason that *we didn't give it time!* We charged down on its phantom lakes and disproved them and forgot them. We broke right in on the dignified and deliberate scene shifting of mountains and *mesas*, showed them up for the brittle, dry hills they were, and left them behind. It was pitiful! It was as though a revered tragedian should overnight find that his vogue had departed; that he was no longer getting over; that an irreverent upstart, breaking in on his most sonorous periods, was getting laughs with slang. We had lots of water; the dust we left behind; it wasn't even hot in the wind of our going!

In the shallow crease of hills a shimmer of white soon changed to evident houses. We drew into a straggling desert town.

It was typical—thirty miles from the railroad, a distributing point for the cattle country. Four broad buildings with peeled, sunburned faces, a wooden house or so, and a dozen flat-roofed adobe huts hung pleasingly with long strips of red peppers. Of course one of the wooden buildings was labelled General Store; and another, smaller, contained a barber shop and postoffice combined. The third was barred and unoccupied. The fourth had been a livery stable but was now a garage. Six saddle horses and six Fords stood outside the General Store, which was a fair division.

Bill slowed down.

"Have a drink," I observed, hospitably.

"Arizona's a dry state," Bill reminded me; but nevertheless stopped and uncoiled. That unbelievable phenomenon had escaped my memory. In the old days I used to shut my eyes and project my soul into what I imagined was the future. I saw Arizona, embottled, dying in the last-wet ditch, while all the rest of the world, even including Milwaukee, bore down on her carrying the banners of Prohibition. So much for prophecy. I voiced a thought.

"There must be an awful lot of old timers died this spring. You can't cut them off short and hope to save them."

Bill grunted.

We entered the store. It smelled good, as such stores always do—soap, leather, ground coffee, bacon, cheese—all sorts of things. On the right ran a counter and shelves of dry goods and clothing; on the left groceries, cigars, and provisions generally. Down the middle saddles, ropes, spurs, pack outfits, harness, hardware. In the rear a glass cubby-hole with a desk inside. All that was customary, right and proper. But I noticed also a glass case with spark plugs and accessories; a rack full of tires; and a barrel of lubricating oil. I did not notice any body polish. By the front door stood a paper-basket whose purport I understood not at all.

Bill led me at once past two or three lounging cow persons to the cubbyhole, where arose a typical old timer.

"Mr. White, meet Mr. Billings," he said.

The old timer grasped me firmly by the right hand and held tight while he demanded, as usual, "What name?" We informed him together. He allowed he was pleased. I allowed the same.

"I want to buy a yard of calico," said Bill.

The old timer reached beneath the counter and produced a strip of cloth. It was already cut, and looked to be about a yard long. Also it showed the marks of loving but brutal and soiled hands.

"Wrap it up?" inquired Mr. Billings.

"Nope," said Bill, and handed out three silver dollars. Evidently calico was high in these parts. We turned away.

"By the way, Bill," Mr. Billings called after us, "I got a little present here for you. Some friends sent her in to me the other day. Let me know what you think of it."

We turned. Mr. Billings held in his hand a sealed quart bottle with a familiar and famous label.

"Why, that's kind of you," said Bill, gravely. He took the proffered bottle, turned it upside down, glanced at the bottom, and handed it back. "But I don't believe I'd wish for none of that particular breed. It never did agree with my stummick."

Without a flicker of the eye the storekeeper produced a second sealed bottle, identical in appearance and label with the first.

"Try it," he urged. "Here's one from a different case. Some of these yere vintages is better than others."

"So I've noticed," replied Bill, dryly. He glanced at the bottom and slipped it into his pocket.

We went out. As we passed the door Bill, unobserved, dropped into the heretofore unexplained waste-basket the yard of calico he had just purchased.

"Don't believe I like the pattern for my boudoir," he told me, gravely.

Stewart Edward White

We clambered aboard and shot our derisive exhaust at the diminishing town.

"Thought Arizona was a dry state," I suggested.

"She is. You cain't sell a drop. But you can keep stuff for personal use. There ain't nothing more personal than givin' it away to your friends."

"The price of calico is high down here."

"And goin' up," agreed Bill, gloomily. He drove ten miles in silence while I, knowing my type, waited.

"That old Billings ought to be drug out and buried," he remarked at last. "We rode together on the Chiracahua range. He ought to know better than to try to put it onto me."

"???" said I.

"You saw that first bottle? Just plain forty-rod dog poison— and me payin' three good round dollars!"

"For calico," I reminded.

"Shore. That's why he done it. He had me—if I hadn't called him."

"But that first bottle was identically the same as the one you have in your pocket," I stated.

"Shore?"

"Why, yes—at least—that is, the bottle and label were the same, and I particularly noticed the cork seal looked intact."

"It was," agreed Bill. "That cap hasn't never been disturbed. You're right."

"Then what objection—"

"It's one of them wonders of modern science that spoils the simple life next to Nature's heart," said Bill, unexpectedly. "You hitch a big hollow needle onto an electric light current. When she gets hot enough you punch a hole with her in the bottom of the bottle. Then you throw the switch and let the needle cool off. When she's cool you pour out the real thing for your own use—mebbe. Then you stick in your forty-cent-a-gallon squirrel poison. Heat up your needle again. Draw her out very slow so the glass will close up behind her. Simple, neat, effective, honest enough for down here. Cork still there, seal still there, label still there. Bottle still there, except for a little bit of a wart-lookin' bubble in the bottom."

It was now in the noon hour. Knowing cowboys of old I expected no lunch. We racketed along, and our dust tried to catch us, and sleepy, accustomed jack rabbits made two perfunctory hops as we turned on them the battery of our exhaust.

We dipped down into a carved bottomland, several miles wide, filled with minarets, peaks, vermilion towers, and strange striped labyrinths of many colours above which the sky showed an unbelievable blue. The trunks of colossal trees lay about in numbers. Apparently they had all been cross-cut in sections like those sawed for shake bolts, for each was many times clearly divided. The sections, however, lay all in place; so the trunks of the trees were as they had fallen. About the ground were scattered fragments of rock of all sizes, like lava, but of all the colours of the giddiest parrots. The tiniest piece had at least all the tints of the spectrum; and the biggest seemed to go the littlest several better. They looked to me like beautiful jewels. Bill cast at them a contemptuous glance.

"Every towerist I take in yere makes me stop while he sags down the car with this junk," he said. Whenever I say "Bill said" or "I said," I imply that we shrieked, for always through that great, still country we hustled enveloped in a profanity of explosions, creaks, rattles, and hums. Just now though, on a level, we travelled at a low gear. "Petrified wood," Bill added.

I swallowed guiltily the request I was about to proffer.

The malpais defined itself. We came to a wide, dry wash filled with white sand. Bill brought the little car to a stop.

Well I know that sort of sand! You plunge rashly into it on low gear; you buzz bravely for possibly fifty feet; you slow down, slow down; your driving wheels begin to spin—that finishes you. Every revolution digs a deeper hole. It is useless to apply power. If you are wise you throw out your clutch the instant she stalls, and thus save digging yourself in unnecessarily. But if you are really wise you don't get in that fix at all. The next stage is that wherein you thrust beneath the hind wheels certain expedients such as robes, coats, and so forth. The wheels, when set in motion, hurl these trivialities yards to the rear. The car then settles down with a shrug. About the time the axle is actually resting on the sand you proceed to serious digging, cutting brush, and laying causeways. Some sand you can get out of by these methods, but not dry, stream-bed sand in the Southwest. Finally you reach; the state of true wisdom. Either you sit peacefully in the tonneau and smoke until someone comes along; or, if you are doubtful of that miracle, you walk to the nearest team and rope. And never, never, never are you caught again! A detour of fifty miles is nothing after that!

While Bill manipulated the makings, I examined the prospects. This was that kind of a wash; no doubt of it!

"How far is the nearest crossing?" I asked, returning.

"About eight feet," said he.

My mind, panic-stricken, flew to several things—that bottle (I regret that I failed to record that by test its contents had proved genuine), the cornered rock we had so blithely charged, other evidences of Bill's casual nature. My heart sank.

"You ain't going to tackle that wash!" I cried.

"I shore am," said Bill.

I examined Bill. He meant it.

"How far to the nearest ranch?"

"'Bout ten mile."

I went and sat on a rock. It was one of those rainbow remnants of a bygone past; but my interest in curios had waned.

Bill dove into the grimy mysteries of under the back seat and produced two blocks of wood six or eight inches square and two strong straps with buckles. He inserted a block between the frame of the car and the rear axle; then he ran a strap around the rear spring and cinched on it until the car body, the block, and the axle made one solid mass. In other words, the spring action was entirely eliminated. He did the same thing on the other side.

"Climb in," said he.

We went into low and slid down the steep clay bank into the waiting sand. To me it was like a plunge into ice water. Bill stepped on her. We ploughed out into trouble. The steering wheel bucked and jerked vainly against Bill's huge hands; we swayed like a moving-picture comic; but we forged steadily ahead. Not once did we falter. Our wheels gripped continuously. When we pulled out on the other bank I exhaled as though I, too, had lost my muffler. I believe I had held my breath the whole way across. Bill removed the blocks and gave her more water. Still in low we climbed out of the malpais.

It was now after two o'clock. We registered 29,328. I was getting humble minded. Six o'clock looked good enough to me now.

One thing was greatly encouraging. As we rose again to the main level of the country I recognized over the horizon a certain humped mountain. Often in the "good old days" I had approached this mountain from the south. Beneath its flanks lay my friend's ranch, our destination. Five hours earlier in my experience its distance would have appalled me; but my standards had changed. Nevertheless, it seemed far enough away. I was getting physically tired. There is a heap of exercise in many occupations, such as digging sewers and chopping wood and shopping with a woman; but driving in small Arizona motor cars need give none of these occupations any odds. And of late years I have been accustoming myself to three meals a day.

For this reason there seems no excuse for detailing the next three hours. From three o'clock until sunset the mirages slowly fade away into the many-tinted veils of evening. I know that because I've seen it; but never would I know it whilst an inmate of a gasoline madhouse. We carried our own egg-shaped aura constantly with us, on the invisible walls of which the subtle and austere influences of the desert beat in vain. That aura was composed of speed, bumps, dust, profane noise, and an extreme and exotic busyness. It might be that in a docile, tame, expensive automobile, garnished with a sane and biddable driver, one might see the desert as it is. I don't know whether such a combination exists. But me—I couldn't get into the Officers' Training Camp because of my advanced years: I may be an old fogy, but I cherish a sneaking idea that perhaps you have to buy some of these things at the cost of the aforementioned thirst, heat, weariness, and the slow passing of long days. Still, an Assyrian brick in the British Museum is inscribed by a father to his son away at school with a lament over the passing of the "good old days!"

At any rate, we drew into Spring Creek at five o'clock, shooting at every jump. My friend's ranch was only six miles farther. This was home for Bill, and we were soon surrounded by many acquaintances. He had letters and packages for many of them; and detailed many items of local news. To us shortly came a cowboy who had evidently bought all the calico he could carry. This person was also long and lean and brown; hard bitten; bedecked with worn brown leather *chaps*, and wearing a gun. The latter he unbuckled and cast from him with great scorn.

"And I don't need no gun to do it, neither!" he stated, as though concluding a long conversation.

"Shore not, Slim," agreed one of the group, promptly annexing the artillery. "What is it?"

"Kill that — Beck," said Slim, owlishly. "I can do it; and I can do it with my bare hands, b' God!"

He walked sturdily enough in the direction of the General Store across the dusty square. No one paid any further attention to his movements. The man who had picked up the gun belt buckled it around his own waist. Bill refilled the ever-thirsty radiator, peered at his gasoline gauge, leisurely turned down a few grease cups. Ten minutes passed. We were about ready to start.

Back across the square drifted a strange figure. With difficulty we recognized it as the erstwhile Slim. He had no hat. His hair stuck out in all directions. One eye was puffing shut, blood oozed from a cut in his forehead and dripped from his damaged nose. One shirt sleeve had been half torn from its parent at the shoulder. But, most curious of all, Slim's face was evenly marked by a perpendicular series of long, red scratches as though he had been dragged from stem to stern along a particularly abrasive gravel walk. Slim seemed quite calm.

His approach was made in a somewhat strained silence. At length there spoke a dry, sardonic voice.

"Well," said it, "did you kill Beck?"

"Naw!" replied Slim's remains disgustedly, "the son of a gun wouldn't fight!"

We reached my friend's ranch just about dusk. He met me at the yard gate.

"Well!" he said, heartily. "I'm glad you're here! Not much like the old days, is it?"

I agreed with him.

"Journey out is dull and uninteresting now. But compared to the way we used to do it, it is a cinch. Just sit still and roll along."

I disagreed with him—mentally.

"The old order has changed," said he.

"Yes," I agreed, "now it's one yard of calico."

THE RANCH

CHAPTER I

THE NEW AND THE OLD

The old ranching days of California are to all intents and purposes past and gone. To be sure there remain many large tracts supporting a single group of ranch buildings, and over which the cattle wander "on a thousand hills." There are even a few, a very few—like the ranch of which I am going to write—that are still undivided, still game haunted, still hospitable, still delightful. But in spite of these apparent exceptions, my first statement must stand. About the large tracts swarm real estate men, eager for the chance to subdivide into small farms—and the small farmers pour in from the East at the rate of a thousand a month. No matter how sternly the old land-lords set their faces against the new order of things, the new order of things will prevail; for sooner or late old land-lords must die, and the heirs have not in them the spirit of the ancient tradition. This is, of course, best for the country and for progress; but something passes, and is no more. So the Chino ranch and more recently Lucky Baldwin's broad acres have yielded.

And even in the case of those that still remain intact, whose wide hills and plains graze thousands of head of cattle; whose pastures breed their own cowhorses; whose cowmen, wearing still with a twist of pride the all-but-vanished regalia of their

Stewart Edward White

all-but-vanished calling, refuse to drop back to the humdrum status of "farm hands on a cow ranch"; even here has entered a single element powerful enough to change the old to something new. The new may be better—it is certainly more convenient—and perhaps when all is said and done we would not want to go back to the old. But the old is gone. One single modern institution has been sufficient to render it completely of the past. That institution is the automobile.

In the old days—and they are but yesterdays, after all—the ranch was perforce an isolated community. The journey to town was not to be lightly undertaken; indeed, as far as might be, it was obviated altogether. Blacksmithing, carpentry, shoe cobbling, repairing, barbering, and even mild doctoring were all to be done on the premises. Nearly every item of food was raised at home, including vegetables, fruit, meat, eggs, fowl, butter, and honey. Above all, the inhabitants of that ranch settled down comfortably into the realization that their only available community was that immediately about them; and so they both made and were influenced by the individual atmosphere of the place.

In the latter years they have all purchased touring cars, and now they run to town casually, on almost any excuse. They make shopping lists as does the city dweller; they go back for things forgotten; and they return to the ranch as one returns to his home on the side streets of a great city. In place of the old wonderful and impressive expeditions to visit in state the nearest neighbour (twelve miles distant), they drop over of an afternoon for a ten-minutes' chat. The ranch is no longer an environment in which one finds the whole activity of his existence, but a dwelling place from which one goes forth.

I will admit that this is probably a distinct gain; but the fact is indubitable that, even in these cases where the ranch life has not been materially changed otherwise, the automobile has brought about a condition entirely new. And as the automobile has fortunately come to stay, the old will never return. It is of the old, and its charm and leisure, that I wish to write.

CHAPTER II

THE OLD WEST

I went to the ranch many years ago, stepping from the train somewhere near midnight into a cold, crisp air full of stars. My knowledge of California was at that time confined to several seasons spent on the coast, where the straw hat retires only in deference to a tradition which none of the flowers seem bound to respect. As my dress accorded with this experience, I was very glad to be conducted across the street to a little hotel. My guide was an elderly, very brown man, with a white moustache, and the bearing of an army regular. This latter surmise later proved correct. Manning was one of the numerous old soldiers who had fought through the General's Apache campaigns, and who now in his age had drifted back to be near his old commander. He left me, after many solicitations as to my comfort, and a promise to be back with the team at seven o'clock sharp.

Promptly at that hour he drew up by the curb. My kit bag was piled aboard, and I clambered in beside the driver. Manning touched his team. We were off.

The rig was of the sort usual to the better California ranches of the day, and so, perhaps, worth description. It might best be defined as a rather wide, stiff buckboard set on springs, and supported by stout running gear. The single seat was set well forward, while the body of the rig extended back to receive the light freight an errand to town was sure to accumulate. An ample hood top of gray canvas could be raised for protection against either sun, wind, or rain. Most powerful brakes could be manipulated by a thrust of the driver's foot. You may be sure they were outside brakes. Inside brakes were then considered the weak expedients of a tourist driving mercenary. Generally the tongue and moving gear were painted cream; and the body of the vehicle dark green.

This substantial, practical, and business-like vehicle was drawn by a pair of mighty good bright bay horses, straight backed, square rumped, deep shouldered, with fine heads, small ears, and alert yet gentle eyes of high-bred stock. When the word was given, they fell into a steady, swinging trot. One felt instinctively the power of it, and knew that they were capable of keeping up this same gait all day. And that would mean many miles. Their harness was of plain russet leather, neat and well oiled.

Concerning them I made some remark, trivial yet enough to start Manning. He told me of them, and of their peculiarities and virtues. He descanted at length on their breeding, and whence came they and their fathers and their fathers' fathers even unto the sixth generation. He left me at last with the impression that this was probably the best team in the valley, bar none. It was a good team, strong, spirited, gentle, and enduring.

We swung out from the little town into a straight road. If it has seemed that I have occupied you too exclusively with objects near at hand, the matter could not be helped. There was nothing more to occupy you. A fog held all the land.

It was a dense fog, and a very cold. Twenty feet ahead of the horses showed only a wall of white. To right and left dim, ghostly bushes or fence posts trooped by us at the ordered pace of our trot. An occasional lone poplar tree developed in the mist as an object on a dry plate develops. We splashed into puddles, crossed culverts, went through all the business of proceeding along a road—and apparently got nowhere. The mists opened grudgingly before us, and closed in behind. As far as knowing what the country was like I might as well have been blindfolded.

From Manning I elicited piecemeal some few and vague ideas. This meagreness was not due to a disinclination on Manning's part, but only to the fact that he never quite grasped my interest in mere surroundings. Yes, said he, it was a pretty flat country, and some brush. Yes, there were mountains, some ways off, though. Not many trees, but some—what you might call a few. And so on, until I gave it up. Mountains, trees, brush, and flat land! One could construct any and all landscapes with such building blocks as those.

Now, as has been hinted, I was dressed for southern California; and the fog was very damp and chill. The light overcoat I wore failed utterly to exclude it. At first I had been comfortable enough, but as mile succeeded mile the cold of that winter land fog penetrated to the bone. In answer to my comment Manning replied cheerfully in the words of an old saw:

"*A winter's fog   Will freeze a dog,*"

said he.

I agreed with him. We continued to jog on. Manning detailed what I then thought were hunting lies as to the abundance of game; but which I afterward discovered were only sober truths. When too far gone in the miseries of abject cold I remembered his former calling, and glancing sideways at his bronzed, soldierly face, wished I had gumption enough left to start him going on some of his Indian campaigns. It was too late; I had not the gumption; I was too cold.

Now I believe I am fairly well qualified to know when I really feel cold. I have slept out with the thermometer out of sight somewhere down near the bulb; I once snowshoed nine miles; and then overheated from that exertion, drove thirty-five without additional clothing. On various other occasions I have had experiences that might be called frigid. But never have I been quite so deadly cold as on that winter morning's drive through the land fog of semi-tropical California. It struck through to the very heart.

I subsequently discovered that it takes two hours and three quarters to drive to the ranch. That is a long time when one has nothing to look at, and when one is cold. In fact, it is so long that one loses track of time at all, and gradually relapses into that queer condition of passive endurance whereto is no end and no beginning. Therefore the end always comes suddenly, and as a surprise.

So it was in this case. Out of the mists sprang suddenly two tall fan palms, and then two others, and still others. I realized dimly that we were in an avenue of palms. The wheels grated strangely on gravel. We swung sharply to the left between hedges. The mass of a building loomed indistinctly. Manning applied the brakes. We stopped, the steam from the horses' shining backs rising straight up to mingle with the fog.

"Well, here we are!" said Manning.

So we were! I hadn't thought of that. We must be here. After an appreciable moment it occurred to me that perhaps I'd better climb down. I did so, very slowly and stiffly, making the sad mistake of jumping down from the height of the step. How that did injure my feelings! The only catastrophe I can remember comparable to it was when a teacher rapped my knuckles with a ruler after I had been making snowballs bare handed. My benumbed faculties next swung around to the proposition of proceeding up an interminable gravel walk—(it is twenty-five feet long!) to a forbidding flight of stairs—(porch steps—five of them!) I put this idea into execution. I reached the steps. And then—

The door was flung open from within, I could see the sparkle and leap of a fine big grate fire. The Captain stood in the doorway, a broad smile on his face; my hostess smiled another welcome behind him; the General roared still another from somewhere behind her.

Now I had never met the Captain. He held out both hands in greeting. One of those hands was for me to shake. The other held a huge glass of hot scotch. The hot scotch was in the right hand!

CHAPTER III

THE PEOPLE AND THE PLACE

They warmed me through, and then another old soldier named Redmond took me up to show me where I lived. We clambered up narrow boxed stairs that turned three ways; we walked down a narrow passage; turned to the right; walked down another narrow passage, climbed three steps to open a door; promptly climbed three steps down again; crossed a screened-in bridge to another wing; ducked through a passageway, and so arrived. The ranch house was like that. Parts of it were built out on stilts. Five or six big cottonwood trees grew right up through the verandahs, and spread out over the roof of the house. There are all sorts of places where you hang coats, or stack guns, or store shells, or find unexpected books; passageways leading to outdoor upstairs screened porches, cubby holes and the like. And whenever you imagine the house must be quite full of guests, they can always discover to you yet another bedroom. It may, at the last, be a very tiny bedroom, with space enough only for a single bed and not much else; and you may get to it only by way of out of doors; and it may be already fairly well occupied by wooden decoys and shotgun shells, but there it is, guests and guests after you thought the house must be full.

Belonging and appertaining unto the house were several fixtures. One of these was old Charley, the Chinese cook. He had been there twenty-five years. In that time he had learned perfect English, acquired our kind of a sense of humour, come to a complete theoretical understanding of how to run a ranch and all the people on it, and taught Pollymckittrick what she knew.

Pollymckittrick was the bereaved widow of the noble pair of yellow and green parrots Noah selected for his ark. At least I think she was that old. She was certainly very wise in both Oriental and Occidental wisdom. Her chief accomplishments, other than those customary to parrots, were the ability to spell, and to sing English songs. "After the Ball" and "Daisy Bell" were her favourites, rendered with occasional jungle variations. She considered Charley her only real friend, though she tolerated some others. Pollymckittrick was a product of artificial civilization. No call of the wild in hers! She preferred her cage, gilded or otherwise. Each afternoon the cage was placed out on the lawn so Pollymckittrick could have her sun bath. One day a big redtail hawk sailed by. Pollymckittrick fell backward off her perch, flat on her back. The sorrowing family gathered to observe this extraordinary case of heart failure. After an interval Pollymckittrick unfilmed one yellow eye.

"Po—o—or Pollymckittrick!" she remarked.

At the sight of that hawk Pollymckittrick had fainted!

The third institution having to do with the house was undoubtedly Redmond. Redmond was another of the old soldiers who had in their age sought out their beloved General. Redmond was a sort of all-round man. He built the fires very early in the morning; and he did your boots and hunting clothes, got out the decoys, plucked the ducks, saw to the shells, fed the dogs, and was always on hand at arrival and departure to lend a helping hand. He dwelt in a square room in the windmill tower together with a black cat and all the newspapers in the world. The cat he alternately allowed the most extraordinary liberties or disciplined rigorously. On the latter occasions he invariably seized the animal and hurled it bodily through the open window. The cat took the long fall quite calmly, and immediately clambered back up the outside stairway that led to the room. The newspapers he read, and clipped therefrom items of the most diverse nature to which he deprecatingly invited attention. Once in so often a strange martial fervour would obsess him. Then the family, awakened in the early dawn, would groan and turn over, realizing that its rest was for that morning permanently shattered. The old man had hoisted his colours over the windmill tower, and now in a frenzy of fervour was marching around and around the tower beating the long roll on his drum. After one such outbreak he would be his ordinary, humble, quiet, obliging, almost deprecating self for another month or so. The ranch people took it philosophically.

The fourth institution was Nobo. Nobo was a Japanese woman who bossed the General. She was a square-built person of forty or so who had also been with the family unknown years. Her capabilities were undoubted; as also her faith in them. The hostess depended on her a good deal; and at the same time chafed mildly under her calm assumption that she knew perfectly what the situation demanded. The General took her domination amusedly. To be sure nobody was likely to fool much with the General. His vast good nature had way down beneath it something that on occasion could be stern. Nobo could and would tell the General what clothes to wear, and when to change them, and such matters; but she never ventured to inhibit the General's ideas as to going forth in rains, or driving where he everlastingly dod-blistered pleased, or words to that effect, across country in his magnificently rattletrap surrey, although she often looked very anxious. For she adored the General. But we all did that.

As though the heavy curtain of fog had been laid upon the land expressly that I might get my first impressions of the ranch in due order, about noon the weather cleared. Even while we ate lunch, the sun came out. After the meal we went forth to see what we could see.

The ranch was situated in the middle of a vast plain around three sides of which rose a grand amphitheatre of mountains.

The nearest of them was some thirty miles away, yet ordinarily, in this clear, dry, Western atmosphere they were always imminent. Over their eastern ramparts the sun rose to look upon a chill and frosty world; behind their western barriers the sun withdrew, leaving soft air, purple shadows, and the flight of dim, far wildfowl across a saffron sky. To the north was only distance and the fading of the blue of the heavens to the pearl gray of the horizon.

So much if one stepped immediately beyond the ranch itself. The plains were broad. Here and there the flatness broke in a long, low line of cottonwoods marking the winding course of a slough or trace of subsoil water. Mesquite lay in dark patches; sagebrush; the green of pasture-land periodically overflowed by the irrigation water. Nearer at home were occasional great white oaks, or haystacks bigger than a house, and shaped like one.

To the distant eye the ranch was a grove of trees. Cottonwoods and eucalyptus had been planted and had thriven mightily on the abundant artesian water. We have already noticed the six or eight great trees growing fairly up through the house. On the outskirts lay also a fruit orchard of several hundred acres. Opposite the house, and separated from it by a cedar hedge, was a commodious and attractive bungalow for the foreman. Beyond him were the bunk house, cook houses, blacksmith shops, and the like.

We started our tour of inspection by examining and commenting gravely upon the dormant rose garden and equally dormant grape arbour. Through this we came to the big wire corrals in which were kept the dogs. Here I met old Ben.

Old Ben was not very old; but he was different from young Ben. He was a pointer of the old-fashioned, stocky-built, enduring type common—and serviceable—before our bench-show experts began to breed for speed, fineness, small size— and lack of stamina. Ben proved in the event to be a good all-round dog. He combined the attributes of pointer, cocker spaniel, and retriever. In other words, he would hunt quail in the orthodox fashion; or he would rustle into the mesquite thorns for the purpose of flushing them out to us; or he would swim anywhere any number of times to bring out ducks. To be sure he occasionally got a little mixed. At times he might try to flush quail in the open, instead of standing them; or would attempt to retrieve some perfectly lively specimens. Then Ben needed a licking; and generally got it. He lacked in his work some of the finish and style of the dogs we used after grouse in Michigan, but he was a good all-round dog for the work. Furthermore, he was most pleasant personally.

Next door to him lived the dachshunds.

The dachshunds were a marvel, a nuisance, a bone of contention, an anomaly, an accident, and a farce. They happened because somebody had once given the hostess a pair of them. I do not believe she cared particularly for them; but she is good natured, and the ranch is large, and they are rather amusing. At the time of my first visit the original pair had multiplied. Gazing on that yardful of imbecile-looking canines, my admiration for Noah's wisdom increased; he certainly needed no more than a pair to restock the earth. Redmond claimed there were twenty-two of them, though nobody else pretended to have been able to disentangle them enough for a census. They were all light brown in colour; and the aggregation reminded me of a rather disentangled bunch of angle-worms. They lived in a large enclosure; and emerged therefrom only under supervision, for they considered chickens and young pigs their especial prey. The Captain looked upon them with exasperated tolerance; Redmond with affection; the hostess, I think, with a good deal of the partisanship inspired not so much by liking as by the necessity of defending them against ridicule; and the rest of the world with amused expectation as to what they would do next. The Captain was continually uttering half-serious threats as to the different kinds of sudden death he was going to inflict on the whole useless, bandylegged, snipe-nosed, waggle-eared—

The best comment was offered last year by the chauffeur of the automobile. After gazing on the phenomenon of their extraordinary build for some moments he remarked thoughtfully:

"Those dogs have a mighty long wheel base!"

For some reason unknown two of the dachshunds have been elevated from the ranks, and have house privileges. Their names are respectively Pete and Pup. They hate each other, and have sensitive dispositions. It took me just four years to learn to tell them apart. I believe Pete has a slightly projecting short rib on his left side—or is it Pup? It was fatal to mistake.

"Hullo, Pup!" I would cry to one jovially.

"G—r—r—r—!" would remark the dog, retiring under the sofa. Thus I would know it was Pete. The worst of it was that said Pete's feelings were thereby lacerated so deeply that I was not forgiven all the rest of that day.

Beyond the dogs lay a noble enclosure so large that it would have been subdivided into building lots had it been anywhere else. It was inhabited by all sorts of fowl, hundreds of them, of all varieties. There were chickens, turkeys, geese, and a flock of ducks. The Captain pointed out the Rouen ducks, almost exactly like the wild mallards.

"Those are my live decoys," said he.

For the accommodation of this multitude were cities of nest houses, roost houses, and the like. Huge structures elevated on poles swarmed with doves. A duck pond even had been provided for its proper denizens.

Thus we reached the southernmost outpost of our quadrangle, and turned to the west, where an ancient Chinaman and an assistant cultivated minutely and painstakingly a beautiful vegetable garden. Tiny irrigation streams ran here and there, fitted with miniature water locks. Strange and foreign bamboo mattings, withes, and poles performed strange and foreign functions. The gardener, brown and old and wrinkled, his cue wound neatly beneath his tremendous, woven-straw umbrella of a hat, possessing no English, no emotion, no single ray of the sort of intelligence required to penetrate into our Occidental world, bent over his work. When we passed, he did not look up. He dwelt in a shed. At least, such it proved to be, when examined with the cold eye of analysis. In impression it was ancient, exotic, Mongolian, the abode of one of a mysterious and venerable race, a bit of foreign country. By what precise means this was accomplished it would be difficult to say. It is a fact well known to all Californians that a Chinaman can with no more extensive properties than a few pieces of red paper, a partition, a dingy curtain, and a varnished duck transform utterly an American tenement into a Chinese pagoda.

Thence we passed through a wicket and came to the abode of hogs. They dotted the landscape into the far distance, rooting about to find what they could; they lay in wallows; they heaped themselves along fences; they snorted and splashed in sundry shallow pools; a good half mile of maternal hogs occupied a row of kennels from which the various progeny issued forth between the bars. I cannot say I am much interested in hogs, but even I could dimly comprehend the Captain's attitude of swollen pride. They were clean, and black, and more nearly approximated the absurd hog advertisements than I had believed possible. You know the kind I mean; an almost exact rectangle on four short legs.

In the middle distance stood a long, narrow, thatched roof supported on poles. Beneath this, the Captain told me, were the beehives. They proved later to be in charge of a mild-eyed religious fanatic who believed the world to be flat.

We took a cursory glance at a barn filled to the brim with prunes; and the gushing, beautiful artesian well; at the men's quarters; the blacksmith shop, and all the rest. So we rounded the circle and came to the most important single feature of the ranch—the quarters for the horses.

A very long, deep shed, open on all sides, contained a double row of mangers facing each other, and divided into stalls. Here stood and were fed the working horses. By that I mean not only the mule and horse teams, but also the utility driving teams and the saddle horses used by the cowboys. Between each two stalls was a heavy pillar supporting the roof, and well supplied with facilities for hanging up the harness and equipments. As is usual in California, the sides and ends were open to the air; and the floor was simply the earth well bedded.

But over against this shed stood a big barn of the Eastern type. Here were the private equipments.

The Captain is a horseman. He breeds polo ponies after a formula of his own; and so successfully that many of them cross the Atlantic. On the ranch are always several hundred head of beautiful animals; and of these the best are kept up for the use of the Captain and his friends. We looked at them in their clean, commodious stalls; we inspected the harness and saddle room, glistening and satiny with polished metal and well-oiled leather; we examined the half dozen or so of vehicles of all descriptions. The hostess told with relish of her one attempt to be stylish.

"We had such beautiful horses," said she, "that I thought we ought to have something to go with them, so I sent up to the city for my brougham. It made a very neat turnout; and Tom was as proud of it as I was, but when it came to a question of proper garb for Tom I ran up against a deadlock. Tom refused point blank to wear a livery or anything approaching a livery. He was perfectly respectful about it; but he refused. Well, I drove around all that winter, when the weather was bad, in a well-appointed brougham drawn by a good team in a proper harness; and on the box sat a lean-faced cow puncher in sombrero, red handkerchief, and blue jeans!"

Tom led forth the horses one after the other—Kingmaker, the

Fiddler, Pittapat, and the others. We spent a delightful two hours. The sun dropped; the shadows lengthened. From the fields the men began to come in. They drove the wagons and hay ricks into the spacious enclosure, and set leisurely about the task of caring for their animals. Chinese and Japanese drifted from the orchards, and began to manipulate the grindstone on their pruning knives. Presently a cowboy jogged in, his spurs and bit jingling. From the cook house a bell began to clang.

We turned back to the house. Before going in I faced the west. The sky had turned a light green full of lucence. The minor sounds of the ranch near by seemed to be surrounded by a sea of silence outside. Single sounds came very clearly across it. And behind everything, after a few moments, I made out a queer, monotonous background of half-croaking calling. For some time this puzzled me. Then at last my groping recollection came to my assistance. I was hearing the calling of myriads of snow geese.

CHAPTER IV

THE EARLY BIRD

I was awakened rather early by Redmond, who silently entered the room, lit a kerosene stove, closed the windows, and departed. As I was now beneath two blankets and an eiderdown quilt, and my nose was cold, I was duly grateful. Mistaking the rite for a signal to arise, I did so; and shortly descended. The three fireplaces were crackling away merrily, but they had done little to mitigate the atmosphere as yet. Maids were dusting and sweeping. The table was not yet set. Inquiry telling that breakfast was more than an hour later, I took a gun from the rack, pocketed the only five shells in sight, and departed to see what I could see.

The outer world was crisp with frost. I clambered over the corral fence, made my way through a hundred acres or so of slumbering pigs, and so emerged into the open country.

In the middle distance and perhaps a mile away was a low fringe of brush; to the left an equal distance a group of willows; and almost behind me a clump of cottonwoods. I resolved to walk over to the brush, swing around to the willows, turn to the cottonwoods, and so back to the ranch. It looked like about four miles or so. Perhaps with my five shells I might get something. At any rate, I would have a good walk.

The mountains were turning from the rose pink of early morning. I could hear again the bickering cries of the snow geese and sandhill cranes away in an unknown distance, the homelier calls of barnyard fowl nearer at hand. Cattle trotted before me and to right and left, their heads high, their gait swinging with the freedom of the half-wild animals of the ranges. After a few steps they turned to stare at me, eyes and nostrils wide, before making up their minds whether or not it would be wise to put a greater distance between me and them. The close sod was green and strong. It covered the slightly rounding irrigation "checks" that followed in many a curve and double the lines of contours on the flat plain.

The fringe of brush did not amount to anything; it was merely a convenient turning mark for my little walk. Arrived there, I executed a sharp "column left—"

Seven ducks leaped into the air apparently from the bare, open, and dry ground!

Every sportsman knows the scattering effect on the wits of the absolutely unexpected appearance of game. Every sportsman knows also the instinctive reactions that long habit will bring about. Thus, figuratively, I stood with open mouth, heart beating slightly faster, and mind making to itself such imbecile remarks as: "Well, *what* do you think of that! Who in blazes would have expected ducks here?" and other futile remarks. In the meantime, the trained part of me had jerked the gun off my shoulder, pushed forward the safety catch, and prepared for one hasty long shot at the last and slowest of the ducks. Now the instinctive part of one can do the preparations, but the actual shooting requires a more ordered frame of mind. By this time my wits had snapped back into place. I had the satisfaction of seeing the duck's outstretched neck wilt; of hearing him hit the ground with a thud somewhere beyond.

Marking the line of his fall, I stepped confidently forward, and without any warning whatever found myself standing on the bank of an irrigation ditch. It was filled to the brim with placid water on which floated a few downy feathers. On this side was dry sod; and on the other was dry sod. Nothing indicated the presence of that straight band of silvery water until one stood fairly at its brink. To the right I could see its sides narrow to the point of a remote perspective. To the left it ran for a few hundred yards, then apparently came to an abrupt stop where it turned at an angle.

In the meantime, my duck was on the other side; I was in my citizen's clothes.

No solution offered in sight, so I made my way to the left where I could look around the bend. Nearing the bend I was seized with a bright idea. I dropped back below the line of sight, sneaked quietly to the bank, and, my eye almost level with the water, peered down the new vista. Sure enough, not a hundred and fifty yards away floated another band of ducks.

I watched them for a moment until I was sure, by various small landmarks, of their exact location. Then I dropped back far enough so that, even standing erect, I would be below the line of vision of those ducks; strolled along until opposite my landmarks; then, bolt upright, walked directly forward, the gun at ready. When within twenty yards the ducks arose. It was, of course, easy shooting. Both fell across the ditch. That did not worry me; if worst came to worst I could strip and wade.

This seemed to be an exceedingly unique and interesting way to shoot ducks. To be sure, I had only two shells left; but then, it must be almost breakfast time. I repeated the feat a half mile farther on, discovered a flood gate over which I could get to the other side, collected my five ducks, and cut across country to the ranch. The sun was just getting in its work on the frost. Long files of wagons and men could be seen disappearing in the distance. I entered proudly, only ten minutes late.

CHAPTER V

QUAIL

The family assembled took my statement with extraordinary calm, contenting themselves with a general inquiry as to the species. I was just a trifle crestfallen at this indifference. You see at this time I was not accustomed to the casual duck. My shooting heretofore had been a very strenuous matter. It had involved arising many hours before sun-up, and venturing forth miles into wild marshes; and much endurance of cold and discomfort. To make a bag of any sort we were in the field before the folk knew the night had passed. Upland shooting meant driving long distances, and walking through the heavy hardwood swamps and slashes from dusk to dusk. Therefore I had considered myself in great luck to have blundered upon my ducks so casually; and, furthermore, from the family's general air of leisure and unpreparedness, jumped to the conclusion that no field sport was projected for that day.

Mrs. Kitty presided beside a copper coffee pot with a bell-shaped glass top. As this was also an institution, it merits attention. A small alcohol lamp beneath was lighted. For a long time nothing happened. Then all at once the glass dome clouded, was filled with frantic brown and racing bubbling. Thereupon the hostess turned over a sand glass. When the last grains had run through, the alcohol lamp was turned off. Immediately the glass dome was empty again. From a spigot one drew off coffee.

But if perchance the Captain and I wished to get up before anybody else could be hired to get up, the Dingbat could be so loaded as to give down an automatic breakfast. The evening before the maid charged the affair as usual, and at the last popped four eggs into the glass dome. After the mysterious alchemical perturbations had ceased, we fished out those eggs soft boiled to the second! One day the maid mistook the gasoline bottle for the alcohol bottle. That is a sad tale having to do with running flames, and burned table pieces, not to speak of a melted-down connection or so on the Dingbat. We did not know what was the matter; and our attitude was not so much that of alarm, as of grief and indignation that our good old tried and trained Dingbat should in his old age cut up any such didoes. Especially as there were new guests present.

After breakfast we wandered out on the verandah. Nobody seemed to be in any hurry to start anything. The hostess made remarks to Pollymckittrick; the General read a newspaper; the Captain sauntered about enjoying the sun. After fifteen minutes, as though the notion had just occurred, somebody suggested that we go shooting.

"How about it?" the Captain asked me.

"Surely," I agreed, and added with some surprise out of my other experience, "Isn't it a little late?"

But the Captain misunderstood me.

"I don't mean blind shooting," said he, "just ram around."

He seized a megaphone and bellowed through it at the stables.

"Better get on your war paint," he suggested to me.

I changed hastily into my shooting clothes, and returned to the verandah. After some few moments the Captain joined me. After some few moments more a tremendous rattling came from the stable. A fine bay team swung into the driveway, rounded the circle, and halted. It drew the source of the tremendous rattling.

Thus I became acquainted with the Liver Invigorator. The Invigorator was a buckboard high, wide, and long. It had one wide seat. Aft of that seat was a cage with bars, in which old Ben rode. Astern was a deep box wherein one carried rubber boots, shells, decoys, lunch, game, and the like. The Invigorator was very old, very noisy, and very able. With it we drove cheerfully anywhere we pleased—over plowed land, irrigation checks, through brush thick enough to lift our wheels right off the ground, and down into and out of water ditches so steep that we alternately stood the affair on its head and its tail, and so deep that we had to hold all our belongings in our arms, while old Ben stuck his nose out the top bars of his cage for a breath of air. It could not be tipped over; at least we never upset it. To offset these virtues it rattled like a runaway milk wagon; and it certainly hit the high spots and hit them *hard*. Nevertheless, in a long and strenuous sporting career the Invigorator became endeared through association to many friends. When the Captain proposed a new vehicle with easier springs and less noise, a wail of protest arose from many and distant places. The Invigorator still fulfills its function.

Now there are three major topics on the Ranch: namely, ducks, quail, and ponies. In addition to these are five of minor interest: the mail, cattle, jackrabbits, coons, and wildcats.

I was already familiar with the valley quail, for I had hunted him since I was a small boy with the first sixteen-gauge gun ever brought to the coast. I knew him for a very speedy bird, much faster than our bob white, dwelling in the rounded sagebrush hills, travelling in flocks of from twenty to several thousand, exceedingly given to rapid leg work. We had to climb hard after him, and shoot like lightning from insecure footing. His idiosyncrasies were as strongly impressed on me as the fact that human beings walk upright. Here, however, I had to revise my ideas.

We drove down the avenue of palms, pursued by four or five yapping dachshunds, and so out into a long, narrow lane between pasture fences. Herds of ponies, fuzzy in their long winter coats, came gently to look at us. The sun was high now, so the fur of their backs lay flat. Later, in the chill of evening, the hair would stand out like the nap of velvet, thus providing for additional warmth by the extra air space between the outside of the coat and the skin. It must be very handy to carry this invisible overcoat, ready for the moment's need. Here, too, were cattle standing about. On many of them I recognized the familiar J-I brand of many of my Arizona experiences. Arizona bred and raised them; California fattened them for market. We met a cowboy jingling by at his fox trot; then came to the country road.

Along this we drove for some miles. The country was perfectly flat, but variegated by patches of greasewood, of sagebrush, of Egyptian-corn fields, and occasionally by a long, narrow fringe of trees. Here, too, were many examples of that phenomenon so vigorously doubted by most Easterners: the long rows of trees grown from original cotton wood or poplar fence posts. In the distance always were the mountains. Overhead the sky was very blue. A number of buzzards circled.

After a time we turned off the road and into a country covered over with tumbleweed, a fine umber red growth six or eight inches high, and scattered sagebrush. Inlets, bays, and estuaries of bare ground ran everywhere. The Captain stood up to drive, watching for the game to cross these bare places.

I stood up, too. It is no idle feat to ride the Invigorator thus over hummocky ground. It lurched and bumped and dropped into and out of trouble; and in correspondence I alternately rose up and sat down again, hard. The Captain rode the storm without difficulty. He was accustomed to the Invigorator; and, too, he had the reins to hang on by.

"There they go!" said he, suddenly, bringing the team to a halt.

I looked ahead. Across a ten-foot barren ran the quail, their crests cocked forward, their trim figures held close as a sprinter goes, rank after rank, their heads high in the alert manner of quail.

The Captain sat down, jerked off the brake, and spoke to his horses. I sat down, too; mainly because I had to. The Invigorator leaped from hump to hump. Before those quail knew it we were among them. Right, left, all around us they roared into the air. Some doubled back; some buzzed low to right or left; others rose straight ahead to fly a quarter mile, and then, wings set, to sail another quarter until finally they pitched down into some bit of inviting cover.

The Captain brought his horses to a stand with great satisfaction. We congratulated each other gleefully; and even old Ben, somewhat shaken up in his cage astern, wagged his tail in appreciation of the situation.

For, you see, we had scattered the covey, and now they would lie. If the band had flushed, flown, and lighted as one body, immediately on hitting the ground they would have put their exceedingly competent little legs into action, and would have run so well and so far that, by the time we had arrived on the spot, they would have been a good half mile away. But now that the covey was broken, the individuals and small bands would stay put. If they ran at all, it would be for but a short distance. On this preliminary scattering depends the success of a chase after California quail. I have seen six or eight men empty both barrels of their guns at a range of more than a hundred yards. They were not insane enough to think they would get anything. Merely they hoped that the racket and the dropping of the spent shot would break the distant covey.

We hitched the horses to a tree, released old Ben, and started forth.

For a half hour we had the most glorious sport, beating back and forth over the ground again and again. The birds lay well in the low cover, and the shooting was clean and open. I soon found that the edges of the bare ground were the most likely places. Apparently the birds worked slowly through the cover ahead of us, but hesitated to cross the open spots, and so bunched at the edge. By walking in a zigzag along some of these borders, we gathered in many scattered birds and small bunches. Why the zigzag? Naturally it covers a trifle more ground than a straight course, but principally it seems to confuse the game. If you walk in a straight line, so the quail can foretell your course, it is very apt either to flush wild or to hide so close that you pass it by. The zigzag fools it.

Thus, with varying luck, we made a slow circle back to the wagon. Here we found Mrs. Kitty and Carrie and the lunch awaiting us with the ponies.

These robust little animals were not miniature horses, but genuine ponies, with all the deviltry, endurance, and speed of their kind. They were jet-black, about waist high, and of great intelligence. They drew a neat little rig, capable of accommodating two, at a persistent rapid patter that somehow got over the road at a great gait. And they could keep it up all day. Although perfectly gentle, they were as alert as gamins for mischief, and delighted hugely in adding to the general row and confusion if anything happened to go wrong. Mrs. Kitty drove them everywhere. One day she attempted to cross an irrigation ditch that proved to be deeper than she had thought it. The ponies disappeared utterly, leaving Mrs. Kitty very much astonished. Horses would have drowned in like circumstances, but the ponies, nothing daunted, dug in their hoofs and scrambled out like a pair of dogs, incidentally dipping their mistress on the way.

In the shade of a high greasewood we unpacked the pony carriage. This was before the days of thermos bottles, so we had a most elaborate wicker basket whose sides let down to form a wind shield protecting an alcohol burner and a kettle. When the water boiled, we made hot tea, and so came to lunch.

Strangely enough this was my first experience at having lunch brought out to the field. Ordinarily we had been accustomed to carry a sandwich or so in the side pockets of our shooting coats, which same we ate at any odd moment that offered. Now was disclosed an astonishing variety. There were sandwiches, of course, and a salad, and the tea, but wonderful to contemplate was a deep dish of potted quail, row after row of them, with delicious white sauce. In place of the frugal bite or so that would have left us alert and fit for an afternoon's work, we ate until nothing remained. Then we lit pipes and lay on our backs, and contemplated a cloudless sky. It was the warm time of day. The horses snoozed, a hind leg tucked up; old Ben lay outstretched in doggy content; Mrs. Kitty knit or crocheted or something of that sort; and Carrie and the Captain and I took cat naps. At length, the sun's rays no longer striking warm from overhead, the Captain aroused us sternly.

"You're a nice, energetic, able lot of sportsmen!" he cried with indignation. "Have I got to wait until sunset for you lazy chumps to get a full night's rest?"

"Don't mind him," Mrs. Kitty told me, placidly; "he was sound asleep himself; and the only reason he waked is because he snored and I *punched* him."

She folded up her fancy work, shook out her skirts, and turned to the ponies.

It was now late in the afternoon. We had disgracefully wasted our time, and enjoyed doing it. The Captain decided it to be too late to hunt up a new covey, so we reversed to pick up some of those that had originally doubled back. We flushed forty or fifty of them at the edge of the road. They scattered ahead of us in a forty-acre plowed field.

Until twilight, then, we walked leisurely back and forth, which is the only way to walk in a plowed field, after all. The birds had pitched down into the old furrows, and whenever a tuft of grass, a piece of tumbleweed, or a shallow grassy ditch offered a handful of cover, there the game was to be found. Mrs. Kitty followed at the Captain's elbow, and Carrie at mine. Carrie made a first-rate dog, marking down the birds unerringly. The quail flew low and hard, offering in the gathering twilight and against the neutral-coloured earth marks worthy of good shooting. At last we turned back to our waiting team. The dusk was coming over the land, and the "shadow of the earth" was marking its strange blue arc in the east. As usual the covey was now securely scattered. Of a thousand or so birds we had bagged forty-odd; and yet of the remainder we would have had difficulty in flushing another dozen. It is the mystery of the quail, and one that the sportsman can never completely comprehend. As we clambered into the Invigorator we could hear from all directions the birds signalling each other. Near, far, to right, to left, the call sounded, repeating over and over again a parting, defiant denial that the victory was ours.

"You *can't* shoot! You *can't* shoot! You *can't* shoot!"

And nearer at hand the contented chirping twitter as the covey found itself.

CHAPTER VI

PONIES

Next morning the Captain decided that he had various affairs to attend to, so we put on our riding clothes and went down to the stables.

The Captain had always forty or fifty polo ponies in the course of education, and he was delighted to have them ridden, once he was convinced of your seat and hands. They were beautiful ponies, generally iron gray in colour, very friendly, very eager, and very lively. Riding them was like flying through the air, for they sailed over rough ground, irrigation checks, and the like without a break in their stride, and without a jar. By the same token it was necessary to ride them. At odd moments they were quite likely to give a wide sidewise bound or a stiff-legged buck from sheer joy of life. One got genuine "horse exercise" out of them.

The Captain, as perhaps I have said, invented these ponies himself. From Chihuahua he brought in some of the best mustang mares he could find; and, in case you have Frederick Remington's pictures of starved winter-range animals in mind, let me tell you a good mustang is a very handsome animal indeed. These he bred to a thoroughbred. The resulting half-breeds grew to the proper age. Then he started to have them broken to the saddle. A start was as far as he ever got, for nobody could ride them. They combined the intelligence and vice of the mustang with the endurance and nervous instability

Stewart Edward White

of the thoroughbred. The Captain tried all sorts of men, even sending at last to Arizona for a good bronco buster on the J-I. Only one or two of the many could back the animals at all, though many aspirants made a try at it. After a long series of experiments, the Captain came to the reluctant conclusion that the cross was no good. It seemed a pity, for they were beautiful animals, up to full polo size, deep chested, strong shouldered, close coupled, and speedy.

Then, by way of idleness, he bred some of the half-bred mares. The three-quarter cross proved to be ideal. They were gentle, easily broken, and to the eye differed in no particular from their pure-blooded brothers. So, ever since, the Captain has been raising these most excellent polo ponies to his great honour and profit and the incidental pleasure of his friends who like riding.

One of these ponies was known as the Merry Jest. He had a terrifying but harmless trick. The moment the saddle was cinched, down went his head and he began to buck in the most vicious style. This he would keep up until further orders. In order to put an end to the performance all one had to do was to haul in on the rope, thrust one's foot in the stirrup, and clamber aboard. For, mark you this, Merry Jest in the course of a long and useful life never failed to buck under the empty saddle—and *never* bucked under a rider!

This, of course, constituted the Merry Jest. Its beauty was that it was so safe.

"Want to ride?" asked the Captain.

"Surely," replied the unsuspecting stranger.

The Merry Jest was saddled, brought forth, and exhibited in action.

"There's your horse," remarked the Captain in a matter-of-course tone.

We rode out the corral gate and directly into the open country. The animals chafed to be away; and when we loosened the reins, leaped forward in long bounds. Over the rough country they skimmed like swallows, their hoofs hardly seeming to touch the ground, the powerful muscles playing smoothly beneath us like engines. After a mile of this we pulled up, and set about the serious business of the day.

One after another we oversaw all the major activities of such a ranch; outside, I mean, of the ranch enclosure proper where were the fowls, the vegetable gardens, and the like. Here an immense hay rick was being driven slowly along while two men pitched off the hay to right and left. After it followed a long line of cattle. This manner of feeding obviated the crowding that would have taken place had the hay not been thus scattered. The more aggressive followed close after the rick, snatching mouthfuls of the hay as it fell. The more peaceful, or subdued, or philosophical strung out in a long, thin line, eating steadily at one spot. They got more hay with less trouble, but the other fellows had to maintain reputations for letting nobody get ahead of *them*!

At another point an exceedingly rackety engine ran a hay press, where the constituents of one of the enormous house-like haystacks were fed into a hopper and came out neatly baled. A dozen or so men oversaw the activities of this noisy and dusty machine.

Down by the northerly cottonwoods two miles away we found other men with scrapers throwing up the irrigation checks along the predetermined contour lines. By means of these irregular meandering earthworks the water, admitted from the ditch to the upper end of the field, would work its way slowly from level to level instead of running off or making channels for itself. This job, too, was a dusty one. We could see the smoke of it rising from a long distance; and the horses and men were brown with it.

And again we rode softly for miles over greensward through

Stewart Edward White

the cattle, at a gentle fox trot, so as not to disturb them. At several points stood great blue herons, like sentinels, decorative as a Japanese screen, absolutely motionless. The Captain explained that they were "fishing" for gophers; and blessed them deeply. Sometimes our mounts splashed for a long distance through water five or six inches shallow. Underneath the surface we could see the short green grass of the turf that thus received its refreshment. Then somewhere near, silhouetted against the sky or distant mountains, on the slight elevation of the irrigation ditch bank, we were sure to see some of the irrigation Chinamen. They were strange, exotic figures, their skins sunburned and dark, their queues wound around their heads; wearing always the same uniform of blue jeans cut China-fashion, rubber boots, and the wide, inverted bowl Chinese sun hat of straw. By means of shovels wherewith to dig, and iron bars wherewith to raise and lower flood gates, they controlled the artificial rainfall of the region. So accustomed did the ducks become to these amphibious people that they hardly troubled themselves to get out of the way, and were utterly careless of how near they flew. Uncle Jim once disguised himself as an irrigation Chinaman and got all kinds of shooting—until the ducks found him out. Now they seem able to distinguish accurately between a Chinaman with a long shovel and a white man with a shotgun, no matter how the latter is dressed. Ducks, tame and wild, have a lot of sense. It must bore the former to be forced to associate with chickens.

Over in the orchard, of a thousand acres or so, were many more Orientals, and hundreds of wild doves. These Chinese were all of the lower coolie orders, and primitive, not to say drastic in their medical ideas. One evening the Captain heard a fine caterwauling and drum beating over in the quarters, and sallied forth to investigate. In one of the huts he found four men sitting on the outspread legs and arms of a fifth. The latter had been stripped stark naked. A sixth was engaged in placing live coals on the patient's belly, while assorted assistants furnished appropriate music and lamentation. The Captain put a stop to the proceedings and bundled the victim to a hospital where he promptly died. It was considered among

Chinese circles that the Captain had killed him by ill-timed interference!

Everywhere we went, and wherever a small clump of trees or even large brush offered space, hung the carcasses of coyotes, wildcats, and lynx. Some were quite new, while others had completely mummified in the dry air of these interior plains. These were the trophies of the professional "varmint killer," a man hired by the month. Of course it would be only too easy for such an official to loaf on his job, so this one had adopted the unique method of proving his activity. Everywhere the Captain rode he could see that his man had been busy.

All this time we had been working steadily away from the ranch. Long zigzags and side trips carried us little forward, and a constant leftward tendency swung us always around, until we had completed a half circle of which the ranch itself was the centre. The irrigated fields had given place to open country of a semi-desert character grown high with patches of greasewood, sagebrush, thorn-bush; with wide patches of scattered bunch grass; and stretches of alkali waste. Here, unexpectedly to me, we stumbled on a strange but necessary industry incidental to so large an estate. Our nostrils were assailed by a mighty stink. We came around the corner of some high brush directly on a small two-story affair with a factory smokestack. It was fenced in, and the fence was covered with drying hides. I will spare you details, but the function of the place was to make glue, soap, and the like of those cattle whose term of life was marked by misfortune rather than by the butcher's knife. The sole workman at this economical and useful occupation did not seem to mind it. The Captain claimed he was as good as a buzzard at locating the newly demised.

Our ponies did not like the place either. They snorted violently, and pricked their ears back and forth, and were especially relieved and eager to obey when we turned their heads away.

Stewart Edward White

We rode on out into the desert, our ponies skipping expertly through the low brush and gingerly over the alkali crust of the open spaces beneath which might be holes. Jackrabbits by the thousand, literally, hopped away in front of us, spreading in all directions as along the sticks of a fan. They were not particularly afraid, so they loped easily in high-bounding leaps, their ears erect. Many of them sat bolt upright, looking at least two feet high. Occasionally we managed really to scare one, and then it was a grand sight to see him open the throttle and scud away, his ears flat back, in the classical and correct attitude of the constantly recurring phrase of the ancients: "belly to earth he flew!"

Jackrabbits are a great nuisance. The Captain had to enclose his precious alfalfa fields with rabbit-proof wire to prevent utter destruction. There was a good deal of fence, naturally, and occasionally the inquiring rabbit would find a hole and crawl through. Then he was in alfalfa, which is, as every Californian knows, much better than being in clover. He ate at first greedily, then more daintily, wandering always farther afield in search of dessert. Never, however, did he forget the precise location of the opening by which he had entered, as was wise of him. For now, behold, enter the dogs. Ordinarily these dogs, who were also wise beasts, passed by the jackrabbit in his abundance with only inhibited longing. Their experience had taught them that to chase jackrabbits in the open with any motive ulterior to that of healthful exercise and the joy of seeing the blame things run was as vain and as puppish as chasing one's tail. But in the alfalfa fields was a chance, for it must be remembered that such fields were surrounded by the rabbit-proof wire in which but a single opening was known to the jack in question. Therefore, with huge delight, the dogs gave chase. Mr. Rabbit bolted back for his opening, his enemies fairly at his heels. Now comes the curious part of the episode. The dogs knew perfectly well that if the rabbit hit the hole in the fence he was safe for all of them; and they had learned, further, that if the rabbit missed his plunge for safety he would collide strongly with that tight-strung wire. When within twenty feet or so of the fence they stopped short in expectation. Probably three times out of five the game made his plunge in safety and scudded away over the open plain outside. Then the dogs turned and trotted philosophically back to the ranch. But the other two times the rabbit would miss. At full speed he would hit the tight-strung mesh, only to be hurled back by its resiliency fairly into the jaws of his waiting pursuers. Though thousands may consider this another nature-fake, I shall always have the comfort of thinking that the Captain and the dogs know it for the truth.

At times jackrabbits get some sort of a plague and die in great numbers. Indeed some years at the ranch they seemed almost to have disappeared. Their carcasses are destroyed almost immediately by the carrion creatures, and their delicate bones, scattered by the ravens, buzzards, and coyotes, soon disintegrate and pass into the soil. One does not find many evidences of the destruction that has been at work; yet he will see tens instead of myriads. I have been at the ranch when one was never out of sight of jackrabbits, in droves, and again I have been there when one would not see a half dozen in a morning's ride. They recover their numbers fast enough, and the chances are that this "narrow-gauge mule" will be always with us. The ranchman would like nothing better than to bid him a last fond but genuine farewell; but I should certainly miss him.

The greasewood and thorn-bush grew in long, narrow patches. The ragweed grew everywhere it pleased, affording grand cover for the quail. The sagebrush occurred singly at spaced intervals, with tiny bare spaces between across which the plumed little rascals scurried hurriedly. The tumbleweed banked high wherever, in the mysterious dispensations of Providence, a call for tumbleweed had made itself heard.

The tumbleweed is a curious vegetable. It grows and flourishes amain, and becomes great even as a sagebrush, and puts forth its blossoms and seeds, and finally turns brown and brittle. Just about as you would conclude it has reached a respectable old age and should settle down by its chimney corner, it decides to go travelling. The first breath of wind that comes along snaps it off close to the ground. The next turns it over. And then, inasmuch as the tumbleweed is roughly globular in shape, some three or four feet in diameter, and exceedingly light in structure, over and over it rolls across the plain! If the wind happens to increase, the whole flock migrates, bounding merrily along at a good rate of speed. Nothing more terrifying to the unaccustomed equine can be imagined than thirty or forty of these formidable-looking monsters charging down upon him, bouncing several feet from the surface of the earth. The experienced horse treats them with the contempt such light-minded senility deserves, and wades through their phantom attack indifferent. After the breeze has died the debauched old tumbleweeds are everywhere to be seen, piled up against brush, choking the ditches, filling the roads. Their beautiful spherical shapes have been frayed out so that they look sodden and weary and done up. But their seeds have been scattered abroad over the land.

Wherever we found water, there we found ducks. The irrigating ditches contained many bands of a dozen or fifteen; the overflow ponds had each its little flock. The sky, too, was rarely empty of them; and the cries of the snow geese and the calls of sandhill cranes were rarely still. I remarked on this abundance.

"Ducks!" replied the Captain, wonderingly. "Why, you haven't *begun* to see ducks! Come with me."

Thereupon we turned sharp to the left. After ten minutes I made out from a slight rise above the plain a black patch lying across the distance. It seemed to cover a hundred acres or so, and to represent a sort of growth we had not before encountered.

"That," said the Captain, indicating, "is a pond covered with ducks."

I did not believe it. We dropped below the line of sight and rode steadily forward.

All at once a mighty roar burst on our ears, like the rush of a heavy train over a high trestle; and immediately the air ahead of us was filled with ducks towering. They mounted, and wheeled, and circled back or darted away. The sky became fairly obscured with them in the sense that it seemed inconceivable that hither space could contain another bird. Before the retina of the eye they swarmed exactly as a nearer cloud of mosquitoes would appear.

Hardly had the shock of this first stupendous rise of wildfowl spent itself before another and larger flight roared up. It seemed that all the ducks in the world must be a-wing; and yet, even after that, a third body arose, its rush sounding like the abrupt, overwhelming noise of a cataract in a sudden shift of wind. I should be afraid to guess how many ducks had been on that lake. Its surface was literally covered, so that nowhere did a glint of water show. I suppose it would be a simple matter to compute within a few thousand how many ducks would occupy so much space; but of what avail? Mere numbers would convey no impression of the effect. Rather fill the cup of heaven with myriads thick as a swarm of gnats against the sun. They swung and circled back and forth before making up their minds to be off, crossing and recrossing the various lines of flight. The first thrice-repeated roar of rising had given place to the clear, sustained whistling of wings, low, penetrating, inspiring. In the last flight had been a band of several hundred snow geese; and against the whiteness of their plumage the sun shone.

"That," observed the Captain with conviction, "is what you might call ducks."

By now it was the middle of the afternoon. We had not thought of lunch. At the ranch lunch was either a major or a minor consideration; there was no middle ground. If possible, we ate largely of many most delicious things. If, on the other hand, we happened to be out somewhere at noon, we cheerfully omitted lunch. So, when we returned to the ranch, the Captain, after glancing at his watch and remarking that it was rather late to eat, proposed that we try out two other ponies with the polo mallets.

This we proceeded to do. After an hour's pleasant exercise on the flat in the "Enclosure," we jogged contentedly back into the corral.

Around the corner of the barn sailed a distracted and utterly stampeded hen. After her, yapping eagerly, came five dachshunds.

Pause and consider the various elements of outrage the situation presented. (A) Dachshunds are, as before quoted, a bunch of useless, bandylegged, snip-nosed, waggle-eared—, anyway, and represent an amiable good-natured weakness on the part of Mrs. Kitty. (B) Dachshunds in general are *not* supposed to run wild all over the place, but to remain in their perfectly good, sufficiently large, entirely comfortable corral, Pete and Pup excepted. (C) Chickens are valuable. (D) Confound 'em! This sort of a performance will be a bad example for Young Ben. First thing we'll know, he'll be chasing chickens, too!

The Captain dropped from his pony and joined the procession. The hen could run just a trifle faster than the dachshunds; and the dachshunds just a trifle faster than the Captain. I always claimed they circled the barn three times, in the order named. The Captain insists with dignity that I exaggerate three hundred per cent. At any rate, the hen finally blundered, the dachshunds fell upon her—and the Captain swung his polo mallet.

Five typical "sickening thuds" were heard; five dachshunds literally sailed through the air to fall in quivering heaps. The Captain, his anger cooled, came back, shaking his head.

"I wouldn't have killed those dogs for anything in the world!"

he muttered half to me, half to himself as we took the path to the house. "I don't know what Mrs. Kitty will say to this! I certainly am sorry about it!" and so on, at length.

We turned the corner of the hedge. There in a row on the top step of the verandah sat five dachshunds, their mouths open in a happy smile, six inches of pink tongue hanging, their eyes half closed in good-humoured appreciation.

The Captain approached softly and looked them over with great care. He felt of their ribs. He stared up at me incredulously.

"Is this the same outfit?" he whispered.

"It is," said I, "I know the blaze-face brute."

"But—but—"

"They played 'possum on you, Captain."

The Captain arose and his wrath exploded.

"You miserable hounds!" he roared.

With a wise premonition they decamped.

"I'm going to clean out the whole bandylegged tribe!" threatened the Captain for the fiftieth time in the month. "I won't have them on the ranch!"

That was seven years ago. They are still there—they and numerous descendants.[G]

CHAPTER VII

DINNER

We washed up and came down stairs. All at once it proved to be drowsy time. The dark had fallen and the lamps were lit. A new fire crackled in the fireplace, anticipating the chill that was already descending. Carrie played the piano in the other room. The General snorted over something in his city paper. Mrs. Kitty had disappeared on household business. Pete and Pup, having been mistaken one for the other by some innocent bystander, gloomed and glowered under chairs.

Both the Captain and myself made some sort of a pretence of reading the papers. It was only a pretence. The grateful warmth, the soothing crackling of the fire, the distant music— and, possibly, our state of starvation—lulled us to a half doze. From this we were aroused by an announcement of dinner.

We had soup and various affairs of that sort; and there was brought on a huge and baronial roast, from which the Captain promptly proceeded to slice generous allowances. With it came vegetables. They were all cooked in cream; not milk, but rich top cream thick enough to cut with a knife. I began to see why all the house servants were plump. Also there were jellies, and little fat hot rolls, and strange pickled products of the soil. I was good and hungry; and I ate thereof.

The plates were removed. I settled back with a sigh of repletion—

The door opened to admit the waitress bearing a huge platter on which reposed, side by side, five ducks. That meant a whole one apiece! To my feeble protest the family turned indignantly.

"Of course you must eat your duck!" Mrs. Kitty settled the whole question at last.

So I ate my duck. It was a very good duck; as indeed it should have been, for it was fattened on Egyptian corn, hung the exact number of days, and cooked by Charley. It had a little spout of celery down which I could pour the abundant juice from its inside; and it was flanked right and left respectively by a piece of lemon liberally sprinkled with red pepper and sundry crisp slabs of fried hominy. Every night of the shooting season each member of the household had "his duck." Later I was shown the screened room wherein hung the game, each dated by a little tag.

After I had made way with most of my duck, and other things, and had had my coffee, and had lighted a cigar, I was entirely willing to sink back to disgraceful ease. But the Captain suddenly developed an inexcusable and fiendish energy.

"No, you don't," said he. "You come with me and Redmond and get out the decoys."

"What for?" I temporized, feebly.

"To keep the moths out of them, of course," replied the Captain with fine sarcasm. "Do you mean to tell me that you can sit still and do nothing after seeing all those ducks this afternoon? You're a fine sportsman! Brace up!"

"Let me finish this excellent cigar," I pleaded. "You gave it to me."

To this he assented. Carrie went back to the piano. The lights were dim.

Stewart Edward White

Mrs. Kitty went on finishing her crochet work or whatever it was. Nobody said anything for a long time. The Captain was busy in the gun room with one of the ranch foremen.

But this could not last, and at length I was haled forth to work.

The crisp, sharp air beneath the frosty stars, after the tepid air within, awakened me like the shock of cold water. Redmond was awaiting us with a lantern. By the horse block lay the mass of something indeterminate which I presently saw to be sacks full of something knobby.

"I have six sacks of wooden decoys," said Redmond, "with weights all on them."

The Captain nodded and passed on. We made our way down past the grape arbour, opened the high door leading into chickenville, and stopped at the border of the little pond. On its surface floated a hundred or so tame ducks of all descriptions. By means of clods of earth we woke them up. They came ashore and waddled without objection to a little inclosure. We followed them and shut the gate.

One after another the Captain indicated those he wished to take with him on the morrow. Redmond caught them, inserted them in gunny sacks, two to the sack. They made no great objection to being caught. One or two youngsters flopped and flapped about, and had to be chased into a corner. In general, however, they accepted the situation philosophically, and snuggled down contentedly in their sacks.

"They are used to it," the Captain explained. "Most of these Rouen ducks are old hands at the business; they know what to expect."

He was very particular as to the colouring of the individuals he selected. A single white feather was sufficient to cause the rejection of a female; and even when the colour scheme was otherwise perfect, too light a shade proved undesired.

"I don't know just why it is," said he, "but the wild ducks are a lot more particular about the live decoys than about the wooden. A wooden decoy can be all knocked to pieces, faded and generally disreputable, but it does well enough; but a live decoy must look the part absolutely. That gives us six apiece; I think it will be enough."

Redmond took charge of our capture. We left him with the lantern, stowing away the decoys, live and inanimate, in the Invigorator. Within fifteen minutes thereafter I was sleeping the sleep of the moderately tired and the fully fed.

CHAPTER VIII

DUCKS

The Captain rapped on my door. It was pitch dark, and the wind, which had arisen during the night, was sweeping through the open windows, blowing the light curtains about. Also it was very cold.

"All right," I answered, took my resolution in my hands, and stepped forth.

Ten minutes later, by the light of a single candle, we were manipulating the coffee-and-egg machine, and devouring the tall pile of bread-and-butter sandwiches that had been left for us over night. Then, stepping as softly as we could in our clumping rubber boots, our arms burdened with guns and wraps, we stole into the outer darkness.

It was almost black, but we could dimly make out the treetops whipped about by the wind. Over by the stable we caught the intermittent flashes of many lanterns where the teamsters were feeding their stock. Presently a merry and vigorous *rattle—rattle—rattle* arose and came nearer. The Invigorator was ready and under way.

We put on all the coats and sweaters, and climbed aboard. The Captain spoke to his horses, and we were off.

That morning I had my first experience of a phenomenon I

have never ceased admiring—and wondering at. I refer to the Captain's driving in the dark.

The night was absolutely black, so that I could hardly make out the horses. In all the world were only two elements, the sky full of stars and the mass of the earth. The value of this latter, as a means of showing us where we were, was nullified by the fact that the skyline consisted, not of recognizable and serviceable landmarks, but of the distant mountains. We went a certain length of time, and bumped over a certain number of things. Then the Captain pulled his team sharp around to the left. Why he did so I could not tell you. We drove an hour over a meandering course.

"Hang tight," remarked the Captain.

I did so. The front end of the Invigorator immediately fell away from under me, so that if I had not been obeying orders by hanging tight I should most certainly have plunged forward against the horses. We seemed to slide and slither down a steep declivity, then hit water with a splash, and began to flounder forward. The water rose high enough to cover the floor of the Invigorator, causing the Captain to speculate on whether Redmond had packed in the shells properly. Then the bow rose with a mighty jerk and we scrambled out the other side.

"That's the upper ford on the Slough," observed the Captain, calmly.

Everywhere else along the Slough, as I subsequently discovered, the banks fell off perpendicular, the water was deep, and the bottom soft. The approach was down no fenced lane, but across the open, with no other landmarks even in daylight than the break of low willows and cottonwoods exactly like a hundred others. Ten minutes later the Captain drew rein.

"Here you are," said he, cautiously. "You can dump your stuff off right here. I can't get through the fence with the team; but it's only a short distance to carry."

Accordingly, in entire faith, I descended and unloaded my three sacks of wooden decoys and my three sacks of live ducks and my gun and shells.

"I'll drive on to another hole," said the Captain. "Good luck!"

"Would you mind," I suggested, meekly, "telling me in which direction this mythical fence is situated; what kind of a fence it is; and where I carry to when I get through it?"

The Captain chuckled.

"Why," he explained, "the fence is straight ahead of you; and it's barbed wire; and as for where you're headed, you'll find the pond where we saw all those ducks last night about a hundred yards or so west."

Where we saw all those ducks! My blood increased its pace through my veins. Now that I was afoot, I could begin to make out things in the starlight—the silhouettes of bushes or brush, and even three or four posts of the fence.

The Invigorator rattled into the distance. I got my stuff the other side of the wires, and, shouldering a sack, plodded away due west.

But now I made out the pond gleaming; and by this and by the dim grayness of the earth immediately about me knew that dawn was at last under way. The night had not yet begun to withdraw, but its first strength was going. Objects in the world about became, not visible, but existent. By the time I had carried my last load the rather liberal hundred yards to the shores of the pond the eastern sky had banished its stars.

My movements had, of course, alarmed the ducks. There were not many of them, as I could judge by the whistling of their departing wings and by the silvery furrows where they had left the water. It is curious how strong the daylight must become before the eye can distinguish a duck in flight. The comparative paucity of numbers, I reflected, was probably due to the fact that the ducks used this pond merely as a loafing place during the day. Therefore I should anticipate a good flight as soon as feeding time should be over; especially as one end of the pond proved to be fairly well sheltered from the high wind.

At once I set to work to build me a blind. This I constructed of tumbleweed and willow shoots, with a lucky sagebrush as a good basis. I made it thick below and thin on top, so I could crouch hidden, and rise easily to shoot. Also I made it hastily, working away with a concentration that would prove very valuable could it be brought to a useful line of work. There can nothing equal the busyness of a man hastening to perfect his arrangements before a flight of ducks is due to start. Every few moments I would look anxiously up to see how things were going with the morning. The light was indubitably increasing. That is to say, I could make out the whole width of the pond, for example, although the farther banks were still in silhouette, and the sky was almost free of stars. Also the perpendicular plane of the mountains to the west, in some subtle manner, was beginning to break. It was not yet daylight; but the dawn was here.

I reached cautiously into one of the sacks and brought forth one of the decoy ducks. Around his neck I buckled a little leather collar to a ring in which had been attached a cord and weight. Then I cautiously waded out and anchored him.

He was delighted, and proceeded immediately to take a bath, ducking his head under and out again, ruffling his wings, and wagging his absurd little tail. Apparently the whole experience was a matter of course to him; but he was willing to show pleasure that this phase of it was over. I anchored out his five companions, and then proceeded to arrange the wooden decoys artistically around the outskirts. By now it was quite genuinely early daylight. Three times the overhead whistle of wings had warned me to hurry; and twice small flocks of ducks had actually swung down within range only to discover me at the last moment and tower away again. When younger, I used, at such junctures, to rush for my gun. That is a puppy stage, for by the time you get your gun those ducks are gone; and by the time you have regained your abandoned task more ducks are in. Therefore one early learns that when he goes out from his blind to pick up ducks, or catch cripples, or arrange decoys, he would better do so, paying no attention whatever to the game that will immediately appear. So now the whistle of wings merely caused me to work the faster. At length I was able to wade ashore and sink into my blind.

Immediately, as usual, the flights ceased for the time being. I had nothing to do but sit tight and wait.

This was no unpleasant task. The mountains to the west had become lucent, and glowed pink in the dawn; those to the east looked like silhouettes of very thin slate-coloured cardboard stuck up on edge, across which a pearl wash had been laid. The flatter world of the plains all about me lay half revealed in an unearthly gray light. The wind swooped and tore away at the brush, sending its fan-shaped cat's-paws across the surface of the pond. My ducks, having finished their ablutions, now gave a leisurely attention to smoothing out their plumes ruffled by the night in the gunnysack. They ran each feather separately through their bills, preening and smoothing. All the time they conversed together in low tones of voice. Whenever one made a rather clever remark, or smoothed to glossiness a particularly rumpled feather, he wagged his short tail vigorously from side to side in satisfaction.

Suddenly the one farthest out in the pond stilled to attention and craned forward his neck.

"*Mark!*" quoth he, loudly, and then again: "*Mark! quok—quok—quok!*"

The other five looked in the same direction, and then they,

too, lifted up their voices. Cautiously I turned my head. Low against the growing splendour of the sunrise, wings rigidly set, came a flock of mallards. My ducks fairly stood up on their tails the better to hurl invitations and inducements at their wild brethren. The chorus praising this particular spot was vociferous and unanimous, I wonder what the mallards thought of the other fifty or sixty in my flock, the wooden ones, that sat placidly aloof. Did they consider these remarkably exclusive; or did they perhaps look upon the live ones as the "boosters" committee for this particular piece of duck real estate? At any rate, they dropped in without the slightest hesitation, which shows the value of live decoys. The mallard is ordinarily a wily bird and circles your pond a number of times before deciding to come in to wooden decoys. At the proper moment I got to my feet, and, by good fortune, knocked down two fat green-heads.

They fell with a splash right among my ducks. Did the latter exhibit alarm over either the double concussion of the gun or this fall of defunct game from above? Not at all! they were tickled to death. Each swam vigorously around and around at the limit of his tether, ruffling his plumage and waggling his tail with the utmost vigour.

"Well, I rather think we fooled that bunch!" said they, one to another. "Did you ever see an easier lot? Came right down without a look! If the Captain had been here he'd have killed a half dozen of the chumps before they got out of range!" and so on. For your experienced decoy always seems to enjoy the game hugely, and to enter into it with much enthusiasm and intelligence. And all the while the flock of wooden decoys headed unanimously up wind, and bobbed in the wavelets; and the sun went on gilding the mountains to the west.

Next a flock of teal whirled down wind, stooped, and were gone like a flash. I got in both barrels; and missed both. The dissatisfaction of this was almost immediately mitigated by a fine smash at a flock of sprig that went by overhead at extreme long range, but from which I managed to bring down a fine

Stewart Edward White

drake. When the shot hit him he faltered, then, still flying, left
the ranks at an acute angle, sloping ever the quicker
downward, until he fell on a long slant, his wings set, his neck
still outstretched. I marked the direction as well as I could, and
immediately went in search of him. Fortunately he lay in the
open, quite dead. Looking back, I could see another good flock
fairly hovering over the decoys.

The sun came up, and grew warm. The wind died. I took off
my sweater. Between flights I basked deliciously. The affair
was outside of all precedent and reason. A duck shooter ought
to be out in a storm, a good cold storm. He ought to break the
scum ice when he puts out his decoys. He ought to sit half
frozen in a wintry blast, his fingers numb, his nose blue, his
body shivering. That sort of discomfort goes with duck
shooting. Yet here I was sitting out in a warm, summerlike day
in my shirt sleeves, waiting comfortably—and the ducks were
coming in, too!

After a time I heard the mighty rattle of the Invigorator, and
the Captain's voice shouting. Reluctantly I disentangled myself
from my blind and went over to see what all the row was
about.

"Had enough?" he demanded, cheerily.

I saw that I was supposed to say yes; so I said it. The ducks
were still coming in fast. You see, I was not yet free from the
traditions to which I had been brought up. Back in Michigan,
when a man went for a day's shoot, he stayed with it all day. It
was serious business. I was not yet accustomed to being so
close to the game that the casual expedition was after all the
most fun.

So I pulled up my rubber boots, and waded out, gathering in
the game. To my immense surprise I found that I had thirty-
seven ducks down. It had not occurred to me that I had shot
half that number, which is perhaps commentary on how fast
ducks had been coming in. It was then only about eight

o'clock. After gathering them in, next we performed the slow and very moist task of lifting the wooden decoys and winding their anchor cords around their placid necks. Lastly we gathered in the live ducks. They came, towed at the end of their tethers, with manifest reluctance; hanging back at their strings, flapping their wings, and hissing at us indignantly. I do not think they were frightened, for once we had our hands on them, they resumed their dignified calm. Only they enjoyed the fun outside; and they did not fancy the bags inside; a choice eminently creditable to their sense.

So back we drove to the ranch. The Captain, too, had had good shooting. Redmond appeared with an immense open hamper into which he dumped the birds two by two, keeping tally in a loud voice. Redmond thoroughly enjoyed all the small details.

CHAPTER IX

UNCLE JIM

Each morning, while we still sat at breakfast, Uncle Jim drove up from the General's in his two-wheeled cart to see if there might be anything doing. Uncle Jim was a solidly built elderly man, with the brown complexion and the quizzical, good-humoured eye of the habitual sportsman. He wore invariably an old shooting coat and a cap that had seen younger, but perhaps not better, days. His vehicle was a battered but serviceable two-wheeled cart drawn by a placid though adequate horse. His weapon for all purposes was a rather ponderous twelve-gauge.

If we projected some sporting expedition Uncle Jim was our man; but if there proved to be nothing in the wind, he disappeared promptly. He conducted various trapping ventures for "varmints," at which he seemed to have moderate success, for he often brought in a wildcat or coyote. In fact, he maintained one of the former in a cage, to what end nobody knew, for it was a harsh and unsociable character. Uncle Jim began to show signs of life about July fifteenth when the dove season opened; he came into his own from the middle of October until the first of February, during which period one can shoot both ducks and quail; he died down to the bare earth when the game season was over, and only sent up a few green shoots of interest in the matter of supplying his wildcat with that innumerable agricultural pest, the blackbird.

Sometimes I accompanied Uncle Jim, occupying the other side of the two-wheeled cart. We never had any definite object in view; we just went forth for adventure. The old horse jogged along very steadily, considering the fact that he was as likely to be put at cross country as a road. We humped up side by side in sociable silence, spying keenly for what we could see. A covey of quail disappearing in the brush caused us to pull up. We hunted them leisurely for a half hour and gathered in a dozen birds. Always we tried to sneak ducks, no matter how hopeless the situation might seem. Once I went on one hand and my knees through three inches of water for three hundred yards, stalking a flock of sprig loafing in an irrigation puddle. There was absolutely no cover; I was in plain sight; from a serious hunting standpoint the affair was quixotic, not to say imbecile. If I had been out with the Captain we should probably not have looked twice at those sprig. Nevertheless, as the general atmosphere of Uncle Jim's expeditions was always one of adventure and forlorn hopes and try-it-anyway, I tried it on. Uncle Jim sat in the cart and chuckled. Every moment I expected the flock to take wing, but they lingered. Finally, when still sixty yards distant, the leaders rose. I cut loose with both barrels for general results. To my vast surprise three came down, one dead, the other two wing-tipped. The two latter led me a merry chase, wherein I managed to splatter the rest of myself. Then I returned in triumph to the cart. The forlorn hope had planted its banner on the walls of achievement. Uncle Jim laughed at me for my idiocy in crawling through water after such a fool chance. I laughed at Uncle Jim because I had three ducks. We drove on, and the warm sun dried me off.

In this manner we made some astonishing bags; astonishing not by their size, but by the manner of their accomplishment.

We were entirely open minded. Anything that came along interested us. We investigated all the holes in all the trees, in hopes of 'coons or honey or something or other. We drove gloriously through every patch of brush. Sometimes an unseen hummock would all but upset us; so we had to scramble hastily to windward to restore our equilibrium.

The country was gridironed with irrigation ditches. They were eight to ten feet deep, twenty or thirty feet wide, and with elevated, precipitous banks. One could cross them almost anywhere—except when they were brimful, of course. The banks were so steep that, once started, the vehicle had to go, but so short that it must soon reach bottom. On the other side the horse could attain the top by a rush; after which, having gained at least a front footing over the bank, he could draw the light vehicle by dead weight the rest of the distance. Naturally, the driver had to take the course at exactly right angles, or he capsized ingloriously.

One day Uncle Jim and I started to cross one of these ditches that had long been permitted to remain dry. Its bottom was covered by weeds six inches high, and looked to be about six feet down. We committed ourselves to the slope. Then, when too late to reconsider, we discovered that the apparent six-inch growth of weeds was in reality one of four or five feet. The horse discovered it at the same time. With true presence of mind, he immediately determined that it was up to him to leap that ditch. Only the fact that he was hitched to the cart prevented him from doing so; but he made a praiseworthy effort.

The jerk threw me backward, and had I not grabbed Uncle Jim I would most certainly have fallen out behind. As for Uncle Jim, he would most certainly have fallen out behind, too, if he had not clung like grim death to the reins. And as for the horse, alarmed by the check and consequent scramble, he just plain bolted, fortunately straight ahead. We hit the opposite bank with a crash, sailed over it, and headed across country.

Consider us as we went. Feet in air, I was poised on the end of my backbone in a state of exact equilibrium. A touch would tumble me out behind; an extra ounce would tip me safely into the cart; my only salvation was my hold on Uncle Jim. I could not apply that extra ounce for the simple reason that Uncle Jim also, feet in air, was poised exactly on the end of his backbone. If the reins slackened an inch, over he went; if he could manage to pull up the least bit in the world, in he came! So we tore across country for several hundred yards, unable to recover and most decidedly unwilling to fall off on the back of our heads. It must have been a grand sight; and it seemed to endure an hour. Finally, imperceptibly we overcame the opposing forces. We were saved!

Uncle Jim cursed out "Henry" with great vigour. Henry was the mare we drove. Uncle Jim, in his naming of animals, always showed a stern disregard for the female sex. Then, as usual, we looked about to see what we could see.

Over to the left grew a small white oak. About ten or twelve feet from the ground was a hole. That was enough; we drove over to investigate that hole. It was not an easy matter, for we were too lazy to climb the tree unless we had to. Finally we drove close enough so that, by standing on extreme tip-toe atop the seat of the cart, I could get a sort of sidewise, one-eyed squint at that hole.

"If," I warned Uncle Jim, "Henry leaves me suspended in mid-air I'll bash her fool head in!"

"No, you won't," chuckled Uncle Jim, "it's too far home."

It was a very dark hole, and for a moment I could see nothing. Then, all at once, I made out two dull balls of fire glowing steadily out of the blackness. That was as long as I could stand stretching out my entire anatomy to look down any hole.

On hearing my report, Uncle Jim phlegmatically thrust the flexible whip down the hole.

"'Coon," he pronounced, after listening to the resultant remarks from within.

And then the same bright idea struck us both.

"Mrs. Kitty here makes good with those angleworms," Uncle Jim voiced the inspiration.

We blocked up the hole securely; and made rapid time back to the ranch.

CHAPTER X

THE MEDIUM-SIZE GAME

Against many attacks and accusations of uselessness cast at her dachshunds, Mrs. Kitty had always stoutly opposed the legend of "medium-size game." The dachshunds may look like bologna sausages on legs, ran the gist of her argument; and they may progress like rather lively measuring worms; and the usefulness of their structure may seem to limit itself to a facility for getting under furniture without stooping, *but*—Mrs. Kitty's eloquence always ended by convincing herself, and she became very serious—but that is not the dogs' fault. Rather it is the fault of their environment to which they have been transplanted. Back in their own native vaterland they were always used for medium-sized game. And what is more they are *good* at it! Come here, Pete, they shan't abuse you!

Coyotes and bobcats are medium-size game, someone ventured to point out.

Not at all, medium-size game should live in holes, like badgers. Dachshunds are evidently built for holes. They are long and low, and they have spatulate feet for digging, and their bandy legs enable them to throw the dirt out behind them. Their long, sharp noses are like tweezers to seize upon the medium-size game. In short, by much repetition, a legend had grown up around the dachshunds, a legend of fierceness inhibited only by circumstances, of pathetic deprivation of the sports of their native land. If only we could have a badger, we could almost hear them say to each other in dog language, a strong, morose, savage badger! Alas! we are wasting our days in idleness, our talents rust from disuse! Finally, Uncle Jim remained the only frankly skeptical member.

At this time there visited the ranch two keen sportsmen whom we shall call Charley and Tommy; as also several girls. We burst on the assembled multitude with our news. Immediately a council of war was called. After the praetors and tribunes of the people had uttered their opinions, Uncle Jim arose and spoke as follows:

"Here is your chance to make good," said he, addressing Mrs. Kitty. "Those badger hounds of yours, according to you, have just been fretting for medium-size game. Well, here's some. Bring out the whole flock, and let's see them get busy."

The proposition was received with a shout of rapture Uncle Jim smiled grimly.

"Well, they'll do it!" cried Mrs. Kitty, with spirit.

Preparations were immediately under way. In half an hour the army debouched from the ranch and strung out single file across the plain.

First came Uncle Jim and myself in the two-wheeled cart as scouts and guides.

Followed the General in his surrey. The surrey had originally been intended for idle dalliance along country lanes. In the days of its glory it had been upholstered right merrily, and around its flat top had dangled a blithesome fringe. Both the upholstery and fringe were still somewhat there. Of the glory that was past no other reminder had persisted. The General sat squarely in the middle of the front seat, very large, erect, and imposing, driving with a fine military disregard of hummocks or the laws of equilibrium. In or near the back seat hovered a tiny Japanese boy to whom the General occasionally issued short, sharp, military comments or commands.

Then came Mrs. Kitty and the ponies with Carrie beside her. Immediately astern of the pony cart followed a three-seated carry-all with assorted guests. This was flanked by the Captain and Charley as outriders. The rear was closed by the Invigorator rilled with dachshunds. Their pointed noses poked busily through the slats of the cage, and sniffed up over the edge of the wagon box.

The rear, did I say? I had forgotten Mithradates Antikamia Briggs. The latter polysyllabic person was a despised, apologetic, rangy, black-and-white mongrel hound said to have belonged somewhere to a man named Briggs. I think the rest of his name was intended as an insult. Ordinarily Mithradates hung around the men's quarters where he was liked. Never had he dared seek either solace or sympathy at the doors of the great house; and never, never had he remotely dreamed of following any of the numerous hunting expeditions. That would have been lese-majesty, high treason, sublime impudence, and intolerable nuisance to be punished by banishment or death. Mithradates realized this perfectly; and never did he presume to raise his eyes to such high and shining affairs.

But to-day he followed. Nobody was subsequently able to explain why Mithradates Antikamia should on this one occasion so have plucked up heart. My private opinion is that he saw the dachshunds being taken, and, in his uncultivated manner, communed with himself as follows:

"Well, will you gaze on that! I don't pretend to be in the same class with Old Ben or Young Ben, or even of the fox terriers; but if I'm not more of a dog than that lot of splay-footed freaks, I'll go bite myself! If they're *that* hard up for dogs, I'll be cornswizzled if I don't go myself!"

Which he did. We did not want him; this was distinctly the dachshunds' party, and we did not care to have any one messing in. The Captain tried to drive him back. Mithradates Antikamia would not go. The Captain dismounted and tried force. Mithradates shut both eyes, crouched to the ground, and immediately weighed a half ton. When punished he rolled over and held all four paws in the air. The minute the Captain turned his back, after stern admonitions to "go home!" and "down, charge!" and the like, Mithradates crawled slowly forward to the waiting line, ducking his head, wrinkling his upper lips ingratiatingly, and sneezing in the most apologetic tones. Finally we gave it up.

"But," we "saved our face," "you'll have to behave when we get there!"

So, as has been said, Mithradates Antikamia Briggs brought up the rear.

Arrived at the tree the whole procession drew into a half circle. We unblocked the opening, and the Invigorator was driven to a spot beneath it so each person could take his turn at standing on the seat and peering down the hole. The eyes still glowed like balls of fire.

Next the dachshunds were lifted up one by one and given a chance to smell at the game. This was to make them keen. Held up by means of a hand held either side their chests, they curled up their hind legs and tails and seemed to endure. Mrs. Kitty explained that they had never been so far off the ground in their lives, and so were naturally preoccupied by the new sensation. This sounded reasonable, so we placed them on the ground. There they sat in a circle looking up at our performances, a solemn and mild interest expressing itself in their lugubrious countenances. A dachshund has absolutely no sense of humour or lightness of spirits. He never cavorts.

By sounding carefully with a carriage whip we determined the depth of the hole, and proceeded to cut through to the bottom. This was quite a job, for the oak was tough, and the position difficult. Tommy had ascended the tree, and proclaimed loudly the first signs of daylight as the axe bit through. Mine happened to be the axe work; so when I had finished a neat little orifice, I swung up beside Tommy, and the Invigorator drove out of the way.

My elevated position was a good one; and as Tommy was peering eagerly down the hole, I had nothing to do but survey the scene.

The rigs were drawn up in a semi-circle twenty yards away. Next the horses' heads stood the drivers of the various vehicles, anxious to miss none of the fun. The dachshunds sat on their haunches, looking up, and probably wondering why their friend, Tommy, insisted on roosting up a tree. The Captain and Charley were immediately below, engaged in an earnest effort to poke the 'coon into ascending the hole. Tommy was reporting the result of these efforts from above. The General, his feet firmly planted, had unlimbered a huge ten-bore shotgun, so as to be ready for anything. Uncle Jim stood by, smoking his pipe. Mithradates Antikamia Briggs sat sadly apart.

The poking efforts accomplished little. Occasionally the 'coon made a little dash or scramble, but never went far. There was a great deal of talking, shouting, and advice.

At last Uncle Jim, knocking the ashes from his pipe, moved into action. He plucked a double handful of the tall, dry grass, touched a match to it, and thrust it in the nick.

Without the slightest hesitation the 'coon shot out at the top!

Now just at that moment Tommy happened to be leaning over for a right *good* look down the hole. He received thirty pounds or so of agitated 'coon square in the chest. Thereupon he fell out of the tree incontinently, with the 'coon on top of him.

We caught our breath in horror. Although we could plainly see that Tommy was in no degree injured by his short fall, yet we all realized that it was going to be serious to be mixed up with a raging, snarling beast fight of twenty-two members. When the dachshunds should pounce on their natural prey, the medium-size game, poor Tommy would be at the bottom of the heap. Several even started forward to restrain the dogs, but stopped as they realized the impossibilities.

Tommy and the 'coon hit with a thump. The dachshunds took one horrified look; then with the precision of a drilled man[oe]uvre they unanimously turned tail and plunged into the tall grass. From my elevated perch I could see it waving agitatedly as they made their way through it in the direction of the distant ranch.

For a moment there was astounded silence. Then there arose a shriek of delight. The Captain rolled over and over and clutched handfuls of turf in his joy. The General roared great salvos of laughter. Tommy, still seated where he had fallen, leaned weakly against the tree, the tears coursing down his cheeks. The rest of the populace lifted up their voices and howled. Even Uncle Jim, who rarely laughed aloud, although his eyes always smiled, emitted great Ho! ho!'s. Only Mrs. Kitty, dumb with indignation, stared speechless after that wriggling mess of fugitives.

The occasion was too marvellous. We enjoyed it to the full. Whenever the rapture sank somewhat, someone would gasp out a half-remembered bit of Mrs. Kitty's former defences.

"Their long, sharp noses are like tweezers to seize the game!" declaimed Charley, weakly. [Spasm by the audience.]

"Their spatulate feet are meant for digging," the Captain took up the tale. [Another spasm.]

"Their bandy legs enabled them to throw the dirt out behind them—as they ran," suggested Tommy.

"If *only* they could have had a badger they'd have beaten all records!" we chorused.

And then finally we wiped our eyes and remembered that there used to be a 'coon. At the same time we became conscious of a most unholy row in the offing: the voice of Mithradates Antikamia.

"If you people want your 'coon," he was remarking in a staccato and exasperated voice, "you'd better come and lend a hand. *I* can't manage him alone! The blame thing has bitten me in three places already. Of course, I like to see people have a good time, and I hope you won't curtail your enjoyment on my account; but if you've had *quite* enough of those made-in-Germany imitations, perhaps you'll just stroll over and see what one good American-built DOG can do!"

CHAPTER XI

IN SEARCH OF ADVENTURE

Uncle Jim had friends everywhere. Continually we were pulling up by one of the tiny two-roomed shacks wherein dwelt the small settlers. The houses were always of new boards, unpainted, perched on four-by-fours, in the middle of bare ground, perhaps surrounded by young poplars or cotton-woods, but more likely fully exposed to the sun. A trifling open shed protected a battered buggy on the thills and wheels of which perched numerous chickens. A rough corral and windmill completed the arrangements. Near the house was usually a small patch of alfalfa. Farther out the owner was engaged in the strenuous occupation of brushing and breaking a virgin country.

To greet us rushed forth a half-dozen mongrel dogs, and appeared a swarm of children, followed by the woman of the place. Uncle Jim knew them all by name, including even the dogs. He carefully wound the reins around the whip, leaned forward comfortably, and talked. Henry dozed; and I listened with interest. Uncle Jim had the natural gift of popularity. By either instinct or a wide experience he knew just what problems and triumphs, disappointments and perplexities these people were encountering; and he plunged promptly into the discussion of them. Also, I was never able to make out whether Uncle Jim was a conscious or unconscious diplomat; but certainly he knew how judiciously to make use of the subtle principle, so well illustrated by Moliere, that it pleases people to confer small favours. Thus occasionally he gravely "borrowed" a trifle of axle grease, which we immediately applied, or a cup of milk, or a piece of string to mend something. When finally our leisurely roadside call was at an end, we rolled away from unanimously hearty signals of farewell.

In accordance with our settled feeling of taking things as they came, and trying for everything, we blundered into varied experiences, none of which arrange themselves in recollection with any pretence of logical order. Perhaps it might not be a bad idea to copy our method, to set forth and see where we land.

One of the most amusing happened when we were out with my younger, but not smaller, brother. This youth was at that time about eighteen years old, and six feet two in height. His age *plus* his stature *equalled* a certain lankiness. As we drove peacefully along the highway we observed in the adjacent field a coyote. The animal was some three or four hundred yards away, lying down, his head between his paws, for all the world like a collie dog. Immediately the lad was all excitement. We pointed out the well-known facts that the coyote is no fool and is difficult to stalk at best; that while he is apparently tame as long as the wagon keeps moving, he decamps when convinced that his existence is receiving undue attention; that in the present instance the short grass would not conceal a snake; and that, finally, a 16-gauge gun loaded with number-six shot was not an encouraging coyote weapon. He brushed them aside as mere details. So we let him out.

He dropped into the grass and commenced his stalk. This he accomplished on his elbows and knees. A short review of the possibilities will convince you that the sight was unique. Although the boy's head and shoulders were thus admirably close to the ground, there followed an extremely abrupt apex. Add the fact that the canvas shooting coat soon fell forward over his shoulders.

Stewart Edward White

The coyote at first paid no attention. As this strange object worked nearer, he raised his head to take a look. Then he sat up on his haunches to take a better look. At this point we expected him to lope away instead of which he trotted forward a few feet and stopped, his ears pricked forward. There he sat, his shrewd brain alive with conjecture until, at thirty-five yards, the kid emptied both barrels. Thereupon he died, his curiosity as to what a movable brown pyramid might be still unsatisfied.

Uncle Jim, the kid, and I had great fun cruising for jackrabbits. Uncle Jim sat in the middle and drove while the kid and I hung our feet over the sides and constituted ourselves the port and starboard batteries. Bumping and banging along at full speed over the uneven country, we jumped the rabbits, and opened fire as they made off. Each had to stick to his own side of the ship, of course. Uncle Jim's bird dog, his head between our feet, his body under the seat, watched the proceedings, whining. It looked like good fun to him, but it was forbidden. A jackrabbit arrested in full flight by a charge of shot turns a very spectacular somersault. The dog would stand about five rabbits. As the sixth turned over, he executed a mad struggle, accomplished a flying leap over the front wheel, was rolled over and over by the forward momentum of the moving vehicle, scrambled to his feet, pounced on that rabbit, and most everlastingly and savagely shook it up! Then Uncle Jim descended and methodically and dispassionately licked the dog.

Jackrabbits were good small-rifle game. They started away on a slow lope, but generally stopped and sat up if not too seriously alarmed. A whistle sometimes helped bring them to a stand. After a moment's inspection they went away, rapidly. With a .22 automatic one could turn loose at all sorts of ranges at all speeds. It was a good deal of fun, too, sneaking about afoot through the low brush, making believe that the sage was a jungle, the tiny pellets express bullets, the rabbits magnified—I am sorry for the fellow who cannot have fun sometimes "pretending!" In the brush, too, dwelt little cottontails, very good to eat. The jackrabbit was a pest, but the cottontail was worth getting. We caught sight of him first in the bare open spaces between the bushes, whereupon he proceeded rapidly to cover. It was necessary to shoot rather quickly. The inexperienced would be apt to run forward eagerly, hoping to catch a glimpse of the cottontail on the other side; but always it would be in vain. That would be owing to the fact that the little rabbit has a trick of apparently running through a brush at full speed, but in reality of stopping abruptly and squatting at the roots. Often it is possible to get a shot by scrutinizing carefully the last place he was seen. He can stop as suddenly as a cow pony.

Often and often, like good strategic generals, we were induced by circumstances to change our plans or our method of attack at the last moment. On several occasions, while shooting in the fields of Egyptian corn, I have killed a quail with my right barrel and a duck with my left! Continually one was crouching in hopes, when some unexpected flock stooped toward him as he walked across country. These hasty concealments were in general quite futile, for it is a fairly accurate generalization that, in the open, game will see you before you see it. This is not always true. I have on several occasions stood stock still in the open plain until a low-flying mallard came within easy range. Invariably the bird was flying toward the setting sun, so I do not doubt his vision was more or less blinded.

The most ridiculous effort of this sort was put into execution by the Captain and myself.

Be it premised that while, in the season, the wildfowl myriads were always present, it by no means followed that the sportsman was always sure of a bag. The ducks followed the irrigation water. One week they might be here in countless hordes; the next week might see only a few coots and hell divers left, while the game was reported twenty miles away. Furthermore, although fair shooting—of the pleasantest sort, in my opinion—was always to be had by jumping small bands and singles from the "holes" and ditches, the big flocks were quite apt to feed and loaf in the wide spaces discouragingly free of cover. Irrigation was done on a large scale. A section of land might be submerged from three inches to a foot in depth. In the middle of this temporary pond and a half dozen others like it fed the huge bands of ducks. What could you do? There was no cover by which to sneak them. You might build a blind, but before the ducks could get used to its strange presence in a flat and featureless landscape the water would be withdrawn from that piece of land. Only occasionally, when a high wind drove them from the open, or when the irrigation water happened to be turned in to a brushy country, did the sportsman get a chance at the great swarms. Since a man could get all the ducks he could reasonably require, there was no real reason why he should look with longing on these inaccessible packs, but we all did. It was not that we wanted more ducks; for we held strictly within limits, but we wanted to get in the thick of it.

On the occasion of which I started to tell, the Captain and I were returning from somewhere. Near the Lakeside ranch we came across a big tract of land overflowed by not deeper than two or three inches of water. The ducks were everywhere on it. They sat around fat and solemn in flocks; they swirled and stooped and lit and rose again; they fed busily; they streamed in from all points of the compass, cleaving the air with a whistling of wings.

Cover there was none. It was exactly like a big, flat cow pasture without any fences. We pulled up the Invigorator and eyed the scene with speculative eyes. Finally, we did as follows:

Into the middle of that field waded we. The ducks, of course, arose with a roar, circled once out of range, and departed. We knew that in less than a minute the boldest would return to see if, perchance, we might have been mere passers-by. Finding us still there, they would, in the natural course of events, circle once or twice and then depart for good.

Now we had noticed this: ducks will approach to within two

or three hundred yards of a man standing upright, but they will come within one hundred—or almost in range—if he squats and holds quite still. This, we figured, is because he is that much more difficult to recognize as a man, even though he is in plain sight. We had to remain in plain sight; but could we not make ourselves more difficult to recognize?

After pulling up our rubber boots carefully, we knelt in the two inches of water, placed our chests across two wooden shell boxes we had brought for the purpose, ducked our heads, and waited. After a few moments overhead came the peculiar swift whistle of wings. We waited, rigid. When that whistle sounded very loud indeed, we jerked ourselves upright and looked up. Immediately above us, already towering frantically, was a flock of sprig. They were out of range, but we were convinced that this was only because we had mistakenly looked up too soon.

It was fascinating work, for we had to depend entirely on the sense of hearing. The moment we stirred in the slightest degree away went the ducks. As it took an appreciable time to rise to our feet, locate the flock, and get into action, we had to guess very accurately. We fired a great many times, and killed a very few; but each duck was an achievement.

Though the bag could not be guaranteed, the sight of ducks could. When my brother went with me to the ranch, the duck shooting was very poor. This was owing to the fact that sudden melting of the snows in the Sierras had overflowed an immense tract of country to form a lake eight or nine miles across. On this lake the ducks were safe, and thither they resorted in vast numbers. As a consequence, the customary resorts were deserted. We could see the ducks, and that was about all. Realizing the hopelessness of the situation we had been confining ourselves so strictly to quail that my brother had begun to be a little sceptical of our wildfowl tales. Therefore, one day, I took him out and showed him ducks.

They were loafing in an angle of the lake formed by the banks of two submerged irrigating ditches, so we were enabled to measure them accurately. After they had flown we paced off their bulk. They had occupied a space on the bank and in the water three hundred yards long by fifty yards wide; and they were packed in there just about as thick as ducks could crowd together. An able statistician might figure out how many there were. At any rate, my brother agreed that he had seen some ducks.

There was one thing about Uncle Jim's expeditions: they were cast in no rigid lines. Their direction, scope, or purpose could be changed at the last moment should circumstances warrant.

One day Uncle Jim came after me afoot, with the quiet assurance that he knew where there were "some ducks."

"Tommy is down there now," said he, "in a blind. We'll make a couple more blinds across the pond, and in that way one or the other of us is sure to get a shot at everything that comes in. And the way they're coming in is scand'lous!"

Therefore I filled my pockets with duck shells, seized my close-choked 12-bore, and followed Uncle Jim. We walked across three fields.

"Those ducks are acting mighty queer," proffered Uncle Jim in puzzled tones.

We stopped a moment to watch. Flock after flock stooped toward the little pond, setting their wings and dropping with the extraordinary confidence wildfowl sometimes exhibit. At a certain point, however, and while still at a good elevation, they towered swiftly and excitedly.

"Doesn't seem like they'd act so scared even if Tommy wasn't well hid," puzzled Uncle Jim.

We proceeded cautiously, keeping out of sight behind some greasewood, until we could see the surface of the pond. There were Tommy's decoys, and there was Tommy's blind. We could not see but that it was a well-made blind. Even as we looked another flock of sprig sailed down wind, stopped short at a good two hundred yards, towered with every appearance of lively dismay, and departed. Tommy's head came above the blind, gazing after them.

"They couldn't act worse if Tommy was out waving his hat at 'em," said Uncle Jim.

We climbed a fence. This brought us to a slight elevation, but sufficient to enable us to see abroad over the flat landscape.

Immediately beyond Tommy was a long, low irrigation check grown with soft green sod. On the farther slope thereof were the girls. They had brought magazines and fancy work, and evidently intended to spend the afternoon in the open, enjoying the fresh air and the glad sunshine and the cheerful voices of God's creatures. They were, of course, quite unconscious of Tommy's sporting venture not a hundred feet away. Their parasols were green, red, blue, and other explosive tints.

Uncle Jim and I sat for a few moments on the top of that fence enjoying the view. Then we climbed softly down and went away. We decided tacitly not to shoot ducks. The nature of the expedition immediately changed. We spent the rest of the afternoon on quail. To be sure number-five shot in a close-choked twelve is not an ideal load for the purpose; but by care in letting our birds get far enough away we managed to have a very good afternoon's sport. And whenever we would make a bad miss we had ready consolation: the thought of Tommy waiting and wondering and puzzling in his blind.

Stewart Edward White

CHAPTER XII

THE GRAND TOUR

Almost always our sporting expeditions were of this casual character, sandwiched in among other occupations. Guns were handy, as was the game. To seize the one and pursue the other on the whim of the moment was the normal and usual thing. Thus one day Mrs. Kitty drove me over to look at a horse I was thinking of buying. On the way home, in a corner of brush, I hopped out and bagged twelve quail; and a little farther on, by a lucky sneak, I managed to gather in five ducks from an irrigation pond. On another occasion, having a spare hour before lunch, I started out afoot from the ranch house at five minutes past eleven, found my quail within a quarter mile, had luck in scattering them, secured my limit of twenty-five, and was back at the house at twelve twenty-five! Before this I had been to drive with Mrs. Kitty; and after lunch we drove twelve miles to call on a neighbour. Although I had enjoyed a full day's quail shoot, it had been, as it were, merely an interpolation.

Occasionally, however, it was elected to make a grand and formal raid on the game. This could be either a get-up-early-in-the-morning session in the blinds, a formal quail hunt, or the Grand Tour.

To take the Grand Tour we got out the Liver Invigorator and as many saddle horses as might be needed to accommodate the shooters. On reaching the hog field it was proper to disembark, and to line up for an advance on the corner of the irrigation ditch where I had so unexpectedly jumped the ducks my first morning on the ranch. In extended order we approached. If ducks were there, they got a great hammering. Everybody shot joyously—whether in sure range or not, it must be confessed. The birds went into a common bag, for it would be impossible to say who had killed what. After congratulations and reproaches, both of which might be looked upon as sacrifices to the great god Josh, we swung to the left and tramped a half mile to the artesian well. The Invigorator and saddle horses followed at a respectful distance. When we had investigated the chances at the well, we climbed aboard again and rattlety-banged across country to the Slough.

The Slough comprised a wide and varied country. In proper application it was a little winding ravine sunk eight or ten feet below the flat plain, and filled with water. This water had been grown thick with trees, but occasionally, for some reason to me unknown, the growth gave space for tiny open ponds or channels. These were further screened by occasional willows or greasewood growing on the banks. They were famous loafing places for mallards.

It was great fun to slip from bend to bend of the Slough, peering keenly, moving softly, trying to spy through the thick growth to a glimpse of the clear water. The ducks were very wary. It was necessary to know the exact location of each piece of open water, its surroundings, and how best it was to be approached. Only too often, peer as cautiously as we might, the wily old mallards would catch a glimpse of some slight motion. At once they would begin to swim back and forth uneasily. Always then we would withdraw cautiously, hoping against hope that suspicion would die. It never did. Our stalk would disclose to us only a troubled surface of water on which floated lightly a half dozen feathers.

But when things went right we had a beautiful shot. The ducks towered straight up, trying to get above the level of the brush, affording a shot at twenty-five or thirty yards' range. We always tried to avoid shooting at the same bird, but did not always succeed. Old Ben delighted in this work, for now he had a chance to plunge in after the fallen. As a matter of fact, it would have been quite useless to shoot ducks in these circumstances had we not possessed a good retriever like Old Ben.

The Slough proper was about two miles long, and had probably eight or ten "holes" in which ducks might be expected. The region of the Slough was, however, a different matter.

It was a fascinating stretch of country, partly marshy, partly dry, but all of it overgrown with tall and rustling tules. These reeds were sometimes so dense that one could not force his way through them; at others so low and thin that they barely made good quail cover. Almost everywhere a team could be driven; and yet there were soft places and water channels and pond holes in which a horse would bog down hopelessly. From a point on the main north-and-south ditch a man afoot left the bank to plunge directly into a jungle of reeds ten feet tall. Through them narrow passages led him winding and twisting and doubting in a labyrinth. He waded in knee-deep water, but confidently, for he knew the bottom to be solid beneath his feet. On either side, fairly touching his elbows, the reeds stood tall and dense, so that it seemed to him that he walked down a narrow and winding hallway. And every once in a while the hallway debouched into a secret shallow pond lying in the middle of the tule jungle in which might or might not be ducks. If there were ducks, it behooved him to shoot very, very quickly, for those that fell in the tules were probably not to be recovered. Then more narrow passages led to other ponds.

Always the footing was good, so that a man could strike forward confidently. But again there are other places in the Slough region where one has to walk for half a mile to pass a miserable little trickle only just too wide to step across. The watercress grows thick against either oozy bank, leaving a clear of only a foot. Yet it is bottomless.

The Captain knew this region thoroughly, and drove in it by landmarks of his own. After many visits I myself got to know the leading "points of interest" and how to get to them by a set route; but their relations one to another have always remained a little vague.

For instance, there was an earthen reservoir comprising two circular connecting ponds, elevated slightly above the surrounding flats, so that a man ascended an incline to stand on its banks. One half of this reservoir is bordered thickly by tules; but the other half is without growth. We left the Invigorator at some hundreds of yards distance; and, single file, followed the Captain. We stopped when he did, crawled when he did, watched to see what dry and rustling footing he avoided, every sense alert to play accurately this unique game of "follow my leader." He alone kept watch of the cover, the game, and the plan of attack. We were like the tail of a snake, merely following where the head directed. This was not because the Captain was so much more expert than ourselves, but so as to concentrate the chances of remaining undiscovered. If each of us had worked out his own stalk we should have multiplied the chances of alarming the game; we should have created the necessity for signals; and we should have had the greatest difficulty in synchronizing our arrival at the shooting point. We moved a step at a time, feeling circumspectly before resting our weight. At the last moment the Captain motioned with his hand. Wriggling forward, we came into line. Then, very cautiously, we crawled up the bank of the reservoir and peered over! That was the supreme moment! The wildfowl might arise in countless numbers; in which case we shot as carefully and as quickly as possible, reloading and squatting motionless in the almost certain hope of a long-range shot or so at a straggler as the main body swung back over us. Or, again, our eager eyes were quite likely to rest upon nothing but a family party of mud-hens gossiping sociably.

Stewart Edward White

Just beyond the reservoir on the other side was an overflowed small flat. It was simply hummocky solid ground with a little green grass and some water. Behind the hummocks, even after a cannonade at the reservoir, we were almost certain to jump two or three single spoonbills or teal. Why they stayed there, I could not tell you; but stay they did. We walked them up one at a time, as we would quail. The range was long. Sometimes we got them; and sometimes we did not.

From the reservoir we drove out into the illimitable tules. The horses went forward steadily, breasting the rustling growth. Behind them the Invigorator rocked and swayed like a small boat in a tide rip. We stayed in as best we could, our guns bristling up in all directions. The Captain drove from a knowledge of his own. After some time, across the yellow, waving expanse of the rushes, we made out a small dead willow stub slanted rakishly. At sight of this we came to a halt. Just beyond that stub lay a denser thicket of tules, and in the middle of them was known to be a patch of open water about twenty feet across. There was not much to it; but invariably a small bunch of fat old greenheads were loafing in the sun.

It now became, not a question of game, for it was always there, but a question of getting near enough to shoot. To be sure, the tiny pond was so well covered that a stranger to the country would actually be unaware of its existence until he broke through the last barrier of tules; but, by the same token, that cover was the noisiest cover invented for the protection of ducks. Often and often, when still sixty or seventy yards distant, we heard the derisive *quack, quack, quack*, with which a mallard always takes wing, and, a moment later, would see those wily birds rising above the horizon. A false step meant a crackle; a stumble meant a crash. We fairly wormed our way in by inches. Each yard gained was a triumph. When, finally, after a half hour of Indian work, we had managed to line up ready for the shot, we felt that we had really a few congratulations coming. We knew that within fifteen or twenty feet floated the wariest of feathered game; and *absolutely unconscious of our presence.*

"Now!" the Captain remarked, aloud, in conversational tones.

We stood up, guns at present. The Captain's command was answered by the instant beat of wings and the confused quicker calling of alarm. In the briefest fraction of a second the ducks appeared above the tules. They had to tower straight up, for the pond was too small and the reeds too high to permit of any sneaking away. So close were they that we could see the markings of every feather—the iridescence of the heads, the delicate, wave-marked cinnamons and grays and browns, even the absurd little curled plumes over the tails. The guns cracked merrily, the shooters aiming at the up-stretched necks. Down came the quarry with mighty splashes that threw the water high. The remnant of the flock swung away. We stood upright and laughed and joked and exulted after the long strain of our stalk. Ben plunged in again and again, bringing out the game.

Of these tule holes there were three. When we had visited them each in turn we swung back toward the west. There, after much driving, we came to the land of irrigation ditches again. At each new angle one of us would descend, sneak cautiously to the bank and, bending low, peer down the length of the ditch. If ducks were in sight, he located them carefully and then we made our sneak. If not, we drove on to the next bend. Once we all lay behind an embankment like a lot of soldiers behind a breastwork while one of us made a long detour around a big flock resting in an overflow across the ditch. The ruse was successful. The ducks, rising at sight of the scout, flew high directly over the ambuscade. A battery of six or eight guns thereupon opened up. I believe we killed three or four ducks among us; but if we had not brought down a feather we should have been satisfied with the fact that our stratagem succeeded.

So at the last, just as the sun was setting, we completed the circle and landed at the ranch. We had been out all day in the warm California sun and the breezes that blow from the great mountains across the plains; we had worked hard enough to deserve an appetite; we had in a dozen instances exercised our wit or our skill against the keen senses of wild game; we had used our ingenuity in meeting unexpected conditions; we had had a heap of companionship and good-natured fun one with another; we had seen a lot of country. This was much better than sitting solitary anchored in a blind. To be sure a man could kill more ducks from a blind; but what of that?

CHAPTER XIII

RANCH ACTIVITIES

Big as it was, the ranch was only a feeder for the open range. Way down in southeastern Arizona its cattle had their birth and grew to their half-wild maturity. They won their living where they could, fiercely from the fierce desert. On the broad plains they grazed during the fat season; and as the feed shortened and withered, they retired slowly to the barren mountains. In long lines they plodded to the watering places; and in long, patient lines they plodded their way back again, until deep and indelible troughs had been worn in the face of the earth. Other living creatures they saw few, save the coyotes that hung on their flanks, the jackrabbits, the prairie dogs, the birds strangely cheerful in the face of the mysterious and solemn desert. Once in a while a pair of mounted men jog-trotted slowly here and there among them. They gave way to right and left, swinging in the free trot of untamed creatures, their heads high, their eyes wild. Probably they remembered the terror and ignominy and temporary pain of the branding. The men examined them with critical eye, and commented technically and passed on.

This was when the animals were alive with the fat grasses. But as the drought lengthened, they pushed farther into the hills until the boldest or hardiest of them stood on the summits, and the weakest merely stared dully as the mounted men jingled by. The desert, kind in her bounty, was terrible in her wrath. She took her toll freely and the dried bones of her

Stewart Edward White

victims rattled in the wind. The fittest survived. Durham died, Hereford lived through, and turned up after the first rains wiry, lean, and active.

Then came the round-up. From the hidden defiles, the buttes and ranges, the hills and plains, the cowboys drew their net to the centre. Each "drive" brought together on some alkali flat thousands of the restless, milling, bawling cattle. The white dust rose in a cloud against the very blue sky. Then, while some of the cowboys sat their horses as sentinels, turning the herd back on itself, others threaded a way through the multitude, edging always toward the border of the herd some animal uneasy in the consciousness that it was being followed. Surrounding the main herd, and at some distance from it, other smaller herds rapidly formed from the "cut." Thus there was one composed entirely of cows and unbranded calves; another of strays from neighbouring ranges; and a third of the steers considered worthy of being made into beef cattle.

In due time the main herd was turned back on the range; the strays had been cut out and driven home by the cowboys of their several owners; the calves had been duly branded and sent out on the desert to grow up. But there remained still compact the beef herd. When all the excitement of the round-up had died, it showed as the tangible profit of the year.

Its troubles began. Driven to the railroad and into the corrals, it next had to be urged to its first experience of sidedoor Pullmans. There the powerful beasts went frantic. Pike poles urged them up the chute into the cars. They rushed, and hesitated, and stopped and turned back in a panic. At times it seemed impossible to get them started into the narrow chute. On the occasion of one after-dark loading old J.B., the foreman, discovered that the excited steers would charge a lantern light. Therefore he posted himself, with a lantern, in the middle of the chute. Promply the maddened animals rushed at him. He skipped nimbly one side, scaled the fence of the chute. "Now keep 'em coming, boys!" he urged.

The boys did their best, and half filled the car. Then some other impulse seized the bewildered rudimentary brains; the cattle balked. J.B. did it again, and yet again, until the cars were filled.

You have seen the cattle trains, rumbling slowly along, the crowded animals staring stupidly through the bars. They are not having a particularly hard time, considering the fact that they are undergoing their first experience in travelling. Nowadays they are not allowed to become thirsty; and they are too car sick to care about eating. Car sick? Certainly; just as you or I are car sick, no worse; only we do not need to travel unless we want to. At the end of the journey, often, they are too wobbly to stand up. This is not weakness, but dizziness from the unwonted motion. Once a fool S.P.C.A. officer ordered a number of the Captain's steers shot on the ground that they were too weak to live. That greenhorn got into fifty-seven varieties of trouble.

Arrived at their journey's end the steers were permitted to get their sea legs off; and then were driven slowly to a cattle paradise—the ranch.

For there was flowing water always near to the thirsty nose; and rich grazing; and wonderful wagons from which the fodder was thrown abundantly; and pleasant shade from a mild and beneficent sun. The thin, wiry beasts of the desert lost their angles; they became fat, and curly of hair, and sleek of coat, and much inclined to kink up their tails and cavort off in clumsy buck jumps just from the sheer joy of living. For now they were, in good truth, beef cattle, the aristocracy of fifty thousand, the pick of wide ranges, the total tangible wealth of a great principality. To see them would come red-faced men with broad hats and linen dusters; and their transfer meant dollars and dollars.

I have told you these things lest you might have concluded that the Captain did nothing but shoot ducks and quail and ride the polo ponies around the enclosure. As a matter of fact, the

Captain was always going to Arizona, or coming back, or riding here or driving there. When we went to the ranch, he looked upon our visit as a vacation, but even then he could not shoot with us as often as we all would have liked. On the Arizona range were the [JH] ranch, and the Circle I, and the Bar O, and the Double R, and the Box Springs, and others whose picturesque names I have forgotten. To manage them were cowpunchers; and appertaining thereunto were Chinese cooks, and horses, and pump mules, and grub lists, and many other things. The ranch itself was even more complicated an affair; for, as I have indicated, it meant many activities besides cattle. And then there was the buying and selling and shipping. The Captain was a busy man.

And the ranch was a busy place. Its population swung through the nations. Always the aristocracy was the cowboy. There were not many of him, for the cattle here were fenced and fattened; but a few were necessary to ride abroad in order that none of the precious beef be mired down or tangled in barbed wire; and that all of it be moved hither and yon as the pasture varied. And of course the driving, the loading and unloading of fresh shipments in and out demanded expert handling.

Some of them came from the desert, lean, bronzed, steady-eyed men addicted to "double-barrelled" (two cinch) saddles, ox-bow stirrups, straight-shanked spurs, tall-crowned hats, and grass ropes. They were plain "cowpunchers." Between them and the California "vaqueros," or "buckeroos", was always much slow and drawling argument. For the latter had been "raised different" in about every particular. They used the single-cinch saddle; long *tapaderos*; or stirrup hoods; curve-shanked spurs with jingling chains; low, wide-brimmed sombreros and rawhide ropes. And you who have gauged the earnestness of what might be called "equipment arguments" among those of a gentler calling, can well appreciate that never did bunk-house conversation lack.

Next to these cow riders and horse riders came probably the mule drivers. There were many teams of mules, and they were used for many things: such as plowing, cultivating, harvesting, haying, the building of irrigation checks and ditches, freighting, and the like. A team comprised from six to twelve individuals. The man in charge had to know mules—which is no slight degree of special wisdom; had to know loads; had to understand conditioning. His lantern was the first to twinkle in the morning as he doled out corn to his charges.

Then came the ruck of field hands of all types. The average field hand in California is a cross between a hobo and a labourer. He works probably about half the year. The other half he spends on the road, tramping it from place to place. Like the common hobo, he begs his way when he can; catches freight train rides; consorts in thickets with his kind. Unlike the common hobo, however, he generally has money in his pocket and always carries a bed-roll. The latter consists of a blanket or so, or quilt, and a canvas strapped around the whole. You can see him at any time plodding along the highways and railroads, the roll slung across his back. He much appreciates a lift in your rig; and sometimes proves worth the trouble. His labour raises him above the level degradation of the ordinary tramp; the independence of his spirit gives his point of view an originality; the nomadic stirring of his blood keeps him going. In the course of years he has crossed the length and breadth of the state a half dozen times. He has harvested apples in Siskiyou and oranges in Riverside; he has chopped sugar pine in the snows of the Sierras and manzanita on the blazing hillsides of San Bernardino; he has garnered the wheat of the great Santa Clara Valley and the alfalfa of San Fernando. And whenever the need for change or the desire for a drink has struck him, he has drawn his pay, strapped his bed roll, and cheerfully hiked away down the long and dusty trail.

That is his chief defect as a field hand—his unreliability. He seems to have no great pride in finishing out a job, although he is a good worker while he is at it. The Captain used to send in the wagon to bring men out, but refused absolutely to let any man ride in anything going the other way. Nevertheless the hand, when the wanderlust hit him, trudged cheerfully the long distance to town. I am not sure that a new type is not thus developing, a type as distinct in its way as the riverman or the cowboy. It is not as high a type, of course, for it has not the strength either of sustained and earnest purpose nor of class loyalty; but still it makes for new species. The California field hand has mother-wit, independence, a certain reckless, you-be-damned courage, a wandering instinct. He quits work not because he wants to loaf, but because he wants to go somewhere else. He is always on the road travelling, travelling, travelling. It is not hope of gain that takes him, for in the scarcity of labour wages are as high here as there. It is not desire for dissipation that lures him from labour; he drinks hard enough, but the liquor is as potent here as two hundred miles away. He looks you steadily enough in the eye; and he begs his bread and commits his depredations half humorously, as though all this were fooling that both you and he understood. What his impelling motive is, I cannot say; nor whether he himself understands it, this restlessness that turns his feet ever to the pleasant California highways, an Ishmael of the road.

But this very unreliability forces the ranchman to the next element in our consideration of the ranch's people—the Orientals. They are good workers, these little brown and yellow men, and unobtrusive and skilled. They do not quit until the job is done; they live frugally; they are efficient. The only thing we have against them is that we are afraid of them. They crowd our people out. Into a community they edge themselves little by little. At the end of two years they have saved enough capital to begin to buy land. At the end of ten years they have taken up all the small farms from the whites who cannot or will not live in competition with Oriental frugality. The valley, or cove, or flat has become Japanese. They do not amalgamate. Their progeny are Japanese unchanged; and their progeny born here are American citizens. In the face of public sentiment, restriction, savage resentment they have made head. They are continuing to make head. The effects are as yet small in relation to the whole of the body politic; but more and more of the fertile, beautiful little farm centres of California are becoming the breeding grounds of Japanese colonies. As the pressure of population on the other side increases, it is not difficult to foresee a result. We are afraid of them.

The ranchmen know this. "We would use white labour," say they, "if we could get it, and rely on it. But we cannot; and we *must* have labour!" The debt of California to the Orientals can hardly be computed. The citrus crop is almost entirely moved by them; and all other produce depends so largely on them that it would hardly be an exaggeration to say that without them a large part of the state's produce would rot in fields. We do not want the Oriental; and yet we must have him, must have more of him if we are to reach our fullest development. It is a dilemma; a paradox.

And yet, it seems to me, the paradox only exists because we will not face facts in a commonsense manner. As I remember it, the original anti-Oriental howl out here made much of the fact that the Chinaman and Japanese saved his money and took it home with him. In the peculiar circumstances we should not object to that. We cannot get our work done by our own people; we are forced to hire in outsiders to do it; we should expect, as a country, to pay a fair price for what we get. It is undoubtedly more desirable to get our work done at home; but if we cannot find the help, what more reasonable than that we should get it outside, and pay for it? If we insist that the Oriental is a detriment as a permanent resident, and if at the same time we need his labour, what else is there to do but pay him and let him go when he has done his job?

And he will go *if pay is all he gets*. Only when he is permitted to settle down to his favourite agriculture in a fertile country does he stay permanently. To be sure a certain number of him engages in various other commercial callings, but that number bears always a very definite proportion to the Oriental population in general. And it is harmless. It is not absolute restriction of immigration we want—although I believe immigration should be numerically restricted, but absolute prohibition of the right to hold real estate. To many minds this may seem a denial of the "equal rights of man." I doubt whether in some respects men have equal rights. Certainly Brown has not an equal right with Jones to spank Jones's small boy; nor do I believe the rights of any foreign nation paramount to our own right to safeguard ourselves by proper legislation.

These economics have taken us a long distance from the ranch and its Orientals. The Japanese contingent were mainly occupied with the fruit, possessing a peculiar deftness in pruning and caring for the prunes and apricots. The Chinese had to do with irrigation and with the vegetables. Their broad, woven-straw hats and light denim clothes lent the particular landscape they happened for the moment to adorn a peculiarly foreign and picturesque air.

And outside of these were various special callings represented by one or two men: such as the stable men, the bee keeper, the blacksmith and wagon-wright, the various cooks and cookees, the gardeners, the "varmint catcher," and the like.

Nor must be forgotten the animals, both wild and tame. Old Ben and Young Ben and Linn, the bird dogs; the dachshunds; the mongrels of the men's quarters; all the domestic fowls; the innumerable and blue-blooded hogs; the polo ponies and brood mares, the stud horses and driving horses and cow horses, colts, yearlings, the young and those enjoying a peaceful and honourable old age; Pollymckittrick; Redmond's cat and fifty others, half-wild creatures; vireos and orioles in the trees around the house; thousands and thousands of blackbirds rising in huge swarms like gnats; full-voiced meadowlarks on the fence posts; herons stalking solemnly, or waiting like so many Japanese bronzes for a chance at a gopher; red-tailed hawks circling slowly; pigeon hawks passing with their falcon dart; little gaudy sparrow hawks on top the telephone poles; buzzards, stately and wonderful in flight, repulsive when at rest; barn-owls dwelling in the haystacks, and horned owls in the hollow trees; the game in countless numbers; all the smaller animals and tiny birds in species too numerous to catalogue, all these drew their full sustenance of life from the ranch's smiling abundance.

And the mules; I must not forget them. I have the greatest respect for a mule. He knows more than the horse; just as the goose or the duck knows more than the chicken. Six days the mules on the ranch laboured; but on the seventh they were turned out into the pastures to rest and roll and stand around gossiping sociably, rubbing their long, ridiculous Roman noses together, or switching the flies off one another with their tasselled tails. Each evening at sunset all the various teams came in from different directions, converging at the lane, and plodding dustily up its length to the sheds and their night's rest. Five evenings thus they come in silence. But on the sixth each and every mule lifted up his voice in rejoicing over the morrow. The distant wayfarer—familiar with ranch ways—hearing this strident, discordant, thankful chorus far across the evening peace of the wide country, would thus have known this was Saturday night, and that to-morrow was the Sabbath, the day of rest!

Stewart Edward White

CHAPTER XIV

THE HEATHEN

This must be mainly discursive and anecdotal, for no one really knows much more than externals concerning the Chinese. Some men there are, generally reporters on the big dailies, who have been admitted to the tongs; who can take you into the exclusive Chinese clubs; who are everywhere in Chinatown greeted cordially, treated gratis to strange food and drink, and patted on the back with every appearance of affection. They can tell you of all sorts of queer, unknown customs and facts, and can show you all sorts of strange and unusual things. Yet at the last analysis these are also discursions and anecdotes. We gather empirical knowledge: only rarely do we think we get a glimpse of how the delicate machinery moves behind those twinkling eyes.

I am led to these remarks by the contemplation of Chinese Charley at the ranch. He has been with Mrs. Kitty twenty-five years; he wears American clothes; he speaks English with hardly a trace of either accent or idiom; he has long since dropped the deceiving Oriental stolidity and weeps out his violent Chinese rages unashamed. Yet even now Mrs. Kitty's summing up is that Charley is a "queer old thing."

If you start out with a good Chinaman, you will always have good Chinamen; if you draw a poor one, you will probably be cursed with a succession of mediocrities. They pass you along from one to another of the same "family"; and, short of the adoption of false whiskers and a change of name, you can find no expedient to break the charm. When one leaves of his own accord, he sends you another boy to take his place. When he is discharged, he does identically that, although you may not know it. Down through the list of Gins or Sings or Ungs you slide comfortably or bump disagreeably according to your good fortune or deserts.

Another feature to which you must become accustomed is that of the Unexpected Departure. Everything is going smoothly, and you are engaged in congratulating yourself. To you appears Ah Sing.

"I go San Flancisco two o'clock tlain," he remarks. And he does.

In vain do you point to the inconvenience of guests, the injustice thus of leaving you in the lurch; in vain do you threaten detention of wages due unless he gives you what your servant experience has taught you is a customary "week's warning." He repeats his remark: and goes. At two-fifteen another bland and smiling heathen appears at your door. He may or may not tell you that Ah Sing sent him. Dinner is ready on time. The household work goes on without a hitch or a tiniest jar.

"Ah Sing say you pay me his money," announces this new heathen.

If you are wise, you abandon your thoughts of fighting the outrage. You pay over Ah Sing's arrears.

"By the way," you inquire of your new retainer, "what's your name?"

"My name Lum Sing," the newcomer replies.

That is about the way such changes happen. If by chance you are in the good graces of heathendom, you will be given an involved and fancy reason for the departure. These generally have to do with the mysterious movements of relatives.

"My second-uncle, he come on ship to San Flancisco. I got to show him what to do," explains Ah Sing.

If they like you very much, they tell you they will come back at the end of a month. They never do, and by the end of the month the new man has so endeared himself to you that Ah Sing is only a pleasant memory.

The reasons for these sudden departures are two-fold as near as I can make out. Ah Sing may not entirely like the place; or he may have received orders from his tong to move on—probably the latter. If both Ah Sing and his tong approve of you and the situation, he will stay with you for many years. Our present man once remained but two days at a place. The situation is an easy one; Toy did his work well; the relations were absolutely friendly. After we had become intimate with Toy, he confided to us his reasons:

"I don' like stay at place where nobody laugh," said he.

As servants the Chinese are inconceivably quick, deft, and clean. One good man will do the work of two white servants, and do it better. Toy takes care of us absolutely. He cooks, serves, does the housework, and with it all manages to get off the latter part of the afternoon and nearly every evening. At first, with recollections of the rigidly defined "days off" of the East, I was a little inclined to look into this. I did look into it; but when I found all the work done, without skimping, I concluded that if the man were clever enough to save his time, he had certainly earned it for himself. Systematizing and no false moves proved to be his method.

Since this is so, it follows, quite logically and justly, that the Chinese servant resents the minute and detailed supervision some housewives delight in. Show him what you want done; let him do it; criticize the result—but do not stand around and make suggestions and offer amendments. Some housekeepers, trained to make of housekeeping an end rather than a means, can never keep Chinese. This does not mean that you must let them go at their own sweet will: only that you must try as far as possible to do your criticizing and suggesting before or after the actual performance.

I remember once Billy came home from some afternoon tea where she had been talking to a number of "conscientious" housekeepers of the old school until she had been stricken with a guilty feeling that she had been loafing on the job. To be sure the meals were good, and on time; the house was clean; the beds were made; and the comforts of life seemed to be always neatly on hand; but what of that? The fact remained that Billy had time to go horseback riding, to go swimming, to see her friends, and to shoot at a mark. Every other housekeeper was busy from morning until night; and then complained that somehow or other she never could get finished up! It was evident that somehow Billy was not doing her full duty by the sphere to which woman was called, etc.

So home she came, resolved to do better. Toy was placidly finishing up for the afternoon. Billy followed him around for a while, being a housekeeper. Toy watched her with round, astonished eyes. Finally he turned on her with vast indignation.

"Look here, Mis' White," said he. "What a matter with you? You talk just like one old woman!"

Billy paused in her mad career and considered. That was just what she was talking like. She laughed. Toy laughed. Billy went shooting.

After your Chinaman becomes well acquainted with you, he develops human traits that are astonishing only in contrast to his former mask of absolute stolidity. To the stranger the Oriental is as impassive and inscrutable as a stone Buddha, so that at last we come to read his attitude into his inner life, and to conclude him without emotion. This is also largely true of the Indian. As a matter of fact, your heathen is rather vividly alive inside. His enjoyment is keen, his curiosity lively, his emotions near the surface. If you have or expect to have visitors, you must tell Ah Sing all about them—their station in life, their importance, and the like. He will listen, keenly interested, gravely nodding his pig-tailed, shaven head. Then, if your visitors are from the East, you inform them of what every Californian knows—that each and every member of a household must say "good morning" ceremoniously to Ah Sing. And Ah Sing will smile blandly and duck his pig-tailed, shaven head, and wish each member "good morning" back again. It is sometimes very funny to hear the matin chorus of a dozen people crying out their volley of salute to ceremony; and to hear again the Chinaman's conscientious reply to each in turn down the long table—"*Good* mo'ning, Mr. White; *good* mo'ning, Mis' White; *good* mo'ning, Mr. Lewis—" and so on, until each has been remembered. There are some families that, either from ignorance or pride, omit this and kindred little human ceremonials. The omission is accepted; but that family is never "my family" to the servant within its gates.

For your Chinaman is absolutely faithful and loyal and trustworthy. He can be allowed to handle any amount of money for you. We ourselves are away from home a great deal. When we get ready to go, we simply pack our trunks and depart. Toy then puts away the silver and valuables and places them in the bank vaults, closes the house, and puts all in order. A week or so before our return we write him. Thereupon he cleans things up, reclaims the valuables, rearranges everything. His wonderful Chinese memory enables him to replace every smallest item exactly as it was. If I happen to have left seven cents and an empty .38 cartridge on the southwestern corner of the bureau, there they will be. It is difficult to believe that affairs have been at all disturbed. Yet probably, if our stay away has been of any length, everything in the house has been moved or laid away.

Furthermore, Toy reads and writes English, and enjoys greatly sending us wonderful and involved reports. One of them ended as follows: "The weather is doing nicely, the place is safely well, and the dogs are happy all the while." It brings to mind a peculiarly cheerful picture.

One of the familiar and persistent beliefs as to Chinese traits is that they are a race of automatons. "Tell your Chinaman exactly what you want done, and how you want it done," say your advisors, "for you will never be able to change them once they get started." And then they will adduce a great many amusing and true incidents to illustrate the point.

The facts of the case are undoubted, but the conclusions as to the invariability of the Chinese mind are, in my opinion, somewhat exaggerated.

It must be remembered that almost all Chinese customs and manners of thought are the direct inverse of our own. When announcing or receiving a piece of bad news, for example, it is with them considered polite to laugh; while intense enjoyment is apt to be expressed by tears. The antithesis can be extended almost indefinitely by the student of Oriental manners. Contemplate, now, the condition of the young Chinese but recently arrived. He is engaged by some family to do its housework; and, as he is well paid and conscientious, he desires to do his best. But in this he is not permitted to follow his education. Each, move he makes in initiative is stopped and corrected. To his mind there seems no earthly sense or logic in nine tenths of what we want; but he is willing to do his best.

"Oh, well," says he to himself, "these people do things crazily; and no well-regulated Chinese mind could possibly either anticipate how they desire things done, or figure out why they want them that way. I give it up! I'll just follow things out exactly as I am told"—and he does so!

This condition of affairs used to be more common than it is now. Under the present exclusion law no fresh immigration is supposed to be possible. Most of the Chinese servants are old timers, who have learned white people's ways, and—what is more important—understand them. They are quite capable of initiative; and much more intelligent than the average white servant.

But a green Chinaman is certainly funny. He does things forever-after just as you show him the first time; and a cataclysm of nature is required to shake his purpose. Back in the middle 'eighties my father, moving into a new house, dumped the ashes beside the kitchen steps pending the completion of a suitable ash bin. When the latter had been built, he had Gin Gwee move the ashes from the kitchen steps to the bin. This happened to be of a Friday. Ever after Gin Gwee deposited the ashes by the kitchen steps every day; and on Friday solemnly transferred them to the ash bin! Nor could anything persuade him to desist.

Again he was given pail, soap, and brush, shown the front steps and walk leading to the gate, and set to work. Gin Gwee disappeared. When we went to hunt him up, we found him half way down the block, still scrubbing away. I was in favour of letting him alone to see how far he would go, but mother had other ideas as to his activities.

These stories could be multiplied indefinitely; and are detailed by the dozen as proof of the "stupidity" of the Chinese. The Chinese are anything but stupid; and, as I have said before, when once they have grasped the logic of the situation, can figure out a case with the best of them.

They are, however, great sticklers for formalism; and disapprove of any short cuts in ceremony. As soon leave with the silver as without waiting for the finger bowls. A friend of mine, training a new man by example, as new men of this nationality are always trained, was showing him how to receive a caller. Therefore she rang her own doorbell, presented a card; in short, went through the whole performance. Tom understood perfectly. That same afternoon Mrs. G—, a next-door neighbour and intimate friend, ran over for a chat. She rang the bell. Tom appeared.

"Is Mrs. B— at home?" inquired the friend.

Tom planted himself square in the doorway. He surveyed her with a cold and glittering eye.

"You got ticket?" he demanded. "You no got ticket, you no come in!"

On another occasion two ladies came to call on Mrs. B— but by mistake blundered to the kitchen door. Mrs. B—'s house is a bungalow and on a corner. Tom appeared.

"Is Mrs. B— at home?" they asked.

"This kitchen door; you go front door," requested Tom, politely.

The callers walked around the house to the proper door, rang, and waited. After a suitable interval Tom appeared again.

"Is Mrs. B— at home?" repeated the visitors.

"No, Mrs. B— she gone out," Tom informed them. The proper ceremonials had been fulfilled.

To one who appreciates what he can do, and how well he does it; who can value absolute faithfulness and honesty; who confesses a sneaking fondness for the picturesque as nobly exemplified in a clean and starched or brocaded heathen; who understands how to balance the difficult poise, supervision, and interference, the Chinese servant is the best on the continent. But to one who enjoys supervising every step or who likes well-trained ceremony, "good form" in minutiae, and the deference of our kind of good training the heathen is likely to prove disappointing. When you ring your friend's door-bell, you are quite apt to be greeted by a cheerful and smiling "hullo!" I think most Californians rather like the entirely respectful but freshly unconventional relationship that exists between the master and his Chinese servant. I do.[H]

CHAPTER XV

THE LAST HUNT

Of all ranch visits the last day neared. Always we forgot it until the latest possible moment; for we did not like to think of it. Then, when the realization could be no longer denied, we planned a grand day just to finish up on. The telephone's tiny, thin voice returned acceptances from distant neighbours; so bright and early we waited at the cross-roads rendezvous.

And from the four directions they came, jogging along in carts or spring-wagons, swaying swiftly in automobiles whose brass flashed back the early sun. As each vehicle drew up, the greetings flew, charged electrically with the dry, chaffing humour of the out of doors. When we finally climbed the fence into the old cornfield we were almost a dozen. There were the Captain, Uncle Jim, and myself from the ranch; and T and his three sons and two guests from Stockdale ranch; the sporting parson of the entire neighbourhood, and Dodge and his three beautiful dogs.

Spread out in a rough line we tramped away through the dried and straggling ranks of the Egyptian corn. Quail buzzed all around us like angry hornets. We did not fire a shot. Each had his limit of twenty-five still before him, and each wanted to have all the fun he could out of getting them. Shooting quail in Egyptian corn is, comparatively speaking, not much fun. We joked each other, and whistled and sang, and trudged manfully along, gun over shoulder. The pale sun was

Stewart Edward White

strengthening; the mountains were turning darker as they threw aside the filmy rose of early day; in treetops a row of buzzards sat, their wings outspread like the heraldic devices of a foreign nation. Thousands of doves whistled away; thousands of smaller birds rustled and darted before our advancing lines; tens of thousands of blackbirds sprinkled the bare branches of single trees, uttering the many-throated multitude call; underneath all this light and joyous life the business-like little quail darted away in their bullet flight.

Always they bore across our front to the left; for on that side, paralleling our course, ran a long ravine or "dry slough." It was about ten feet deep on the average, probably thirty feet wide, and was densely grown with a tangle of willows, berry vines, creepers, wild grape, and the like. Into this the quail pitched.

By the time we had covered the mile length of that cornfield we had dumped an unguessable number of quail into that slough.

Then we walked back the entire distance—still with our guns over our shoulders—but this time along the edge of the ravine. We shouted and threw clods, and kicked on the trees, and rattled things, urging the hidden quail once more to flight. The thicket seemed alive with them. We caught glimpses as they ran before us, pacing away at a great rate, their feathers sleek and trim; they buzzed away at bewildering pitches and angles; they sprang into the tops of bushes, cocking their head plumes forward. Their various clicking undercalls, chatterings, and chirrings filled the thicket as full of sound as of motion. And in the middle distance before and behind us they mocked us with their calls.

"You *can't* shoot! You *can't* shoot!"

Some of them flew ever ahead, some of them doubled-back and dropped into the slough behind us; but a proportion broke through the thicket and settled in the wide fields on the other side. After them we went, and for the first time opened our guns and slipped the yellow shells into the barrels.

For this field on the other side was the wide, open plain; and it was grown over by tiny, half-knee high thickets of tumbleweed with here and there a trifle of sagebrush. Between these miniature thickets wound narrow strips of sandy soil, like streams and bays and estuaries in shape. We knew that the quail would lie well here, for they hate to cross bare openings.

Therefore, we threw out our skirmish line, and the real advance in force began.

Every man retrieved his own birds, a matter of some difficulty in the tumbleweed. While one was searching, the rest would get ahead of him. The line became disorganized, broke into groups, finally disintegrated entirely. Each man hunted for himself, circling the tumbleweed patches, combing carefully their edges for the quail that sometimes burst into the air fairly at his feet. When he had killed one, he walked directly to the spot. On the way he would flush two or three more. They were tempting; but we were old hands at the sport, and we knew only too well that if we yielded so far as to shoot a second before we had picked up the first, the probabilities were strong that the first would never be found. In this respect such shooting requires good judgment. It is generally useless to try to shoot a double, even though a dozen easy shots are in the air at once; and yet, occasionally, on a day when Koos-ey-oonek is busy elsewhere, it may happen that the birds flush across a wide, bare space. It is well to keep a weather eye open for such chances.

With a green crowd and in different cover such shooting might have been dangerous; but with an abundance of birds, in this wide, open prairie, cool heads knew enough to keep wide apart and to look before they shot. The fun grew fast and furious; and the guns popped away like firecrackers. In fact, the fun grew a little too fast and furious to suit Dodge.

Dodge had beautiful and well-trained dogs. Ordinarily any one

Stewart Edward White

of us would have esteemed it a high privilege to shoot over them. In fact, I have often declared myself to the effect that of the three elements of pleasure comprehended in field shooting that of working the dogs was the chief. Just as it is better to catch one yellowtail on a nine-ounce rod than twenty on a hand line, so it is better to kill one quail over a well-trained dog than a half dozen "Walking 'em up." But this particular case was different. We were out for a high old time; and part of a high old time was a wild and reckless disregard of inhibitive sporting conventions. The birds were here literally in thousands. Not a third had left the slough for this open country; we could not shoot at a tenth of those flushed, yet the guns were popping continuously. Everybody was shooting and laughing and running about. The game was to pelt away, retrieve your bird as quickly as you could, and pelt away again. The dogs, working up to their points carefully and stylishly, as good dogs should, were being constantly left in the rear. They drew down to their points—and behold nobody but their devoted master would pay any attention to their bird! Everybody else was engaged busily in popping away at any one of the dozen-odd other birds to be had for the selection!

Poor Dodge, being somewhat biased by the accident of ownership, looked on us as a lot of barbarians—as, for the time being, we were; nice, happy barbarians having a good time. He worked his dogs conscientiously, and muttered in his beard. The climax came when, in the joyous excitement of the occasion, someone threw out a chance remark on "those — dogs" being in the way. Then Dodge withdrew with dignity. Having a fellow-feeling as a dog-handler I went over to console him. He was inconsolable; and so remained until after lunch.

In this manner we made our way slowly down the length of the slough, and then slowly back again. Of the birds originally flushed from the Egyptian corn into the thicket but a small proportion had left that thicket for the open country of the tumbleweed and sage; and of the latter we had been able to shoot at a very, very small percentage. Nevertheless, when we emptied our pockets, we found that each had made his bag.

We counted them out, throwing them into one pile.

"Twenty-four," counted the Captain.

"Twenty-four," Tom enumerated.

"Twenty-four," Uncle Jim followed him.

We each had twenty-four. And then it developed that every man had saved just one bird of his limit until after lunch. No one wanted to be left out of *all* the shooting while the rest filled their bags; and no one had believed that anybody but himself had come so close to the limit.

So we laughed, and shouldered our guns, and trudged across country to the clump of cottonwood where already the girls had spread lunch.

That was a good lunch. We sat under shady trees, and the sunlit plains stretched away and away to distant calm mountains. Near at hand the sparse gray sagebrush reared its bonneted heads; far away it blurred into a monochrome where the plains lifted and flowed molten into the canons and crevices of the foothills. Numberless crows, blackbirds, and wildfowl crossed and recrossed the very blue sky. A gray jackrabbit, thinking himself concealed by a very creditable imitation of a *sacatone* hummock, sat motionless not seventy yards away.

After lunch we moved out leisurely to get our one bird apiece. Some of the girls followed us. We were now epicures of shooting, and each let many birds pass before deciding to fire. Some waited for cross shots, some for very easy shots, some for the most difficult shots possible. Each suited his fancy.

"I'm all in," remarked each, as he pocketed his bird; and followed to see the others finish.

*   *   *   *   *

Stewart Edward White

Next day, our baggage piled in most anywhere, our farewells all said, we bowled away toward town in the brand-new machine. Redmond sat in the front seat with the chauffeur. It was his first experience in an automobile, and he sat very rigidly upright, eyes front, his moustaches bristling.

Now at a certain point on the road lived a large black dog—just plain ranch dog—who was accustomed to come bounding out to the road to run alongside and bark for an appropriate interval. This was an unvarying ceremony. He was a large and prancing dog; and, I suppose from his appearance, must have been named Carlo. In the course of our many visits to the ranch we grew quite fond of the dog, and always looked as hard for him to come out as he did for us to come along.

This day also the dog came forth; but now he had no steady-trotting ranch team to greet. The road was smooth and straight, and the car was hitting thirty-five miles an hour. The dog bounded confidently down the front walk, leaping playfully in the air, opened his mouth to bark—and, behold! the vehicle was not within range any more, but thirty yards away and rapidly departing. So Carlo shut his mouth and got down to business. For three hundred yards he managed to keep pace alongside; but the effort required all his forces; not once did he manage to gather wind for even a single bark.

Redmond in the front seat sat straighter than ever. From his lordly elevation he waved a lordly hand at the poor dog.

"Useless! Useless!" said he, loftily.

And looking back at the dog seated panting in a rapidly disappearing distance, we saw that he also knew that the Old Order had changed.

FOOTNOTES

Footnote A: Oiler = Greaser = Mexican.

Footnote B: Saddle pockets that fit on the pommel.

Footnote C: 3,350, to be exact. We later measured it.

Footnote D: 3,350 feet—later measurement.

Footnote E: 355 paces.

Footnote F: Somewhere between 500 and 700 yards. I am very practised at pacing and guessing such distances.

Footnote G: Ten years later sentence of death was passed and carried out after they had killed *one wheelbarrow* load of broilers!

Footnote H: This chapter was written in the—alas—vanished past!

Choose from Thousands of 1stWorldLibrary Classics By

A. M. Barnard
Ada Leverson
Adolphus William Ward
Aesop
Agatha Christie
Alexander Aaronsohn
Alexander Kielland
Alexandre Dumas
Alfred Gatty
Alfred Ollivant
Alice Duer Miller
Alice Turner Curtis
Alice Dunbar
Allen Chapman
Alleyne Ireland
Ambrose Bierce
Amelia E. Barr
Amory H. Bradford
Andrew Lang
Andrew McFarland Davis
Andy Adams
Angela Brazil
Anna Alice Chapin
Anna Sewell
Annie Besant
Annie Hamilton Donnell
Annie Payson Call
Annie Roe Carr
Annonaymous
Anton Chekhov
Archibald Lee Fletcher
Arnold Bennett
Arthur C. Benson
Arthur Conan Doyle
Arthur M. Winfield
Arthur Ransome
Arthur Schnitzler
Arthur Train
Atticus
B.H. Baden-Powell
B. M. Bower
B. C. Chatterjee
Baroness Emmuska Orczy
Baroness Orczy
Basil King
Bayard Taylor
Ben Macomber
Bertha Muzzy Bower
Bjornstjerne Bjornson

Booth Tarkington
Boyd Cable
Bram Stoker
C. Collodi
C. E. Orr
C. M. Ingleby
Carolyn Wells
Catherine Parr Traill
Charles A. Eastman
Charles Amory Beach
Charles Dickens
Charles Dudley Warner
Charles Farrar Browne
Charles Ives
Charles Kingsley
Charles Klein
Charles Hanson Towne
Charles Lathrop Pack
Charles Romyn Dake
Charles Whibley
Charles Willing Beale
Charlotte M. Braeme
Charlotte M. Yonge
Charlotte Perkins Stetson
Clair W. Hayes
Clarence Day Jr.
Clarence E. Mulford
Clemence Housman
Confucius
Coningsby Dawson
Cornelis DeWitt Wilcox
Cyril Burleigh
D. H. Lawrence
Daniel Defoe
David Garnett
Dinah Craik
Don Carlos Janes
Donald Keyhoe
Dorothy Kilner
Dougan Clark
Douglas Fairbanks
E. Nesbit
E. P. Roe
E. Phillips Oppenheim
E. S. Brooks
Earl Barnes
Edgar Rice Burroughs
Edith Van Dyne
Edith Wharton

Edward Everett Hale
Edward J. O'Biren
Edward S. Ellis
Edwin L. Arnold
Eleanor Atkins
Eleanor Hallowell Abbott
Eliot Gregory
Elizabeth Gaskell
Elizabeth McCracken
Elizabeth Von Arnim
Ellem Key
Emerson Hough
Emilie F. Carlen
Emily Bronte
Emily Dickinson
Enid Bagnold
Enilor Macartney Lane
Erasmus W. Jones
Ernie Howard Pie
Ethel May Dell
Ethel Turner
Ethel Watts Mumford
Eugene Sue
Eugenie Foa
Eugene Wood
Eustace Hale Ball
Evelyn Everett-green
Everard Cotes
F. H. Cheley
F. J. Cross
F. Marion Crawford
Fannie E. Newberry
Federick Austin Ogg
Ferdinand Ossendowski
Fergus Hume
Florence A. Kilpatrick
Fremont B. Deering
Francis Bacon
Francis Darwin
Frances Hodgson Burnett
Frances Parkinson Keyes
Frank Gee Patchin
Frank Harris
Frank Jewett Mather
Frank L. Packard
Frank V. Webster
Frederic Stewart Isham
Frederick Trevor Hill
Frederick Winslow Taylor

Friedrich Kerst
Friedrich Nietzsche
Fyodor Dostoyevsky
G.A. Henty
G.K. Chesterton
Gabrielle E. Jackson
Garrett P. Serviss
Gaston Leroux
George A. Warren
George Ade
Geroge Bernard Shaw
George Cary Eggleston
George Durston
George Ebers
George Eliot
George Gissing
George MacDonald
George Meredith
George Orwell
George Sylvester Viereck
George Tucker
George W. Cable
George Wharton James
Gertrude Atherton
Gordon Casserly
Grace E. King
Grace Gallatin
Grace Greenwood
Grant Allen
Guillermo A. Sherwell
Gulielma Zollinger
Gustav Flaubert
H. A. Cody
H. B. Irving
H.C. Bailey
H. G. Wells
H. H. Munro
H. Irving Hancock
H. R. Naylor
H. Rider Haggard
H. W. C. Davis
Haldeman Julius
Hall Caine
Hamilton Wright Mabie
Hans Christian Andersen
Harold Avery
Harold McGrath
Harriet Beecher Stowe
Harry Castlemon
Harry Coghill
Harry Houidini

Hayden Carruth
Helent Hunt Jackson
Helen Nicolay
Hendrik Conscience
Hendy David Thoreau
Henri Barbusse
Henrik Ibsen
Henry Adams
Henry Ford
Henry Frost
Henry James
Henry Jones Ford
Henry Seton Merriman
Henry W Longfellow
Herbert A. Giles
Herbert Carter
Herbert N. Casson
Herman Hesse
Hildegard G. Frey
Homer
Honore De Balzac
Horace B. Day
Horace Walpole
Horatio Alger Jr.
Howard Pyle
Howard R. Garis
Hugh Lofting
Hugh Walpole
Humphry Ward
Ian Maclaren
Inez Haynes Gillmore
Irving Bacheller
Isabel Cecilia Williams
Isabel Hornibrook
Israel Abrahams
Ivan Turgenev
J.G.Austin
J. Henri Fabre
J. M. Barrie
J. M. Walsh
J. Macdonald Oxley
J. R. Miller
J. S. Fletcher
J. S. Knowles
J. Storer Clouston
J. W. Duffield
Jack London
Jacob Abbott
James Allen
James Andrews
James Baldwin

James Branch Cabell
James DeMille
James Joyce
James Lane Allen
James Lane Allen
James Oliver Curwood
James Oppenheim
James Otis
James R. Driscoll
Jane Abbott
Jane Austen
Jane L. Stewart
Janet Aldridge
Jens Peter Jacobsen
Jerome K. Jerome
Jessie Graham Flower
John Buchan
John Burroughs
John Cournos
John F. Kennedy
John Gay
John Glasworthy
John Habberton
John Joy Bell
John Kendrick Bangs
John Milton
John Philip Sousa
John Taintor Foote
Jonas Lauritz Idemil Lie
Jonathan Swift
Joseph A. Altsheler
Joseph Carey
Joseph Conrad
Joseph E. Badger Jr
Joseph Hergesheimer
Joseph Jacobs
Jules Vernes
Julian Hawthrone
Julie A Lippmann
Justin Huntly McCarthy
Kakuzo Okakura
Karle Wilson Baker
Kate Chopin
Kenneth Grahame
Kenneth McGaffey
Kate Langley Bosher
Kate Langley Bosher
Katherine Cecil Thurston
Katherine Stokes
L. A. Abbot
L. T. Meade

L. Frank Baum
Latta Griswold
Laura Dent Crane
Laura Lee Hope
Laurence Housman
Lawrence Beasley
Leo Tolstoy
Leonid Andreyev
Lewis Carroll
Lewis Sperry Chafer
Lilian Bell
Lloyd Osbourne
Louis Hughes
Louis Joseph Vance
Louis Tracy
Louisa May Alcott
Lucy Fitch Perkins
Lucy Maud Montgomery
Luther Benson
Lydia Miller Middleton
Lyndon Orr
M. Corvus
M. H. Adams
Margaret E. Sangster
Margret Howth
Margaret Vandercook
Margaret W. Hungerford
Margret Penrose
Maria Edgeworth
Maria Thompson Daviess
Mariano Azuela
Marion Polk Angellotti
Mark Overton
Mark Twain
Mary Austin
Mary Catherine Crowley
Mary Cole
Mary Hastings Bradley
Mary Roberts Rinehart
Mary Rowlandson
M. Wollstonecraft Shelley
Maud Lindsay
Max Beerbohm
Myra Kelly
Nathaniel Hawthrone
Nicolo Machiavelli
O. F. Walton
Oscar Wilde

Owen Johnson
P.G. Wodehouse
Paul and Mabel Thorne
Paul G. Tomlinson
Paul Severing
Percy Brebner
Percy Keese Fitzhugh
Peter B. Kyne
Plato
Quincy Allen
R. Derby Holmes
R. L. Stevenson
R. S. Ball
Rabindranath Tagore
Rahul Alvares
Ralph Bonehill
Ralph Henry Barbour
Ralph Victor
Ralph Waldo Emmerson
Rene Descartes
Ray Cummings
Rex Beach
Rex E. Beach
Richard Harding Davis
Richard Jefferies
Richard Le Gallienne
Robert Barr
Robert Frost
Robert Gordon Anderson
Robert L. Drake
Robert Lansing
Robert Lynd
Robert Michael Ballantyne
Robert W. Chambers
Rosa Nouchette Carey
Rudyard Kipling
Saint Augustine
Samuel B. Allison
Samuel Hopkins Adams
Sarah Bernhardt
Sarah C. Hallowell
Selma Lagerlof
Sherwood Anderson
Sigmund Freud
Standish O'Grady
Stanley Weyman
Stella Benson
Stella M. Francis

Stephen Crane
Stewart Edward White
Stijn Streuvels
Swami Abhedananda
Swami Parmananda
T. S. Ackland
T. S. Arthur
The Princess Der Ling
Thomas A. Janvier
Thomas A Kempis
Thomas Anderton
Thomas Bailey Aldrich
Thomas Bulfinch
Thomas De Quincey
Thomas Dixon
Thomas H. Huxley
Thomas Hardy
Thomas More
Thornton W. Burgess
U. S. Grant
Upton Sinclair
Valentine Williams
Various Authors
Vaughan Kester
Victor Appleton
Victor G. Durham
Victoria Cross
Virginia Woolf
Wadsworth Camp
Walter Camp
Walter Scott
Washington Irving
Wilbur Lawton
Wilkie Collins
Willa Cather
Willard F. Baker
William Dean Howells
William le Queux
W. Makepeace Thackeray
William W. Walter
William Shakespeare
Winston Churchill
Yei Theodora Ozaki
Yogi Ramacharaka
Young E. Allison
Zane Grey